# THE SWISS
# ACCOUNT

May

# PAUL·ERDMAN

# THE SWISS ACCOUNT

**TOR**

*A Tom Doherty Associates Book*

*New York*

THE SWISS ACCOUNT

Copyright © 1992 by Paul Erdman

*Book design by Judith A. Stagnitto*

A Tor Book
Published by Tom Doherty Associates, Inc.
175 Fifth Avenue
New York, N.Y. 10010

Tor ® is a registered trademark of Tom Doherty Associates, Inc.

Library of Congress Cataloging-in-Publication Data

Erdman, Paul Emil
    The Swiss Account / Paul Erdman.
        p.   cm.
    ISBN 0-312-85321-1
    I. Title.
PS3555.R4S94   1992
813'.54—dc20

92-24131
CIP

First edition: October 1992

Printed in the United States of America

0 9 8 7 6 5 4 3 2 1

# PREFACE

This novel leans heavily on historical events and personae. In order to help the reader separate real events from fiction, I have provided footnotes.

The "real" characters include Allen Dulles, head of the American espionage efforts in Switzerland in World War II; General Walter Schellenberg, in charge of the foreign intelligence operations of the Nazi SS during the war; and the Swede, Per Jacobsson of the Bank for International Settlements, the central bank of the world's central banks.

The two tarts who travel with Schellenberg are fictional, as are the three protagonists. Two of the latter are Swiss: Peter and Felicitas Burckhardt, brother and sister; and the third is an American, Nancy Reichman, who represented the United States as vice-counsul in Basel, Switzerland, between 1940 and 1945.

# PART·ONE

# ONE

The dense fog rising off the River Rhine enveloped the night train. Thoughts of death consumed Per Jacobsson as he sat in his darkened compartment. He could not see the bodies of the American G.I.'s that lay frozen in the Ardenne Forest. But he knew they were there. It was January, 1945.

At Lörrach, everybody but Jacobsson and a heavy contingent of German military guards left the train, which then continued its slow journey across the border into neutral Switzerland. Ten minutes later, the train came to a second halt at the Badische Bahnhof in the ancient Swiss city of Basel.

Nazi guards watched the Swede as he descended from the train. There had been no porters at the station since September 3, 1939, the day World War II began.

After walking through fifty meters of eerie emptiness, Jacobsson came to a high fence of steel mesh, where he was met by three officials. One of them was an Oberst in the SS.

"Geben Sie mir bitte Ihren Pass," came the order.

The Swede handed over his passport.

"Sie sind ja sehr weit weg von zu Hause Herr Jacobsson. Warum?"

Before the Swede could even begin to explain his presence so far from his native land, the man with the skull-and-bones insignia on his black uniform stepped forward.

"We have been expecting you, sehr geehrter Herr Jacobsson. I trust your journey from Berlin was uneventful?"

The Swede nodded, motioning toward his unopened suitcase.

"Nicht nötig," said the SS Oberst, indicating that Per Jacobsson could proceed through the gate, suitcase unopened.

A loud buzzer sounded, and the gate through the steel-mesh fence swung open. On the other side of the gate there was a small wooden table. Behind it stood a Swiss corporal in the ugly green uniform of the Swiss military. When Jacobsson handed over his passport, it was carefully examined. Then a huge book that lay on the table was opened and pages were turned to the section that dealt with Swedish nationals. The passport was again checked, numbers compared, and the passport returned without comment. But this time, the suitcase was not only opened, but thoroughly inspected.

"In Ordnung," the Swiss corporal finally said.

It was almost midnight when Per Jacobsson finally emerged from the train station and stepped onto Swiss soil. He crossed the Rosenthalstrasse and approached a man and a woman who waited for him in front of the Kleinbasler Weinstube. Seconds later, they entered the restaurant together. Another man who had watched silently from an old black Fiat drove off, apparently satisfied that the connection had been made.

Jacobsson ordered a carafe of Dole, a heavy Swiss red wine appropriate on this icy winter night.

The American woman was the first to speak. "Mr. Dulles was unable to come over from Bern this evening. So he asked me to come."

The Swede nodded. He knew that the American woman worked with Dulles. The three of them had dined together in Basel on one occasion.

"Were you able to find out where Heisenberg is?" the woman asked.

"No," answered the Swede. "Mr. Dulles' information was correct. Heisenberg, Hahn, and von Weizsäcker have disappeared from Berlin. And all the equipment they were using at the Kaiser Wilhelm Institute has likewise disappeared."

"Did you get any indication of how close they were to their goal before they disappeared?"

"Very close. I don't quite understand what it means, but I was told that for a while there was a lack of heavy water, and also a minor design problem. They now have an adequate supply of heavy water, and the design problem will be corrected shortly."

"Mr. Dulles will want to hear about this immediately."

"You must handle this information with the utmost of discretion. It was only at enormous risk that Herr Doktor Puhl could find this out. Doktor Puhl is the director of the Reichsbank in Berlin and one of the directors of my bank, the Bank for International Settlements here in Basel. He is not a physicist. At times, however, physicists seek out his financial advice. But if any of this gets back to the Gestapo . . ."

"We understand, Herr Jacobsson," the American woman replied.

"Speaking of the Gestapo, they have people all over Basel," Peter Burckhardt, the young Swiss, added. "I don't think that the three of us should be seen together any longer than necessary."

"You're right," the American woman said "Would you mind dropping me off first? I know it might be out of the way, but . . ."

Peter Burckhardt motioned to the waiter and paid the bill. His Mercedes was parked in front of the restaurant. All three climbed in.

After a five-minute ride, they crossed the Rhine over the Mittlere-brücke, the eleventh-century bridge that connected the two parts of the city of Basel. From there Burckhardt drove to the Marktplatz, the center of the city, where each morning since the Middle Ages, the Baslers came to buy fresh produce in the open-air market. There the American woman asked to be let out. She checked to see if anyone was watching—in fact, the square was totally deserted—and then climbed out of the car The Mercedes moved on.

She walked briskly up a steep, narrow passageway, the Martins-gasse, leading to an ancient cobblestoned street, the Augustiner-gasse. The houses on the north side, dating back to the thirteenth and fourteenth centuries, looked down on the Rhine. The woman lived in a small apartment on the third floor, the top floor, of Augustinergasse 11.

After climbing the stairs and letting herself in, she flung her coat onto the sofa and picked up the phone. Despite the hour, somebody at the American Embassy in Bern immediately answered.

"This is Nancy Reichman, the vice-consul in Basel. Please let Mr. Dulles know that I will be calling him at eight o'clock tomorrow morning."

"Will do," said a cheerful voice on the other end.

She then sat back anxiously. She was one of the few people in the world who had ever heard the adjective "atomic" applied to the noun "bomb." Not even Harry Truman, the vice-president of the

United States, had been brought into the know. She was also among the few people in the world who knew that Herr Professor Dr. Werner Heisenberg was thought to be, in the words of the Swede banker, "close, very close" to manufacturing one that would work.

# TWO

Allen Dulles was having breakfast in his apartment, situated in Bern high above the ravine formed by the Aare River, when Nancy Reichman's call came through. After he had thanked her and suggested to her that she make no immediate plans that could not be easily canceled, he hung up. He already had the germ of an idea.

Back in Washington, patience with the Swiss had just about run out in view of that country's continuing economic cooperation with Nazi Germany. When the Administration found out that he himself had arranged through the Bank for International Settlements yet another deal involving the swapping of looted Nazi gold for American dollars in Switzerland, God knew how they would react. Which made everything he was about to undertake all the more dangerous, the more delicate; it was almost tantamount to consorting with the enemy. Yet there was no choice. Somebody had to find out where Heisenberg was, and how far he had gotten, before it was too late. Dulles desperately needed the help of the Swiss. Yet again.

And if he found out what he feared he might, he might very well have to arrange for some people to be killed, quickly. Those who might have to act as the executioners might themselves have to pay dearly. Even if it cost the life of a nice young American girl like Nancy Reichman, he had no choice. Peter Burckhardt was of less concern. In addition to being a banker, Burckhardt was a lieutenant attached to Section 5 of the General Staff of the Swiss High Command, and as such, one of the most responsible officers in Swiss Intelligence. Running high risks went with the job.

■

Callous thoughts for an American diplomat in the official service of his country!

Allen Dulles lived and worked in a world that was really totally new for Americans—the underworld of active intelligence, where the rules of diplomacy did not apply and where, in fact, moral and ethical principles were often ignored because, it was reasoned, they had to be ignored if the Western democracies were to survive in the face of both Fascism and Communism. For Allen Dulles and his colleagues in the Office of Strategic Services, the Nazis and the Soviets were regarded as being in the same class: mortal enemies of the United States. If *either* were about to produce an atomic bomb, it had to be stopped. From the very beginning, he had been fighting a two-front war against both the Nazis and the Soviets. From his post in Bern, he directed all OSS activities on the continent of Europe, and if he needed the help of the Swiss, or of the devil himself, to win that war, he had no qualms whatsoever about seeking that help, one way or the other.

He and the Swiss had already used each other on quite a few occasions . . . to their mutual profit. In fact, were the truth to ever come out, it was Dulles' highly secret connection with Swiss Intelligence—a secret often kept from their superiors on both sides—that had made the difference between his success or failure.

# THREE

The origins of the OSS dated back to June of 1942. "Wild Bill" Donovan had convinced President Roosevelt that the United States needed an organization that could not only gather intelligence, but also conduct "unconventional" wartime operations.[1]

One of Donovan's first recruits had been Allen Dulles, a Princeton graduate, professional diplomat, and a nephew of former Secretary of State Robert Lansing. Dulles had been associated with the Foreign Service since World War I and had served in various European countries, including Switzerland. In his Swiss post in the final years of World War I, his real activity had been in providing Washington with intelligence about what was happening in Germany, Austria, and the Balkans. Dulles was, therefore, perfectly qualified to run the OSS's operations in central Europe. Neutral Switzerland, which he knew well, was the obvious place from which to do it. He arrived there on November 7, 1942, and immediately began recruiting aides.

Among those recruited were Americans already stationed in Switzerland whose original assignments had become outdated now that Switzerland was isolated: men and women from various departments of the American government dealing with commercial matters, or those involved with consular activities—providing visas for Swiss businessmen intending to visit the United States, or giving aid to American tourists visiting Switzerland.[2]

1. See Dunlop, Richard, *Donovan, America's Master Spy* (New York, 1982), for the definitive history of the OSS and the role played by Allen Dulles.
2. Allen Dulles, *The Secret Surrender* (New York, 1966), p. 16.

■

One of the first to be signed up was the American vice-consul in Basel, Nancy Reichman.

The consulate in Basel could not have been more strategically placed from the standpoint of the OSS, located as it was in the center of that Swiss city which bordered on both Germany and France and was one of central Europe's most important transportation hubs. The problem was that the consulate had been staffed with only two Foreign Service officers, and one of them, the consul, had just retired and had not been replaced. Nor could he be replaced now that Switzerland was sealed off. There was a "problem" also where the vice-consul was concerned: she was a woman. Not only that, she was a Jewish woman.

But Dulles was desperate. So exactly thirty days after he arrived in Bern he invited her to visit him at his apartment on the Herrengasse.

When he opened the door to greet her, he was stunned by her appearance. She was a petite, dark-haired beauty, extremely well dressed. Dulles' first irreverent thought was that Donovan, who had an eye for young women, would have recruited her on the spot without a further word.

"Coffee?" he asked.

She hesitated.

"It's real American coffee, not the ersatz stuff," Dulles immediately added. "I brought some with me on the Clipper. And let's sit over there by the window while we drink it."

The window looked out over the ravine that had been formed by the Aare River below, and beyond that, the whole stretch of the Alps of the Bernese Oberland.

"Beautiful, isn't it?"

She agreed.

"And an added feature is that vineyard that you see down there between my apartment and the river. It provides an ideal cover for any visitors who might not wish to be seen entering the front door on the Herrengasse."[3]

Nancy Reichman said nothing.

"Nancy, has anyone in the department told you about me?"

"No, sir," replied Nancy Reichman. "Although I did read in the

---

3. *Ibid.*, p. 15. In this autobiographical book, it is obvious that Allen Dulles relished the role of being a "spy."

*Neue Zürcher Zeitung* that the Swiss regard you as the personal representative of President Roosevelt."[4]

Allen Dulles laughed. "That's not quite true. What I am is an intelligence officer attached to the Office of Strategic Services under William Donovan. We report to both the President and the Joint Chiefs of Staff. We are a relatively new organization, and brand new where Switzerland is concerned. We're looking for help here, and that's why I asked you to come over from Basel. I must impress on you from the very outset, however, that all I am about to tell you is highly confidential. You understand?"

"Yes, sir."

Dulles was a man in his fifties, of medium build, and dressed rather informally. He wore a tie, but rather than the blue suit so prevalent in diplomatic circles, he had on a brown sports jacket and tan slacks. His gray hair was impeccably groomed, his head squarer and larger than normal. But it was his penetrating gray eyes behind the rimless glasses that set him apart from other men. He was a man who invariably made others uneasy.

"You said that you read about me in the Swiss newspapers. Are you that fluent in German?"

"Yes. Also in Schwyzerdeutsch, the Swiss dialect."

"Why German?"

"My parents emigrated from Germany, and we still speak German at home."

"Where is home?"

"Palo Alto, California."

"Why Palo Alto?"

"My father teaches economics—the history of economic thought, to be more precise—at Stanford. He studied under Max Weber at Heidelberg."

Allen Dulles nodded approvingly. He was becoming more interested by the minute.

"And your fluency in the Swiss dialect?"

"After I finished my undergraduate work at Stanford, I came to Switzerland for postgraduate studies in Basel. In fact, last year I resumed taking lectures and seminars there—part-time of course—and made a deliberate effort to learn Schwyzerdeutsch. You see, the Swiss students hated the Germans at the university. The Germans

---

4. *Ibid*. Dulles notes here that he had no idea as to how this false rumor was started.

were arrogant and standoffish. The more successful Hitler became, the more superior their attitude. The Swiss referred to them as 'chaibe Schwobe.'"

"Translation?"

"A loose translation would be 'Kraut bastards.'"

"When did you join the Foreign Service?"

"In the summer of nineteen thirty-nine, just before the war started. My father insisted I break off my studies and return home. So I did. I took the Foreign Service exams, passed, and after an initial stint in Washington at the State Department, was sent to Basel in August of nineteen forty as vice-consul. I guess for obvious reasons."

"Who do you know in Basel?" Dulles asked.

"You mean Swiss?"

Dulles waves his hand. "Important people, Swiss or foreign."

"The Swiss keep to themselves, as I am sure you know, but through the university, I have met some interesting people."

"Such as?"

"Lawyers. People active in the arts. Also bankers . . . from the Bank for International Settlements, for example."

"Such as?"

"You mean from the BIS?"

"Yes."

"Per Jacobsson and his personal assistant, Dr. Peter Burckhardt."

"Who else?"

"Former students who have taken positions with the chemical companies in Basel, such as CIBA, Geigy, Hoffmann La Roche, Sandoz. They all have operations throughout Europe and around the world. Or people with commercial banks, like the Swiss Bank Corporation, which is Switzerland's largest and has its headquarters in Basel. And ex-students who live in other cities, like Zürich. They are among Switzerland's elite since they came to Basel to study under professors who are among the greatest thinkers of our time. Men like Professor Karl Barth, the Protestant theologian; Professor Karl Jaspers, the German existentialist philosopher; and Professor Carl Gustav Jung, the psychiatrist. Jung comes over from Zürich twice a month to lecture, as does Wolfgang Pauli, the physicist. Then there is Professor Edgar Bonjour, the Swiss historian who is chronicling the history of Swiss neutrality, and—"

Dulles interrupted, "And your professor . . . what is his name?"

"Salin. Edgar Salin."

"And who is he exactly?"

"He is German, from Frankfurt am Main. He studied under the Webers at Heidelberg. He knows my father from there. In the early nineteen thirties both Salin and my father left Germany. Like Jaspers and so many other German academics, they could see what was coming. A lot of them went to America, including Albert Einstein. My father went to Stanford, as I already mentioned. Others, like Jaspers and Salin, wanted to stay in Europe, in German-speaking Europe if possible, and so when Salin was invited to head the economics department at the University of Basel, he immediately accepted. He seems to know everybody: émigrés like my father and Siegmund Warburg, the Hamburg banker who now lives in London, or the Seligman family, who have a bank in Basel. But Professor Salin also maintains close contact with a lot of people in Germany, former students now often in high places in that country, or academics who still teach there. When these people come to Basel, he usually puts on private dinner parties for them."

"And you are usually included?"

"Yes."

Dulles had heard enough. "Miss Reichman, I would like you to work for me. It would be a part-time job. You would, of course, continue with your duties as vice-consul in Basel. Your setup, location, and background could not be better. I can think of no one better qualified to help us. Our work can, at times, be dangerous. Among other things, it is rumored that Jews are being systematically deported to Polish work camps. No one knows for sure, but I feel it my duty, Miss Reichman, to point these things out to you before you make a decision. You may want to take a few days to think about it, although I must insist that you consult no one, including your father or your Professor Salin . . . or anybody else, for that matter. If you decline, both you and I will forget we ever had this discussion. And that loss of memory will be permanent. Understood?"

"Yes, sir. I do understand, but if you don't mind. I would prefer not to wait. I have no reservations whatsoever about working for you, and I fully understand the risks."

Dulles rose from his chair and extended his hand. "Welcome aboard, Miss Reichman." He was surprised by the firmness of her handshake.

Dulles then looked at his watch. "It's four o'clock. When were you planning on returning to Basel?"

"At six o'clock, but—"

"That gives us ample time to work out some of the details, including what we tell, or don't tell, the people at the State Department, especially the chief of mission here in Switzerland, Minister Harrison. Leland Harrison and I don't see eye to eye on a lot of things. He belongs to that school of thought in the State Department which feels that gentlemen do not read other people's mail. Needless to say, that's the only kind of mail I like to read. Understood?"

Nancy Reichman nodded. "I understand."

# FOUR

Nancy Reichman made the six-o'clock train back to Basel on that early December night in 1942, and in the weeks that followed, she began her first "mission" on behalf of the OSS: to cultivate those contacts in Basel who could provide firsthand information about what was happening in the country that lay immediately to the north of that city, a country almost totally sealed off, access being impossible for all but a few. It was those few whom Nancy Reichman was to seek out.

Dulles' confidence in her ability to do just what was justified almost immediately. Two weeks after their first meeting in Bern, Nancy Reichman came up with information so startling that even Dulles was hesitant to pass it along to Washington without confirmation from other sources.

It came to her after a dinner that Professor Edgar Salin, her mentor at the University of Basel, put on in a private room of one of the finest restaurants in Basel, Zum Sternen, on the Sankt Alban Vorstadt. Attendance was small due to the Christmas break at the university. In fact, Nancy Reichman was one of only two ex-students who had been asked to join the men who met at eight that evening. All but one were residents of Basel: the professor, Salin; the private banker, Seligman; a local lawyer, Karl Meyer. Then there was Dr. Peter Burckhardt, former student of Salin and now assistant to Per Jacobsson, chief economist of the Bank for International Settlements. The fifth man was Professor Arthur Sommer, a member of the wartime German Army, wherein he served as an officer with the General Staff in Berlin. He had a third job as a

•

member of the permanent Swiss-German Economic Commission, that body which regulated those immensely important—important to both countries—trade and financial flows between Nazi Germany and neutral Switzerland. The commission met often, almost always in Switzerland, so Sommer crossed the Swiss-German border at Basel almost every other week.

During the dinner itself, nothing unusual had come up. It being December of 1942, the main subjects of discussion were the battles raging on Germany's Eastern front in Russia and the success of the Americans in North Africa after their landing on November 8th. Salin was of the opinion that the tide had definitely turned against the Nazis. It was now just a matter of time. Professor Sommer was less optimistic. Though anti-Nazi to the core, he was highly critical of the Allies' failure to begin establishing a second front on the continent of Europe. Despite some of the recent setbacks the German Army had taken, the Nazis still considered themselves invincible and, in fact, were embarking on some new programs of a truly frightening nature. However, when Salin tried to get him to further explain what he meant, Sommer had suddenly backed off. The presence of the Swiss lawyer, with his known German connections, might have been the reason. In any case, the discussion had moved on to other matters.

But afterward, on the way home, Salin had persisted. Salin, as was his custom, had offered to drop Nancy Reichman off on the Marktplatz before proceeding to his house on the Hardstrasse. But first he brought his guest to the Hotel Euler, located directly vis-à-vis Basel's central railroad station. The two professors sat in the front seat of Salin's massive BMW; Nancy Reichman sat alone in the back.

"Die Entscheidung war am zwanzigsten Januar dieses Jahres getroffen worden," Sommer began. The decision was made on January 20th of the current year, 1942.

"It was taken at a meeting held in Wahnsee, just outside of Berlin, convened by Reinhard Heydrich, who, as I am sure you know, Edgar, is the number-two man in the SS. He explained to the men gathered there that his special squads had, so far, managed to eliminate five hundred thousand Jews in Nazi-occupied Russia."

"A half million!" Salin exclaimed. "Das ist ja wahnsinnig!"

"Crazy or not, it's true. They were shot and then buried in mass graves dug by the next batch of Jews scheduled to be shot. And therein lay the problem. The process, according to Heydrich, was simply too slow, too cumbersome. A better solution to the Jewish problem was required. And that is when Heydrich first used the word 'Endlösung.'"

"Endlösung," Salin repeated. "Am I right in interpreting this as meaning—"

Arthur Sommer interrupted him. "It means exactly what it says. The Final Solution. The Nazis intend to totally eliminate the Jews in all of Europe."

"But that means killing five, maybe six million people."

"Exactly. Heydrich then described how he proposed going about this. He was going to gas them. He already had the right gas: Zyklon B. IG Farben had developed it and was prepared to produce it in large quantities. All that was now required were gas chambers. Heydrich proposed that a prototype be built, and if all went well, he would embark upon a full-scale program that could soon handle thousands of Jews a day. He had the place: a small town in Poland by the name of Auschwitz. Heydrich also had the right man to run it, his 'Jewish expert' . . . a man by the name of Adolph Eichmann. He was there, sitting beside Heydrich. '

"But how do you know all this so exactly?" Salin asked.

"Because Eichmann kept precise minutes of the meeting. I have seen a copy of those minutes. To continue, everybody gathered there at Wahnsee thought all this was brilliant, so Heydrich immediately began to implement his plan. By mid-July of this year, he finished construction of what he termed his 'experimental plant' at Auschwitz. He invited his boss. Heinrich Himmler, to join him in witnessing the first mass execution there, the gassing of four hundred and forty-nine Dutch Jews. After that, the Final Solution went into full gear."[5]

Professor Sommer then finished his story with the ultimate in "Galgenhumor"—gallows humor, for which the Germans are known. "Auschwitz must have developed into one of the biggest cities in Europe, since so many people enter it and no one ever leaves."

Salin left the car running as he stepped out to say good-bye to the German visitor, and they exchanged their final words.

5. See MacDonald, Callum, *The Killing of SS Übergruppenführer Reinhard Heydrich* (New York, 1989), pp. 40 ff. Also Laccuer, Walter, and Breitman, Richard, *Breaking the Silence* (New York, 1986), pp. 154 ff and pp. 138 ff.

"Aber haben Sie Beweis?" Salin had asked. Did the German have evidence?

"Leider nein," came the answer. Regretfully, no.[6]

6. In *Breaking The Silence*, Lacqueur and Breitman tell the story of a German industrialist, Eduard Schulte. He was, they claim, the heretofore "unknown man" who, to use their words, "first passed on to the outside world the unbelievable news that Hitler's extermination of the Jews had begun." These historians determined that Minister Leland Harrison, Chief of Mission in Switzerland, was the initial recipient of this information. When Harrison passed it on to the State Department in late 1942, they relayed it on further to the OSS in Washington, terming the legation's message a "wild rumor inspired by Jewish fears." Later, in early 1943, after Schulte established contact with Dulles, he convinced him, the OSS, and President Roosevelt of the awful truth.

However, there are other historians who dispute that it was Schulte alone who first informed the Allies of the nature and scope of the Final Solution, suggesting that its origins could be found rather in the Sommer/Salin connection. The dispute arose due to the fact that Schulte's name was never in the cables sent from Switzerland transmitting the information passed on by the German informant: only the letter "S." In fact, it was the mystery of the identity of the man behind that letter "S" that Walter Lacqueur set out to solve and that led to his co-authoring the book on Schulte under the title *Breaking the Silence*. In a postscript to that book, Laqueur wrote the following:

"Through an accident I established that the man's name began with the letter 'S.' At the time this did not help very much, for 'S' is the most common initial for German last names. A great many Schmidts, Schöllers, Strausses, and Stumms had been in Basel, Zürich, and Bern during the war. I inquired among surviving German and Swiss industrialists whether they could give me any clues. I wrote dozens of letters and made scores of phone calls but without success.

"Meanwhile, some other historians had reached the conclusion that Arthur Sommer was the mysterious messenger. Sommer was a German economist who had belonged to the circle of admirers of the German poet Stefan George. Another member of this circle was Count Claus von Stauffenberg, the brave officer who almost killed Hitler on July 20, 1944 . . . . Sommer was not a Nazi, and from time to time he met with Jewish friends in Switzerland, including Professor Edgar Salin, a native of Frankfurt, who taught economics in Basel. According to postwar evidence provided by Salin, Sommer sent Salin a letter in 1942 to the effect that extermination camps had been established in Eastern Europe to kill all the European Jews (and also most Russian prisoners) by means of poison gas."

Lacqueur then goes on to point out that according to Dr. Haim Pazner, a historian who had studied under Salin, Salin got the word to the Americans in Bern, who then disseminated the information to Washington and the Allies. Laqueur says this thesis is "interesting but wrong."

I had the privilege of studying under Professor Edgar Salin, and, in fact, it was he who was my "Doktor Vater" (roughly, thesis supervisor) when I received a Ph.D. in economics at the University of Basel in 1958. I personally heard this story from him, but I have no way of knowing whether or not this information ever reached Washington or, if it did, whether it was believed.

"But could you at least repeat in writing what you have told me?" Salin asked.

Sommer hesitated. "I will write you a letter this evening, Edgar, and hand-deliver it to your home tomorrow morning."

The two professors had then shaken hands, and Salin had returned to the car and taken Nancy Reichman home.

Nancy Reichman called Dulles in Bern the following morning, explaining that she had something of extreme importance but would prefer to discuss it in person. Dulles concurred. So she took the next train to Bern, and a taxi to Dulles' apartment.

He listened intently as she repeated the conversation she had overheard in the car. "You have a remarkable memory," he said.

"Yes, I do."

"You also believe what you overheard, don't you?"

"Yes."

"In our first conversation, I mentioned that all kinds of rumors are afloat about what is happening to Europe's Jews. But like the German professor, Sommer, we have no evidence. And there is another problem. Were I to transmit this information to Washington, there is a strong possibility that you and your sources would be compromised. You see, we have just found out that the Nazis have cracked the code our legation here is using for both its radio and telephone transmissions."

Nancy was shocked.

"Still, this Endlösung—this Final Solution—is a matter that I am pursuing with the highest priority. And you should, too. There are many people in Washington who don't want to believe these things. They feel that they are being fed misinformation, intended to pressure the United States to open its doors to unlimited Jewish immigration. The Swiss attitude is even more hostile. The country is literally tossing Jews back across the border into Germany and Austria. 'Das Boot ist voll,' they have claimed. The Swiss lifeboat is full."

"That's awful," Nancy said.

Dulles gave her a long, hard stare. Finally he stood. "I could use a drink." He crossed the room and returned from the refrigerator with a bottle of Aigle. "We've recently learned of an increase in the amount of gold Germany is shipping into Switzerland. Secretary of the Treasury Morganthau wants confirmation of this. If it is true, the Bank for International Settlements is bound to know about it, since the BIS is usually right in the middle of Europe's gold transactions. So cultivate your contacts there—carefully—and see what develops. It's just a fishing expedition, but you never know what you'll catch unless you put a line in the water. There are still a lot of highly placed Germans operating in the BIS. Maybe one of them can shed some light on this Final Solution."

# FIVE

Nancy Reichman made slow progress until mid-February, when she received a phone call from Peter Burckhardt He told her how much he had enjoyed seeing her at Professor Salin's dinner in December and suggested that they might get together again.

Afterward, she wondered what had prompted his call. They had known each other since 1938 when both were students at the university, but it had just been a passing relationship of students. Burckhardt, she knew, had gone on to receive his doctorate in 1939 and join the Bank for International Settlements as a junior staff member in its economics research department. There he had caught the attention of Per Jacobsson, the Swede who was not only chief economist at the BIS, but one of its chief policymakers. If Dulles wanted her to sniff around about intergovernmental financial matters, the BIS was the place to do it.

The origins of the BIS dated back to World War I and the billions of dollars of reparations that the victorious Allies had forced Germany to pay. Postwar Germany had lurched from near revolution to hyperinflation to massive unemployment, with the result that by the end of the 1920s, the country was experiencing such great financial difficulties that it had to suspend further payments to its international creditors.

The "solution" to the German reparations payment problem came in the form of the Young Plan in 1929 (named after the president of General Electric, Owen D. Young), under which the Allies arranged for Germany to borrow enough money, through the issue of bonds, to resume payments. The establishment of the Bank of International Settlements was part and parcel of the plan,

■

aimed at "depoliticizing" the reparations process. It replaced the old Reparations Committee and took over the administration of the flow of funds into and out of Germany. The apolitical nature of the new institution was reinforced by its location in neutral Switzerland in the traditional financial center, Basel.[7]

Almost immediately after its founding in 1930, however, it became obvious that the BIS would go far beyond its original purpose. This had, in fact, been foreshadowed by the unique nature of the ownership of the BIS: the controlling shareholders were the leading central banks of the world, initially those of Belgium, England, France, Italy, Germany, and Japan.[8] The American participation came from a consortium of American commercial banks—J.P. Morgan, the National Bank of New York, and the First National Bank of Chicago—with the Federal Reserve Bank staying in the background in order to avoid any possible political interference from its supervisor, the American Congress. Gradually the list of participating nations was expanded to include Sweden, Rumania, Poland, Holland, and Switzerland.

Since the men who ran these central banks were also responsible, ultimately, for the running of the BIS, they were now obligated to gather regularly in Basel. Net result: the BIS became the Club of Clubs, the Central Bankers Club, a place where they could secretly confide in one another, cut deals with one another, and often involve the BIS in the execution of these deals. Consequently, the BIS developed into the central bank of central banks, a powerful link between the most important financial systems of the world.

Per Jacobsson was the man in charge of the bank's economic policy, and it was he who had single-handedly made the BIS and Basel the place where the most powerful financial men on earth regularly gathered to coordinate their control of the world's money and finance. Jacobsson was staunchly anti-Nazi and pro-Anglo-Saxon. In fact, his sister was married to a key figure in Britain's military establishment, Sir Archibald Nye, who, during World War

7. For a history of the founding and early years of the BIS, see Einzig, Paul, *The Bank for International Settlements* (London, 1930). Also, Dulles, Eleanor Lansing, *The Bank for International Settlements at Work* (New York, 1932). Note that Eleanor Lansing Dulles was the sister of Allen and John Foster Dulles, which shows that the links between the Dulles family and the BIS go back to the bank's very beginnings.

8. The First National City Bank, *Bank for International Settlements—Documents* (Chicago, 1930).

II, held the post of vice-chief of the Imperial General Staff. But Jacobsson kept his views to himself, especially because he felt that he was a "guest" of neutral Switzerland. Despite the outbreak of war, he encouraged his staff—the Germans and British, the Italians and Americans, the Poles and the Czechs—who worked there to continue to lunch together though, unfortunately, they were no longer able to golf together since Basel's only golf course was located across the border in France (where land was plentiful and cheap), a border that had been sealed since September of 1939.[9]

The bank was physically located in a most unassuming building— formerly a small hotel—vis-à-vis Basel's main railroad station and immediately next door to one of the city's famous coffee houses, Frey. Since the staff of the BIS came to Frey's regularly for morning coffee or afternoon tea, Peter Burckhardt suggested that he and Nancy Reichman meet for coffee in the late afternoon of that Tuesday, February 16, 1943.

Arriving first, she took a table looking out on the Centralbahnstrasse and ordered tea and some chocolate patisserie. Minutes later, Peter Burckhardt walked in, deep in thought and carrying the afternoon edition of the *Basler Nachrichten.* When he saw Nancy, the seriousness was replaced by a broad smile.

"Salut, Nancy," he said as she stood up to shake his hand. "Das isch aber nett dass Du ko bisch." He used the familiar "Du" as was customary in Switzerland between former fellow students.

She decided to switch to English. "It was a nice surprise when you called, Peter. Would you like to share some of my tea?"

"No thanks," he said with a grimace. "Can't stand the stuff." He ordered coffee and Kirschwasser.

"I noticed in the telephone book that you live on the Augustinergasse. Wie schön," he added, reverting momentarily to Swiss German. "Sorry, but somehow it seems more natural talking to you in dialect. At the Uni we always admired you for how quickly you picked it up."

"I'm glad I made the effort," she replied. "The Germans turned out to be as bad as we all thought."

Peter Burckhardt at first said nothing. "Not all of them. The man at Professor Salin's dinner was all right."

9. See Jacobsson, Erin E., *A Life for Sound Money: Per Jacobsson, His Biography* (Oxford, 1979), where the author describes her father's passion for golf.

She noticed that he did not mention Sommer's name. "Have you seen him since?" she asked.

"No. But I hear that he will be back in Switzerland next week for a meeting of the German–Swiss economic committee. In Bern, though, not here. Do you want to meet with him?"

"I don't think it would be healthy for him to be seen with an American Foreign Service officer. But you've aroused my curiosity. Does he do business with the BIS?"

"Not directly. His connection is with the Swiss government. And now, so is mine. I've assumed a new job at the BIS. I've become responsible for overseeing the relationship between the BIS and the Swiss National Bank."

"That must be fascinating."

"Yes, but I really shouldn't be telling you all this, Nancy. You know how paranoid we Swiss are these days. Nobody is supposed to know anything, or if they do, to ever talk about it. Especially with foreigners."

"Like that poster tells you," Nancy Reichman interjected, pointing out the window at the wall of the train station. The poster depicted the huge shadow of a Swiss soldier in his battle helmet, his index finger in front of his lips, looking down on three working-class Swiss. The warning was clear. Keep your mouth shut. Or else. And the authority behind that warning was equally clear: another reminder that Switzerland was a state under martial law. Its citizens did as the military told them to do, or they would disappear behind barbed wire.

Peter Burckhardt looked at his watch.

"It's four-thirty," he said, "and it's already getting dark out there. Let's go see a movie. There's a new Jean Gabin thriller playing at the Rex. And I think the first showing starts at five."

Five minutes later, they paid separately, donned their coats and scarfs, and left the coffee house. As they stepped onto the Bahnhofstrasse, it began to snow lightly.

"We could take the tram, or we could walk," Peter said. "It's only about ten minutes."

'Let's walk" she replied.

They walked quickly to the Margarethenstrasse, then downhill to the Heuwaage and across the small square to the Steinenvorstadt, the street where Basel's first-run movie houses were situated.

"You know what I used to call this street when we were students?" she asked. "Broadway. When all the movie houses were lit up with their neon lights, it looked just like the downtown of an American city. They even played the same movies."

"They still do," Peter said, "except that it takes longer for the American films to get here. But it hardly looks like Broadway anymore, does it?"

"No. It's too bad."

"But necessary. Electricity is in very short supply here. Normally we have ample domestic supplies of hydroelectricity from our generating plants on the Rhine and below our Alpine dams. But now we export immense amounts to Germany."

"What for?"

"They use it to produce aluminum for their fighter aircraft and bombers."

It was only ten to five when they arrived in front of the Rex, but already there was a long line for tickets. Across the street in front of the Capitol it was the same. Where else could the Swiss turn for a little escape from their grim reality? For over three years now, they had been locked up in their tiny country, their borders sealed. The only window on the outside world was the screen in their movie theaters.

At seven, the movie was over. As Peter and Nancy left the theater, they had to work their way through the long line of people waiting to get in for the second showing. Burckhardt took her arm for the first time as they pushed their way down the sidewalk.

"I've got another idea. Do you know the Witwe Hunziger's place?"

"No."

"It's a small restaurant in the old city, owned and run by a little old lady known as the Widow Hunziger. All she serves is wine, dark bread, and for special clients, the best entrecôte in town. Are you game?"

"Do we qualify for the entrecôte?"

"Frau Hunziger knows us."

There was no arrogance in his statement. He was a member of that elite Basel society known as the "Daig"—the "crust," the upper crust. They controlled the city's private banks and its legal establishment, as well as the choice real estate both in the city and in the countryside surrounding it. The power of the families even extended to the military establishment. Their sons volunteered for officers' training school, so they inevitably held the highest ranks in the Swiss Army. This upper crust stuck together, they protected each other, and intermarriage had been the rule among these families for centuries.

They were, however, also elitist in the positive sense. The opera—one of the best provincial operas in Europe—was their creation, as was the ballet. Chamber music flourished in Basel as in few other cities. The art museum was superb. The university in Basel was one of the world's oldest. Founded in 1456, it ranked with those in Bologna, Prague, Oxford, Cambridge, and the Sorbonne. Yet the "Daig" that supported all of this consisted of only a few thousand citizens.

Nancy also knew about two other characteristics of the "Daig": they were staunch Protestants, and they were Anglophiles. And so she could hardly help but wonder what a Peter Burckhardt was doing taking an American–Jewish woman out to dinner.

They were seated near the restaurant's coal-burning stove. Almost immediately both decided to take off their heavy sweaters. Nancy noted that her companion observed her figure as she did so. He was well worth looking at himself, she thought. In contrast to most Swiss, he was tall—at least six feet—slim, yet muscular, with blond, slightly curly hair—and a bearing that reflected his patrician status.

The black bread and a carafe of Dole were placed automatically on their table.

"Nancy, could I ask you a strictly professional question?"

"Sure." Here it comes, she thought.

"Are you in regular contact with your embassy in Bern?"

"Not unless something unusual comes up."

"Like what?"

"Arranging an emergency visa. Or if some unusual information comes to my attention."

"Like a visit by—" and this time, in the privacy of Widow Hunziger's restaurant, which was his home turf, he named the name "—Herr Doktor Sommer?"

"Maybe." Now she was afraid that they had entered dangerous territory. "In fact, I sometimes wonder why Professor Salin invited me to that dinner."

"Because we have no channel of communication with either the British or the Americans. We are much more isolated here in Basel than you might think."

"You know as well as I do where our embassies are, Peter," she said.

"If a Swiss like me, or for that matter, even like Professor Salin, were seen entering the British or American Embassy, we would soon have people asking why."

"Well, what about being seen with me?"

"You're different. After all . . ."

And then he stopped.

So she continued his sentence for him. "After all, I'm just a woman. Right?"

He appeared embarrassed. "You know Swiss men. We do not even allow our women to vote. A woman's place in Switzerland is still in the home, and if a Swiss wife does not obey her husband in all matters, he has the perfect right, under law, to punish her. She is to be seen and not heard, like children in your country. So women are not taken seriously where political matters are concerned. They are regarded in our society as, well, as 'harmlos.'"

"I'm not harmless."

"I didn't mean that. I only wanted to know whether you know Allen Dulles."

"Why do you ask?"

"Some of us are unhappy about Switzerland's behavior in this war. Our leaders know certain things that the rest of the world should also know. Yet we remain silent. Many in government have been ambivalent about Fascism since its inception—Marcel Pilet, our Foreign Minister, and Otto Rottemund, the head of our national police force, to name just two. My family, and most of our family's friends, consider this attitude despicable. Some on purely theological grounds, the rest for political reasons. After all, we are a democracy . . . at least we were until this war broke out. We were a democracy long before the Anglo-Saxons got around to it."

Burckhardt stopped talking suddenly, realizing that his voice had been rising. He looked around the small room. Nobody was taking any notice of them. So he continued, but now in a voice that was barely above a whisper.

"Some of us have information about what's happening in Germany, because we maintain relationships, personal and otherwise, with certain men who have key positions there. Some of that information, some of those men, could potentially be helpful in defeating Fascism, provided we can get their information to the Allies. We have decided that you may be exactly the conduit we have been searching for."

"I've never been called a conduit before."

After a slight pause, he continued. "In Switzerland, intelligence is the responsibility of the army. The army shares the responsibility for counterintelligence with the various political police units in the country. These tasks have been specifically assigned to Section Five of the General Staff. It is a very small group. Just over a hundred men are involved. Some—not all—of them do not appreciate our so-called neutrality. They want to align themselves with the Allies, with the British and the Americans, and help where they can, but with the understanding that their first and foremost loyalty is to Switzerland. As a side benefit—not as a condition—they hope that this will be remembered. Especially if the Russians try to stir up trouble for our country either during the war or after it is over."

Nancy nodded.

"I work for them. Two officers in charge of our intelligence, Colonel Masson and Captain Waibel, want to get into contact with Mr. Dulles. As soon as possible. A direct approach by my superiors in Bern was considered, but rejected. If Foreign Minister Pilet, whom we consider Fascist, found out, he might disband the entire organization and start over with his own people. Bern is like a village. So we thought it better to approach Mr. Dulles indirectly via Basel."

"Enter Nancy Reichman."

"Exactly. You might represent the beginning of the solution, depending upon how well you know Mr. Dulles."

"I know him well enough."

"And you are willing to help?"

"Of course." Should she tell him how ironic this all was? That it was *she* who had intended to use *him*. No, she decided.

But then she asked, "Were you and Professor Salin by any chance looking me over at dinner with this in mind?"

"I was. Not Salin. He is not connected with us. He helps, but he is not connected."

"What kind of trouble could you get into by doing this sort of thing?"

"That is not the issue."

"Do you trust me that much?"

"I certainly trust *you* that much. Those behind you, or above you, well, we will just have to hope, won't we?"

He looked at his watch. "Let's order two entrecôtes. Then I'm going to walk you home. And after that, I'm going to be on the phone with my superiors in Bern. I trust you will be doing the same."

"Yes, I will."

"Anything else we should discuss?"

"One small thing, Peter, that I've been asked to check out. We've heard some disturbing stories about the Nazis making huge gold shipments to Switzerland, perhaps with the help of the BIS. Can that somehow be verified?"

"It goes right to the heart of the dilemma we face: how to help you without hurting Switzerland."

"I assume, however, you mean the real Switzerland. Not the ruling clique in Bern," she responded.

"I'll look into it."

He walked her home an hour later, kissing her ever so lightly on the cheek when he left.

Five minutes later, Nancy Reichman was on the phone, leaving a message for Allen Dulles. When she hung up, she could not help but wonder about who was manipulating whom. Had Dulles, somehow, known about the desire of Swiss Intelligence to contact him? Had he set all this up?

At dawn the next morning, she received a phone call telling her that Mr. Dulles would be out of town until the beginning of the following week and that she would be expected on Tuesday, February 23rd, at the usual time and place.

# SIX

That afternoon Nancy Reichman arranged to meet Peter Burckhardt at her favorite place, Spielman's, situated on the Rhine next
to the Middle Bridge. Spielman's was where the ladies who
belonged to Basel society gathered for afternoon tea. It was also
frequented by the City's wealthier Jewish women, thereby making
it one of the last places where Nazi sympathizers would ever be
found.

"Problems?" Burckhardt asked after she sat down.

"I'm coming from the Fremdenpolizei. They have a Jewish
woman in custody. She slipped across the border from Austria and
somehow ended up finding refuge with a local Jewish family. They
kept her in their attic."

"How did the police find her?"

"She would take a walk occasionally. According to the police, a
neighbor saw her 'sneaking in and out of the house' on two
occasions and 'because she did not look or dress like a Swiss,'
tipped them off."

"Why are you involved?"

"In desperation, the woman claimed to have American relatives
who would sponsor her emigration to the United States. They
phoned me, and I went to see her."

"And?"

"She's just trying to buy time. In two weeks they will hand her
back to the German authorities. And . . ." She could not continue.
After having overheard that conversation while in the backseat of
Professor Salin's BMW, she knew what would happen.

"If I can help—"

■

She shook her head, and then the waitress came to take their order.

"About the gold," he began after the waitress left. "This is very touchy stuff."

"Don't worry. I left a message for Mr. Dulles last night, as I promised. He's out of town right now, but I will be going to Bern next Tuesday to meet with him. I thought you should know this. That's why I called you."

"I'll pass that along right away," Peter replied. Then, hesitantly, "I have another meeting that I would like to arrange. It has absolutely nothing to do with business. I would like you to meet my parents."

This left Nancy Reichman literally speechless. In Switzerland, such a meeting was highly irregular.

He handed her a small map. "This will show you how to get to our family's place in Riehen." Riehen was a small suburb of Basel, where the estates of many of the "Daig" were located. "In fact, it was my parents' idea. They would like to invite you to join us for dinner next Monday."

They stayed together at Spielman's for another forty-five minutes, discussing skiing, what it was like living in California, the latest novel by Remarque; anything but the war. A casual observer of the pair could see that what kept them lingering was their obvious pleasure in being together—two young people in the middle of a world that seemed to have forgotten everything but war.

# SEVEN

The six-acre Burckhardt estate was comprised of the main house, stables, servants' quarters, a tennis court, and, unusual for Switzerland, a swimming pool. The grounds were covered with snow, but it was easy to imagine lazy summer days spent on the lawn beneath the huge chestnut trees. The house itself was French provincial; the statuary adjacent to the main entrance, three Rodins. As Nancy Reichman would soon find out, the Burckhardt home was furnished in the style of Louis XV. The paintings were mostly eighteenth-century, but they also included two Renoirs and a Pissarro.

She arrived at seven-thirty on Monday evening in her tiny Fiat Topolino. The CC license plates designated her as a member of the Consulate Corps.

"Guten Abend, Fräulein. Darf ich Ihren Mantel nehmen?" The maid who had opened the door spoke high German with difficulty. As she took Nancy Reichman's coat, an extremely elegant woman in her mid-fifties appeared. Her clothes could have come from nowhere else than a pre-1940 Paris boutique; her hair was exquisitely coiffed; the pearl necklace that swooped into her rather deep decolletage was perfection itself.

"How very nice of you to come," the woman said in impeccable Oxford English. "I'm Peter's mother. He said that you were a beautiful young woman, and you are. May I call you Nancy?" She took Nancy's arm. "Let's have something to drink."

Together they crossed the marble floor of the entrance hall and entered the salon. The two men who had been sitting in front of the fireplace rose immediately. Peter greeted her with a handshake. "Nancy, I would like to introduce you to my father."

■

Herr Doktor Maximilian Burckhardt–Von der Mühl, tall, and like his son, impeccably tailored, stepped forward. "We are honored to have an American in our home." His handshake was firm, his gray eyes warm.

"Now," he said, "in celebration of having you in our presence, I propose we all indulge in a dry martini. Are you game?"

"I'd love one," Nancy answered.

Peter's father picked up a small silver bell from one of the end tables and rang it. Almost immediately a male servant appeared, the butler that Nancy had been anticipating with such trepidation before her arrival. But now those fears had totally disappeared, and when Peter suggested she join him on the sofa, she took her place beside him with confidence.

Peter's mother now took over. "Peter has told us that your family lives in Palo Alto. We visited there in nineteen thirty-eight. We were staying at the Mark Hopkins in San Francisco in September, and we drove down. We loved the campus at Stanford. Peter tells us that your father teaches there."

"He does. The history of economic thought."

And so it went through cocktails and then through a magnificent dinner accompanied by, first, a 1939 Meursault, and then a 1933 Lynch Bages. It ended with a Grand Marnier soufle.

Afterward, they gathered in the library for coffee and cognac, and for the men, Cuban cigars. At nine o'clock, pleading a long day at the bank, Peter's father rose, the signal for his mother to do the same. They said good night to Nancy, graciously suggesting their hope that this evening would be only the first of many. Peter and Nancy were finally alone in front of the fireplace, which had just been reattended to by one of the maids.

"Your parents are wonderful."

"They liked you from the first moment," Peter replied.

Then the door to the library swung open once more, and in plunged a young woman in her mid-twenties, dressed in a ski parka. Peter Burckhardt looked up in surprise, and with the grin that was already beginning to endear him to Nancy Reichman, rose to introduce the intruder. "My sister, Felicitas. And this, dear sister, is Nancy Reichman."

"I didn't want to interrupt, Peter," Felicitas said, "but I did have to . . . have to see what your mysterious American woman looked like. She's smashing!"

That would have been the correct word to describe Felicitas

Burckhardt as well. In contrast to the dark, petite beauty of the "American woman," Peter's sister was tall, blonde, and blue-eyed, and exuded a warmth and an enthusiasm rare in subdued, controlled Switzerland.

"Would you have lunch with me one day?" she asked.

"I'd love to," Nancy said, taking an immediate liking to the young woman.

"Then I can tell you all of Peter's secrets," Felicitas said. And with that, blowing her brother a kiss, she disappeared.

"I didn't know you had a sister," Nancy said as soon as the door to the library had closed again. "What does she do?"

"She's studying at the University. Physics," Peter replied. "But I have the feeling that it bores her. I think she wishes she could do things like you are able to do. But this is Switzerland. Maybe you could help cheer her up."

"She doesn't look like she needs cheering up."

Peter shrugged. "Have lunch with her soon. She'd appreciate it. Now, how about us having another cognac?"

Nancy Reichman looked at her watch. "I'd love to, Peter, but it's getting late. The blackout starts at ten, and I have to take an early train to Bern."

He dutifully went to get her coat. "By the way, when you see Mr. Dulles, you might tell him that we know about the back-door approach to his apartment through the vineyard, so it's hardly worth the trouble."

"I will."

"You're coming back from Bern tomorrow?"

"Yes."

"May I call you at seven tomorrow evening? At your apartment?" he asked as he opened the door of the Topolino for her.

"Yes. But now, Peter, I'd better go."

The good-night kiss he gave her was on the cheek and barely perceptible.

She went to bed that night thinking of Peter Burckhardt.

# EIGHT

In Bern the next morning, it took Nancy Reichman less than twenty minutes to describe the conversation at the Witwe Hunziger's a week earlier.

"Excellent," Allen Dulles said when she finally fell silent. "I trust you understand how delicate this is. If certain people found out about it, you would be declared persona non grata and kicked out of Switzerland within a matter of days. Which could well mean the end of your career in the Foreign Service."

"I understand, sir."

"Good. What Bruckhardt told you about Section Five checks out. Colonel Masson and Captain Waibel run the show. Waibel and Burckhardt are especially important to us; they are attached to the unit within Section Five that runs all operations directed at Germany. Tell Burckhardt that I will meet Masson at any time and at any place that is convenient to him, since he might have more of a problem there than I do. And suggest that Waibel and your Peter Burckhardt join us. I'd especially like to meet Burckhardt."

"I'll speak to him right away."

Dulles looked at his watch. "I have another appointment in a few minutes. As soon as Burckhardt gets back to you, let me know. Should I call you a taxi?"

"No. I think I'll walk. By the way, the Swiss are on to the back-door approach to your apartment through the vineyard."

Pleased with herself, she left by the front door, which led onto the Herrengasse. She might have been less pleased had she known that she was being observed by *two* men, only one of whom worked

■

for Colonel Masson. The other was a member of an organization known to Swiss Intelligence as the "Rote Kapelle," the Red Orchestra. The head of that organization in Switzerland was also a colonel. In the NKGB.[10]

10. We know this organization today as the KGB. Originally its name was the NKVD. That was changed to NKGB in 1943 and finally shortened to KGB in 1953.

# PART·TWO

# NINE

That evening, at precisely seven o'clock, Peter Burckhardt called.

"Have you eaten?" he immediately asked.

She said she had.

"Then let's go to the Three Kings. We can walk there, have a drink, and maybe dance. Lothar Löffler's orchestra plays there, and he's the best we have in Basel."

"All right, but not too late."

"I'll pick you up at eight and have you home by eleven"

"I'll be waiting downstairs. It's Augustinergasse Eleven, by the way."

"I know."

As she shed her vice-consul uniform, she weighed the merits of the only two dresses she owned suitable for dancing. While doing so, she realized that she was nervous.

Peter Burckhardt arrived as the bells of the ancient cathedral, the Basler Münster, finished chiming eight. He was driving a black Mercedes. When he stepped out of the car, he greeted her with a firm Swiss handshake. No kiss this time. Slightly relieved, Nancy turned the conversation to business.

"Let me tell you what I was able to accomplish today. I went to Bern this morning and spent a short time with Mr. Dulles."

"We know. Twenty-three minutes."

This startled her. Then she remembered.

"Right. You know about the back-door approach to Herrengasse Twenty-three."

"And Colonel Masson was anxious to know how serious you and Mr. Dulles are."

.

"You can tell your Colonel Masson that Mr. Dulles is *very* serious and that he is prepared to meet with him at his earliest convenience."

"Where?"

"He will leave that up to your people. He had a further request. He said that if you could accede to it, it might be helpful . . . in the longer run."

"And that is?"

"That Captain Waibel also be present. And you."

Now it was Peter Burckhardt's turn to be startled.

So Nancy Reichman added, "I think he would like to look you over."

"The way we looked you over last month? Fine with me. But you should tell him it will be up to Colonel Masson."

By this time they had pulled up in front of the Three Kings, the city's premier hotel, located in the center of the city on the southern bank of the Rhine River. Statues of the biblical Three Kings were mounted above the main entrance on the Blumenrain.

They were no sooner inside the lobby than a huge bear of a man approached them.

"Peter," he said. "Was für eine nette Überraschung!" Then he noticed Nancy Reichman at Peter Burckhardt's side and switched immediately to a heavily accented English. "You are the vice-consul, aren't you? I remember you from one of Professor Salin's dinners. Per Jacobsson is my name."

"Of course I remember you, sir. My name is Nancy Reichman."

He took her hand and bowed slightly. "How very nice to see you again."

Peter Burckhardt, watching all this, appeared to be flustered, not quite knowing what the next move should be. His boss at the Bank for International Settlements immediately resolved the problem.

"Now don't worry," Jacobsson continued. "I'm not going to bother you any further. I'm going to bed, since I have to take the early morning train to Berlin. Otherwise," and now he turned back to Nancy, "I certainly would have asked for a dance. Perhaps some other time?"

"I would love that," Nancy replied.

"Maybe the occasion will arise when I return," Jacobsson added, and he glanced at Burckhardt as he said it. Then he bade them good night and disappeared up the hotel stairway.

Peter Burckhardt noticed the puzzled look on Nancy's face.

"Something's bothering you," he said as they started to move toward the bar.

"What is he doing here?"

"He lives in the hotel now. He felt that his family would be safer in Sweden, and after they left, he closed up his apartment and moved into the Three Kings."

"Why would he feel that his family is threatened here?"

"Let's get a drink first. Then I'll explain."

They left their coats at the cloakroom, and when the maitre d' asked Peter whether he preferred to sit at a table or at the bar, Burckhardt suggested a table by the window, overlooking the Rhine. A waiter appeared immediately and took his drink order: a bottle of Veuve Cliquot.

Only then did he return to Nancy's questions. He leaned across the table and spoke in a low voice. "Rumors indicate that the Germans may be planning to invade Switzerland in March. It may be just a matter of weeks."

"From whom have you heard this?"

"That does not matter. Suffice to say that it comes from a source very close to the top in Berlin."

"Why should the Germans invade Switzerland now?"

"Because the whole strategic situation has changed. As late as last September, it appeared that Germany was on the verge of winning the war. Their Sixth Army had just crossed the Don River and was moving into the suburbs of Stalingrad. After that, Moscow and Hitler would have totally controlled Europe, from the Atlantic to the Urals. The last holdout in Europe, Switzerland, under those circumstances would have been just a detail, one that could be taken care of at any time, almost at leisure.

"But then came the landing of the Americans and the British in North Africa on November eighth, and now the German Sixth Army had no choice but to surrender to the Russians at Stalingrad at the end of January. The roles have been reversed. It will now be the Russian army in Eastern Europe and the Americans and the British in North Africa who will be on the offense. And the German Army will be on the *defensive*. The strategic importance of Switzerland has dramatically increased. If the Allies invade Sicily or Sardinia, all of Italy will eventually become a war zone. And the only direct transportation link the Nazis have between Germany and Italy that is controlled by the Nazis is Austria's Brenner Pass. It is extremely vulnerable to bombing attack. So Hitler needs

Switzerland's two north-south railroad tunnels, the Gotthardt and the Simplon, as well as our Alpine passes and roads that go through them. He must ensure that his troops in Italy will not be cut off from their only source of supply, Germany proper."

"And how does this relate to Mr. Dulles?"

"We want his help."

"Can you be more specific?"

"I can be very specific. We are interested in troop movements within Germany. Anything that points to an increasing concentration of military forces in the south of that country would tend to confirm these rumors. What we are specifically watching out for are unusual movements of troop trains and of freight trains moving large numbers of camouflaged flatcars—that's how they transport their tanks and armored personnel carriers to the front. If they are suddenly diverted to the south instead of going east to the Russian front, we will know that serious trouble lies ahead for Switzerland. The Americans and the British are constantly monitoring such movements from the air. We, of course, are unable to conduct aerial surveillance of Germany. But still, we do rather well from the ground. Much of this type of movement take place at night, when aerial cameras are useless anyway.

"What is critical is a very specific piece of information that we need as soon as possible. But first let me back up just slightly to explain. If military intelligence has one key function, it is to help prevent military surprises. Pearl Habor, for instance. We are convinced that if there is one prime 'indicator' of Nazi military intentions vis-à-vis Switzerland, it is the location of the special mountain warfare units of their army. These units would be an essential component of any invasion of our country. For the Nazis know full well that should they attack us from the north, the basic military response of our commander in chief, General Guisan, will be to fall back across the flatlands south of the Rhine to our reduit, our mountain fortress in the Alps, which is centered around and beneath the Gotthardt Pass. From there, our military forces will take their stand and flight, literally, to the death."

Burckhardt paused and briefly looked around the room. More people, most of them young, were arriving, but nobody as yet had taken the adjacent tables.

"Now back to my boss, Per Jacobsson. He heard from his sources in Stockholm a week ago that a significant number of the troops that were concentrated on the Finnish-Russian front have 'disappeared.' The Swedes are worried that they might be moving in their direction. The Wehrmacht unit in question is the Twentieth Alpine Army, under the command of General Eduard Dietl. We want to know where that unit is, and Mr. Dulles can help us. My boss, Colonel Masson, would have preferred to put the request to Mr. Dulles in person, but time is of the essence. We are therefore depending on you, Nancy. If you could . . ."

Lothar Löffler and his orchestra had taken their places on the stage in front of the dance floor. They began to play a Glenn Miller piece in the Glenn Miller style.

"That's 'Moonlight Serenade,'" Nancy observed.

"A pause is in order," he said.

They were the first, and for a time, the only couple to approach the dance floor. It took a few seconds for them to adjust to each other. He became aware of the slimness of her waist and the fullness of her breasts. She pressed closer. The orchestra played "At Last," and Nancy Reichman hoped the music would never stop.

But suddenly Peter Burckhardt stiffened and drew back. When the orchestra finally paused, he steered her back to their table.

"What is it?" she asked when they were once again seated.

"The two men who just sat down at the bar. Don't look now."

"Who are they?"

"One of them is German, a major in the Waffen SS. His name is Hans Wilhelm Eggen. He's watching us, and I don't like it."

"Maybe it's just a coincidence."

"Maybe. But maybe not."

"What's a major in the SS doing in Basel?"

"He's a big wheel in the Beschaffungsamt, the procurement agency of the Waffen SS. They operate under the cover of a company they secretly own—the Warenvertriebs G.m.b.H. Berlin. Two years ago, Eggen signed a contract with a Swiss company located here in Basel, Extroc S.A., for the delivery over a two-year period of two thousand wooden barracks made in Switzerland.[11] Eggen comes here regularly to make sure that everything is on schedule. We're also told that he is currently negotiating for another thousand units. But nobody believes that that's all he does when he visits Switzerland. There was an attempt to kill the British ambas-

11. See Braunschweig, Pierre-Th., *Geheimer Draht nach Berlin* (Zurich, 1989), pp. 179 ff.

sador to Switzerland eighteen months ago. Eggen was in Basel the night it happened."

Then all of a sudden he smiled. "Another new arrival at the bar. And this time it's good news. One of ours. From Lucerne."

Now, despite his warning, Nancy Reichman looked directly at the bar.

"Why is one of ours talking to one of theirs?" she asked. "He's hardly supposed to talk to them first, is he?"

"Perhaps there's a special reason."

Five minutes later, the German got up and left the bar.

"Now our man is also leaving," Burckhardt said. The shocked look on his face indicated that something was wrong.

"I think we had better call it a night, Nancy," he said. After paying the bill, they went to the cloakroom to collect their coats.

As they waited, a man approached Burckhardt from the rear and took firm grip of his right arm. "If you will please excuse us for a moment," he said to Nancy Reichman in English.

The two men then walked to the far corner of the lobby and exchanged what were obviously heated words. After a few minutes, their conversation ended and the intruder turned to leave. But before he did so, he directed one last verbal salvo at Burckhardt, shaking a finger in his face.

When Burckhardt returned, his face was red with anger. "Let's get the hell out of here," he said, taking Nancy's arm.

"Who . . ." she began to ask as he steered her out the door of the hotel.

"The police," he answered. "The head of the political police of the canton of Basel. He wanted to know what 'we' are doing secretly consorting with the Nazis on Swiss soil. And while he was at it, he asked about you. He wants to see me at eight o'clock tomorrow morning in his office for a full explanation, or it is going to be my head."

"What did you tell him?"

"To piss off." He paused. "Sorry. It just slipped out. However, he said something else. He has people who have infiltrated the local groups of Nazi sympathizers. They have heard questions being raised about you during the past couple of days. He warned that if anything happens to you, all hell would break out with the American government and I would be held directly responsible. Eggen's presence in Switzerland, he said, is very bad news, as the British ambassador nearly found out a year and a half ago."

By this time, they had reached his Merceces. Five minutes later, they were back in front of her apartment building. He got out, leaving the motor running.

"I'll see you up."

She did not protest. After she had unlocked her door, he entered the apartment with her. As she turned on the lights, he scanned the room. "Let's check the rest of it," he said. "First the bedroom, then the bath."

"Everything's fine, Peter," she finally assured him.

"All right. But be careful. Speak to Mr. Dulles right away."

"I will. I will also tell him everything first thing in the morning."

She saw him to the door, and as he turned to say good night, she knew that this time it would be more than before. They first kissed tentatively, then deeply. When he finally withdrew and started down the stairs, Nancy discovered that she was trembling.

A man watched all of this through binoculars from the attic of a house directly across the Rhine from Augustinergasse 11. He also watched her undress a few minutes later . . . until she suddenly remembered that the blackout had been in effect for at least an hour and drew the heavy draperies.

# TEN

Despite his bravado the previous evening, Peter Burckhardt showed up five minutes before the eight A.M. deadline that had been put to him. The chief of the political section of the police department of the city and canton of Baselstadt, Dr. Wilhelm Lützelschwab, received him immediately.

"Herr Doktor, nehmen Sie bitte Platz," were Lützelschwab's opening words.

"Danke, Herr Doktor," was Burckhardt's reply. Both men had studied at the university at the same time and had earned their doctorates in the same year, Lützelschwab in law, Burckhardt in economics.

"I'll come directly to the heart of the matter. What are you idiots in the D Bureau doing consorting with a man who reports directly to Heinrich Himmler and who is reputed to be the right-hand man of Walter Schelleberg?[12]

"And what in God's name was that young American woman doing there? She's the vice-consul of the United States. Need I point out to you that the consulate in question is located on *my* territory and that *I* am responsible for keeping her alive? That's diffcult enough in a city that seems to be full of goddamn Germans

---

12. The D Bureau that he referred to was the Swiss Intelligence unit, run chiefly out of Basel, from which all espionage directed at the Deutschland originated. The intelligence "acquisition" was the responsibility of Captain Waibel, who reported to the head of all Swiss espionage operations, Colonel Masson, who operated out of the Hotel Schweizerhof in Lucerne under the code name "Rigi." For a detailed description of the activities of Bureau D (for Deutschland), see Braunschweig, *op. cit.*, pp. 101–150.

■

and Communist sympathizers. But no, you've got to bring in a major in the Waffen SS so he can watch you two walzing around the dance floor. Are you setting her up or what? I thought that the Americans were supposed to be our friends and the Germans our enemies. Or have I somehow gotten things mixed up?"

"I had nothing to do with Eggen's presence at the bar last night," Peter Burckhardt said. "Furthermore, that was not one of our men in the narrow sense of the word. He works out of Lucerne and as far as I know, reports directly to Colonel Masson."

"Are you suggesting that the left hand here in Basel doesn't know what the right hand is up to in Lucerne?"

"It's been known to happen before."

"Did you know that the three of them met later in a room at the Schweizerhof Hotel?"

"No. By the way, who was the man with Eggen?"

"A local lawyer by the name of Rudolph Widmer. Really bad news, in our opinion. And our opinion is based on telephone taps that we maintain on his lines, both in his opulent office downtown and in his fancy apartment in the Gellertquartier."

"Is he German or Swiss?"

"Swiss. He's purportedly Eggen's lawyer here. Advises him on contracts, like the one for the military barracks. Are you guys familiar with that?"

"With the barracks, yes. With this Widmer fellow, no. Should we be?"

Lützelschwab shrugged. Then: "Leave him to us. We want to know what's going on with Eggen so that we can determine whether or not to arrest him. And I want you to pass those exact words on to Lucerne. Immediately. Have I made myself clear?"

"I'll see what I can do. But in the meantime, Herr Doktor, I would like to suggest that perhaps something has come up involving our national interests. Maybe that's why the Lucerne man was here. My suggestion is that you lay off Eggen until you know exactly what's going on."

The two men stared at each other while Peter Burckhardt rose from his chair and headed for the exit without another word.

Burckhardt left the Spiegelhof and walked down the hill to the market square, where he headed for the phone booth. Captain Waibel answered immediately. Burckhardt explained what had just happened. Waibel said he would contact Lucerne, then take care of Lützelschwab.

But he did not sound convincing.

Leaving the phone booth, Burckhardt, who had intended to board a tram for the Bank for International Settlements, changed his mind and instead headed up the Freie Strasse. A few minutes later he stood in front of the world headquarters of the Swiss Bank Corporation. He had an idea.

After announcing himself to the porter, he took the private elevator to the fourth floor, where he was met by another uniformed porter, who ushered him into his father's office, the office of the chairman of the board. His father rose to greet him and they shook hands.

"What a surprise. Sit down over there. I'll get us some coffee." His father went back to his desk and after saying a few words on the intercom to his secretary, joined his son at the coffee table.

"I can stay only a minute," Peter said. "I have two favors to ask of you. Could you call Lützelschwab over at the police department? Tell him we've just talked and that you would appreciate it if he would simply let things be for the moment."

Peter Burckhardt knew that his father had influence that went far beyond Basel. Maximilian Burckhardt was a member of an elite clique made up of Switzerland's most prominent bankers and industrialists, men who advised and assisted Swiss Intelligence. They had contacts at the highest levels in Berlin, Rome, Paris, London, and New York, and they used them to gather information and to constantly reasure *both sides* that Switzerland intended to remain strictly neutral, and to defend that neutrality with its armed forces, if necessary. Since they were regularly briefed by both the Swiss Foreign Office and the military, they were as informed as anybody in the country.

"May I inquire as to what you mean by 'things'?" Herr Doktor Maximilian Burckhardt–Von der Mühl asked his son.

He had obviously been kept in the dark on this one. "That's all you will have to tell him."

His father smiled. "All right. But can you tell me?"

"Yes. And that relates to the second request. May I use our place in Benken for a very private meeting, either tomorrow or the next day?" The "place" Peter Burckhardt referred to was a medieval Schloss ten kilometers outside of Basel, a castle that the Burckhardts had bought and restored forty years earlier.

"I'll send some people up this morning to make sure that

everything is shipshape. And to light some of the fireplaces. It's cold up there this time of year."

"They will need to prepare four or five bedrooms, including the master suite."

"For whom will that be?"

"Allen Dulles, if everything works out."

Burckhardt, Senior, let out a low whistle. "What's the occasion?"

"We've heard, from an excellent source, that Hitler may be planning to attack us in March. We want the Americans to find out if that's true."

His father's face turned grim, but he said nothing.

"One other thing," Peter said. "Can you find out who's all involved with a company by the name of Extroc S.A.?"

"What do they do?"

"Make wooden barracks and sell them to the German Army."

"You're full of news this morning, aren't you, Peter? If they bank with us, I can tell you within minutes."

He went back to his desk, picked up the phone and gave his instructions. Minutes later, a man knocked on the door and entered. He handed a dossier to Peter's father and left. The banker Burckhardt glanced through it rapidly.

"They bank with us. Sales this year are twelve million Swiss francs. Decent profit. It says that they are involved in the manufacture of prefabricated wooden structures, but nowhere does it say that they are selling them to the Nazis." Abruptly he stopped reading.

"If you were looking for trouble, you've found it, son. Guess who's on the board of directors? The son of our commander in chief. If this comes out, this country could be dumped into one hell of a political crisis."

"The man who is in charge of *buying* those barracks, a major in the Waffen SS by the name of Eggen, was in town last night. And Lützelschwab caught one of our men meeting him in the bar of the Three Kings."

"How do you know all this?"

"I happened to be in the Three Kings last night also. Dancing, for God's sake. Which led Lützelschwab to call me on the carpet earlier this morning."

"Don't worry. I'll take care of him as soon as we're done. But what the hell is going on here?"

"I don't know, but I'm increasingly concerned that our people in Lucerne, with the help of Guisan and his son, have gotten into business with some high-ranking Nazis."

"Such as?"

"My guess would be the SS major's boss, Heinrich Himmler."

"Do you mean that the general has been meeting with *Himmler?*"

"Perhaps not yet. But that's where things seem to be heading."

His father's face turned even grimmer. "And now," he said, "Lützelschwab has gotten wind of it and is trying to stop it. Christ, they're all playing with fire. If the general is serious . . ." He paused. "No, it can't be. He isn't trying to work out a deal, surely. Especially now that the German Army has finally been stopped."

"Which may be *why* Masson and the general are running this risk. They want someone to tell Hitler that if he tries to 'consolidate' central Europe by invading Switzerland, he's going to face one hell of a battle."

"If the general is taking those invasion rumors *that* seriously, maybe I should get your mother and sister out of here."

"They would never leave, and you know it," Peter said.

His father's secretary peeked into the room, prompting him to look at his watch. Peter stood up. After she left, the banker said: "Before you leave, I've got a suggestion. Tell your people that if they need a private venue for that other meeting, one that even Lützelschwab and his hound dogs won't be able to penetrate, they can have the Schloss in Benken any time they want, even on short notice. Although I'm not sure that it would be advisable to have both Dulles and Himmler there on the same weekend."

"I'll pass the word along today. And thanks."

# ELEVEN

When Peter Burckhardt arrived at his office at the Bank for International Settlements shortly after nine A.M., there were two messages for him. One asked that he call his aunt — the prearranged signal that he call Captain Waibel. The other came from Nancy Reichman. He called her first.

"About that meeting," she began right after they had exchanged greetings, "our suggestion is tomorrow night. Seven o'clock. You should name the place. And I've passed on the word about the other matter."

Burckhardt immediately phoned his superior in Bureau D of Section 5 of the General Staff of the Swiss Army. He arranged with Captain Waibel for them to use his family's place in Benken as the meeting place. Waibel said he would contact Colonel Masson right away. He also suggested that Burckhardt drop by his office later that morning.

The Basel operations of Bureau D of Swiss Intelligence enjoyed luxurious surroundings — an eighteenth-century patrician mansion located on the Petersplatz, across the park from the new building that now housed the lecture halls of the university. It was less than half a block from the university library. Peter Burckhardt drove there in his Mercedes, and Captain Waibel received him immediately.

"You've kicked up a hornet's nest," were the captain's first words. He was a good-looking man in his late thirties, and despite his officer's rank, he had an easygoing, nonmilitary way about him. "But before I get into that, I want to officially inform you that

.

Colonel Masson has agreed to meet with Mr. Allen Dulles tomorrow evening at seven o'clock at the venue you suggested."

Peter Burckhardt looked at his watch. "I will confirm that to the American vice-consul right away, if I may use your phone. How many from our side? And how many will spent the night?"

"I don't know for sure," Waibel answered, "but I assume that there will be just three of us, including you. My guess is that Masson will probably not want to spend the night, but I will. It's not every day that I get invited to your family's Schloss. Where the Americans are concerned, that's your call."

After talking to Nancy Reichman, Peter hung up and called his father. "It's on for seven tomorrow night," he told him. "Three of us, of which two will stay the night. Two Americans, Dulles and Nancy, and both will stay over."

"Does anybody need travel arrangements?" Waibel asked after Peter hung up.

"I can take care of the Americans," Burckhardt said.

"All right. I'm sure that Masson will arrange to be driven directly to Benken from Lucerne. And I'll drive myself. So we'll all meet there tomorrow night at seven."

"Done."

"Now topic number two," Waibel said. "Heikel, sehr, sehr heikel. Waffen SS Major Eggen, whom you spotted in the Three Kings last night, delivered a request to one of our men from Lucerne: Heinrich Himmler would like to meet with our commander in chief, General Guisan, in Switzerland as soon as possible."

Peter Burckhardt said nothing.

"You don't look very surprised."

"I'm not," Burckhardt answered. "And what was our reply?"

"Himmler? Our man simply told them that it would be suicidal for our general if it ever came out. He sensed that Eggen anticipated this answer since he immediately came up with an alternate suggestion: General Walter Schellenberg, Himmler's deputy and the head of their intelligence operations. It was made clear that the Germans would be very put off if this request was refused. So it wasn't . . . in view of the rumors that have been swirling around."

"When?"

"That has yet to be determined."

"Where?"

"The Germans suggested Arosa. Or Davos. Apparently the good

General Schellenberg likes to ski. We nixed that since the last thing
we want is any public knowledge of this. The Swiss press would kill
us. I talked with Masson this morning at considerable length. When
the question of venue came up for a potential meeting with
Schellenberg, and we are talking here about a *preliminary* meeting,
without General Guisan, I suggested that Masson might consider
using your family's place in Benken again. He said he would want
to check it out first. Which he will do tomorrow evening."

"What about Lützelschwab? He'll go up the goddamn wall if he
finds out that an SS *general* is about to set foot on Basel soil. A
*major* like Eggen was bad enough. But now a Schellenberg?"

"Look, Peter, I'm basically on Lützelschwab's side. And so are
you, I'm sure."

Burckhardt nodded.

"I also talked to Lützelschwab this morning and made it crystal
clear that all the goings-on last night were instigated by Lucerne,
not us. I think he also got the message that the people in Bureau
D, meaning specifically you and me, think that Masson and the
general are being led down the garden path. By the way, he brought
up the subject of the American girl and asked what you were up to
with her at the Three Kings last night."

"What did you tell him?"

"That it had nothing to do with us. That it was a date, pure and
simple."

"Did he believe you?"

"I doubt it. Which reminds me: did she pass on our request to
Dulles?"

"Yes."

"I'll relay that immediately to Masson. You've done all right with
her, Peter, and we're all grateful. She could develop into one of the
most important assets we've got."

"Then we'd better have our people keep an eye on her, especially
at night and over weekends, when she's not inside the consulate."

"I've already thought of that, Peter. Arrangements are being
made."

# TWELVE

In fact, such arrangements had already been made. But not by the Swiss. Other eyes had been watching Nancy Reichman for weeks from the top floor of a house located not across the street from her, but across the Rhine. At that point the river was just over one hundred meters wide. The three-story house from which she was watched was situated in Kleinbasel, home to the city's working-class bars and its nightclubs.

Assisted by Zeiss binoculars, her observers viewed her in minute detail, day and night. The owner of Rhinegasse 37 was Werner Lentz. He represented one of the last remnants of the Rote Kapelle, the Red Orchestra, the espionage network that the Soviets had installed throughout central Europe in the decade prior to the outbreak of World War II. Most of his colleagues had been hunted down and put out of business by the counterespionage unit of the SS—under the leadership of General Walter Schellenberg.[13]

Lentz had come to Basel in 1929, purportedly a returnee from Russia, where his Swiss parents, who were in the watch-repair business, had taken him as a boy. He had learned the skills of watch repair from his father and had no trouble in finding a job with Basel's premier jeweler, Seiler's on the Barfüsserplatz. In 1935, Lentz had opened his own small jewelry shop in Kleinbasel. In 1939, shortly before the war broke out, he had bought that house

13. For the best histories of the Red Orchestra, see Perrault, Gilles, *Auf den Spuren der roten Kapelle* (Zurich, 1956); Flicke, W.F., *Spionagegruppe Rote Kapeile* (Kreuzlingen, 1954); Hoehne, Heinz, *Codeword: Direktor* (New York, 1971); Trepper, Leopold, *The Great Game: Memoirs of the Spy Hitler Couldn't Silence* (New York, 1977).

■

on the Rhine. In reality, Werner Lentz was a full colonel in the NKGB and had been assigned the "operational alias" name of Igor Scitovsky; he was the man whom the Soviets had planted in Switzerland under deep cover.

The prime job of Igor Scitovsky, alias Werner Lentz, was military espionage, and the prime target was Germany. He was part of the Red Orchestra, as were the three Swiss Communists who worked for him. One was a bartender at the Three Kings Hotel, one a room clerk at the Schweizerhof Hotel, and the third an assistant in the jewelry store in Kleinbasel, owned by Lentz/Scitovsky. Together these four monitored Nazi military shipments through Switzerland. Using Zeiss binoculars, they counted the number and types of rail cars coming from Germany through the Badische Bahnhof, the German railroad station located in Basel ten blocks from where Lentz lived. This almost endless string of trains transported war materials destined for deployment in Italy or North Africa. Why such monitoring? According to the Moscow Center, the more war materials that headed south through Switzerland, the less there would be available to resupply the German armies fighting the Soviets on the Eastern front.

That type of information was easy to come by and involved little risk. Accurate information about military movements—troops, armor, and other materials—in Germany proper was of greater importance and more difficult to obtain. By 1943, Schellenberg had eliminated most of their agents, and the Soviets had few "assets" on the ground in Germany. Those who had survived were turning in next to nothing . . . which was why Moscow had decided to infiltrate the other intelligence services operating in Switzerland.

Allen Dulles had just begun to build up a new network. Slipping a double agent inside his fold might be relatively easy to accomplish, and a new agent might help fill the intelligence vacuum. The first step was the surveillance by the Red Orchestra of Dulles' apartment, which was how they had learned about Nancy Reichman.

So far, the surveillance of Nancy Reichman's apartment had turned up nobody, except for a young Swiss aristocrat who worked for the Bank for International Settlements and was thus an unlikely candidate for recruitment by the Soviets. But, it was reasoned, somebody, something, was bound to turn up inside Augustinergasse 11. And on February 25th, they produced a winner.

It set the machinery of the Red Orchestra in full motion for the second night in a row. And it would lead to another flurry of radio traffic between Basel and Moscow, traffic that was already at a dangerously high level that week. Scitovsky agents had reported the presence of an SS colonel in Basel in the company of Swiss agents. The bartender at the Three Kings had overhead elements of their brief conversation and alerted the room clerk at the Schweizerhof. After the special guests arrived fifteen minutes later and collected the key, the Red Orchestra's man inside the Schweizerhof had determined that the room reservation had come from the headquarters of General Guisan himself.

Something was underway—something that could undermine the strategic objectives of Soviet Union.

Allen Dulles arrived at the Bahnhof in Basel at 5:07 that evening. He was met there by Nancy Reichman and Peter Burckhardt. After Nancy had introduced the two men, the three walked to Burckhardt's car across from the station in front of the Bank for International Settlements. Dulles had come with a small black overnight bag that he insisted upon carrying himself.

"Would you like me to put that in the trunk for you, sir?" Burckhardt asked when they arrived at his Mercedes.

"Please."

As Burckhardt did so, Dulles stood back to look at the building that housed the bank. "Did you know that my sister Eleanor wrote her dissertation about the BIS?" he asked Burckhardt.[14]

"No, sir."

"You might look it up some time and give me your opinion. By the way, I understand that you work directly under Per Jacobsson."

"Yes, sir. I do."

"I'd be most interested in meeting him. Is he here?"

"No. He's in Stockholm right now. But he plans to return to Basel next Monday."

"Would you let him know I will be calling him?"

"I will. I'm sure he will be very eager to meet you."

"Good. Then I'll suggest that we dine together. What's his favorite restaurant here in Basel?"

"Unquestionably the Schützenhaus. It was formerly a hunting lodge, but now it's the city's premier restaurant."

14. Her book was published in 1933 by Macmillan under the title, *The Bank for International Settlements at Work*.

Dulles turned to Nancy, who had been standing silent, listening as the two men became acquainted. "Could you arrange that?"

"Certainly."

"Let's tentatively aim for next Tuesday or Wednesday."

Dulles turned back to Burckhardt. "Now, what's the drill for this evening?"

"We are scheduled to meet Colonel Massor at seven. At my family's country home outside of Basel."

"So Nancy told me. How long will it take us to get there?"

"Thirty minutes."

Dulles looked at his watch. "So we have time to spare."

"How about a coffee at my apartment?" Nancy interjected.

"Splendid idea," Dulles replied. "I need a little warming up."

Once they were inside Nancy's apartment and had shed their overcoats, Nancy went into the kitchen to prepare the coffee. The men stood in front of the French doors that led out to the terrace overlooking the Rhine. Darkness had fallen, and the lights of the city—the preblackout lights—were reflected in the swiftly flowing water below. A very dimly lit huge barge came in o view, followed immediately by another, and yet another.

Dulles watched, curious, and then asked, "What are they carrying?"

"Coal, no doubt."

"This happens every night?"

"Yes, sir."

"Where does the coal originate?"

"Germany. The Ruhr. The barges you see down there were probably loaded at Duisburg four or five nights ago. They move only at night, and run with lights only when traveling this very short distance through Basel, where both banks of the Rhine are in neutral Switzerland. As you can imagine, with their size and at the speed with which they move, they are easy targets for any Allied aircraft in the area, bombers or fighters. So they travel at night, and at dawn they pull up to preselected spots on the banks of the Rhine, out in the countryside. They spend the daylight hours there, under heavy camouflage."

"Who owns them?"

"They are Swiss-registered, Swiss-owned, and fly the Swiss flag. Most offload downstream at the Rhine harbor here in Basel, but some, like the ones you are now watching, proceed farther up the Rhine to Augst or Schaffhausen."

"Isn't coal part of the compensation agreements your government has been entering into with the Germans?"

"Yes, but the most recent trade agreement is just about to run out."

"Really?" Dulles paused. "How interesting. Will that come up during our discussion this evening with Colonel Masson?"

"Perhaps."

"Tell me something else if you can, Dr. Burckhardt . . . or may I call you Peter?"

"By all means, sir."

"Good. These barges. Do they return empty?"

"Usually. Although sometimes they carry back some Swiss exports. Bulk cargoes. Like cement."

"But they also move by night and hide by day?"

"Yes, sir."

"What about checkpoints?"

"Normally the barges are kept clear of all harbor facilities in between because such ports are prone to bomber attack at any time."

Nancy entered the living room with a tray bearing coffee. "It's getting late, sir. Perhaps . . ."

They joined her at the coffee table as she poured.

Twenty minutes later they were on their way once again. Nancy Reichman was the last to leave, turning out the lights before she closed and then carefully double-locked the door. The man across the Rhine who had been watching the whole time checked his watch. It would be a close call, but Colonel Scitovsky, whom he had alerted by phone, would probably have had time to get over there before they left.

# THIRTEEN

The Augustinergasse was a dead end for automobiles; it narrowed to a pedestrian passage just fifty meters down the street from Nancy Reichman's apartment. So Peter Burckhardt had to go through a series of maneuvers to turn his Mercedes around before heading back out to the square in front of the cathedral a hundred meters up the street. The Opel van driven by Colonel Scitovsky pulled up immediately behind it. Because there was still a good deal of traffic on the streets of the city—full blackout restrictions would not go into effect until ten o'clock—Scitovsky was not concerned about following the Mercedes too closely.

But ten minutes later he was less confident. As they drove farther into the outskirts of Basel, he dropped farther behind, even letting first one and then another vehicle, the second with military markings, come in between. By the time they had passed beyond city limits, he had dropped so far behind the Mercedes that its taillights were barely visible. Fortunately, it was a fog-free night. The moon was but a sliver in the night sky, so his van would be all but invisible in the rearview mirror of the cars ahead.

They first passed through Binningen, Bottmingen, and Oberwil. One of the cars between Scitovsky's van and the Mercedes had turned off in Bottmingen; the second, the military vehicle, had pulled to the side in Oberwil. The Swiss countryside took over after Oberwil, and during the next seven kilometers, the only lights to be seen were those of the two remaining vehicles, both of them moving fast despite that fact that the road was now becoming increasingly narrow, the terrain more hilly, and the curves more frequent. The

■

next road sign indicated that they were entering the twin villages of Biel and Benken, referred to locally as Biel/Benken.

Suddenly the brake lights of the Mercedes lit up. Scitovsky, a full half kilometer behind, slammed on his brakes and pulled to the side of the road. He switched off the van's lights. From this vantage point, he could easily follow the progress of the Mercedes as it turned right and began climbing a road leading up into the hills west of Biel/Benken. When Scitovsky got out of the van, a crisp layer of snow cracked beneath his boots. He raised the Zeiss night glasses, scanning the western horizon. There, at an elevation of probably four hundred meters and directly in line with the direction the Mercedes was taking, was light. Minutes later the two light sources appeared to merge.

Mr. Allen Dulles, it seemed, had reached his destination.

Colonel Scitovsky had no sooner gotten back into his van than the headlights of another vehicle appeared in his rearview mirror. It was the same vehicle that had stopped at the side of the road two villages back, probably to allow the driver to check his bearings. A half kilometer farther down the road, its brake lights lit up and the vehicle appeared to have once again pulled over to the side of the road, its lights remaining on. Three minutes later it began to move again, turning right off of the main road and then moving up the hill to the west, following the same route the Mercedes had taken. Scitovsky remained in his van in the darkness for another twenty minutes, wondering if there were more vehicles to come. Not a single vehicle passed him in either direction.

Finally he started up the Opel. He turned on the lights and proceeded slowly into the village of Biel, then into Benken. In the center of Benken there was an intersection, and at the near corner of that crossing, on the right, was a restaurant—"Zum Ochsen." Scitovsky pulled up right in front of the dimly lit sign that hung above its entrance and bore the image of a huge oxen. He looked at his watch: 7:22. Plenty of time before the blackout would be enforced.

It was a typical Swiss village inn, with ancient beams crisscrossing the ceiling, wooden floors, and pewter plates and mugs mounted on the walls. In the front of the room there were a dozen tables covered with red-and-white tablecloths and immaculately set for dinner. Only one was occupied. To the rear were another five tables—no tablecloths there. The waitress, clad in a peasant costume, immediately approached his table.

"Guete n'Obe, Fräulein," Scitovsky began. "Ich hät gärn e Bier und e Paar Würschtli." He was speaking in the dialect of the urban half-canton of Baselstadt.

The waitress returned immediately with the beer Scitovsky had ordered. She delivered it with an inviting smile . . . for Scitovsky was a good-looking man in his late thirties, and a quick glance at his right hand confirmed the absence of a wedding band.

"I'll be back with the wieners in a few minutes."

"I'm in no hurry." And he smiled right back at her. "After all, it's nice and warm in here. It must be ten below freezing outside."

"It's actually twelve below," she said. "I'm not looking forward to walking home tonight."

"I hope you don't live too far away."

"No, no. It's just a few hundred meters. Benken is not Basel, you know."

"Be happy it isn't."

"They all say that. But since the war started, it has been very quiet here. Even on weekends. Because of the gas rationing, you know."

"I can understand that. It must get to be very lonely at times. Although I did notice at least two cars ahead of me on the road from Basel. And both turned off here."

"Ja. But that's because of the Schloss. Those people have nothing to do with us."

"Really. Who owns it?"

"One of those families in Basel. You know, the 'Dorig.'"

"A Sarasin? Or perhaps a Von der Mühl?" And he spoke in imitation of the haughty form of the Basel dialect used by that city's aristocrats.

She giggled. "You don't like them either."

"Not too many do."

"Well, these are Burckhardts."

"Which ones?"

"The old one is the big banker. You must know of him."

"Of course. He runs, or some say he rules, the Swiss Bank Corporation."

"That's the one. You know, it's really quite odd. This is the second time this evening that this subject has come up. Right before you arrived, somebody else came in to ask how to get to the Burckhardts' Schloss. A big shot in the army. A colonel, I think. Something's obviously going on. Probably a big dinner party. I saw two of the maids shopping for food in the Migros store this morning." She paused. "Now I've got to go and see after your wieners."

The wieners came with potato salad, hard rolls, and a tube of mustard. When he was through eating, Scitovsky looked directly at the waitress, who had been watching him most of the time from her perch behind the bar. She immediately came over.

"I think I'll switch to wine. After all, 'Wein nach Bier, das rat ich Dir.' What would you suggest?"

"Something local?"

"Yes. And why don't you bring a glass for yourself? That is, if the Wirt allows it. It does not look like you're going to be busy tonight."

"The Wirt's not here tonight." She looked over at the occupied table. "And they're taken care of for a while. Sure. Why not?"

During the next half hour, over a slightly sour though quite drinkable Baselbieter Riesling, he learned that her name was Liselotte. She was twenty-seven. Her family were farmers and had owned and worked several parcels of land outside of Benken for generations. They had cows and chickens, and some cherry trees from which her father made Kirschwasser every spring. She not only worked as a waitress at "Zum Ochsen" six days a week—she had Sundays off—but was also expected to help out at home, including taking her turn milking those stupid cows and even cleaning out the disgusting chicken pen.

She had a pretty face, and beneath the peasant costume there was apparently a very full peasant body that seemed ready for some robust animal activity that had nothing to do with either cows or chickens.

The first glass of wine was followed by a second. She continued to talk—about her brother, who was a lazy bum, about her three sisters, all still in school, and about how she would move to Basel in a second if only she could find some kind of job there. She punctuated her remarks by reaching over to touch Scitovsky's hand. And it was an increasingly hot little hand that did so . . . especially after he revealed that he owned a small jewelry store in Basel and might need more help there. Maybe someone to work at the counter, to clean up in the evening.

By nine o'clock, the other couple had left and they were alone. Lentz checked his watch.

"I've got to get back to Basel before the blackout starts, Lise-

lotte." He looked into her eyes as he said it. "So as much as I hate
to do so, I'm afraid I must ask you for the check."

When she came back, he laid two ten-franc notes on top of the
tab and rose to collect his coat. When she returned with his change,
he waved it aside.

"Will I hear from you again?" she asked as he began shrugging
into his overcoat.

"Definitely," he said, thinking that this was too good to pass up
in any case. "Maybe we could take in a movie together. In Basel. I
could pick you up. On a Sunday. Maybe this Sunday?"

"Oh, I'd love that."

They walked to the door together, and when he stepped outside
into the darkness, she followed him.

"But you'll catch cold," he protested.

"I just want to thank you for the wine. And to tell you how much
I am looking forward to Sunday."

He stepped toward her and, very hesitantly, kissed her on the
cheek. She moved into him—all the way. And now he kissed her
fully on the lips. She responded by pressing even closer. His hand
moved over her back. And then to her breasts.

Liselotte was ready. Scitovsky guessed that with little encourage-
ment, she would end up in his bed after the Sunday matinee.

And, as a bonus, Colonel Igor Scitovsky would have another
"asset on the ground" just down the hill from the Bruckhardts'
Schloss.

# FOURTEEN

Peter Burckhardt served as Nancy Reichman and Allen Dulles' tour guide. Leading them through the Schloss, he described its history.

"The Benkener Schloss was built by a local mercenary in the employ of King Louis the Twelfth of France. By the eighteenth century, the founder's family had become impoverished and had fallen back into obscurity. The Schloss remained abandoned thereafter, right up to nineteen three, when my great-grandfather gained control of the castle and, parcel by parcel, the land surrounding it, land that now extends up to the Swiss frontier with France. Most of the land is kept as a hunting reserve, although a small section, about twenty hectares, is planted in Riesling grapes, just as it was centuries earlier. In fact, the house wine of the local inn, 'Zum Ochsen,' is made from grapes grown on the estate. It took almost ten years for the castle to be fully restored. But since the beginning of World War One, it has served as our summer home. I spent every summer of my childhood here."

"How I envy you for that," said Nancy Reichman.

They returned to the main living room, dominated by a fireplace in which huge logs were burning. When they entered, the two Swiss army officers who had been sitting before its blazing hearth rose from their chairs. The greeting formalities had been taken care of earlier, when both parties—the Swiss and the Americans—had arrived within five minutes of each other.

"If you all agree, I would like to suggest that we sit down to dinner," Burckhardt said.

Entering the dining room was like stepping back into the fifteenth century. An immense oak table was the centerpiece. Gobelin tapestries adorned the walls, and medieval arms—from crossbows to pikes—seemed to be there for a purpose rather than for mere display.

There were five elegant places set at the table. Baccarat crystal glasses accompanied blue Meissen china atop pewter underplates. Jetzler silverware shone at each setting. Peter Burckhardt immediately put Allen Dulles between himself and Nancy Reichman, with Nancy to his right, of course, directly across from the two Swiss army officers, Colonel Roger Masson and Captain Max Waibel. They were no sooner seated than a manservant appeared and poured white wine. He was immediately followed by two serving girls bearing smoked trout and Alsatian goose-liver pâté.

It was Dulles who broke the ice. "Colonel Masson, it is an honor to meet you. I know how difficult it must have been for you to come here this evening, and I appreciate it. I am here to offer our support in maintaining the neutrality and independence of Switzerland."

Masson's response, given ostentatiously in French, made it clear that he intended to proceed cautiously. Nancy Reichman, aware that Allen Dulles was not fluent in French, translated into English, murmuring the words as the Swiss army officer spoke.

"We Swiss appreciate your sentiments, Mr. Dulles. I am personally honored that you are here this evening. We have a great respect for you and your country. As you know, we Swiss take our neutrality seriously and would defend that neutrality against any belligerent action, by military force if necessary. It is the closeness of that possibility that prompted me to suggest this meeting."

Peter Burckhardt sprang into the breach of silence that followed. "What I have to offer is a humble Baselbieter Riesling and the suggestion that we raise our glasses in celebration of the friendship that has always existed between the two oldest democracies on earth, Switzerland and the United States."

After the five glasses were half emptied, Nancy Reichman began a conversation in impeccable French with Colonel Masson. They began by noting how well the Swiss population was coping with such wartime hardships as rationing and blackouts, then moved on to more serious matters, such as the role of the Swiss Red Cross in monitoring the prisoner-of-war camps in Germany, where many downed American fliers were being held.

Nancy's appreciation of their efforts pleased Masson. He began to gradually relax.

This process was enhanced by the arrival of the red wine, a superb 1934 Pomerol. The main course consisted of marinated wild boar, accompanied by mashed potatoes and carrots. A second bottle of Pomerol was needed almost immediately. By the time dessert was served—Schwarzwäldertorte—the atmosphere had changed to one of congeniality.

At nine o'clock Peter Burckhardt consulted his watch and then addressed his military superiors seated across the table. "If you agree, I would suggest that we retire to the library and move on to the more serious part of the evening."

Colonel Masson nodded his agreement. And as soon as the only woman present rose from the table, assisted by her boss, Allen Dulles, the two American diplomats and the two Swiss military officers followed Peter Burckhardt into the library. A valet offered a choice of cognac or Kirschwasser. All went for the Kirschwasser except Nancy Reichman, who accepted the suggestion of a glass of champagne.

The room, warmed by a lively flame in the huge fireplace, was dominated by leather-bound objects: hundreds of books on the ancient oaken shelves. The massive furniture was grouped in three areas defined by huge Persian rugs that partially covered the original stone floor. Peter Burckhardt led them to the stuffed leather chairs arranged in front of the fireplace. Dulles and Nancy Reichman took their places on the left side of that semicircle, facing the two uniformed Swiss officers, with Peter Burckhardt in the middle. All eyes turned to the Swiss colonel, for all knew that the next move was his.

Masson was a portly man with a kind face. A native of the French-speaking part of Switzerland, he had been a career military officer all his life. He had received his principal military training at the *Ecole supérieure de guerre* in Paris in the 1920s. In 1936, he was appointed head of Section 5 of the General Staff of the Swiss High Command, the military intelligence unit. At that time, the entire intelligence service of Switzerland was made up of just two people, Masson and his secretary. In February of 1938, however, just weeks before the annexation of neighboring Austria by the Nazis, the intelligence service was radically upgraded in importance, at least by Swiss standards, and by early 1943, it had a full-time staff of a hundred and thirty professional intelligence officers. But these numbers greatly understated the capability of Swiss Intelligence under the leadership of Colonel Masson.

In the eighteen months between its reorganization and the outbreak of war in September of 1939, Colonel Masson's organization had recruited hundreds of part-time informants and agents abroad, predominantly Swiss nationals who lived and worked as architects, doctors, teachers, and housewives in France, Italy, Austria, and Germany. This network of agents was for the most part situated in a hundred-kilometer-wide zone on the other side of the Swiss border, and the greatest concentration was in south Germany, north of that stretch of the Rhine that flowed between Basel and the Lake of Constance. The man in charge of this network of agents—in fact, in charge of all espionage conducted against Germany—sat to the left of Colonel Masson: Captain Max Waibel.

"I am sure you know," Masson began in French, "that we in Swiss Intelligence regard the detection of a potential surprise military attack on our country as our prime mission. We have reason to believe that such an attack is being organized right now. We would have no problem in verifying this were conditions today similar to those that prevailed in World War One, when troops moved on foot and artillery was often horse-drawn. Prior to any assault, there was a massive military buildup relatively close to the territory to be attacked, and this buildup would give it away. Unfortunately, the nature of warfare has changed so much during the past thirty years that an attacking army can now cover a hundred kilometers a day. Which means that if they intend to invade us, the massing of their forces will no doubt take place beyond the range of our surveillance capability . . . which generally extends no more than a hundred kilometers beyond our border.

"However, we do have sources of information in high places. Two of these sources—impeccable sources, I might add—have informed us that an attack is planned for either March sixth or March twenty-fifth."

For some reason, this last sentence caused Captain Waibel's eyebrows to raise ever so slightly, though nobody except Nancy Reichman appeared to notice it.

Masson continued, looking directly at Allen Dulles as he spoke. "To be truthful, Mr. Dulles, and I pride myself on always being so, we have been unable to verify this from any third source. Which leave us in a quandary. If we, and I refer now to the General Staff of the Swiss Army under the command of General Guisan, are to take this threat seriously, we have no choice but to order a general

mobilization on a scale similar to that undertaken at the outbreak
of the war. At that time, we put a half-million Swiss under arms
and at full alert, and this in a country with a population of less than
five million. Needless to say, the cost was enormous, both in direct
costs incurred by the defense department and even more so in the
loss of national output, because so many able-bodied men of this
country had to leave their factories and farms and desks to join
their military units in the field. Right now our troop strength stands
at one hundred thousand men. We are a much weaker nation today
than we were in nineteen thirty-nine and nineteen forty. If we went
back to a full mobilization now, we would become economically
paralyzed. Our liquid fuel supply would be almost totally depleted
as we moved troops and armor into place. The effect of mobilization
on our future foodstuff supply could be equally disastrous if our
farm population were to be diverted into the army just when spring
planting must begin. Yet not to mobilize would be tantamount to
surrender."

He paused, and as soon as Nancy Reichman had completed the
translation, Allen Dulles tried to interrupt. But to no avail.

"Then there is the other danger to be considered. *If* our information regarding the invasion plans of the Wehrmacht proves in
the end to be incorrect, but *if*, nevertheless, we have mobilized
before we could make that determination, our actions could be
regarded as a serious act of provocation by the leaders of
Germany. And rightly so. They could regard a mobilization now as
indicative of our reassessment of the possible outcome of this war—
following your recent victories in North Africa and their defeat at
Stalingrad. This could prod the Führer into making a preemptive
attack on us. Our mobilization could end up as a self-fulfilling
prophecy."

"What can we offer you?" Dulles asked.

"What we have already asked for—reliable information about
German intentions during the coming three weeks. A mistake now
could prove fatal for you as well as for us, Mr. Dulles. If the
Germans were to ultimately gain control of the entire Alps, it
would make attacks on Germany from the south extremely difficult, even impossible. I don't have to tell you what that would
mean."

"You've made your situation abundantly clear, Colonel Masson,"
Dulles said.

He reached into the inside pocket of his suit jacket and extracted a brown envelope. Rising from his chair, he stepped across the semicircle facing the fireplace and handed it to the colonel. Masson opened it and took out its contents: two single sheets of paper. As he began reading, Dulles, who had returned to his chair, resumed talking.

"The top sheet you are now reading gives a summary of our aerial surveillance of Germany, conducted during the past seventy-two hours, as it relates to your specific problem. The report was personally transmitted to me from London by Vice-Marshal Matthew Kelly, who is in charge of such matters for the RAF."

Captain Waibel interrupted for the first time since the "official" part of the evening had begun. "Those seventy-two hours. When did they end?"

"At nightfall yesterday. But if anything new, startlingly new, had come up since dawn today, I would have been informed before I came over here this afternoon. I left my office in Bern at fifteen twenty-five." Dulles had his eyes on Colonel Masson. "As for the Twentieth Army, we went to the Russians on that one. After all, it is they who are engaged with the Germans—and the Finns—on that battle line along the border between Russia and northeastern Finland. The best intelligence on the situation in that part of the world comes from the *Glovnoye Razvedyvatelnoye Upravlenie*, the Soviet Military Intelligence. They informed us—yesterday—that the Twentieth Army, the German Wehrmacht's crack Alpine unit under the command of General Eduard Dietl, is fully in place in Lapland."

"Your conclusion?" Waibel asked.

"That this is a false alarm. And that it would be folly for your general to order a general mobilization at this time. Or to accept any 'deal' that the Nazis may suggest. We believe that somebody in Berlin is cooking this whole thing up in order to strengthen their hold over you."

Colonel Masson's face turned to stone. He folded the two sheets of paper, slowly, deliberately, and inserted them back into the yellow envelope. He got up, returned the envelope to Allen Dulles, and then spoke once again—this time in English.

"Thank you, Mr. Dulles. Your help is greatly appreciated. We shall be evaluating your information immediately. I would appreciate it if you and your people keep our conversation this evening confidential. I also would recommend that you report back to your superiors in Washington by courier. Your other means of communication, sir, are not secure."[15]

He then offered his hand to Allen Dulles who, caught by surprise, rose hastily from his chair to grasp it.

The rest of them were on their feet, and it was to Captain Max Waibel that Colonel Masson now turned. He reverted to French. "J'aimerais bien que vous et Lieutenant Burckhardt m'accompagniez à ma voiture."

His last act before leaving the library was to kiss the hand of Nancy Reichman while murmuring how great his pleasure had been at having had the opportunity to meet her. Then the three Swiss officers left the room, leaving Allen Dulles and Nancy Reichman standing side by side in front of the fireplace.

"What was that all about?" she asked.

"My guess is that Masson's intentions tonight were to somehow draw me into his negotiations with the Germans. And when he realized that he had failed, he simply left in a huff."

Dulles reached into the side pocket of his jacket and withdrew first a pipe and then a small packet of tobacco. "Do you mind?"

"Of course not," Nancy Reichman answered.

Dulles took his time lighting the pipe, and after a few puffs, he said, "I'm afraid that some influential Germans have decided to really put the pressure on Switzerland. These are men who have come to the reluctant conclusion that the war will be lost if they must continue fighting both us and the Russians. So they are seeking a diplomatic alternative, which would involve Switzerland as the intermediary. To gain Switzerland's support, they are using the bad-cop, good-cop approach. If the Swiss cooperate with the good cops, maybe they can convince the bad cops to lay off."

"What do they want specifically from the Swiss?" she asked.

"That they use their good services to work out a deal between the Anglo-Saxons and Germany—a deal that would allow the Germans to devote all of their resources to the single purpose of defeating Russia and preventing all of Europe from coming under the influence of the Bolsheviks."

"But that's absurd!"

"Not in the view of the foreign minister of Switzerland, Marcel Pilet. He actually summoned our ambassador, and your official

---

15. See Dulles, *Germany's Underground* (New York, 1947), p. 130.

boss—Leland Harrison—to his office yesterday afternoon to discuss just that. Apparently the German ambassador to Switzerland, Otto Karl Köcher, had put him up to it.[16] As for Masson, he has already met twice with the head of SS Intelligence, once last November just across the border in Waldshut, and a second time in Switzerland, near Schaffhausen, in January. Which brings me to those mysterious goings-on you witnessed at the Three Kings Hotel the other night. We think they were in the process of setting up a third meeting. Probably near here. One that will no doubt take place very soon, with or without my presence."

"But why would Masson get so deeply involved with the Nazis?"

"Naiveté, my dear. Plus a thorough mistrust of Soviet intentions after this war is over . . . a mistrust that I fully share, I might add."[17]

"But what if all this gets back to the Russians?"

However, the library door opened once again, and Peter Burck-hardt and Captain Max Waibel reentered the room.

16. See Bonjour, Edgar, *Geschichte der Schweizerishen Neutralität* (hereafter cited as "Bonjour"), Vol. V (Basel, 1970), p. 188. Bonjour is the official chronicler of Swiss neutrality during World War II. I had the opportunity to study under him at the University of Basel in the second half of the 1950s.

17. For a history of Swiss-Soviet relations, see Bonjour, Vol. V, pp 373 ff.

# FIFTEEN

Waibel immediately approached Dulles. "My apologies for the behavior of Colonel Masson," he said.

"Not to worry. We are all under stress."

"I think that the circumstances call for a strong dose of cognac," said Peter Burckhardt. "By the way, you are still staying the night, aren't you?"

"Of course," Dulles answered. He sat down in front of the fireplace and relit his pipe.

The cognac arrived. This time Nancy Reichman accepted a glass.

"I would like to make it clear," Waibel said, "that my views are not necessarily always those of Colonel Masson. I would also like to ask you a question."

"Surely," Dulles answered.

"You suggested that someone in Berlin is leading us down the garden path. Perhaps you could elaborate."

"By 'someone in Berlin' I mean General Walter Schellenberg, acting on behalf of Heinrich Himmler."

Waibel stared at him grimly. "Our second 'impeccable' source."

"You disapprove of him?" Dulles asked.

"I and my entire staff thoroughly disapprove of Masson consorting with the likes of Schellenberg," Waibel answered.

"Then allow me a question, Captain Waibel."

"Max."

"All right, Max it is. Who is your other source?"

Max shook his head. "All I can tell you is that it is the best single source we have."

■

"Our British colleagues tell me you have given that source a code name: you call it the 'Viking Line.'"[18]

"British Intelligence is seldom wrong." Waibel fell silent for a moment. Then: "I will tell you this. Viking is privy to the deliberations of the General Staff of the German Wehrmacht. And sometimes privy to the actual military decisions made in Berlin and, more important, at the Führer's command post in the Wolfschanz in East Prussia, where he now spends most of his time. Although I thoroughly mistrust *any* information that comes down the line from Himmler and Schellenberg, I have *complete* trust in the Viking Line."

"I assume that the Viking Line is one of your personal 'accounts.'"

"It is. And it will stay that way."

"Following up on what Colonel Masson said, can you be more specific about the information you've had from the Viking source? And when you received it?"

"It first came through to me on January sixteenth. And it has subsequently been reconfirmed twice."

"Specifics," Dulles repeated.

"That should the Allies invade Italy, and I quote the exact words that came from Viking: 'Since the Swiss Army will act as a shield, protecting the Anglo-Saxon military forces as they move toward us, Switzerland will be attacked in two stages.'

"Viking goes on to say that the battle plans were worked out by General Dietl, acting under direct orders from Hitler. His Twentieth Alpine Army will spearhead the attack in night parachute drops and glider landings aimed at securing the Gotthardt Redoubt. Other drops will be made in the northern foothills of the Alps. This first wave will involve a hundred thousand men. Simultaneously, there will be a massive bomber attack on the major Swiss cities north of the Alps—Zürich, Basel, Bern, Lucerne, and Schaffhausen. An hour after Dietl confirms that his attack behind the main

---

18. This "Viking Line" is alluded to in all histories of Switzerland's role in World War II, but in no case is the exact identity of the German or Germans who were providing the Swiss with their most important intelligence during this war ever revealed. It is thought, however, that he or they were attached to Hitler's personal communications center and were thus privy to all of Hitler's decisions as soon as they were communicated to the German High Command, or directly to the commanding generals on the various fronts.

Swiss line of defense has been successful, a Panzer column, stationed five hundred kilometers north of the Swiss border, will begin to move south at a speed of seventy kilometers an hour. These units will secure the major centers of population. Immediately behind it, motorized units of the Waffen SS will follow. Once on Swiss soil, their primary task will be to enter these population centers and 'eliminate' any Swiss, military and civilian, who might be inclined to organize partisan activities after the invasion is over. The main invasion force, which will follow the Waffen SS units across the Rhine, will be the new 'Southern Army' of the Wehrmacht, now in formation, composed of a million regular troops. And all this will begin on March sixth."

"And you believe it?"

"Yes, sir. Maybe not the exact date, but the rest, yes."

"We don't. In fact, we have been aware of this almost from the beginning and were highly skeptical even *before* receiving the latest information I gave to Colonel Masson this evening." Dulles reached into the breast pocket of his jacket and extracted another single-page document. "This is a message relayed to Washington by our military attaché in Bern, Captain Legge. Legge and I don't talk much directly since the chief of our legation here tries to keep me out of his embassy."[19]

Weibel read it and appeared shaken. "I don't know how Legge found out about this. But I'll take Viking's word over his any day."

"That is your choice. In any case, we'll keep you informed if our intelligence assessment changes. That is, if you want to remain in contact."

"Of course I do. I would suggest, however, that we leave Masson and Lucerne out of this."

"Agreed. And may I further suggest that Miss Reichman and your Lieutenant Burckhardt continue to serve as intermediaries?"

"Perfect."

"Good. And if this arrangement continues to work for you where this 'March alarm' is concerned, it could be used for other purposes."

"Such as?"

"Some joint ventures. In areas where our interests overlap."

"Do you have something specific in mind?"

19. See p. 82 for a copy of this document, (Braunschweig, Pierre-Th., *Geheimer Draht nach Berlin* [Zurich, 1989], p. 269).

"Yes. In two areas particularly. We want a pipeline straight to the Führer, one similar to the Viking Line. We also could use your help in estimating the efficacy of our bombing. This interest goes beyond its effect on industrial output and disruptions in transportation. We are equally interested in knowing how the bombing is affecting the morale of the German people. That type of assessment can only come from agents on the ground, which you apparently have."

"You're right. We do have such resources. However, our 'range' is limited. It includes such cities as Stuttgart, Mannheim, Karlsruhe, Munich. But frankly, north of that, our capability diminishes rapidly."

"Any help would be welcomed."

"I understand."

Now Peter Burckhardt, after receiving a nod from his superior, broke out of his role as the neutral host for the first time that evening. "I don't know how familiar you are with the BIS, Mr. Dulles, but we have a constant flow of visitors from Germany, men who operate at the highest level and are in regular personal contact with Hitler. Perhaps, for whatever reason, one or more of them might help."

"Can you name names?"

"Yes. Hermann Schmitz. He's chairman of IG Farben. And Baron Kurt von Schröder, head of the J. H. Stein Bank in Cologne. He's supposed to be the financier of the Gestapo. Both are on the board of directors of the BIS. Then, more important, there are Dr. Walther Funk and Emil Puhl. They co-run Germany's central bank, the Reichsbank. They were Hitler's personal appointees to the board of the BIS, and it is well known that their brief is to make sure that the BIS continues to function as Germany's back door to international finance, no matter what happens."

"How do you rate them?"

"Of the four, I would say that Puhl is the most interesting. He was close to Hjalmar Schacht. In fact, the two of them helped found the BIS. Schacht, as you must know, is now in a concentration camp. We understand that Puhl is a member of the 'Mitwochgesellschaft' in Berlin. Have you heard of it?"

"No."

"It is a discussion group of the kind that today can be found only in central Europe. The Wednesday Society was started in the middle of the nineteenth century and has always been confined to

EC 30
filed 29/1920Z
dm

Jan 29
2108Z

*G-2 report on rumors of German invasion of Switzerland*

From: Bern
To:   Milid

No. 450  January 29, 1943

Following 609:303 has been aware some for
Special General Staff studying new plan invasion
of Switzerland under direction Diete recently
in Munich latter reports have stated event invasion of Italy by Allies Germany could not have
large part mountainous frontier held by a nation
which was only advance guard of Allies.

Plans based on surprise air invasion before
Swiss could concentrate in National Redoubt
parachute and air landings troops neutralizes
troops concentration, Deny roads and destroys
critical points. Motorized and mechanized ground
invading forces in order to retain surprise makes
last march considerable distance from frontier.

1:25000 scale map of Redoubt prepared by
Germans have been obtained by 303 agent.

Situation German Army precludes this as
present danger but Swiss alert to possibility.

Legge

ACTION:  G-2 -H

INFORMATION:  OPD
              CG AAF

CM-IN-14129  (30 Jan 43)  1210Z  ems

| | DISTRIBUTION | |
|---|---|---|
| | | STRONG |
| RS | | KRONER |
| BRATTON | MA | |
| SIT | FL | |
| MIB | CIG | |
| SW | SSB | |
| AIR | FIN | |
| NA | TRNG | |
| FE | POW | |
| EA | PERS | |
| AIC | CC | |
| PUBL | ONI | |
| COLL | | |
| PWB | | |

sixteen members, who dine together weekly in Berlin . . . obviously on Wednesdays. Its purpose is to bring scientists together with other intellectuals, although at present it includes a general of the Wehrmacht. He was admitted, I am told, only because of his knowledge of military history."[20]

Dulles was alert.

"You said *scientists* and other intellectuals?"

"Yes," Burckhardt replied.

"What kind of scientists? We are especially interested in them."

"Chemists most probably," Burckhardt said. "Although I must tell you that we Swiss regard it unlikely that the Germans will revert to gas warfare."

"I tend to agree. Yet contacts with chemists would still be useful. And with physicists. Especially with physicists. This is all very interesting. How can we go about pursuing these ideas further?"

"May I suggest that you activate the Reichman-Burckhardt Line?"

Dulles laughed. "I like that." He looked at his watch. "But now I must go to bed."

He rose from his armchair, and the three younger people immediately did the same.

"I will show you to your room, sir," Burckhard said.

Dulles shook hands first with Nancy Reichman and then with Max Waibel. "Be careful of that fellow Schellenberg. He's liable to get all of you into trouble. Also keep your eyes open for the Russians. Switzerland is not exactly their favorite country."

20. See Dulles, Allen, *Germany's Underground*, p. 27.

# SIXTEEN

The next morning, breakfast was served in everybody's room. At eight sharp the exodus from the Benkener Schloss began. Captain Waibel returned to his office in a Swiss army car, and Peter Burckhardt drove the two Americans to Basel in his Mercedes, dropping Allen Dulles at the central train station, where he caught the nine-o'clock train back to Bern. After taking Nancy Reichman to her apartment at Augustinergasse 11, he headed for his office at the Bank for International Settlements.

Peter Burckhardt had barely sat down behind his desk when the phone rang. It was Colonel Masson. Contrary to Burckhardt's expectations, the colonel seemed to be in the best of moods.

"I hadn't expected to find you back in the office already, Peter. You must have gone to bed earlier than I thought you would. How did the evening end up?"

"Very well. Mr. Dulles went to bed no more than ten minutes after you left. I dropped him off at the station about half an hour ago. The only business discussed this morning was his request again that I set up a meeting for him with Per Jacobsson next Tuesday or Wednesday . . . after Jacobsson gets back from Stockholm."

"I assume you'll ask Jacobsson if he's heard anything further about the situation in Finland."

"Yes, sir. I'll talk to him as soon as I can."

"And you'll report to me immediately thereafter, even if it's late."

"Yes, sir."

"Good. Now, Peter, the arrangements you made for our meeting with Mr. Dulles yesterday were absolutely perfect. The venue ensured total privacy, and the ambiance could not have been better. I want you to do it again. Next Tuesday."

"Same procedure?"

"Yes. You can count on the visitors to arrive in Benken around six o'clock in the evening. We expect two of them, and there will undoubtedly be a second car with security personnel. Two of my staff will meet them at the border. I'll be coming alone with my driver in a separate vehicle. All will be staying overnight at the Schloss, if that is convenient."

"No problem, sir. What about the drivers?"

"They can take care of themselves."

"Do you want me present?"

"Of course. Although I think our guests will feel more comfortable if you were to retire before any serious discussions began."

"Yes, sir."

"Good. Then I'll hear from you after you've spoken to Jacobsson on Monday?"

"Yes, sir."

"Then have a good weekend."

"Thank you, sir."

Burckhardt did not have to ask who it was. The fact that no mention had been made of Waibel cinched it. It had to be Schellenberg. And the second man? It could be either Schellenberg's boss, Heinrich Himmler, or that SS Major Eggen. It now appeared that Masson helped set this thing up. He must have known for days that they were coming. Which explains, Burckhardt thought, Masson's skeptical attitude toward Dulles last night. Whatever Dulles said had to come, by definition, from secondary sources. Masson, however, was dealing with primary sources. *Men who sat at the right hand of the Führer,* for God's sake. Men who not only knew Hitler's plans regarding Switzerland, but who were in a position to influence Hitler on the execution of such plans.

It's worth the gamble, Burckhardt thought, despite the words of warning that Dulles had expressed.

He called his father to let him know that the Benkener Schloss would be needed again, since "some visitors from the north" would be arriving the following Tuesday.

His father understood immediately. 'We will show those scum how things are run in a civilized country. I'll send our people out on Sunday to prepare for them."

"They were returning to Basel this morning on the bus."

"They'll have to get back on the bus. In fact, I will go to Benken myself on Sunday to make sure that things are done properly. You have to realize, Peter, that the Nazis, all of them, are thugs. Had their boss not grabbed power through intimidation, the likelihood of their ever being invited to the Benkener Schloss would have remained zero. So this is our chance to intimidate *them.*"

"If you say so, Father." Peter sounded less than convinced.

"I definitely say so."

# SEVENTEEN

Two days later, Colonel Igor Scitovsky, alias Werner Lentz, picked up Liselotte Maurer in front of the restaurant "Zum Ochsen" in Benken. She was dressed in her Sunday best and bubbling with enthusiasm. She had barely taken her place beside Lentz in the front seat of his van when she began.

"Oh, what a morning it's been so far!"

"What happened?" Lentz asked as he turned the van around in front of the restaurant and started to head back toward Basel.

"First we were late for church because two of the cows got out and onto the highway, and all of us—Mutti, Vatti, my sisters, and I—and mind you, all dressed like this!—had to round them up and bring them back to the barn. Then at church the Pfarrer sneezed right in the middle of his sermon, and my sister and I started to giggle. Everybody looked at us. Mutti could have killed us. Then after church, we walked home as usual, and as we passed in front of the restaurant, the Wirt saw me and asked if I could help out, just for a little while. The restaurant is always busy on Sundays, but then on top of that, totally unexpectedly, the banker Burckhardt, the old one who owns the Schloss, turned up for lunch with his wife. They said that a separate party would be arriving later on the bus and that we should prepare a special lunch for them, too, and to send the bill up to the Schloss. So I helped in the kitchen, peeling potatoes, cutting carrots, that sort of thing." She paused, out of breath.

"Who was in that separate party?"

"The Burckhardts' servants. They are all in there right now. The maids, the valet, the driver, two gardeners! Can you imagine! But when you think of it, isn't that nice of the old Burckhardt. They always say that he is very stuck-up—talks to nobody in Benken. Just comes and goes like an English lord. But I'll bet English lords don't treat *their* help to lunch on Sundays."

"But why are they all here in Benken?"

"Well, I put exactly that same question to Heidi—she's one of their maids, the cousin of a girl I went to school with here in Benken. Heidi said that they had all just left on Friday after a big do with some big-shot Americans and now here they are again, getting ready for some Germans arriving on Tuesday."

"Germans!"

"Germans. Old man Burckhardt said that he wanted everything— the castle, the gardens, everything—to be in absolutely tip-top condition to show some 'chaibe Schwobe' how things are done in Switzerland."

Now she had the full attention of Lentz/Scitovsky. "'Chaibe Schwobe,' huh. German bastards right here in Benken! That is something."

Liselotte, having unburdened herself of her news, now settled back in the front seat of the Opel van as it sped toward Basel. But she did not remain quiet for long.

"Du, Werner, what kind of movie are we going to?"

"That was supposed to be a surprise. But I'll tell you. We're not going to the kino after all."

He saw a pout starting to develop. "But—" she began.

"We're going to the opera."

The beginnings of a pout were instantly replaced by a frown.

"Now don't worry. It's an operetta. 'Die Lustige Witwe.'"

"I love that music," she exclaimed.

And to show that she meant it, Liselotte began to sing, in her little girl's soprano, the first lines of that operetta's theme. She ran out of the words after that but continued to hum as she slid across the front seat of the van until her thigh met his. When he put his right hand on her thigh and let it stay there, she made no effort to remove it. Quite the contrary. As they passed through Biel and then Oberwil, she snuggled ever closer. By the time they reached the center of Basel, her hand was on his thigh. It was a chubby peasant hand with a firm grip. Werner Lentz wished that they could just skip the goddamn operetta and get on with it.

Lentz was able to park his van within a half block of the theater, and he and Liselotte immediately rushed to join the crowd entering the Stadttheater. As soon as the auditorium darkened and the overture began, Liselotte found Lentz's hand. As Lentz gave her hand a squeeze, his thoughts were already focused on the upcoming meeting at Benkener Schloss. It had surely been arranged during the conversation between Eggen and Swiss Intelligence at the Three Kings and the Schweizerhof Hotel. If Eggen was to be one of the Germans present, was it possible that another there might be his boss — Schellenberg?

*It had to be Schellenberg!*

There was no man alive more feared and more despised by the Rote Kapelle. It was Schellenberg who had personally supervised the hunting down and summary execution of dozens of Scitovsky's colleagues in Germany, Belgium, Holland, and France. His manhunt had been so relentless and so successful that almost all that was left of the Soviet Union's espionage apparatus in Western Europe was its operation in Switzerland.

Such an opportunity would never present itself again. He had to move now, and move decisively.

*He would kill Schellenberg on Tuesday and then get out.* The situation in Benken was perfect for both an ambush and then an escape over the border into France, where he could find refuge with the underground. He could then wait out the end of the war and return to Moscow as the man who had assassinated General Walter Schellenberg and dealt a blow to the Nazi leadership on a scale equal to that which had followed the assassination of that other symbol of the SS elite: SS Obergruppenfuehrer and Reichsprotektor of Czechoslovakia, Reinhard Heydrich, in Prague. What made it all the more beautiful, the more symmetrical, was the fact that Schellenberg had been Heydrich's protégé.

Rumors of a German invasion filled the country. The death of Schellenberg on Swiss soil would make that invasion inevitable. That maniac Hitler would retaliate immediately! And from his safe haven in France, he, Igor Scitovsky, could then watch as the hypocritical, double-dealing Swiss went down in flames!

*Both* Adolf Hitler *and* Josef Stalin would be delighted! The Soviet Union would be the prime beneficiary of all this. A German attack on Switzerland would divert at least a million troops from the Eastern front — just at a time when the very outcome of the Nazis' war against Russia was hanging in the balance. Without reinforcements, the defeat of the German Sixth Army at the gates of Stalingrad could now be followed by a massive Soviet offensive.

The Soviets could achieve victory over the Third Reich *without* the help of the capitalist powers, who kept promising the establishment of a second front in Europe but never fulfilling that promise.

In fact, now that he thought of it, the consequences of the assassination of General Walter Schellenberg might go deeper still.

Was it not possible—no, *likely*—that the two meetings at the Benkener Schloss, organized by Swiss Intelligence, were linked? That their purpose was to open the way for a *third* meeting, one between Schellenberg and Dulles? And to what end was perfectly clear: to set up a deal for a separate peace between the Western Allies and the Germans, allowing the Nazis to direct their entire war machine against Mother Russia, which harbored their common enemy, Communism—the enemy of not just the Germans, but also of the Americans and the British, and last but not least, of the ultracapitalistic Swiss. No wonder that the banker Burckhardt was in essence cosponsoring the whole conspiracy at his Benkener Schloss!

And all this would now come to naught!

Scitovsky-Lentz was so carried away with the enormity of the havoc that he personally was about to wreak that, involuntarily, his grip on Liselotte's hand tightened to the point where she squirmed with pain and, yes, with pleasure. At this precise moment, the curtain came down on the first act. The theater lights came on.

"Isch das nit toll gsi!" she exclaimed.

"Wonderful," he responded. "I need a cigarette."

In the lobby he immediately lit up a Gitane and headed for the bar. He ordered a Warteck beer for himself and a tea for Liselotte. She, for once, remained silent, basking in the joy of being in the midst of the matinee theater crowd in the big city. He, ever wary, scanned the crowd. His eyes suddenly stopped moving. There, across the lobby, also smoking a cigarette—was that not one of Lützelschwab's men? Why would a man from the *political* police force be in the Stadttheater for a Sunday matinee instead of at the football stadium, where all the cops got in free?

Nervous now, he took a last drag on his first cigarette and immediately lit another. Even Liselotte noticed.

"Something wrong?" she asked.

"No. It's just getting a bit stuffy here. Let's sit down." He drank the rest of his beer, crushed out his second cigarette in an ashtray, waited impatiently while she finished her tea, and then escorted her back to their seats.

As the crowd settled in, the curtain rose for the second act. Scitovsky's thoughts were jumping all over the place. Were they keeping an eye on him? Could there be any connection between the police presence here and his two trips to Benken? Not a chance. There had been nobody there the first time—just one couple, who had not even noticed him. And if anybody had made any inquiries about him or his van, Liselotte would have told him. So what other angle could there be? The radio traffic that week from the attic of the house on the Untere Rhinegasse had been heavy, but there had been other weeks when traffic was at the same level. The much more likely explanation was that Lützelschwab's man was observing somebody else. After all, they now had a hundred and twenty men in the city of Basel alone. They had to be watching hundreds, even thousands, to justify that force strength.

The only way to be sure was to test it. Leave early in the middle of the third act. Before anybody could get lost in the crowd. Simple. In fact, he could test it twice. First by taking Liselotte to his place. And then, afterward, by taking her back to Benken. He would be able to spot them if indeed he was being watched. After all, *he* was a professional and *they* were a bunch of local cops.

In the middle of the third act, just as the merry widow was about to latch on to the man of her dreams, Scitovsky leaned over to tell Liselotte that he needed some fresh air and thought it best that they leave. Since they had aisle seats, they were able to get out without creating any undue commotion. Within minutes, they had collected their coats from the garderobe and were out on the Theaterstrasse. It was now four in the afternoon, and although the sun still shone, it was already turning cold. As they hurried toward Scitovsky's van, Liselotte looked at him anxiously.

"Are you feeling better, Werner?"

"A little bit. But I would like something to drink . . . the stronger, the better."

"A Kirschwasser," she suggested. "Mutti always has one when she feels faint. Let's find a restaurant."

"I've got a better idea," he said, "Let's go to my place. It's not far, and it will be a lot more comfortable than a restaurant."

Liselotte agreed, and when they reached the van, as he opened the door for her, he checked, then rechecked, the Theaterstrasse in both directions. No one, he was certain, had followed them out of the theater. And there were but two pedestrians on the street: a young couple walking arm in arm in their direction. As they passed,

Scitovsky judged their age at no more than eighteen years. No problem there.

As soon as he entered the van, he checked the rearview mirror, and as he pulled out into the Theaterstrasse, he kept his eyes glued to it. Nothing. He turned right on the Steinenberg, still nothing; a block later, he turned left into the Freie Strasse. Since the Freie Strasse was the main street of downtown Basel, Scitovsky immediately found himself in traffic. Three blocks later, they passed through the Marktplatz. He did not like the looks of a black Citroën that had been parked there and then abruptly pulled out behind him.

"Du. Werner," Liselotte began at just this moment, pointing out the window on her side. "Look at that display in the window of Globus department store. Isn't it—"

"I'm trying to drive," he said.

A minute later they were on the Mittlere Rheinbrücke, the twelfth-century bridge that took them across to Kleinbasel. The black Citroën was still behind them. Then came the critical moment. At the first intersection on the other side of the bridge, Scitovsky turned right onto the Rheingasse and then immediately pulled up to the curb, stopped, and turned off the engine.

Nothing. No black Citroën. No traffic whatsoever. A minute passed. Two minutes.

"May I finally say something now?"

Scitovsky was so relieved that he laughed out loud before leaning across the seat to give Liselotte a big hug.

"My dear," he said, "you can say anything you want."

"*Finally*! What I want to say first is that I'm starting to freeze! Why in the world are we just sitting here?"

"Because this is where we are getting out. My house is just fifty meters up the street."

"Then why stop here?"

"Because . . . I like to park under the street lamp here. Now let's go and get that Kirschwasser."

As they walked up the Rheingasse, now arm in arm, Scitovsky was still on full alert for anything unusual: a parked car that was normally not seen on that street; a curtain that twitched; a vehicle that might enter the street from the other end and stop there. Still nothing. So it had been a false alarm. At least it appeared so thus far.

When they reached the front door of Rheingasse 37, Liselotte watched in amazement as Scitovsky produced a rather large key-chain from his pocket and then proceeded to select three different keys and insert them into three different locks before the door could finally be opened.

She had another uneasy moment when she found herself inside. The room they entered was absolutely pitch-black despite the fact that outside, darkness had only begun to fall. When Scitovsky finally turned on a lamp, she could see why: all of the windows in the living room were hidden behind thick, impenetrable drapes. The third moment of surprise came when a man suddenly appeared on the staircase that led from the living room to the second floor, a man dressed in black and carrying binoculars. He appeared to be as startled as she was.

"I'm sorry," he blurted out to an obviously annoyed Scitovsky. "I had no idea that you intended to bring her back here."

"I must have a word with you. Now!" was Scitovsky's response. Then, turning to Liselotte, he said, "My dear, allow me to take your coat."

She surrendered it. Reluctantly. He took off his own coat and proceeded to hang both garments in the closet.

"Now just make yourself at home. I'll be back in a few minutes."

With that, Scitovsky mounted the staircase, and along with the strange man, disappeared into the darkness of the second floor.

# EIGHTEEN

Minutes after Scitovsky had disappeared up the stairs behind his radio man, there was action in another van. It was parked two hundred meters away in the secluded courtyard of Basel's Waisenhaus, the city orphanage. There, sitting hunched in the middle of an array of radio equipment and wearing earphones, was Dieter Wenger, the sergeant in the Basel political police who was in charge of shortwave radio-monitoring activities.

It had been in late December of 1942 when, as a result of their constant random sweeps of the shortwave bands, Sergeant Wenger's unit had first detected the presence of a powerful illegal shortwave transmitter in the region of Basel. On January 24, 1943, his mobile short-range monitoring devices had pinpointed its exact location. From the call signals being employed, they had subsequently deduced that it was a unit of the Rote Kapelle. Since then, Lützelschwab's men had been monitoring every movement to and from the house on Rheingasse 37 from an observation point in the attic of a house across the street.

"They're at it again," he whispered to another policeman, a corporal sitting beside him and monitoring a separate frequency. Wenger pressed his earphones as tightly as possible to his head.

Just as he did so, somebody opened the back door of the van. Without even looking to see who it was, Wenger waved a hand for silence. Seconds later, he took off the earphones in dismay, for now he saw who was standing at the rear of the van. "Entschuldigen Sie, Herr Doktor," he stammered. "I did not know it was you."

Lützelschwab ignored the apology. "What went wrong?"

"Nothing, sir. They're at it again. But it's so damned frustrating.

■

They keep transmitting, and we keep intercepting and taking notes. But we still don't know what they're saying."

"When did this transmission start?"

"Just when you opened the door, sir. One short burst and *finis*."

"What does that mean?"

"We think they're alerting Moscow that they will be transmitting at length later tonight."

"On the same frequency?"

"I hope so, at least initially. The one they use used is 8,750 kilohertz, and I lucked out because that was the one I was monitoring today. My guess, knowing the past pattern, is that they will switch back and forth between that frequency and 10,365 kilohertz later tonight."

"What time tonight?"

"Again, if they follow the same pattern, they will start transmitting at exactly twenty-three twenty." Then he asked: "Herr Doktor, are you having any luck deciphering any of their signals?"

"Not yet. But we think that certain events tonight, if they come off as planned, may allow us to decipher at last. Maybe as early as tomorrow night. That is why you and your men in the other van must take exact notes of each transmission."

The other van, with the familiar markings and colors that designated them as part of the large fleet of the PT&T vehicles, was positioned in a pattern designed to triangulate the source, the second van being parked on the Claraplatz in Kleinbasel. The house at Rheingasse 37 was in the exact middle of the triangle.

"How are we going to proceed this evening, Herr Doktor?"

"I want your men to take time out for dinner and some rest. But I want you all back at your posts no later than twenty-three hours this evening. After that, I want you constantly monitoring all of the frequencies known to be used by the Rote Kapelle until twenty-three twenty."

"And if nothing starts to happen then?"

"Stay with 8,750 kilohertz in case, for some reason, the start of transmission was just delayed beyond the usual time. With our limited resources, we cannot cover all the contingencies, Sergeant. We have to hope that tonight they stick to their usual pattern."

"Maybe this is out of line, Herr Doktor, but some of my men have been wondering why we don't simply go in and shut them down."

"If we could guarantee a clean sweep, we would go in and get them right now. But we don't know exactly how many of them are involved . . . others perhaps at another location of which we are not aware. But I will tell you this: I already have a very, very good idea of what's going on, but I need confirmation. And that, Sergeant, is why you and your colleague are going to be spending the next few nights camped out in this van."

The key to what would happen next, Lützelschwab knew, was in the hands of the man who owned Rheingasse 37, Werner Lentz. After his people had detected the illegal transmitter there, Lützelschwab had pulled the man's police file. Lentz's family hisory, his people's emigration to Russia, and his subsequent return, elevated him to the status of prime suspect. Every member of the Basel political police force was now thoroughly familiar with Lentz's particulars—thus the phone call to police headquarters from the lobby of the Stadttheater less than an hour ago by one of his men, there on a totally unrelated matter, reporting that he had just seen "Der rote Lentz" in a most improbable place and in the most improbable company. When Lützelschwab heard about this—as the result of a routine call to his office—on pure instinct he had decided to immediately put Lentz under intensive surveillance. With his men now in place all around the house, and with Lentz inside, whatever Lentz's next move might be, they would be right behind him.

Satisfied, Dr. Lützelschwab looked at his watch and left.

Back at police headquarters, Lützelschwab had barely taken off his overcoat when he was on the phone to his counterpart in the canton of Geneva.

He went right to the point. "This is Lützelschwab in Basel. Is that raid you told me about last week still on for tonight?"

The answer was affirmative.

"Would you mind if I send one of our men over to Geneva right away tomorrow morning? If you're lucky, you're going to get everything we need: radio frequencies, call signs, and, most important for us, the Rote Kapelle's code book."

Again the answer was affirmative.

"His name is Rudolph Merian. He's our resident cryptanalyst. I assume that he will be working with your Marc Payot. You can expect him to show up at your place before noon. Et merci bien."

That accomplished, Lützelschwab, a pedantic man—as were most of Basel's Lützelschwabs, who inevitably, it seemed, ended up as postmen, firemen, clerks, or in this case, with the police — decided to memorialize where he was and where this might all be leading to. He wrote:

*1. SS Major Eggen meets Massor's man at Bar of Three Kings Hotel observed by me, Burckhardt, the American vice-consul, and — the bartender, who is a frequent caller at Fheingasse 37!*

*2. Eggen and Masson's man go to Schweizerhof Hotel observed by us, and the room clerk — who is a frequent caller at Fheingasse 37!*

Lützelschwab paused. Scratching his head, he then continued.

*3. Question: Why this meeting?*
*Answer: To set up a further meeting between Swiss and Nazi Intelligence, but at a much higher level. Purpose? to establish a framework for future collaboration with SS Intelligence.*

Lützelschwab reread what he had just written — and shook his head in disgust.

*4. Who? Where? When?*

Then he wrote his answers:

*5. Schellenberg + Himmler?? Masson + Waibel?? + Burckhardt??*

*In Switzerland? In or near Basel???*
*Very soon.*

And added:

*6. Who knows about this?*
*Answer: Swiss Intelligence: Masson/Waibel??/Burckhardt??*
*SS: Eggen, Schellenberg/Himmler??*
*Rote Kapelle: Lentz + at least two. But how much?*
*Americans?? : Vice-consul/Dulles?? How much?*
*Basel Political Police: Lützelschwab.*

Finally:

7. *Is Rote Kapelle planning action against Eggen/Schellenberg/*
*Himmler???*
*Answer in radio intercepts. Makes it* imperative *we can decipher*
*immediately (Geneva).*
*If confirmed, two options: a. Intervene*
                                   *b. Not intervene*

8. *But first must know: Where? and When?*

Lützelschwab looked over his finished work, fished a small box
of wooden matches out of his jacket pocket, and lit the piece of
paper containing his notes. He put it in his ashtray and watched it
burn. It left very little ash.

Then he picked up his phone once again and dialed the internal
number that connected him with the corporal who had the all-night
watch.

"This is Lützelschwab. Inform Rudolph Merian that he is due
in Geneva tomorrow to meet Marc Payot. I put surveillance on
Lentz . . . the Rote Kapelle Lentz. I'm going home now. If they
report in with anything unusual, I want you to call me there.
Immediately. No matter what the hour."

# NINETEEN

Liselotte Maurer waited a full twenty minutes before finally being rejoined by Werner Lentz. By that time she was as mad as hell, but also increasingly fearful. Had this happened to her in Benken, she would have simply walked out the door and walked home. But this was Basel. And she was with a stranger. Worse still, she was alone in the house of a stranger. And nobody knew where she was or with whom — not Vatti, nor Mutti, not even the innkeeper of "Zum Ochsen."

When Scitovsky offered her the long-ago promised cognac, she burst into tears and demanded, "Ich will jetzt Heim! Und sofort!"

She punctuated her demand to be taken home — and right away! — by going to the closet, taking out her coat and putting it on. Lentz was not about to argue with her. The last thing he needed now was an angry woman interfering in a process that had just been set, irrevocably, in motion. Moscow Central had been alerted to the fact that a priority-one transmission would be coming their way at 23.20 that evening. In fact, he had just spent twenty minutes dictating the contents of that message to his radio man upstairs, who was now in the process of coding it.

"Liselotte," he said, "I must explain. You know I didn't feel well. So I had to spend some time . . . in the bathroom. I'm sorry. You know how it is." He actually managed to look embarrassed.

She stopped sniffling. But the set of her peasant chin made it obvious that she was not going to change her mind about leaving. Scitovsky now had much more important matters on his mind anyway. He took his coat out of the closet and walked Liselotte down the street to his van . . . watched all the way by Lützel-

■

schwab's man in the attic of the house across the street from
Rheingasse 37. And the watching man picked up the phone that
was positioned right in front of the window and dialed the number
that connected him with the headquarters of Basel's political police.

"This is Roth," he said. "The Rote Kapelle Lentz is about to
move out in his van. He's got a girl with him. Better let the boys up
the street know right away."

Seconds later, the shortwave radio in a gray Peugeot parked a
block away crackled out the message to the two plainclothes
policemen inside. A half-minute after that, the Opel van passed
them going in the opposite direction and already moving fairly
fast. The driver of the Peugeot made a fast U turn, but by then
the van was gone. This part of Basel was a warren of narrow,
medieval streets, and the police knew that they could lose Lentz
very easily . . . if they had not already done so.

"Let's take a chance on the Wettsteinbrücke," the second policeman suggested to the driver of the Peugeot.

As soon as they turned right onto the Wettsteinstrasse, which led
to the bridge, they could see Lentz's van a hundred meters to the
south, already halfway over the Rhine. From there, they were on
modern thoroughfares, and tailing them was a breeze.

Twenty minutes later, when the Opel van pulled up in front of
the restaurant "Zum Ochsen" in Benken, it was carefully watched
by a man on a bicycle. The man was Benken's one and only
policeman. Fifteen minutes earlier, while he was in the middle of
dinner, he had received a totally unprecedented call from the head
of Basel's political police. Lützelschwab wanted him out on the
street immediately. To watch for an Opel van with the license
number BS 49672. Biel's policeman had received a similar call. As
had his counterparts in the villages of Bättwil, Therwil, Ettingen,
and Witterswil. All the bases were now covered, but Lützelschwab
already knew what the answer would be: Benken, or, more specifically, the Schloss in Benken owned by Peter Burckhardt's family.
His earlier suspicions concerning Peter Burckhardt—after he had
spotted him that night in the Three Kings Hotel—had been fully
justified. The man was in this thing with Masson, and right up to
his ears!

But how in the world had the Rote Kapelle found out about that
location?

His phone suddenly rang. It was the return call from the village
policeman in Benken. The van had stopped in front of the res-

taurant "Zum Ochsen." Then it had turned around and begun heading back toward Basel. A man in his mid-forties was driving. A girl? Ja, ja. A girl had gotten out of the van and gone directly into the restaurant. Did he know her name? Of course. It was Liselotte. Liselotte Maurer. A local girl who served in the restaurant. A nice girl. Always thought of as being perfectly harmless. Everybody liked her. Hardly the type to get mixed up with anything shady. When he told her father about this, there was going to be hell to pay, that was for sure.

Lützelschwab said that was out; there would be no mention of this to Liselotte's father, or to anybody else.

After he hung up, Lützelschwab decided he would call it an evening . . . unless he heard from his man who was spending the night in the courtyard of the orphanage with earphones attached to his head.

At exactly 23:30, Lützelschwab's phone rang again. It was his chief radio man, Sergeant Dieter Wenger. He had just intercepted a lengthy transmission emanating from Rheingasse 37.

"Good. Very, very good," was his boss's response. "Now you can all call it a night. But on the way back, I want you to drop off your transcripts of the intercept with Sergeant Meian. He's going to Geneva first thing tomorrow morning, and I want him to take them along. He lives with his parents on the Bruderholz . . . Bruderholzallee twenty-six. And, Dieter, thank your men for a job very well done."

One half-hour later, the Geneva political police made two midnight raids: one on a villa—a secluded, private villa—located at 192 Route de Florissant, owned and occupied by a Swiss couple by the name of Olga and Edmond Hamel; the other on an apartment located at No. 8 rue Henri Mussard, rented by a woman, also Swiss, by the name of Margrit Bolli, who operated under the code name of "Rosa". In charge of these raids was Inspector Charles Knecht of the canton of Geneva's political police. Earlier that evening, Wilhelm Lützelschwab had spoken to Knecht's boss.

The reason for the raids: to close down two of the now four known transmitters being operated by the Rote Kapelle in Switzerland: two in Geneva, one in Luausanne, and the fourth in Basel, at Rheingasse 37. Two weeks earlier, using the same methodology as that employed by Lützelschwab's unit in Basel—namely, triangulation—the location of the Geneva-based transmitters of the Rote Kapelle had been narrowed down to these two locations. Two days after that, visits purportedly from the Geneva electricity board had allowed the police to get men inside. Their objectives were to establish the floor plans of the two dwellings and to identify any and, one hoped, all possible escape routes. For the intention of the raids was not just to seize and thus close down the transmitters, but also to put everybody on the two premises into immediate and secret custody. Subsequently, at least for a few days, both locations would become traps for anybody who showed up. This method of operation had become standard Gestapo practice throughout Europe, and the Swiss police were nothing if not quick studies when it came to entrapment.

Due to the secluded location of the villa, the police had been able to apply full force. Two dozen armed men, half of them aided by police dogs, had surrounded the place at 23:45, and at precisely five minutes before midnight, Inspector Knecht had personally entered the villa, flanked by four other policemen. After determining that the ground floor was deserted, they had silently made their way up the stairs to the second floor, and after moving a few meters down the upstairs corridor, had burst through the first door on the right, opening directly into the master bedroom. And there was Olga Hamel in her nightgown, actually seated at the transmitter. The reason: just as Lentz/Scitovsky in Basel always began his transmissions to Moscow at precisely 23.20, Olga Hamel always began hers at 24:00 on the second, as Inspector Knecht's monitoring activities during the past fourteen days had established. The Geneva station was, it seemed, the *primus inter pares* among the Red Orchestra's Swiss establishments. Therefore, it controlled the midnight hour.

Olga's husband was, as usual for that hour, lying in the adjacent bed sleeping while his wife was about to toil for the good of her adopted fatherland—she being a member of the "Partei der Arbeit," the Swiss Communist Party. But both were soon in handcuffs. The police search for evidence of treasonous activities proved to be extraordinarily productive; everything lay exposed in front of Olga, who was rather exposed herself, since her choice of nightgowns was not above reproach, at least as judged by Swiss standards. Among the items seized was a large notebook containing the texts of previous transmissions and—most important of all—a list of call signs, three code tables, and two code books.

The raid on Margrit Bolli's apartment was less successful. The visit by the men from the electricity board had apparently alerted her to what was about to happen. She was not there, and the transmitter was gone, although they did find various radios and two code books—one of which subsequently proved to be the same as that found at the villa on the Route de Florissant. Fortunately, the Geneva police had been keeping her under surveillance during the prior two weeks and had determined that she had a boyfriend, a hairdresser of German nationality by the name of Hans Peters. One hour later they raided his Geneva apartment and caught them both in bed. The transmitter was in the bedroom closet. By three o'clock that morning, all four were being held incommuncado in Geneva's Saint-Antione prison.

This left just two Rote Kapelle transmitters still operating in Switzerland: one in Lausanne, the other in Basel.

# TWENTY

Fourteen hours later, the last express train of the day bound for Bâle, as the city is known in the French-speaking world, left Geneva's train station at 5:00 P.M. on Monday, March 1st. Two cryptologists were the sole occupants of a compartment in the first-class section of the second car: Marc Payot, a civilian who acted as a consultant to Geneva's police, and Sergeant Rudolph Merian of Basel's political police force.

Merian had met Payot at noon in Geneva's central police station, where Merian had gone directly after arriving on the morning train. It had taken four hours of negotiation and five phone calls from Basel to convince the Geneva authorities to release some of the material seized during the midnight raid into the official custody of Merian's boss, Dr. Wilhelm Lützelschwab. Permission had also been given to Marc Payot to accompany that booty, and Merian, on the next train back to Basel.

Upon boarding the train, Merian had arranged for the conductor to post a "Reserved" sign on the outside of the sliding door leading from the corridor into their compartment. Then, after getting two cups of coffee from the dining car, Merian had drawn the shade on the window in that door, sealing himself and his colleague off from the eyes of other passengers using the corridor.

Then Marc Payot opened the suitcase that he had brought with him and began extracting the code sheets, two copies of an obscure thriller published in France decades earlier, and a notebook containing the clear texts of transmissions. He placed these on top of the table that he had folded out from its storage space beneath the outside window of the compartment. Sergeant Merian, who sat vis-

∎

à-vis him on the other side of the small table, could not keep his eyes off of the "evidence" as it was placed, one by one, in front of him. But protocol forced him to keep his hands away. After all, it was still in the sole preserve of the police force of another canton . . . until otherwise indicated.

They were almost halfway to Lausanne, the first stop on the Genève-Bâle route, when Payot gave that indication.

"C'est tout à vous," he said. Merian now opened his briefcase. It was filled with documents, transcripts of the signals sent during the preceding thirty days by the Rote Kapelle's Basel transmitter. All they contained were numbers, blocks of numbers separated by minuscule pauses that in the absence of a *means* to decode them, represented communications to Moscow that were unintelligible babble.

Merian took two documents from the top of the small stack and handed one—a copy— across to his colleague from Geneva, keeping the original for himself. Then he started to talk "shop."

"That is a transcript of their most recent transmission to Moscow. They have abandoned the traditional Russian method of cryptology in favor of using books at each end and transmitting ciphers indicating sequences of letters or numbers on those pages, which, when strung together, would form the message in clear text."

"I see."

"Good. Then we probably agree that if by using the code novel we are able to find key words that make sense when put in sequence, we are going to be successful."

Payot agreed.

"We each have a copy of the same code novel, found in both places in Geneva," Merian pointed out.

"Yes."

"Then let's both start with one of the messages that we have found in the clear and work through the code novel. Why don't you work from the front while I work from the back? If one of us succeeds, then we can start working on the ciphers sent from Basel. All right?"

"Bien sur," Payot said when Merian had finished, "et maintenant, au travail."

The men worked in total silence, referring occasionally to copies of earlier Geneva transmissions contained in the notebook seized from the villa on the Route de Florissant. After stopping briefly in Lausanne, the train began to move at a much higher speed. As it accelerated, the cars began to periodically lurch, and to lurch rather sharply, as they rounded the many curves on the main line between Lausanne and Bern. But neither man took notice. They were like chess players: totally absorbed by the intellectual exercise.

The train arrived in Bern at 18:45 and left at 18:49.

At 19:23, Sergeant Rudolph Merian announced, "I've got one!"

After hearing Merian's excited words, Marc Payot immediately got up and took his place beside him.

"Here," Merian said as he pointed to the top of page 185 of the code book found at both addresses in Geneva: the 1910 edition of *Le Miracle du Professor Teramond* by Guy de Lacerf.[21]

"Now watch," he said.

Payot watched as Merian began to decode the text of a short message found in the villa on the outskirts of Geneva.[22]

> *RTO to KWT.2/23.2400.29 wds.No.363.*
> *Source:Emil.*
> *Two new German poison-gas substances now in production in IG Farben plant outside of Lyon.*
> *1. Nitrosulfluoride. Formula HC2F. 2. Kakodylisocyanide. Formula (CH3)2AsNC.*
> *Rado*

Payot now began comparing it to the notebook that had also been seized at the villa, the one containing the clear-text messages that had subsequently been coded prior to transmission. It lay open at one message numbered 363 and read:

> *RTO TO KWT 2/23 2400 29 wds no 363*
> *Source:Emil*
> *Two new German poison-gas substances are now in production in IG Farben factory outside of Lyon.*
> *1. Nitrosulfluoride. Formula HC2F. 2. Kakodylisocyanide. Formula: (CH3)2AsNC.*

21. Flicke, *Spionagegruppe Rote Kapelle*, p.61. The use of this particular book was in keeping with the idiosyncratic Soviet practice of using only code books that were rare, old, and of obscure origin. They could just as well have used *Gone with the Wind*.

22. *Ibid.* This is the text of an actual message (slightly edited) as sent by the Red Orchestra, as documented in Flicke's history of that organization.

An hour later, when the two cryptologists stepped onto the platform inside the Bahnhof in Basel, they were met by Sergeant Merian's boss. Without bothering about formal greetings, Lützelschwab immediately put a question.

"Did you get the code book?"

"Yes, sir. In here." Merian lifted his briefcase.

"And?"

"We've already managed to decode one of the messages sent by 'Rado' from Geneva, using the book."

Lützelschwab was all smiles now. "Rudolph," he said, "I've always told your parents that you were a smart kic!"

"Now for the Basel transmissions?" Merian asked.

"That's right," Lützelschwab said, looking at his watch. "Time is of the essence. We must move quickly. If you need something to eat, the Bahnhof buffet is open all night. Otherwise, stop for nothing."

# TWENTY-ONE

Lützelschwab's nerves were getting the better of him. The Basel cell of the Rote Kapelle had stopped transmitting. Their radio silence could mean one of three things: (a) they were lying low for a while as a routine precaution; (b) they had learned about the Geneva raids and had decided to close up shop; (c) they were so involved in a project of such major proportions that transmitting intelligence data had taken a backseat.

When Lützelschwab answered the phone the next day, March 2, 1943, at 16:05, his voice betrayed his anxiety.

"Guete Tag, Herr Doktor," were young Rudolph's first words. 'Do isch dr Rudolph Merian."

"Merian! What have you got?"

"We have been able to decipher the last two messages sent from Rheingasse Thirty-seven."

"Are you absolutely, I stress *absolutely*, sure you've got it right?"

"Yes, sir."

"You have them written out, on paper?"

"Of course."

"Then stop talking and bring them over!" Lützelschwab thundered into the telephone.

But then, immediately, he reversed course. "Rudolph," he yelled, "Are you still there?"

"Yes, sir."

"As a major exception to all the rules we follow in this business, I want you to do something."

■

"Read me those messages. Now."

"I'll have to get them. They're lying on the bed across the room."

"You get them, Rudolph. I'll be here, waiting." Lützelschwab's voice was now soft.

Thirty seconds later, "This is Rudolph again."

"Go ahead."

"The message sent at 23:20 on February twenty-eighth was deciphered as follows: 'SCV to KWT. February twenty-eight. Twenty-three twenty hours. Fifty-seven words. Number One seventy-six. Attention: Director. Source: Igor. Absolutely reliable information that Swiss Intelligence has arranged meeting with SS in Switzerland outside of Basel on the evening of March two, repeat March two. SS group to most probably include Schellenberg, perhaps also Himmler. Know exact venue. Recommend we take action to eliminate both and then exit Switzerland for France. Please advise. Scitovsky.' That's it. Shall I reread it, sir?"

"No need to do that, Rudolph." Lützelschwab's voice was very controlled. "Just read me the second message."

'Yes, sir. It reads as follows: 'SCV to KWT. March one. Twenty-three twenty hours. Forty-two words. Number One seventy-seven. Attention: Director. Source: Igor. Will proceed on March two as directed. Confirm to Lucy that I will seek to contact her in Belfort on March three. Will then report to you results of action. This is our last transmission. Closing down as instructed. Scitovsky.' "

That explained the radio silence, was Lützelschwab's first thought. The signatures on both messages also confirmed his suspicions about Werner Lentz, the obvious leader of the local cell. He was indeed Russian, and his name was Scitovsky.

"Good work, Rudolph. Now check out of that hotel right away and come over here. Needless to say, I do not want one scrap of paper left behind. Is that Payot fellow still with you?"

"Yes, sir."

"Has he communicated any of this back to Geneva?"

"Not that I know of, sir."

"Tell him not to, or it's going to be his hide. And then bring him along. He's going to spend the rest of the day with us."

After hanging up on his resident cryptologist, Lützelschwab immediately dialed the long-distance number of Section 5 of the General Staff of the High Command of the Swiss Army. Upon identifying himself, he asked for Colonel Masson, indicating that it concerned a matter of great urgency. After more than a full minute, another voice came on the line to inform Lützelschwab that Colonel Masson was not available.

"But I insist!" Lützelschwab roared into the phone, putting all of his six feet four inches and two hundred twenty-five pounds behind that roar. It was paramount that he learn as quickly as possible the exact scheduled time of that meeting between Swiss Intelligence and the SS. And while he was at it, he could also reconfirm the venue, although there was not even a shadow of doubt in his mind that they planned to meet at the Benkener Schloss.

"I beg your pardon, sir, but I have my instructions."

Before Lützelschwab could demand the name and rank of the officer with whom he was speaking, the man simply hung up.

"Sauhund!" Lützelschwab bellowed. But the line was dead.

"All right," he said to the room in general. "If that's the way Masson wants to play it, that's the way I'll play it. Each according to his own mandate. And each according to his own rules."

For the next five minutes Lützelschwab sat in silence behind the plain wooden desk in his office on the fourth floor of the Spiegelhof, headquarters of Basel's police department. Ever the deliberate man, he was thinking through his battle plan before issuing any further commands. His thoughts were interrupted when the phone rang, and he was tempted to not answer it. But he finally did, and regretted doing so the moment the caller identified himself. It was only the head of the Verkehrsbureau, the traffic division, which issued drivers' licenses and imposed traffic and parking fines. It was also the place where the residents of Basel had to go to register their vehicles and get their license plates.

"Salut, Hans," Lützelschwab said, adding immediately. "I'd appreciate it if you'd keep it short. I'm very busy."

The caller ignored the admonition and proceeded to tell Lützelschwab an astounding story.

Apparently about ten minutes earlier, at 16:40, three huge automobiles, one a Mercedes and the other two BMWs, each bearing the standards of both the Third Reich and the Waffen SS, had pulled up on the German side of the border-crossing in Lörrach. This crossing was closed to all traffic except that officially sanctioned by both governments. Such exceptions almost always involved trucks transporting goods specifically agreed to under bilateral trade agreements between Bern and Berlin. The guards on both sides were always informed well ahead of the time these crossings actually took place. It was understandable, then, that the unexpected and unprecedented appearance of the three *automobiles* caused a high degree of, first, consternation, then apprehension, when a Waffen SS major emerged from the black Mercedes—its back windows were curtained—and demanded that the barriers be raised: they were expected on the other side, and they were going through!

The officer in charge on the German side of the crossing, also a major, though in the Wehrmacht, immediately appeared on the scene. Politely, but firmly, he demanded to see papers and orders. And just as politely, and just as firmly, the request was denied. Then the SS major walked back to the Mercedes, opened the back door, and with the slightest motion of his hand, indicated that the Wehrmacht officer would be well advised to come over and join whomever was sitting in the back seat. He did so, and after two minutes, emerged a much paler man. Seconds later, up swung the barrier.

At that moment, precisely 16:25, or five minutes ahead of the agreed-upon time, a Fiat, painted in that sickly gray-green typical of Swiss army vehicles, pulled up behind the barrier on the Swiss side of the border. Two lieutenants emerged. One barked an order to the man in charge—a lowly corporal in the Swiss infantry—and up swung the barrier on the Basel side of the crossing.

Three marvels of German automotive engineering left the soil of the Vaterland and rolled onto that of the Swiss Eidgenossenschaft.

But they did not roll very far. The reason: the Swiss Intelligence officers who had just arrived, and who were to serve as escorts to the German visitors, were under strict instructions from Colonel Masson, the head of Section 5: No car bearing German standards or license plates would be allowed through. The standards must be removed, and the German plates *had* to be replaced with Swiss plates.[23] A huge Mercedes bearing German plates as it traveled through the streets of Basel in broad daylight would have stood out like one of Rommel's Panzers moving through the desert of North Africa, and the rabidly anti-Nazi journalists of Basel—despite the heavy censorship under which they labored—would have pounced immediately, jeopardizing the entire process of Nazi-Swiss rapprochement that Swiss Intelligence, at least one faction within Swiss Intelligence, was trying to achieve.[24]

23. See Braunschweig, *Geheimer Draht nach Berlin*. p. 236.
24. For a history of the attitude of the vast majority of the Swiss press—

The problem was that Masson's men, all of them stationed in Lucerne, had anticipated two, not three, vehicles and thus had brought only two sets of license plates with them, each set bearing, in addition to the registration numbers preceded by LU, a lion's head, the emblem of the canton of Lucerne, which the local police department had issued them only after a long bureaucratic hassle.

Where to get a third? Lucerne was two hours away, so that was out. It had to happen fast; it had to be the police department of the canton where they now stood. Thus the phone call to the Verkehrs-bureau in the Spiegelhof at 4:30 P.M. on that first Tuesday in March of 1943, and thus, at 4:40, the phone call from the head of the Verkehrsbureau to the head of Basel's political police, Dr. Wilhelm Lützelschwab.

"Give it to them," was Lützelschwab's immediate response. "No. Hold on, Hans. Give *me* the license plate and *I'll* give it to them myself. I'll be right down!"

---

vehemently anti-Nazi and pro-Allies—and the heavy censorship that the federal government had imposed upon them, see Bonjour, Vol. V, pp. 161–241.

# TWENTY-TWO

On that same Tuesday, March 2, 1943, just as Dr. Wilhelm Lützelschwab, head of Basel's political police, had started driving toward the border-crossing with the extra license plate, the late-afternoon train from Bern was arriving in Basel's main station. When Allen Dulles stepped from the smoking section of the first-class car, Nancy Reichman was waiting for him on the platform.

"Is everything still on schedule?" Dulles asked as he shook her hand.

"Yes. I was not able to contact Mr. Jacobsson directly, but his secretary just reconfirmed both the time and place. We'll be meeting him at the Schützenhaus restaurant, which is Mr. Jacobsson's favorite. It will take us only fifteen or twenty minutes to get there."

"What should we do in the meantime?"

"Check you into your hotel, sir. And then, if you would like, we could go to my apartment for coffee. I'd like to tell you about some peculiar rumors that are making the rounds in intelligence circles here in Basel."

A few minutes later, Dulles checked into the Schweizerhof Hotel. He filled out the registration card and handed over his passport for verification, as the law required. No sooner had he disappeared into the elevator, accompanied by the bell hop, than the desk clerk picked up the phone behind the desk. After seven rings, somebody finally answered on the other end.

"Do ish dr Rolf," the clerk said in a quiet voice. "Guess who just checked in? Mr. Allen Dulles. In person! And our American girl is with him." As he spoke, he watched Nancy Reichman mechanically

■

1 1 3

paging through the afternoon newspaper on the other side of the lobby.

"How does she look close up? Great, even though she now has all her clothes on. Fantastic legs, by the way. We never were able to see that far down, right?"

The desk clerk listened to the response on the other end for a moment, then grinned. "Maybe we'll both get our chance tonight, Urs. But look, you'd better tell Lentz about Dulles right away. It might change his plans for this evening."

He hung up.

# TWENTY-THREE

Minutes later, Allen Dulles reappeared in the lobby; then both he and the American girl disappeared out the door.

"Something wrong, Nancy?" he asked the moment they were outside.

"Nothing really," she said as they walked toward her car. "Just that desk clerk. He watched me the entire time you were upstairs."

After they had walked another fifteen meters, Nancy stopped beside her two-seat Fiat Topolino and said, "Well, here's the limousine!"

They climbed in, and Nancy started up.

"Tell me, how is Peter Burckhardt?" Dulles asked.

"He's fine. He's the one who filled me in on the latest gossip."

"Which is?"

"Just what you thought. Colonel Masson is meeting with Walter Schellenberg. In Switzerland. Today."

"Is Burckhardt going to be involved?"

"Only peripherally. They're meeting in Benken . . . where they met you. So he has to play host again."

"Anything else?"

"The Swiss police closed in on the Rote Kapelle in Geneva. They seized their transmitters and are holding three or four of their agents incommunicado. Peter sees the fine hand of Colonel Masson behind this. The Germans have been trying to force this action on the Swiss for many months to eliminate the last remnants of the Soviet's espionage apparatus still operating in central Europe. And now, just prior to Schellenberg's visit, Masson's given them what they want. And one other thing." She hesitated, clearly nervous.

■

"Go ahead," Dulles said.

"Somebody within Swiss Intelligence has suggested that you were consulted in this matter and acquiesced."

Dulles shrugged. "Why should I do something like that?"

"You would have the opportunity to open the door for negotiations with the Germans. In fact, Peter heard somebody say that you were probably going to be present at the meeting tonight."

"And sure enough, here I am in Basel." He paused and then continued. "Which raises the question: are we being suckered into something? And if so, by whom? You remember, I warned both Burckhardt and his boss, Waibel, about getting mixed up with that gangster Schellenberg. In fact, it was the last thing I said at the close of our evening in Benken last week. Now that son of a bitch— excuse me, Nancy—is going to get all of us into trouble. The Russians will go crazy if they hear about this. It will confirm their worst suspicions."

A few minutes later, they pulled up in front of Nancy's apartment building on the Augustinergasse.

"You know, Nancy, I think I'll skip that coffee. Maybe both of us could use a Scotch. Assuming you have some."

Soon they were in her third-floor apartment, sitting in front of her fireplace, enjoying a good belt of Scotland's finest. Although it had made a big dent in her vice-consul's salary, knowing Allen Dulles' proclivities, she had invested in a bottle just the day before. She hated the stuff, so she took it with a lot of water. He drank his straight.

"How long do you think dinner with Jacobsson will last?" he asked.

"In Basel, such affairs seldom go beyond ten-thirty, maximum eleven."

"Peter Burckhardt still seems eager to cooperate with us. Maybe it would be a good idea if Peter were to join us for a nightcap. We will be sitting at different dinner tables, and it'll give us a chance to compare notes. It will require his coming back from the country. But I have the feeling it'll be worthwhile. Maybe you could call him and suggest eleven-thirty. Here."

Nancy Reichman rose and went to the phone. In Switzerland in 1943, it was already possible to direct-dial the number of every telephone in the country, so there was normally no danger of conversations being overheard by nosy long-distance operators.

Nancy also knew that if her phone were tapped it would probably be monitored by a colleague of the very man she was about to call . . . with his full knowledge and complete acquiescence.

Basel was a complicated place in 1943.

# TWENTY-FOUR

While Nancy Reichman was on the phone extending Dulles' invitation to Peter Burckhardt, Lützelschwab's black Citroën was just pulling up on the Swiss side of the Basel-Lörrach border-crossing. The two Swiss Intelligence officers from Lucerne approached him the minute he stepped out of the car.

"I'm Lieutenant Sannwald, and this is my colleague, Lieutenant Holzer. We are both from Section Five of the General Staff. I assume you know what that means since I also assume you are from the Basel police."

"Indeed I am. What exactly is going on here?"

"What's going on here need not concern you. It is a military matter. Military intelligence. I see you've brought the license plate. Just hand it over, and then you are relieved to go about your business."

"Ah, yes. But perhaps you are my business. You see, my name is Lützelschwab, Doktor Wilhelm Lützelschwab, and I just happen to be head of the political police and responsible for *counter*intelligence here in the canton of Baselstadt. In other words, you are in *my* territory, and when I put a question to you, Lieutenant, I want that question answered. So I will try a second time: what exactly is going on here? And who is in those three cars?"

Lützelschwab noticed a flicker of recognition cross the lieutenant's face. No doubt over the years, word from the chief of Swiss Intelligence, Colonel Masson, had filtered down to the rank and file of Section 5 that the political police in Basel, a city known for its liberals, was dead set against any act that even hinted of cooperation

·

with the Germans. The provincial cops in Basel would see it only as collaboration with the Nazis.

"We are here under the direct orders of General Guisan."

Evoking the name of the commander in chief of the Swiss Army in Switzerland in 1943 was tantamount to citing the authority of Yahveh in Old Testament Israel and normally prompted immediate obedience. But Lützelschwab did not always play by the rules.

"Oh, really?" he said. "Let's see those orders."

"Impossible."

"All right. Let me try another approach. Less han an hour ago, I came into possession of some information that, if correct, would mean that your boss, Masson, is in serious jeopardy. In fact, the people in those three cars might themselves be in jeopardy. Physical danger. Understand?"

No response . . . except for a thinly veiled smirk.

Undeterred, Lützelschwab pressed on. "Let me make a suggestion. You should *either* arrange for me to talk by phone with your Colonel Masson immediately, and I mean right now, *or* let me talk directly to whoever is inside that Mercedes with the Lucerne license plate."

Now the lieutenant came to full attention. "I don't think you understand, Lützelschwab," he said, "or, more likely, you don't *want* to understand. Unless you hand over that license plate right now and then get the hell out of here, I am going to place you under military arrest."

Lützelschwab's eyes narrowed to slits. Practicing all the self-control he could muster, he gave the lieutenant the plates, turned on his heel, and climbed back into his black Citroën, and drove off with a roar.

He didn't roar off very far, however, before he pulled over to the curb and activated the car's shortwave radio.

"Do isch Lützelschwab," he began, before giving the desk sergeant his location. "I want four cars to move out immediately, with four men in each car. I want everybody fully armed, including automatic rifles and grenades. Two cars should station themselves at the intersection of the Wettsteinallee and the Schwarzwald-strasse. The other two I want on the corner of Riehenstrasse and Riehenring. The object of the exercise is to pick up on three German automobiles, a Mercedes and two BMWs, all of them black and traveling together, led by an unmarked Swiss army car, gray-green of course. Whoever spots them first should let the rest of us know by radio immediately. They are all bearing Swiss license plates reading as follows: the Mercedes, LU 14321; one BMW, LU 2131; the second BMW, BS 1146. I didn't get the number on the Swiss army vehicle. All right? Get moving!"

# TWENTY-FIVE

It was now approaching a quarter after five in the afternoon, and Rolf Seiler, desk clerk, was just climbing down from the Number 9 tram at the intersection of the Greifergasse and the Rheingasse. He quickly walked the half block to the house at Number 37. When Scitovsky opened the front door and let him into the semidarkness of the living room—the drapes were, as always, tightly drawn— three other men rose to greet him. One was the bartender from the Three Kings Hotel who had answered the phone when Seiler had called a half hour earlier. The other two, when introduced, spoke in a rather pathetic mix of bad German and worse Schwyzerdeutsch. They were members of the Rote Kapelle's cell in Lausanne, which, after what had just happened in Geneva, was the only other cell still operating in central Europe.

Rolf Seiler was about to quietly take his place on the sofa and allow the four men to resume their conversation when Scitovsky decided otherwise.

"No, Rolf. Based on what you saw at the hotel a half hour ago, I suspect that they will end up at the apartment on the other side of the river. So I want you up in the attic with the binoculars right now. Keep an eye on the place for the next fifteen minutes."

"Yes, sir. But would you mind if I first got something to eat? If there's anything in the kitchen."

"There's bread and salami there. And beer. Just get what you want and take it up to the attic with you."

"Yes, sir."

As soon as Seiler had disappeared, Scitovsky resumed his conversation with the other three men gathered in his living room. "You

■

just asked me if I knew what was going on in Geneva," he said, "and I must confess that I don't know. I can only conclude that they were somehow warned of the raid and got out."

"Got out to where?" one of the men from Lausanne asked.

"To France. Where else? If they had been arrested in Geneva, the press would have been onto it by now. You know how they are in that city. And you would have heard about it in Lausanne immediately thereafter."

Both men from Lausanne look skeptical and worried.

"All right. Then who has a better idea? What does Sandor say?" Scitovsky referred here to Alexander Rado, a Hungarian who had been trained in Moscow by the Soviets and then sent to Switzerland in the 1930s for the purpose of setting up and running the operations of the Red Orchestra in the French-speaking part of that country.

"Rado is extremely worried. In fact, this morning he took the train to Geneva about the same time we took our train to Basel. He'll find out today or tomorrow . . . unless they catch him, too."[25]

Scitovsky said, "When I talked to him yesterday, he did not sound worried."

"How long was your conversation?" one of the men from Lausanne asked.

"Very brief, of course."

"And very guarded. We were both there, you know."

Scitovsky's attitude seemed to change. "Maybe you would be well advised to stay clear of that situation until we find out what is really going on."

"Can we stay here?"

"Nobody's going to stay here."

"Then where?"

"Don't worry. I'll take care of that." He looked at his watch. "We've got to get moving. I am going to tell you exactly what we will be doing tonight and what role each of you is going to play. I want you to listen carefully, and to ask questions if you don't understand. Your life and mine depend on each of us executing our job perfectly. Understood?"

---

25. According to Professor Bonjour, Rado escaped arrest in March of 1943 by immediately going underground in Geneva, protected by the community of local Communists. In 1944, he escaped to France on a milk train. See Bonjour, Vol. V, pp. 99 ff. Also Foot, M.R.D., *Resistance* (London, 1978), p. 216.

They nodded.

"Let's all go into the dining room. I've got my maps and some photographs laid out on the tables there."

Someone shouted down to him from upstairs. "Harry! You must come up here. Now!"

It was the voice of Rolf Seiler.

When Scitovsky burst through the trapdoor that opened up into the attic, Rolf immediately handed him binoculars. "Take a look. Just like you said. They are both there."

Scitovsky looked through the binoculars and then at his watch. It was almost 17:30. "The goddamn Americans must be in on it too. They *must* be; otherwise why would Dulles show up in Basel?" He again raised the binoculars to his eyes. "They don't look like they're about to move, do they?"

"No, sir."

Again Scitovsky referred to his watch. And then he made a decision. "Rolf, I've changed my mind. Instead of coming with the rest of us, I want you to keep an eye on that apartment. It's now obvious that Dulles is going to meet Schellenberg, but not in Benken."

"How will I recognize Schellenberg?"

"He's a lot younger than you would expect. In his early thirties. About six feet tall. Slim. Elegant for a German. And a very stylish dresser. Remember, *if* he shows up, he will be in civilian clothes."

"Yes, sir. But assuming he does show up, what are our plans?"

"I'll either telephone or deliver the news personally. By no later than twenty-three hours. In any case, you must realize, Rolf, that this is the last night that any of us will spend here. More important, this is probably the last night that we can make a *real* difference in the outcome of this war."

"And if I don't hear from you?"

"Kill him. And if the Americans are hit in the process, so be it."

"Yes, sir."

"I'm leaving three different weapons, with ample ammunition for each of them, in the cellar. You know where. All right?"

Scitovsky disappeared down the trapdoor. It was now 5:35 P.M., and there was no time to waste.

The other three members of the Rote Kapelle were waiting for him in the dining room. Scitovsky spread out a map on the dining-room table. "This is a blowup of the western end of the Birsigthal. The valley is formed by the Birsig River, which starts in France and

works its way through Switzerland on its way to the Rhine. Here."
Scitovsky's finger traced the river's path.

"The last Swiss village before the French frontier is Benken.
Here." Again the finger pointed. "Above Benken, at the top of the
ridge overlooking the valley, is the Benkener Schloss." He had
marked the spot with a red X.

"This is where our target will be spending the night. As you can
see, there is only one road leading up to it. Actually, it's more a
lane than a road. It's a half kilometer long and goes through forest
most of the way. Now come over to this end of the table."

This time he had a photograph for them to look at. "That's the
front view of the Schloss. As you can see, it's surrounded by a
moat, and you approach the front entrance across that narrow
bridge. The rather formidable oaken entrance door and the massive
stone structure of the castle itself, with its very small windows, rule
out any attempt at frontal assault. Even grenades would be useless."

Scitovsky knew that the two men from Lausanne were superbly
qualified for assaults of a paramilitary nature. Although in civilian
life one was a butcher and the other a physical-education teacher,
both were members of the elite mountain division of Switzerland's
militia, wherein they spent four months of each year in active
service, one as a sergeant, the other as a corporal.

The mountain troops were accustomed to undertaking all-day
climbs from the valley floors of central Switzerland to the upper
reaches of the Alps that formed the Gotthardt massif, lugging fifty
kilos of weapons and ammunition on their backs, and this on skis
fitted with non-skid chamois skins for the ascent. There they set up
their tents in the snow in sub-zero temperatures, with winds blowing
at forty kilometers an hour, in preparation for spending weeks up
there participating in maneuvers aimed at improving their ability to
respond to an aerial attack on central Switzerland by Nazi paratroopers. The exercises left little to the imagination, since live
ammunition was often used. Scitovsky himself, though out of shape,
had been thoroughly trained in the art of guerrilla warfare as part
of his NKGB training.

The fourth man in that dining room, the bartender from the
Three Kings Hotel, had none of these qualifications. He was,
therefore, the designated driver.

"So," Scitovsky continued, "we are left with two options. Either
we ambush the target's automobile on the way up to or down from
the Benkener Schloss, using the forest as our cover. Or we try to

somehow get inside the Schloss and kill him there. I'm leaving the decision open until I see how things develop."

Turning to the bartender, he said, "Either way, I want you to stay with the van. No matter what happens, I want you to call in to this house, to Rolf, who will be remaining here, at twenty-three hours, and bring him up to date. No matter what. There are two public telephone booths you can use—one in Biel and one in Benken, both of them on the main road. I'll point them out to you on the drive out."

"Yes, sir."

Scitovsky turned to the two men from Lausanne. "I know that you can handle weapons of all types, but I want to be absolutely sure that you are familiar with the ones we will be using this evening. They are down in the cellar. Let's check them out right now."

Twenty-five minutes later, at 18:10, Scitovsky's van pulled away from Rheingasse 37 with four men inside. It was loaded as well with three Russian submachine guns, four German pistols, five kilo of ammunition, plus a dozen Swiss hand grenades. The observer from Basel's political police, stationed in the attic of the house directly opposite Rheingasse 37, immediately alerted headquarters in the Spiegelhof.

His report was duly noted, but no further action was taken. The department's available cars and manpower had already been commandeered by Dr. Wilhelm Lützelschwab to monitor the movements of SS General Walter Schellenberg and entourage as they proceeded farther into Swiss territory.

# TWENTY-SIX

Although the hours during which the Deutsche Generalkonsulat in Basel was open to the public, nine to twelve A.M. Monday through Friday, were long past, the activities within the German consulate were at a pitch not seen there since the outbreak of war in 1939. At five o'clock that afternoon, the German ambassador to Switzerland, Otto Karl Köcher, arrived from Bern. Forty-five minutes later, General Walter Schellenberg and Major Hans Eggen joined him.

They met in the library, where it quickly became apparent to the consul general that the ambassador and the general had an instant mistrust of each other. This was hardly surprising, since they came from completely different worlds.

The ambassador was a diplomat of the old school, who still clung to the principles enunciated at the Council of Vienna in 1815. As such, he was firmly anchored in the assumption that intercourse between governments should take place through established diplomatic channels. He, like his American counterpart in Bern, Minister Leland Harrison, failed to recognize that the world in which he operated in 1943 was radically different from that which had endured, essentially unchanged, for well over a century. A new element had interjected itself into the affairs of state: the intelligence services, a rogue element that paid no attention whatsoever to the old rules of the game.

In the case of the American envoy, the new cross that he now had to bear had been thrust upon him in the person of an intelligence officer by the name of Allen Dulles . . . a *spy* who had arrived four months earlier, and who had immediately let the world know that he and he alone had a direct line to President Roosevelt.

■

It soon became apparent to America's friends and foes alike that if they wanted immediate action, it was Dulles who should be contacted.

Thereafter, it had been only a matter of time before the back channels established by Dulles, channels that ran through the OSS directly to the White House, displaced the diplomatic channels that ran through Harrison back to the State Department, which, more often than not, turned out to be a cul-de-sac. The spy had displaced the diplomat.

SS General Walter Schellenberg, the German ambassador knew, was trying to do exactly the same thing—to circumvent diplomatic channels and establish direct contacts with foreign leaders—and that to this end he had enlisted the help of his intelligence counterpart in Switzerland, Colonel Masson (who was now *also* operating outside of the accepted parameters, which enjoined the interference of the Swiss military in political affairs), leaving him out in the cold. The trouble was, there was nothing he could do about it. Because just as Dulles had the ear of Roosevelt, so Schellenberg had the ear of Hitler. Once a week, every week, he, as the man in charge of Germany's foreign intelligence service, personally delivered the service's intelligence estimates to the Führer.

Despite the fact that Schellenberg was SS, and not a cookie pusher, it was well known that when the situation required it, he knew how to turn on the charm, which he immediately did.[26]

"Herr Köcher," Schellenberg began, "let's sit down together on

26. Compare David Kahn's description of Schellenberg in his book, *Hitler's Spies: German Military Intelligence in World War II* (New York, 1985), p. 260: "He had a quiet way about him, quite different from the bullying pretentious hardness of most SS types. He spoke softly, almost shyly, in a clear tenor with exceptionally precise enunciation and with a boyish charm that was one of his greatest assets . . . . Not everyone liked him. Some of the older, street-brawler types of the SS despised him; some officials regarded him as too pushy . . . . He was bright and perceptive: people meeting him often had the impression he could form a clear picture of people and events on the basis of a few key facts . . . He could lunch smoothly with foreigners and befriended young officials in the Foreign Office and the Propoganda Ministry. He was credited with understanding foreign affairs."

The British historian, Trevor-Roper, had a quite different view. "The excellent reputation which Schellenberg, their youngest general, commanded within the ranks of the most narrow-minded fanatics of the SS was completely without substance . . . . To be sure, he did not believe in the use of force but rather in cunning, since he believed himself to be a cunning man. That was his biggest mistake." *The Last Days of Hitler* (London, 1947), p. 59.

the sofa. I'm sure we can arrange for some coffee to be brought in. In fact," and he addressed these words to his fellow officer in the SS, Rittmeister Eggen, "why don't you see to that?" It was obvious that Schellenberg wanted to hold his conversation with the ambassador in strict privacy.

And only after his man had left the room did Schellenberg continue. "First, I want to extend to you personal greetings from the Führer. I was with him yesterday morning, and he specifically requested that I do so."

That broke the ice. "I am greatly honored, Herr General," the ambassador said. "I hope that the next time you meet the Führer, you will relay to him how much I appreciate his continuing trust in me. My only remaining mission in life is to be able to serve him and the Reich to the best of my abilities."

"I am sure he will be very pleased when I repeat your words to him," Schellenberg replied. "I feel obligated to mention that the Führer is in a rather agitated state. As you know, things are not going well on the Eastern front, at least for the time being. And he is becoming increasingly worried about our exposure on the southern flank, especially now that he must reckon with an Allied landing in Sicily or southern Italy. And that has raised the issue of what to do with Switzerland. As you know, the Führer is not overly fond of this country. I recall being present at the meeting he had with Mussolini in June of nineteen forty-one when the subject of this country came up. And all of us were shocked at how hostile, *emotional*, he was vis-à-vis Switzerland. He described the Swiss as 'das Niederträchtigste und erbärmlichste Volk,' 'the most devious and detestable of people,' and as the 'Todfeinde des neuen Deutschland,' 'the deadly enemies of the new Germany.'[27] Mussolini was the most shocked of all, since he had spent a year or so right here in Basel in the early nineteen twenties and had apparently been treated very well. Our Führer is so distraught that any provocation on the part of the Swiss might tip the scales dangerously in the direction of military intervention. He might like to secure our southern flank by integrating Switzerland into the Reich and then using the Alpine reduit as a bulwark against any invasion that the Anglo-Saxons might contemplate mounting against the fatherland

27. Bonjour, Vol. V, p. 66. His source, in turn, was *Staatsmänner und Diplomaten bei Hitler,* compiled by Andreas Hillgruber (Frankfurt, 1967).

from the Italian peninsula. In the Führer's headquarters, one is already talking about this as 'Aktion Schweiz'—'Campaign Switzerland.'"

At this point, Rittmeister Eggen reappeared, followed by a young woman bearing a tray with coffee and some local Konfisserie.

Ambassador Otto Karl Köcher waited until they had left before responding: "I am fully aware of this danger. In fact, just a month ago I had a long conversation with the Swiss foreign minister and suggested that it would be in everybody's best interest if all of us would begin to work toward a German-American detente before it is too late. The alternative could be the Bolshevization of all of Europe. Minister Pilet was very sympathetic and, I am told, communicated this desire to the American ambassador here, Leland Harrison . . . a fine diplomat of the old school, I should add."[28]

"You did this acting on who's authority?"

"State Secretary Ernst von Weizsäcker's."[29]

"And what was the American response?"

"Negative."[30]

"Maybe you used the wrong channel of communication. Maybe you should have gone through Allen Dulles."

"Is that why you are here?" the ambassador asked. 'What, might I ask, is your mission here, Herr General?"

"I'm here for the same reason you are. To warn the Swiss. To suggest that it is in their best interest to cooperate economically with us. They need to demonstrate that they are truly neutral. In Berlin, there are those in the circle around Hitler who talk about Switzerland's 'Anglo-Saxon' neutrality. If they have their way, the Führer may be talked into 'Aktion Schweiz' right away."

28. Bonjour, Vol. VI, p. 116. This meeting between Köcher and the Swiss foreign minister took place on February 5, 1943.

29. Ernst von Weizsäcker was the father of the current President of Germany, Richard von Weizsäcker.

30. Pilet told Harrison that since the Germans military reserves were almost exhausted, the danger of a "Bolshevization" of Europe was becoming acute, something that was hardly in the interests of the Anglo-Saxons. He then suggested that the Americans and British pull out of the war and let the Russians fight it out with the Germans. The American ambassador relayed these thoughts immediately to the State Department. Their laconic response: Roosevelt had already given his answer in previous statements to the effect that the Americans intended to fight on without compromise until the Axis powers agreed to an unconditional surrender. Bonjour, Vol. VI, pp. 117–18.

These last words appeared to shock the ambassador. "But that would be a great mistake. We have good friends in high places here. Foreign Minister Pilet, for one."

"And Colonel Masson of the Swiss Army's General Staff for another," added Schellenberg.

"So you will be meeting with him?"

"This evening."

"Be careful. There are also people in both high and low places, such as the police in this city, who harbor a deep hatred for us."

"I appreciate your concern, but I believe it is misplaced. Only a very few officers in the High Command of the Swiss military know that I am here. In fact, and you must keep this entirely to yourself, my visit has been sanctioned by no less than their commander in chief, General Guisan. If all goes well, I will meet him tomorrow."

The ambassador was stunned. All he could say as a response to this news was, "Congratulations, Herr General."

Schellenberg looked at his watch. "Regrettably, I must leave in a few minutes. But before I do, I want to ask you how our negotiations are working out with the Swiss with regard to supplying our defense industries, particularly with electricity, turbines for our U-Boots, and aluminum for our aircraft. We are running desperately short of all these, and the Führer himself is concerned. There is also a question of gold and dollars. To fund my operations around the world, I require both. And, as you know, Herr Ambassador, our only remaining reliable source for such financing is the Swiss National Bank. That source cannot be allowed to dry up."

"I am doing my best," the ambassador said. "You can reassure the Führer of that. But the negotiations are not easy. Roosevelt and the Jew Henry Morganthau promise dire consequences if the Swiss continue to cooperate with Germany. The Swiss greatly resent this pressure, especially their Foreign Minister Pilet. We need to encourage men like Pilet, to reassure them. But to also impress them that they really have no option other than not only continuing, but even expanding, our bilateral economic cooperation. I hope you will mention this to your colleague, Colonel Masson, and to General Guisan when you meet with them."

"Allow me to return to the person of Mr. Dulles. How does he fit into all this?"

"I wish I knew. He is an enigma even to the Swiss. Why do you ask?"

"I have the feeling that he might be a reasonable man. One who understands the enormity of the Soviet threat, a man whom one can talk to."

"Then you should talk to him."

"Perhaps. You could also help by dropping a word here, one there, in Bern."

"Perhaps."

General Schellenberg rose from the sofa. The audience was over. Five minutes later, he and his adjutant, Rittmeister Eggen, climbed into the backseat of the long black Mercedes that had been waiting outside the consulate, along with two BMWs and one rather pathetic-looking gray-green Fiat.

As they pulled away from the curb and began to move off, they were observed by twelve Swiss policemen in three different cars.

# TWENTY-SEVEN

But it was not only the Swiss police who were aware of their operation.

At quarter after six on this evening of March 2, 1943, NKGB Colonel Igor Scitovsky, though unaware that the SS general was on Swiss soil three hours earlier, believed that sooner or later that evening, he would show up at the Benkener Schloss. He planned on being ready for him.

Dusk had begun to fall when the Opel van, driven by the bartender at the Three Kings Hotel and carrying Scitovsky and his two colleagues from the Rote Kapelle cell in Lausanne, entered the outskirts of the village of Benken. They pulled up across from the restaurant "Zum Ochsen." Up the road was the lane leading to the Benkener Schloss. The van's lights went out, and its four occupants waited in silence. There was no movement whatsoever in the village. Then Scitovsky gave a curt order. The driver started the engine, pulled out, and immediately turned into the lane to the castle. The full moon enabled him to see the way despite the tall fir trees that lined both sides of the lane.

After three hundred meters, he was once again ordered to stop. Scitovsky and the two other men jumped out, opened the back door of the Opel van and removed, piece by piece, the weaponry stashed there: the three submachine guns, three of the four pistols, all of the ammunition, plus ten of the twelve hand grenades. With these, they disappeared into the forest off to the left.

Ten minutes later they returned empty-handed and climbed back into the van. The driver backed down the narrow lane until he had again reached the main road. After confirming that the streets of

.

Benken were still deserted, he switched on the headlights and pulled forward. About twenty meters farther, he paused in front of the restaurant "Zum Ochsen" just long enough for the three passengers to climb out of the van. He continued on for a kilometer beyond the restaurant and pulled into another lane, which led to the village cemetery. There he shut off the motor, consulted his watch, and decided to take a nap. He had many hours to waste.

# TWENTY-EIGHT

Scitovsky entered the restaurant warily. If Liselotte was working this evening, would she revert to her usual talkative form? He spotted her in the far corner and waved.

She walked right up to him. "So, so," she began, "I thought I had seen the last of *you*!"

"I've missed you," he said, "and I apologize for acting so badly last Sunday. To prove it, I've brought you a little something."

He handed over a small package, elegantly wrapped in silver paper and bearing a red ribbon. An envelope was discreetly attached to the ribbon. She removed the envelope, read the enclosed card, and blushed.

"That is very sweet of you, Werner," she said, "but we can't just stand here. Are these two gentlemen with you?"

"Yes." Scitovsky did not bother to introduce them.

"Are you going to be eating, or just—"

"We've come for a full dinner."

"I can't give you the best table, because it's already reserved. But the one next to it is really just as good." She led them to an alcove area that lay off to the left.

After they had taken their places, she asked, "Now, what can I get you to drink?"

Scitovsky ordered a large carafe of the local Riesling, and Liselotte went to fetch it, carrying the small package with her. After the door leading into the kitchen had closed behind her, she untied the red ribbon and began to work carefully on the wrappings. Once hardly daring to look at the exquisite little leather jewelry box that had been revealed. Finally she opened the lid.

"Du lieber Gott im Himmel! Das isch en ächte Pärlering!" It was indeed a real pearl in the ring, and a rather large one at that. Very slowly—in fact, very shyly—she put it on her ring finger, which had remained a virgin so far. It fit perfectly!

Her immediate impulse was to show it off to the cook and his helper, who were both busy, one chopping vegetables, the other stirring a sauce. But she decided against it; the cook knew her father. Instead, she took the beautiful little box, the wrapping paper, and the ribbon and carefully stuffed them into the pocket of her winter coat.

She let the ring remain on her finger. If somebody noticed it and asked her about it, she would say it was from . . . an aunt. A rich aunt who had lived all alone in Basel for many years and who had just died.

Then Liselotte fetched a carafe of Baselbieter Riesling and after putting it and three glasses—the type known as Römer—on a tray, she returned to the table occupied by her admirer and his two friends.

Once the wine had been poured, she caressed the back of Werner Lentz very briefly, leaned down and whispered in his ear, "Du bisch en Schatz, Werner." Then she added: "I'll take a break in an hour or so. Maybe we could meet for a few minutes outside."

He nodded his agreement. And as soon as she moved away, he looked at his watch. An hour was just about right. If he found out what he wanted to know, it would leave ample time to plan the details of the operation accordingly.

Twenty minutes later there was a pause in the conversations in the restaurant "Zum Ochsen," which was almost full by then. Everybody became aware of unusual noise on the road outside—of cars, heavy cars, being shifted down, and then, after a pause, at least three or four big engines being revved up as the vehicles started to move off again. Liselotte Maurer, nosy as always, could not help but go to the front door and peek out onto the road  In the glare of headlights turning into the lane that led up to the Benkener Schloss, there was the biggest Mercedes she had ever seen in her life, followed by two huge BMWs.

After the cars had passed, she headed for Schovsky's table,

where she leaned down and whispered in his ear. "Remember what I told you on Sunday? About the Germans coming? Well, they must have arrived this very minute. I've never seen such big cars!" Then she straightened and, in a normal voice asked, "Would the gentlemen now like to see the menu?"

They did. And five minutes later they ordered dinner—all three went for the Rehschnitzel with Spätzli—and another carafe of wine, this time a Dole, the heavy red wine from the Valais that would go well with the venison.

A half hour later, the phone behind the bar rang. Liselotte happened to be near, drawing beer from the keg, and so she answered it. After she hung up, she delivered steins of Warteck Lager and then went to the adjacent table and arranged two additional settings. On the way back to the bar, she paused ever so briefly behind Scitovsky and whispered another message.

"Four of them from up there will be here in five minutes. That means I can't take a break until much later, maybe another hour. Are you going to stay that long?"

Scitovsky nodded. Her hand caressed the back of his neck, and then she was off again.

Five minutes later two men and two women entered the restaurant "Zum Ochsen." Immediately every eye in the place was drawn to them. For they were not ordinary men: each stood well over six feet tall, and neither weighed under ninety kilo. But it was not just their size, but also their bearing that was so striking. Each wore a long black-leather coat over civilian clothes, but it was easy to imagine them in military uniform. When one of them beckoned impatiently to the waitress in impeccable high German, everyone in the room could not help but conclude that these men were part of the Wehrmacht. Indeed, they were members of the military elite in their German homeland: they were Fallschirmjäger, paratroopers. One of Hitler's own "ten commandments" to his Fallschirmjäger had been: "Against an open foe, fight with chivalry, but extend no quarter to a guerrilla."[31] As Schellenberg's bodyguards in a neutral but hostile country, they were definitely in guerrilla territory.

But it was their two companions who caused an even greater stir as Liselotte showed all four new patrons to their reserved table.

31. Quarie, Bruce, *German Airborne Troops 1939–45* (London, 1983), p. 6.

# TWENTY-NINE

The four-car convoy had reached the drawbridge in front of the Schloss forty minutes earlier, at precisely 1900 hours, as had been prearranged. As soon as the convoy had stopped, two Swiss officers had sprung out to meet Peter Burckhardt, who was standing under the bright light of the lamp posts.

Simultaneously, the driver of the black Mercedes opened the back doors of his vehicle and out stepped General Walter Schellenberg and his adjutant, Sturmbannführer Rittmeister Hans Eggen. As Burckhardt approached them, four heels clicked and two closely shorn heads nodded. For a split second, it looked as if they were also going to salute, Nazi-style, but instead, Schellenberg took one step forward and merely extended his right hand. For another split second it appeared as if Burckhardt were hesitating. But then he grasped that hand firmly, very firmly.

"Willkommen in der Schweiz, Herr General," he said. Then he also shook hands with Eggen, and addressing both, continued. "My name is Peter Burckhardt, and I will be your host. Colonel Masson has already arrived and has asked me to tell you that he is eagerly looking forward to meeting you. If you agree, we will all meet for dinner at seven-thirty. In the meantime, one of the servants will escort you to your accommodations for the evening. If there is anything you need, please let me know immediately."

Then, as if on signal, the main entrance to the Schloss opened and two valets, followed by six maids, approached them.

Schellenberg appeared to be not in the slightest fazed by the display put on by the Basel aristocracy. "Your Swiss hospitality is, indeed, overwhelming, Lieutenant Burckhardt. We Germans, as

■

your neighbors and friends, hope that our ties with you, which have always been close and include the language that we share, will become even closer in the days ahead."

His heels clicked and his head nodded yet again. At this moment, the back doors of the first BMW opened. Two strapping examples of classic Aryan breeding emerged and approached Peter Burckhardt.

"These men," Schellenberg explained, "always accompany me. This is Major Gerhardt von Göhler." Göhler stiffly stepped forward and shook Burckhardt's hand. "And this is Lieutenant Reichardt." He did the same. At that moment, the back doors of the second BMW opened for the first time since it had rolled onto Swiss soil. What emerged were two further prime specimens of the Nordic race, equally tall and equally well-built — but in a somewhat different way. Their appearance caused more than a slight stir among the Swiss maids who stiffly waited, clad in their black dresses and white aprons. They had never seen two women quite like this, except perhaps on the screen in the Kino. Both wore silk dresses — one red, the other bright green — that began well below the neck and stopped well above the knee. The bosoms that were displayed were ample; the trim legs were encased in black silk stockings. One of the ladies was blonde; the other had red hair. And both were absolutely gorgeous.

General Schellenberg again proved himself equal to the situation. "Darf Ich vorstellen?" he asked. "These are my two secretaries, although in many ways they are much more than that," and he grinned slightly as he said it. "I think they would like to room together this evening, if that can be arranged." Their names were Hannelore and Marlene, and both of them looked quite boldly at Peter Burckhardt as they were introduced.

"Since neither will be joining us for dinner," Schellenberg continued, "I thought that they might enjoy eating in the village below. I noticed a very quaint inn there. I am sure that Major von Göhler and his colleague would be gallant enough to accompany them."

"In fact," Peter Burckhardt said, "I anticipated that this might arise, and took the liberty of reserving a table at the inn — its name is "Zum Ochsen" — for seven-thirty. The reservation had been for only two, but that can be corrected to four by telephone. Is that convenient?" He addressed the question to Hannelore, the one with the red hair.

She leaned forward to touch his arm while saying in the husky voice that seemed so typical of women from Berlin, "It is very kind of you, Herr Burckhardt. Do you think we could go like this?" The question evoked an inadvertent but understandable response in the young Swiss; his eyes went directly to the red dress and the body it so tightly encased.

"Of course," he said, and then added, "but it being such a lovely moonlit night, I suggest that you walk down through the forest. And since it gets quite chilly here at night, you might consider wearing a coat, or a very warm wrap, over your . . . costume."

# THIRTY

And so it came to pass that a half hour later, the four Berliners were ushered to their table by Liselotte Maurer. At the adjacent table were seated the last three active members of the Soviet Union's espionage network in central Europe. In this year of 1943, a situation such as this could have arisen in only four places: Lisbon, Istanbul, Geneva, and Basel. These were where the agents of all warring parties were free to go about playing their games not only without undue interference on the part of the local authorities, but often under their protection. For it was in the interest of all neutrals in 1943 to ward off any incidents that might draw them into the bloodiest war that mankind had ever waged.

Thus on this March 2nd of 1943, the comings and goings in Benken, specifically at the Benkener Schloss and at the restaurant "Zum Ochsen" in the village itself, were under official surveillance. The head of Basel's political police, Dr. Wilhelm Lützelschwab, supervised the operation personally. He and his men had arrived in the village of Benken in three unmarked police cars just minutes after the four-car convoy transporting Walter Schellenberg and his entourage had turned up the lane leading to the Benkener Schloss. Two of the police had been assigned to watching the restaurant; the rest had fanned out around the Benkener Schloss, taking advantage of the cover provided by the surrounding forest.

Lützelschwab's purpose upon entering the restaurant was two-fold. The first was to verify that the Basel members of the Rote Kapelle were indeed inside. Their arrival in Benken had been observed by the local gendarme and notification duly passed on to Lützelschwab's headquarters an hour earlier. He spotted Lentz

•

immediately but was shocked that he did not recognize either of the other two men sitting with him. Lützelschwab had expected to see the man who doubled as a bartender at the Three Kings Hotel, and the desk clerk from the Schweizerhof. If these other two were not here, where were they? And now, come to think of it, where was Lentz's van? And who were these two strangers? "Dammit," Lützelschwab swore under his breath. He had thought that he had this thing totally under control, and now . . . He went to a table in the back to avoid being recognized.

The second reason for his appearance inside "Zum Ochsen" was to check out the report that two men who appeared to be Schellenberg's Leibwächter had entered the inn a half hour earlier in the company of two women of questionable background. It had hardly required the eye of an eagle to spot the ladies in question. Clad as they were in their low-cut red and green frocks, they could scarcely be mistaken for one of the local Swiss hausfraus in their dowdy dresses buttoned up to the neck. When he was approached by the Serviertochter, he concluded that she was probably none other than the peasant girl his man had spotted in the Stadttheater with the Soviet spy, who, he now realized, was sitting not more than a few meters away from the Nazis.

"Do you want to have dinner, sir?" she asked, and the policeman from Basel could not help but notice that she was a very attractive young lady.

"No," he replied. "In fact, I just came by for a quick beer."

He ordered his Warteck beer "temperiert," meaning that he wanted it to be warmed up, a vulgar custom practiced only by dull Swiss men.

"Dull" was hardly the word that described the behavior of the four Germans seated at their table in the restaurant's alcove, however: boisterous, raucous, in fact downright loudmouthed would have been more accurate adjectives. As a result, "Typische Schwobe"—"typical Germans"—was the phrase that began making the rounds among the Swiss patrons in the restaurant Lützelschwab wondered if this was a criticism of their behavior or more an expression of envy of the Germans' ability to have a good time. Because having a good time they certainly were!

In the half hour following their arrival, and before they had even ordered any food, the Germans had gone through three carafes of white wine. And the more they drank, the louder became the voices in which the two Fallschirmjäger told their jokes. The giggles and shrieks of the two fräuleins became ever shriller. They made it clear that they could not care less what the local peasantry was thinking.

It was the beginning of a night that would long be remembered in the village of Benken.

# THIRTY-ONE

Above the village, in the Benkener Schloss, the atmosphere could not have been more different. Six people at at the table in the dining room, all of them men, and all of them officers in their respective armies: four Swiss—Burckhardt, Masson, and his two staff officers—and two Germans, Schellenberg and his adjutant. But the usual hearty camaraderie that typifies get-togethers of military men, regardless of their nationality, was singularly absent.

Their mood instead was subdued, reserved, even restrained. It was as though several acquaintances from those student days at the Gymnasium or the Universität had suddenly been reunited after many years and were struggling to bridge the gap of time. For despite the fact that Germany and Switzerland shared a common border stretching from France to Austria, since the late summer of 1939, the two nations had lived totally apart. A steel curtain had been dropped between them. And while during these years, the German people had become, perhaps, the most powerful on earth, conquering Europe from the Atlantic almost to the Urals without any outside help (that provided by the Italians being more of a hindrance than a help, as current events in North Africa were now proving), the Swiss had gone into isolation. Switzerland was now a nation held captive within its own boundaries, and the fact that two of its warders now sat in their midst certainly added to the strain.

The six men were finishing their first course of Forellen blau, the local blue trout. Peter Burckhardt had deliberately turned the conversation to the Eastern front to remind their "captors" that they were hardly invincible. For it had been just over a month since the Nazis had suffered their first major defeat. On January 31st,

.

General Friederich von Paulus had surrendered his Sixth Army to the Russians at Stalingrad.

Colonel Masson, a professional soldier who was a graduate of France's military academy, tried to press General Schellenberg on details of the current military situation in Russia. However, it soon became apparent that the general, despite his rank, was ignorant of military tactics and strategies. The conclusions that he drew from the fiasco at Stalingrad showed him to be a political, not a military general.

"Stalingrad," he stated, "is one of the main reasons that I am here this evening, meine Herren. The military catastrophe that occurred there, and no one is denying that it was just that, a catastrophe, has served to further emphasize a truth that is now inescapable: the enemy of *all* of us who are seeking to preserve our common European culture is the Bolsheviks. Should the Russian barbarians be allowed to overrun Europe, it would be the end of the Abendland as we know and love it.

"We Germans stand ready to defend Europe to the death. All that we ask is that as we do so, others who share our European heritage are not preparing to stab us in the back."

The "back" he was referring to was Germany's southern flank, and the "stabbing," a dagger thrust through Switzerland.

Schellenberg became even blunter. "As you know, Colonel Masson, we are in possession of certain documents that are very damaging where your nation's claim of strict neutrality in this conflict is concerned. A secret military pact worked out between General Guisan and the General Staff of the French Army was discovered in a railroad car full of highly sensitive files of the French government. They were obviously being transported to some hiding place when, inexplicably, that railroad car was left abandoned in a siding in the village of La Charité-sur-Loire, a hundred and fifty kilometers west of Dijon. It was discovered by the advancing German troops on June sixteenth, nineteen forty, during their blitzkrieg attack on France. These protocols fully documented that Franco-Swiss joint military planning began as early as October of nineteen thirty-nine immediately after the outbreak of World War Two, and that by late November, precise details of a joint French-Swiss military response to a German attack had already been worked out.

"Phase One would have involved a massive artillery barrage

against the invading Germans in the region by Basel on the part of the Swiss Army. Phase Two would begin three to four hours later and would be triggered by the Swiss High Command granting permission to the French military to cross the border. A full French division would then move through Switzerland and begin its counterattack on the Germans from a totally unexpected direction—from the *south*. This tactic would allow the French to make an end run around the fixed East-West lines of defense that had been built up along both sides of the Maginot Line. In Phase Three, the entire Eighth French Army would have engaged the enemy, as would the Swiss Army, under joint French-Swiss command. The total evacuation of the city of Basel was foreseen, since it would have been right in the middle of the war zone. In the early months of nineteen forty, the units of the French Army that were to be thus deployed had been moved into the southernmost region of the province of Alsace."[32]

"But it never happened that way," Masson said quietly.

"No. For on May seventeenth of nineteen forty, three days after the Dutch had surrendered and Sedan had fallen to the advancing German army, the Eighth French Army was withdrawn under orders to do so 'as secretly as possible.'[33] A few battalions were left in place so that the Swiss would not immediately notice what was going on. The Swiss Army, and particularly General Guisan, was never informed."

Colonel Masson knew all this to be true. The "heroic" French military had lived up to its reputation once again, this time leaving the Swiss in the lurch. But to be confronted with these highly secret and extremely *dangerous* revelations *on Swiss soil* by a general in the SS—and in front of Swiss officers of lesser rank, who, of course, had no knowledge of any of this—was still nightmarish.

Walter Schellenberg continued: "Unless I can convince the Führer that similar plans are not now being made between your General Guisan and the Americans and the British, allowing the Allies entry onto and free passage through Swiss territory for the

32. For a full history of this episode, see Bonjour, Vol. V, pp. 12 ff. Bonjour had to rely completely on German sources since all Swiss documentation of these negotiations were destroyed in 1940 on orders of General Guisan. Bonjour's repeated attempts to gain access to any of the original French documentation were rebuffed by the French government.

33. See Bonjour, Vol. V, p. 16.

purpose of attacking Germany from the south, I am afraid that he will proceed with a preemptive attack—and soon."[34]

There it was, right out in the open: the specter of "Aktion Schweiz!"

When Schellenberg had completed his ultimatum, Masson signaled to Lieutenant Peter Burckhardt. Burckhardt abruptly rose to his feet and suggested that his fellow staff officers and Rittmeister Eggen retire for dessert and coffee in the library.

Once they were alone, Colonel Masson turned to General Schellenberg. "Now let us talk soldier to soldier, Herr General. General Guisan is prepared to meet with you tomorrow in order to personally give you his assurances that despite any conclusions your government may have drawn from those documents found at La Charité-sur-Loire, this nation and this nation's army intend to maintain absolutely strict neutrality toward *all* warring parties. *All*!"

"I am grateful that this meeting was arranged, Colonel Masson," Schellenberg responded, "because I am sure that you must be aware of my deepest admiration for your country and my sympathy for the plight in which you currently find yourselves. You can rest assured that I will do everything in my power to convince the Führer that he has been misinformed concerning the *current* intentions of the Swiss military and that it would be imprudent to proceed with 'Aktion Schweiz,'"

When he used that term, he could not help but notice the reaction on Colonel Masson's face. "I see that you are acquainted with that code name, my dear colleague . . . despite the fact that it has been classified as top secret in Berlin. My congratulations."

Having just demonstrated how easy it was to trap his Swiss counterpart into revealing that his intelligence organization had a pipeline into the innermost circle of the Nazi High Command, Schellenberg began to apply additional pressure.

---

34. According to the then Secretary of State of the Third Reich, Ernst von Weizsäcker, when Hitler received a full report on the documents found at La Charité-sur-Loire in the fall of 1940, it only served to further increase his already highly developed animosity toward Switzerland. This prompted Weizsäcker, as well as Admiral Canaris, who was in charge of German military intelligence (both men being friends of Switzerland and anti-Hitler), to inform Swiss Intelligence that these documents had fallen into Nazi hands and to warn them about the military consequences that might follow any further provocation of the Führer were the Swiss to be again caught compromising their neutrality through any cooperation with the Allies. See *Ernst von Weizsäcker: Erinnerungen* (Munich, 1950), edited by his son, Richard, pp. 301 ff.

"But if I am to help you and your nation, Colonel Masson, I am going to have to return to Berlin with certain items in hand. I must have a written statement, *written and personally signed* by your commander in chief, General Guisan, stating unequivocally that this nation and its army intend to remain neutral, in the strictest sense of that word, for the duration of this war."

Masson nodded his agreement. Thus encouraged, the German general continued. "Now, and this hardly need concern your General Guisan, there are certain concessions in the realms of industry and finance that must also be agreed to if I am to convince our Führer of your nation's good intentions. First there is the matter of our gold shipments to your National Bank, a matter in which I have a personal interest, since, as you know, dear colleague, in order to finance some of my operations abroad, I have a continuing need for hard currencies."

What Schellenberg failed to mention was that he maintained a large espionage network in Switzerland of Swiss nationals willing to accept payment only in the world's hardest currency, the Swiss franc, the source of which was the Swiss National Bank.

"Then there is the vital issue of our rights of transit through the Gotthardt tunnel. We cannot tolerate any backsliding on our agreements, especially now when an Allied landing in Italy appears imminent. The tonnage must, in fact, be increased and . . ."

# THIRTY-TWO

While Schellenberg droned on in the dining room of the Benkener Schloss, Peter Burckhardt found himself alone with Schellenberg's adjutant, Rittmeister Eggen, in his study on the second floor . . . alone because the SS major had insisted on it, suggesting that the junior officers, who had left the dining room with them, take their dessert and coffee elsewhere.

"I understand," Eggen began, "that your father is chairman of the Swiss Bank Corporation."

"Indeed he is," Peter Burckhardt responded.

"I haven't had the pleasure of meeting him, although we have done business with his bank. As you may know, I've been involved in several major business transactions between our two countries, the most recent involving the importation of prefabricated wooden army barracks made here in Switzerland. Our Swiss partner is a firm by the name of Extroc S.A., domiciled here in Basel. Since the name 'Guisan' came up several times this evening, it might interest you to know that General Guisan's son is one of the directors of Extroc."

Major Eggen paused here, no doubt to provide a little time for that last smattering of information to sink in. He was certain that having Colonel Guisan, the general's son, as a reference would automatically elevate him to a privileged status in this country. But Burckhardt merely stared at him in blank silence.

"The reason I wanted to see you in private, Herr Doktor," Eggen continued, "is to discuss some new business that I have been asked to offer to your country. This time, however, it involves pure finance. Banking. Banking in the classic Swiss sense, requiring the

∎

type of discretion that can be found only in your country, since bank secrecy here is backed up by law . . . and by severe sanctions if these secrecy laws are broken. I am talking about large deposits. In hard currencies. If necessary, in noninterest-bearing accounts."

Again he paused, and again Burckhardt deprived him of any reaction.

"Those persons who have asked me to act as an intermediary," Eggen said, "are fully aware that access to such protection is a privilege not extended to everyone. Especially where foreigners are concerned. If, however, I can bring these new private clients to, say, your father's bank, they would be more than willing to discuss, no, to *offer* reciprocity. Such reciprocity might take on unusual forms since these are indeed troubled times for us *all*.

"And if we do not help each other, each in our own way, who will?"[35]

The offer could hardly have been presented more bluntly. And the more Peter Burckhardt thought about it, the more it became apparent that it was an offer that could not be refused.

"I cannot speak on behalf of my father or his bank, as you must realize, Herr Major," Peter said, choosing his words carefully. "Nevertheless, I can tell you, as one professional speaking to another," and this time it was Burckhardt who paused to allow the import of these last words to sink in, "that this matter interests me. So much so that I am willing to take the matter up with my father. Tomorrow, in fact. I can assure you that he would require further information before agreeing even in principle. As you yourself just said, the protection of Swiss bank secrecy is hardly granted to all comers. And contrary to the mythology about numbered accounts, *responsible* Swiss banks, and you can certainly count my father's

---

35. Bonjour confirms that Eggen was deeply involved in secret financial transactions in Switzerland on behalf of the Nazis. "Unter Schellenbergs Schutz konnte sein Adjutant versteckterweise Nazigelder in die Schweiz verschieben and persönlich lukrative Geschäfte machen." Vol. V, p. 89. That there was a connection between this financial deal and intelligence activities *benefiting Switzerland* was revealed in a letter from Swiss Federal Councilor and Minister of Justice Eduard von Steiger to the Generalstabschef of the Swiss Army, Jacob Huber, dated December 20, 1944: "Man weiss nie was nun bei Eggen die Hauptsache ist, sein Nachrichtendienst gegen die Schweiz, seine privaten Geldgeschäfte oder seine Tätigkeit im Nachrichtendienst zugunsten der Schweiz." Translation: "One never knows with Eggen whether his principal interest lies in spying on Switzerland, his private financial transactions, or his intelligence activities on behalf of Switzerland." *Ibid.*, p. 90.

bank as such, *must* know the true identity of its clients. That identity is made known to two executives of the bank, and two executives only, from the time the account is opened until it is closed. Where everybody else within the bank is concerned—from tellers to secretaries to auditors—that account and all transactions made through that account are identified only by a number. And I can assure you, Herr Major, that since nineteen thirty-four, when criminal penalties were attached to any violation of our bank secrecy laws, no serious penetration of the system has occurred. I trust that your clients are familiar with all this?"

Eggen nodded.

"Then might I suggest that you identify one or two of your potential bank clients? This information will be passed on to only one other person, my father."

Peter Burckhardt meant it, and Eggen knew that he meant it.

Eggen then reached into the inside breast pocket of his jacket and removed a small notebook and a pen. He wrote three names on one of the pages, ripped the page out and handed it to Burckhardt. After Burckhardt had read the three names—Schellenberg, Bormann, and the initial H—Eggen reached out his hand to retrieve the paper.

"Where the third party is concerned," Eggen said, "I think it would be wise if he had the protection of both a number and a pseudonym.[36]

36. The "H" that Eggen had so mysteriously listed was *not* Hitler, although there can be no doubt that he was not averse to leaving that impression. Rather, as it later turned out, it was Heinrich Himmler, the head of the SS. According to no less an authority than General Guisan's son (see Braunschweig, *Geheimer Draht nach Berlin*, p. 179), Eggen had a close relationship with Himmler and, no doubt, as the man responsible for SS procurements in Switzerland, shared with him some of the profits resulting from Eggen's dubious business deals there—that share being deposited in Swiss francs in Swiss banks.

Whether Hitler had accounts in Switzerland has never been proven, in spite of reports, such as that which appeared in the *Weltwoche* of March 15, 1990 (the *Weltwoche* being Switzerland's equivalent of *Time* magazine) to the effect that Hitler had deposits of over one million Swiss francs in three different accounts in Switzerland, using a false name. This was reported as early as July 12, 1945, by London's *Evening Standard*, and then somehow forgotten or buried. The reason for this could well be due to the fact that the bank where these deposits were made was, in the highest probability, the Basler Handelsbank, one that specialized in German business. As a result, it failed shortly after the war and was liquidated under Swiss government supervision. No doubt all records that could be potentially damaging to Swiss national interests were destroyed in the process, just as all

Then he asked: "Do you perhaps have an ashtray?"

Burckhardt went over to his desk and returned with a large crystal one. The German officer took a small box of wooden matches from his pocket, placed the sheet of paper in the ashtray, and set it on fire.

While Eggen was going through all this, Burckhardt was trying to think fast, for he knew full well that his father would not even consider taking the men on Eggen's short list as clients. But there was a bank right across the street from the headquarters of the Swiss Bank Corporation—the Basler Handelsbank—that specialized in German business, loans, and deposits. In fact, the bank's exposure in Germany was so great that there were whispers among the most inner circle of banquiers in Basel that if the tide of war continued to turn against Germany, those businesses and those loans, and thus the Basler Handelsbank, could end up in deep trouble. Which would be all the more reason for them to accept new deposits now, from anybody anywhere

"Well?" the SS major asked after the sheet had burned and the ashes crumbled.

"I think something can be arranged," Burckhardt replied.

And with that, he rose and went to fetch a decanter of port, two glasses, and two cigars. He would obviously have to pass a good deal more time with this scum from the SS, and he might as well try to make it as painless as possible.

---

documents relating to the Swiss-French military pact of 1939–40 were destroyed under direct orders of General Guisan. In both instances, the Swiss again proved that they are past masters at revising history in their favor by simply destroying any damaging historical evidence.

In recent times they have been less successful in doing so, however. In the second half of the 1980s alone, it became known that at least five of the worst of the post-World War II dictators had, collectively, deposited *billions* in Swiss banks: Marcos of the Philippines, Duvalier of Haiti, Noriega of Panama, the Ceausescus of Romania, and Honecker of East Germany.

# THIRTY-THREE

At ten o'clock on that evening of March 2, 1943, the discussions in both the dining room and study of the Benkener Schloss ended.

Colonel Masson and General Schellenberg had agreed on the agenda to be followed the next day during Schellenberg's meeting with the Swiss commander in chief. In keeping with the desire of both parties to avoid any publicity, it was further agreed that the meeting would take place in the obscure Swiss village of Biglen, situated in the canton of Bern. The venue there would be the discreet back room of the restaurant "Bären." They would, however, be spending the night in Bern.

Since it promised to be another long day for them, Masson suggested that they adjourn for the evening.

The Swiss colonel and the German general walked to the study on the second floor to inform their host that they would be retiring for the night. To Burckhardt's enormous relief, SS Major Rittmeister Eggen announced his intention to do the same. So after another series of bows and heel clicks, the two Nazi visitors disappeared out into the second-floor corridor of the Benkener Schloss and proceeded to their respective bedrooms. Masson soon retired also, leaving Peter Burckhardt alone in his study, where he decided to sit in the dark for a while and watch the fire burn down while enjoying a last glass of port and one more of Havana's best.

# THIRTY-FOUR

Down in the village the evening had been considerably more boisterous and the amount of alcohol consumed considerably higher than up at the Schloss. By ten o'clock, the two Falschirmjäger and their two fräuleins were roaring drunk.

At the adjacent table, Igor Scitovsky and his two colleagues from Lausanne had been much more judicious in their drinking, nursing first a few beers and then a series of coffees, biding their time as the rest of the restaurant gradually emptied. The final element in his plan of attack had fallen into place as Scitovsky observed the behavior of the Germans; all that its implementation now required was an opening.

That opening arrived very suddenly. Herr Doktor Wilhelm Lützelschwab had also been forced to play the waiting game and had moved on from beer to coffee as the evening progressed. By ten o'clock this had led to a desperate need to seek relief. And so he left for the toilet, situated down a corridor in the rear of the restaurant.

At precisely this moment, one of the German paratroopers called out for his bill, and Liselotte Maurer went behind the bar to fetch it. Scitovsky immediately rose from his table. His two colleagues automatically did likewise and then followed him toward the rear of the restaurant. But instead of entering the corridor that led to the rest rooms, Scitovsky stopped at the end of the bar and addressed no more than a half-dozen words to Liselotte, who was bent over adding up the Germans' tab for the night. She stopped what she was doing, walked quickly to the door leading to the kitchen and pushed it open for Scitovsky and his colleagues. As if

∎

nothing out of the ordinary was going on, she then went back behind the bar, finished her calculations and rushed to present the bill to the tallest of the German men, who was waiting impatiently just inside the front entrance. The other three Germans had already walked out. He looked at the bill in the most cursory fashion, took out his wallet and handed a one hundred franc note to Liselotte with a bow.

"Vielen Dank, gnädiges Fräulein," he said and disappeared out the front door in the wake of the other three, leaving Liselotte with the change and thus the largest tip she had ever received in her life.

Dr. Lützelschwab emerged from the men's room just in time to witness this scene, and without even sitting down at his table, it was he who now called out to Liselotte for the check. His was already prepared and in Liselotte's apron pocket, so she went right over to him with it. He studied it, handed her a ten-franc note and then likewise headed for the front door of the restaurant, also leaving Liselotte with the change, which in this case represented one of the smallest tips she had received in recent memory.

Lützelschwab was halfway out the front door when he stopped short and looked back. *Both* tables in the alcove of the restaurant were now empty, as was the rest of the dining room, meaning that Scitovsky and his two men must have exited the restaurant immediately in front of the Germans. The Swiss policeman plunged out into the night and hurried past the four Germans, who were standing in front of the restaurant engaged in a loud discussion. None of them took any note of him. Once onto the road in front of the restaurant, Lützelschwab frantically looked in all directions for Scitovsky and his friends. Not a trace.

# THIRTY-FIVE

In fact, Igor Scitovsky and his friends were sitting at a table in the kitchen restaurant, waiting for Liselotte Maurer to join them. She did so almost immediately.

A few minutes after that, the back door to the kitchen opened and in came two young women about Liselotte's age. After they had taken off their coats, Scitovsky, with growing certitude that things were going his way, noticed that both were dressed in the black-and-white uniforms of maids. Liselotte brought them over to the communal kitchen table and introduced them to her now-back-in-favor boyfriend from Basel, Werner Lentz. One, it seemed, was Liselotte's best friend, Hilde, who had gone to school in Benken with her and who sometimes helped out at the Schloss when there was a big do there. The other girl was her cousin, Heidi, who was a full-time maid with the Burckhardt, Sr., family in Riehen. She had come out to Benken by train with the other maids that afternoon, but now that dinner was over and her help no longer required, instead of spending the night with the rest of the maids up on the Schloss, Heidi was going to spend the night with her cousin in the village. This all took a long time for Liselotte to explain, but Scitovsky managed to feign eager interest in every word until, finally, he was able to break in.

"I understand," he said, addressing his words to Heidi, "that you are entertaining a very important person up there tonight." He used the German expression "ein grosses Tier."

"Ja," Heidi answered, " a general. And I was responsible for his rooms. He even spoke to me. In High German. He seemed to be a real gentleman, despite the fact that he's a German."

■

"What kind of rooms would they be? I mean, for a person like that, they must be something special."

"He's in what the Frau Doktor Burckhardt calls the 'blue suite' because the wallpaper and all are blue." And then she turned to Liselotte. "You know it, Liselotte. Remember last summer when Hilde and I managed to sneak you into the Schloss through the back door and then up the back stairs? It's right at the top of those stairs on the left, the one with the huge Himmelbett."

Liselotte nodded her head. She definitely remembered the Himmelbett.

Heidi continued in a low voice. "That's why the general spoke to me. While I was turning down that bed for him this evening, just fifteen minutes ago, he came into the bedroom and asked that I bring two additional pillows." She turned to address her fellow maid. "Hilde, I think that one of those fräuleins who are supposed to be staying together in the pink room might be paying him a little visit later on tonight. Maybe both! In the Himmelbett!" And then all three girls broke out into loud giggles.

A minute later, after a short, whispered conversation with Liselotte at the back door of the restaurant, Scitovsky and his two comrades slipped out into the darkness. The moon had disappeared, and a cold drizzle had set in.

# THIRTY-SIX

The drizzle was the reason that the two German fräuleins, Hannelore and Marlene, after stepping outside the restaurant, had resolutely refused to take the path through the forest as they had done earlier in the evening at the suggestion of Peter Burckhardt. Maybe Swiss mädchen liked that sort of thing, but for them, once—downhill—had been enough. After all, they were women from Berlin! Since their two male companions had by now broken into song—"Trink, trink, Brüderlein trink"—it took a bit of shouting before they got the message across, but in the end, they succeeded.

A few minutes later, leaving the two girls from Berlin huddled in the doorway of the restaurant "Zum Ochsen," Major Göhler and his fellow officer began trotting up the hill to get one of the BMWs, and it was a fairly fast trot since, as paratroopers, they were in top condition.

All of this noise and coming and going had left Lützelschwab's surveillance team in a state of disarray. So it was easy for Scitovsky and his two foot soldiers to slip unnoticed into the forest after leaving "Zum Ochsen" through the back door of the kitchen.

# THIRTY-SEVEN

Lützelschwab now had no choice but to rethink his strategy. As he stood in the darkness across the road from the restaurant, joined by the sergeant he had charged with keeping an eye on any and all activities in the village of Benken, he had to admit to himself that he was in trouble . . . that he might have made a strategic error in dealing with this situation.

For days, he had had the option of simply moving in on Rheingasse 37, taking Scitovsky into custody and quietly closing down the Rote Kapelle's operations in Basel at the source. But that would have left an unknown number of Scitovsky's coconspirators still free and more or less in the clear. He had wanted to get them all, and catch them all red-handed. And in the process, teach Colonel Masson and the faction he represented within the Swiss military that they had been playing with fire by bringing a high-ranking Nazi onto Swiss territory. In one respect at least, he had been proven right. There were indeed more active members of the local Communist cell than those who had been identified during the surveillance of Rheingasse 37, as evidenced this evening by two complete unknowns showing up at Lentz's table.

But now all of them had somehow eluded him. He had been sure that Lentz and his two cohorts must have left the restaurant immediately before the Germans. But when he had checked with the sergeant in charge of surveillance of "Zum Ochsen," he had been told that it simply had not happened that way. What about the back? The man he had stationed there had momentarily left his post to see what all the noise was about in front of the restaurant. He had felt that his help might be needed.

.

Then it struck Lützelschwab: that stupid peasant girl! She'd let them out the back way in the middle of all the turmoil. And by now they were probably halfway through the forest on their way up to the Schloss—and to Schellenberg. To be sure, he had six men up there in the forest that surrounded the Schloss. But the Schloss was big and the night dark. And after a phone call to his counterpart in Geneva earlier that evening, he now knew that Lentz was in reality an NKGB man, known by the Geneva cell of the Rote Kapelle as Colonel Scitovsky. The Russian was obviously on his way home to a hero's welcome—provided he succeeded in this one last job on Swiss soil.

Lützelschwab decided to radically change tactics. Speaking in a low voice, he addressed the sergeant at his side: "I'm going into the restaurant through the back door." He did not explain why. "I can only assume that the two Germans have gone to fetch a car to take the ladies back up to the Schloss. If and when they do, we are all going up after them."

"By foot, sir?"

"No, by car."

"But—"

"The plans have changed. I have reason to believe that at least three members of that Communist cell are in the forest right now, working their way up toward the Schloss. And there are probably others who were planted in the forest earlier this evening to join them. I'm going to make one last attempt to surprise them in the act. If it doesn't work, or doesn't work completely, we are going to break out of our cover and openly go after them. Get your men who are down here ready. There's no time left now to alert our men up at the Schloss without alerting the enemy. After all this, Sergeant, I'll be goddamned if I'm going to let them get away."

Both the sergeant and Lützelschwab moved off into the darkness . . . though in opposite directions. Lützelschwab ran a hundred meters down the road and circled back through the pasture behind the three houses adjacent to the restaurant. When he opened the back door of the restaurant and burst into the kitchen, the sudden appearance of this huge man in a dark trenchcoat with a fierce scowl on his face prompted two of the three girls sitting at the communal table to let out shrill shrieks of terror. But not Liselotte. Instead, she went right for the butcher table and was about to pick up the largest knife there when Lützelschwab grabbed her arm and hissed, "Quiet! All of you!" And then, directly addressing Liselotte, now firmly in his grasp, "Is your name Liselotte Maurer?"

She nodded as tears started to pour down her cheeks.

"You stupid little goose! You had those three men back here, didn't you?"

Again she nodded.

"When did they leave?"

When she continued to sob, Lützelschwab increased the pressure on her right arm. "Enough of that, young lady. Now listen to me. I am with the Basel police. Anymore of your hysteria and I'll take you outside, put you in one of our cars, and have you taken to the Lohnhof in Basel, where you will spend the rest of the night."

That did it. Everybody who lived in the region surrounding Basel knew about the Lohnhof, a prison that resembled a dank medieval monastery . . . but with none of its comforts. So the sobbing stopped immediately, and Liselotte Maurer suddenly managed to find her voice.

"No more than ten minutes ago, sir," she said.

"And where were they headed?"

"I don't know, sir. But Werner—Herr Lentz—said that he would be back in less than an hour. That I should wait for him here."

Lützelschwab turned to the other two girls. "What do you do?"

"We're maids from the Schloss, sir."

"Did Lentz talk to you?"

"Yes, sir. About the general who's up there."

That did it.

"Where's the telephone ?"

"Inside the restaurant. Behind the bar."

"Show me."

After Liselotte had done so, he said, "Now I want you back in the kitchen, where you and the other two girls are going to stay until I tell you differently. Understood?"

She nodded, let out one last stifled sob, and then disappeared into the kitchen.

Lützelschwab picked up the receiver from the wall phone and dialed one-one for information. "Benkener Schloss," he said when the operator answered.

A pause. "We do not have such a listing."

"Verdammt nochmal," he swore under his breath. "Try Burck-hardt . . . with a 'ck' and a 'dt' . . . in Benken."

Five seconds later: "Forty-two, thirteen, eighty-one."

He hung up and dialed the number. It rang out twice. A man answered in a low voice: "Burckhardt "

"Is that *Peter* Burckhardt?" Lützelschwab demanded.

"Who is this? Don't you realize what time it is?"

"This is Wilhelm Lützelschwab, and I want you to listen to me very carefully. I'm calling you from the restauran 'Zum Ochsen.' I know that you've got Schellenberg up there in the Schloss. There are at least three men, no doubt very heavily armed by now, on their way up to kill him. All of them are connected with the local cell of the Rote Kapelle."

Suddenly there was the sound of an automobile braking outside the restaurant.

"Hold on!" Lützelschwab said. "And don't even think of hanging up!"

Leaving the receiver dangling from the wall-mounted phone, Lützelschwab ran to the front window of the restaurant, arriving there just in time to see the two German fräuleins getting into the Germans' BMW. Seconds later he was back on the phone. "They are led by a major in the NKGB. Within no more than five minutes—*five minutes*, Burckhardt—they are going to try to get in through the back door, find Schellenberg's bedroom, and kill him. I have men up there, but I can't get to them in time. And I fear that their attention is about to be diverted. So, Peter, it's up to you. My advice: shoot to kill."

"I understand," Burckhardt replied. Then the phone went dead.

After he had hung up the phone, Peter Burckhardt hurried out of his study to his bedroom, directly across the hall. From the closet he took out an experimental "Bergman" Maschiner pistol, a 7.36-caliber Mauser made in Switzerland. He grabbed three clips of ammunition, snapped one in place and stuck the other two under his belt beneath his jacket.

Then he ran out of the door of his bedroom and down the hall to the head of the stairs at the rear of the Schloss, the "back stairs" that led up from the kitchen on the ground floor. There he stopped. And listened. It was dead silent. He could see light coming from the door on his immediate right—the door that led into the rooms that his mother insisted upon calling the "blue suite." Schellenberg was apparently still awake.

The noise began at first very faintly. It came from outside, through the open window at the end of the hall. Seconds later, as it grew in intensity, the source became obvious: the engine of a high-powered car that was coming up the lane from the village below. The squealing of tires was soon heard above the roar of the engine. Somebody was pushing the automobile to the limit.

"It's them!" was the immediate thought that entered Burckhardt's mind. Somehow, the men from the Rote Kapelle had gotten by Lützelschwab's men below and were mounting a frontal attack on the Schloss! His next thought was to simply burst into Schellenberg's rooms to warn him to take cover. But that impulse was instantly suppressed when Burckhardt recalled what Lützelschwab had just told him on the phone . . . that the men he had stationed up near the Schloss were "about to be diverted." And Burckhardt had no doubt that by now, this had already occurred, that Lützelschwab's men had abandoned their earlier lookout positions around the Schloss and were moving to counter the frontal assault that was now so obviously underway.

It was already too late to involve Schellenberg. He might just decide to put himself in the line of fire. He was better off in his bedroom.

Burckhardt raced down the stairs. The kitchen lay in total darkness. He knelt behind the massive butcher-block table that stood in the center of the room.

And waited.

Ninety seconds later, the driver of the automobile that had been roaring up from the village slammed on the brakes and came to a screeching halt in front of the Benkener Schloss. Doors were slammed and loud voices, soon joined by loud *angry* voices—no doubt those of Lützelschwab's men—were heard.

Ten seconds later, the back door leading into the kitchen of the Benkener Schloss opened. A man entered, followed immediately by two others.

"Halt! Oder ich schiesse!" Burckhardt shouted.

They did not stop. So he opened fire, using up the entire ammunition clip in one long burst. Igor Scitovsky was killed immediately. One of the men behind him was hit in the chest and dropped to the kitchen floor, barely alive and bleeding profusely. The third man was unscathed and escaped through the back door.

Burckhardt shoved a new clip into the Mauser but maintained his cover behind the table until he was sure that no second wave of attackers had been held in reserve.

A minute later, he heard more gunfire and a voice from outside the kitchen door.

"This is Major von Göhler. I want everybody inside this room to identify himself. Then I want somebody to turn on the light in there. Right now. Otherwise, I'm going to come in firing." The words were spoken in impeccable high German.

"Herr Major," Burckhardt answered, "hier ist Peter Burckhardt. And I'm alone. Hold your fire. I'm going to turn on the light."

The light went on, and a German paratrooper was revealed poised in the doorway, a submachine gun at the ready. The first thing he did was to kick the two men on the floor. Neither moved. But taking no chances, the German soldier tossed their guns, one by one, into the far corner of the kitchen, took the grenades from their belts and carefully carrying them to the butcher-block table, deposited them directly in front of Burckhardt.

"Where's Schellenberg?" von Göhler asked.

Without turning his head, Burckhardt pointed his thumb up the back stairs. The German major charged across the room and up those stairs.

The next thing Peter Burckhardt did was to ensure that the door leading from the kitchen to the servants' quarters remained closed. To be absolutely sure, he bolted it. He wanted no maids wailing over the dead as a prelude to spreading war stories through the village of Benken and later through the entire city of Basel.

The next man to arrive through the back door of the Schloss was one of Lützelschwab's men, and he entered the kitchen carefully, with pistol drawn. He first checked out the room, taking special note of the two bodies, then addressed Burckhardt. "Your're Burckhardt. Right? And you're alone? Except for these? Right?"

When Burckhardt nodded affirmatively, the policeman said, "We just got the third one. And we're checking out the forest for more." Then he knelt down to assess the condition of the two men lying there.

"This one's dead," he said after a brief examination of Scitovsky. And after taking the pulse and raising the eyelids of the second man, he added, "This one's dying." Satisfied, he put away his pistol. "One of our men is a medic. I'll get him in here right away." He disappeared out the back door.

He returned a few minutes later with the medic and their boss, Lützelschwab, who pumped Peter's hand vigorously. 'Damn well-done, Burckhardt. Where's Schellenberg?"

"I assume he's still in his rooms. Eggen's probably with him. One of their bodyguards just went up the stairs."

"And Colonel Masson?"

As if on cue, the head of Section 5 of the General Staff of the Swiss Army appeared on the back stairs. When he saw Lützelschwab, he was visibly startled. Ignoring him, he addressed Peter Burckhardt. "Is the situation under control, Lieutenant?"

"Yes, sir," Peter said.

"They were obviously after Schellenberg. Do you have any idea of who they are?"

"Yes, sir. Members of the local cell of the Rote Kapelle. Doktor Lützelschwab can explain it better than I can."

"In a minute," Masson answered, still avoiding even looking at Lützelschwab. "Who are these men?" He pointed at the two policemen who were bent over the dying man.

"They're my men," Lützelschwab said.

"Well, tell them to get the two wounded out of here. Immediately."

"One's dead, sir," Burckhardt interjected.

"All the more reason. I don't want Schellenberg to see this."

Lützelschwab chose not to argue with Masson and went over to his men to relay the order.

As he did so, Colonel Masson, quietly and with his back turned to Lützelschwab, kept up his interrogation of Burckhardt. "Who did the shooting?"

"I did, sir," Burckhardt answered.

"How did you happen upon them?"

"I didn't. Doktor Lützelschwab alerted me by phone from the village."

"Were just these two involved?"

"No, sir. There was a third one. Lützelschwab's men have him."

"Lützelschwab is going to have a lot of explaining to do," Colonel Masson said.

Peter Burckhardt mulled this over for a moment. Then he said: "May I suggest something, sir?"

"By all means. After all, you have been the host to all this."

Ignoring the implied insult, Burckhardt plunged on. "It is obviously in everybody's interest to keep this thing contained." He paused, and taking Masson's silence as an indication of his agreement, went on. "That will require Lützelschwab's full cooperation." Masson still said nothing. "If you agree, sir, I'll have a word with him to that end. It may be necessary to evoke the name of General Guisan, and to mention the meeting he will be having with Schellenberg tomorrow. In order to drive home the point that whether Lützelschwab likes it or not, our national security interests are at stake. With your permission, sir."

"Hold on, Burckhardt. Lützelschwab obviously knew that something like this was being planned. Why, for God's sake, did he let it go so far?"

"Let's face it, sir. To embarrass you. If they had succeeded in killing Schellenberg, God knows how Hitler would have reacted."

"All right. I'll have a brief word with Schellenberg and tell him that the incident is over. That you will brief his Major von Göhler on the details. And then I'll suggest that we go back to bed. Where Lützelschwab is concerned, do what you feel is necessary. Just don't involve me."

The chief of the Swiss Intelligence Service disappeared up the back stairs.

Lützelschwab's men began hauling the two bodies—the second had just been declared dead—and their weapons out of the kitchen. After they were gone, Lützelschwab crossed the room to talk with Peter Burckhardt.

"If you agree, I'll leave five men here for the rest of the night. They'll be outside. Three in front and two in back. Just in case."

This startled Burckhardt. "Why?"

"We're still missing two members of the cell. One's driving a van. Probably been parked somewhere outside the village, waiting for his compatriots. When they don't show up, he'll move out. And we'll get him. We've just set up road blocks."

"And the other one?"

Lützelschwab shrugged. "No idea. Probably in Basel. We know who he is. So it will be only a matter of time. After all, he can hardly leave the country."

Lützelschwab turned as if to leave, which prompted Burckhardt to say, "Before you go, Herr Doktor, I would like to ask that we meet as soon as possible, preferably tomorrow morning, to discuss how we handle this incident."

"What's to discuss? It's been handled."

"You know what I mean."

"All right. Nine o'clock. My office."

"Ten."

"All right."

"By the way, what are you going to do with those two bodies?" Peter asked.

"What bodies?"

He'd already gotten the message, Burckhardt realized.

Lützelschwab, being Lützelschwab, then added: "Which means that since nothing happened up here this evening, I'm no longer indebted to you for saving my ass. Right?" He grinned and left the Benkener Schloss without looking back.

# THIRTY-EIGHT

Peter Burckhardt suddenly remembered: Nancy Reichman! Dulles! And looked at his watch: 11 P.M. exactly.

When he reached the top of the back stairs on the way to get his overcoat, he was immediately challenged: by the German paratrooper, Major von Göhler, as well as by one of the Swiss army lieutenants who had been charged with escorting the Germans during their secret mission to Switzerland. The lieutenant, keenly aware of his own failure, stood asher-faced. When Burckhardt suggested that he spend the rest of the night in the kitchen below, armed and ready, he was off like a shot.

Burckhardt turned to the German paratrooper. "Alles in Ordnung?" he asked. Then he heard the loud giggling of a girl, or girls, from behind the door that led into the rooms of General Walter Schellenberg.

"In bester Ordnung," the German replied, "as you can no doubt hear. I assume that everything else is also now under control?"

"It is."

"Then could you, perhaps, spare a minute or two with me? *Alone*?"

"Certainly. In my study, just down the hall."

"First I have to get my colleague to replace me on guard duty."

"I'll wait."

As soon as Göhler had returned with his fellow paratrooper, who now assumed the watch in the corridor outside of Schellenberg's door, he followed Peter Burckhardt into his study. Burckhardt immediately went to fetch two glasses and a bottle of cognac. He poured a more than generous portion into one of the glasses and

■

offered it to the German officer. Then he did the same for himself. Both men stood in front of the fireplace, where the dying embers were still radiating enough heat to keep the study comfortable despite the increasingly late hour.

"I'll be blunt," von Göhler began. 'I have given the general very few details on what happened tonight. Yet he seems to be under the impression that I played a key role in preventing his assassination." He paused and took a good slug of cognac. "Needless to say, my dear colleague, nothing could be farther from the truth. In fact, if the truth came out, I'm afraid it would provide me with excellent grounds for seeking political asylum in Switzerland." And he laughed.

Burckhardt took a liking to the man. "So what do you suggest we do in order to remedy the situation and save both of us unnecessary embarrassment? After all, Herr Major, we have too many refugees here already."

"I have the germ of an idea. But first I must ask you something. Those two dead men downstairs—were they not dining in the village inn earlier this evening?"

Burckhardt thought that one over, and recalling that Lützelschwab's warning call had originated from the restaurant in the village below, answered, "I believe so."

"In fact, I am sure that they spent almost the entire evening at the table right next to ours. As you know, my colleague and I, along with the two ladies, also dined at the 'Zum Ochsen' this evening, at your suggestion."

"I'm aware of that, yes."

"Yes, indeed. Good food, by the way. And good wine. In fact, we enjoyed just a wee bit too much of the latter."

"I understand."

"Well, what I'm leading up to is this: would it be at all within the realm of possibility for you to not contradict me if I were to suggest to the general—perhaps *imply* would be the more apt verb—that it was I who became suspicious of the men at the table next to mine and when they suddenly left, alerted you by telephone. Put you on guard, so to say. Allowing you—and you *alone*, that will be stressed, dear colleague—to save my general from an early death at the hands of . . ." And then his voice fell off. When he continued, it was with a question: "Who *were* they, by the way?"

"Members of the local Soviet spy ring, led, I've been told, by an NKGB colonel."

"Du lieber Gott! It was *that* serious?"

"I'm afraid so."

"Could you perhaps spare a drop or two more of that excellent cognac, dear colleague?"

Burckhardt poured him another glass and said, "Upon further reflection, I can now appreciate that when all his comes out, it might, at a very minimum, mean that any promotion to colonel would become a very remote possibility where you are concerned, Herr Major."

"Remote is hardly the word, my dear fellow."

Burckhardt continued: "This may seem a bit obtuse, but your name—von Göhler—am I correct in assuming that your family belongs to what we in the provinces of central Europe might regard as the Prussian landed aristocracy?"

"One could say that, yes."

"I assume then that you regard yourself as a professional soldier."

"Strictly."

"Well, back to our problem. I think I have what might prove to be a useful suggestion. How about this? I came down the stairs at the same moment that you burst in through the back door. We opened fire simultaneously and caught the intruders in our crossfire. You killed one, I killed the other."

"How very chivalrous of you!"

"In fact," Burckhardt continued, "as far as I am concerned, you can have them both."

"No, no. *That* I could not agree to. I think *one* will be more than sufficient. Which one did you have in mind for me?"

"The Russian."

"You are generous to a fault, Lieutenant. I will accept the offer. Vielen, vielen Dank."

Generosity had nothing to do with it. The last thing Burckhardt wanted was for word to get back to the Russians that one of theirs had been killed by a Swiss army officer. Even Dulles had warned of dire consequences if the Swiss should alienate the Soviets any further.

Burckhardt looked at his watch. "I must go, but before I do, I want to ask one more question. And if you do not choose to answer, it will not change my decision to back you up completely in regard to what transpired this evening."

Major von Göhler nodded his head in appreciation.

"We have heard that your General Dietl, acting under direct

orders from Hitler, is now at one of your army's staff headquarters in Freising, just outside of Munich,[37] and that he is there to supervise the transfer of his Twentieth Alpine Army to southern Germany and that within a matter of weeks, they will parachute into the Swiss Alps, spearheading an invasion of our country."

The expression these words produced on the German major's face could not possibly have been anything but spontaneous: he appeared totally flabbergasted.

And when he finally spoke, it was to utter but one word: "Unsinn!" Nonsense.

Then, raising himself to his full height, he added: "I, sir, served as General Dietl's adjutant before being temporarily detached to my current duties in Berlin. We still telephone each other at least once a week. The last time we spoke was two days ago, I from Berlin, he from his command post in Lapland. To be sure, he *did* mention the possibility of the Twentieth Alpine Army being moved. But to the Eastern front, not to southern Germany!"

"Are you totally convinced that this is true?"

"Dietl would never lie to me. And you have my word, sir, as a German officer, that what I have just told you is the truth."

Burckhardt reached out to shake the hand of the German officer. "Thank you," he said.

"It is I who must thank *you*, Herr Burckhardt. And something else before you go. I would like to stay in contact with you. Who knows? There might be other occasions, other reasons, other times . . ." He left the rest unsaid. "Are you traveling with us tomorrow?"

"No, I'm not," Burckhardt answered.

"Then I will leave the details of where and how I can be reached with one of your lieutenants who will be escorting us to the meeting with General Guisan."

"It might be better if you merely left a note on the bureau in your bedroom. I will have it picked up in the morning."

"Then I will do it that way."

Burckhardt again looked at his watch. It was now 23:05. "I must be on my way," he said.

In the corridor outside of Burckhardt's study on the second floor of the Benkener Schloss, the Swiss captain and the German major again shook hands. Minutes later, Peter Burckhardt was in his Mercedes, headed for Basel. The lateness of the hour meant

---

37. See Bonjour, Vol. V, p 57.

nothing to him. For after all, what was involved was the most important mission the Swiss Intelligence Service had been involved in since the outbreak of the war: to determine, beyond any reasonable doubt, whether or not a Nazi invasion of Switzerland was imminent.

If Allen Dulles would be able to reconfirm what he had just been told by the German paratrooper, it would undoubtedly allow for a much firmer negotiating stance on the part of the Swiss government vis-à-vis the Nazis and pull the rug from under those factions within both the Swiss military and the Swiss Intelligence who favored collaboration with the Germans.

# THIRTY-NINE

Rolf Seiler, the member of the Rote Kapelle who had been left behind in Basel to maintain a continuing surveillance of the apartment of the American vice-consul from within the attic of the house on the Rheingasse, had started to get nervous at ten thirty that evening. For before Igor Scitovsky had left for Benken with the rest of the remaining active members of the Swiss cells of the Rote Kapelle, he had made a promise to call him at that time. Seiler knew that where timeliness was concerned, the NKGB colonel was a fanatic.

Seiler began to reexamine his options.

# FORTY

Allen Dulles and the American vice-consul in Basel had spent the entire evening over dinner with the Swedish banker, Per Jacobsson. The restaurant they had gone to was the city's finest, the Schützenhaus, located on the site of a medieval hunting lodge that had for centuries been situated outside of the walled city of Basel. By 1943, the wall had been long gone, although three of the massive gates through which one could enter the city in medieval times still survived: the "Spalentor," the "St. Johanntor," and the "St. Albantor." Copper-plate engravings of each graced one of the walls in Nancy Reichman's apartment, and as the hour approached eleven-fifteen on this March 2nd of 1943, Allen Dulles stood in front of them, cognac glass in hand.

"Jacobsson may be a Swede, but he could just as well be a Swiss. He seems to be completely in love with this city.[38] And when one looks at these engravings and recalls Basel's history, its architecture, its university, and the humanistic tradition it has always stood for, Jacobsson's love affair is certainly understandable. But at times it seems to me that he goes a bit too far in defending some of the Swiss's actions."

38. As Jacobsson's daughter, Erin E. Jacobsson, points out in her biography of him, *A Life for Sound Money*, he loved Basel so much that he planned to retire there. Unfortunately, the six years he spent between 1956 and 1962 as head of the International Monetary Fund in Washington took such a toll that he died in 1963 before he could fulfill that wish. Poignantly, among those whom she lists as sending condolences and tributes at the time of his death, alongside the names of President Charles de Gaulle, President John Kennedy, and Chancellor Ludwig Erhardt, was that of Per Jacobsson's Basel shoemaker.

∎

"You mean when you brought up the subject of the Swiss selling arms to the Nazis in return for gold," Nancy Reichman said. She sat on the sofa, sipping a cup of coffee.

"Precisely."

"But you did offer to pass on to Washington his explanation that the Swiss have no choice. That they are literally under the gun."

Now Dulles turned away from the prints and walked to the windows that faced north and looked out on the Rhine River. It reminded him of how close he was to the enemy, that those German guns were just three kilometers farther north.

"I will do that immediately, but I fear that it will meet with very little understanding in Washington. And much, much less in Moscow. Stalin, I hear, is really starting to get worked up over the Swiss. And when he hears about General Schellenberg's visit here, he's going to be even more agitated."

Dulles looked at his watch. "Speaking of Schellenberg, I assume that we can rely on your friend showing up."

Nancy Reichman looked at her own watch. "He's never been late before. I hope nothing has happened."

# FORTY-ONE

Just one hundred and twenty meters away, on the other side of the Rhine River, a third person, Rolf Seiler, the last member of the Rote Kapelle in Switzerland who was not in police custody, looked at his watch and pondered his comrade's punctuality. He had kept his binoculars directly focused on Nancy Reichman and Allen Dulles from the minute they had stepped into the vice-consul's apartment and turned on the lights. The American woman had obviously forgotten to draw the curtains as was required after ten o'clock in all of Switzerland as a result of the blackout edict in effect since November of 1940. It was probably because that on most nights she was already in bed before that ten-o'clock deadline.[39]

He had already begun to worry a quarter of an hour before that. The exact words of Colonel Scitovsky were perfectly fresh in his mind: "I'll either telephone or deliver the news personally" about the outcome of their mission in Benken. "By no later than twenty-three hours," had been his promise.

After almost three years of experience with the NKGB intelligence officer, Seiler knew that Scitovsky always kept his promises and was, if that was possible, even more punctual than the Swiss. As he continued to watch the two Americans in the living room on

39. The blackout edict was revoked on September 12, 1944, after repeated bombings of Swiss cities, including Basel and Zürich, by British and American planes, piloted, the Swiss government claimed, by young, inexperienced men who erroneously assumed they were still over German territory. As in many cases where the Swiss government was concerned, this was a half-truth; some raids were no doubt deliberate, others accidental.

■

the other side of the river, he could tell by their body language, especially the pacing up and down of Allen Dulles, that they were also becoming increasingly disturbed. They had obviously been expecting the arrival of someone . . . who had not shown up at the appointed hour. If that someone was Walter Schellenberg, the most likely reason for his lack of appearance was that he was dead. They would probably give him until midnight, and then Dulles would return to his hotel, Nancy Reichman would go to bed—he would keep his glasses trained on her until whe was out of her clothes and into her pink nightgown just to make sure—and then he would do what he had told Scitovsky he planned to do in the absence of any new instructions to the contary: he would quietly slip out of the house on the Rheingasse 37 and seek asylum for the duration of the war in the house of his ex-professor and mentor. For him, the war would be over.

At exactly 11:38, all that changed. He watched as Nancy Reichman suddenly rose from the sofa, where she had been sitting during most of the last half hour nursing one cup of coffee after another, and rushed to the front door of the apartment. The entrance itself was out of his view, but there was no doubt in Rolf Seiler's mind that the visitor had arrived and that she was pushing the buzzer that would unlatch the door leading into her apartment building from the Augustinergasse. That meant that the newcomer would appear within minutes.

And sure enough, just two minutes later a man still clad in his overcoat appeared and crossed the living room to shake hands with Allen Dulles. After he had taken off his coat and handed it to Nancy Reichman, he chatted with Dulles in front of the huge panoramic window. The visitor filled Colonel Scitovsky's description of Walter Schellenberg to a T: six feet tall, slim, in his early thirties, and immaculately dressed in a suit that could have been tailored on Savile Row.

It was now 11:41, and still no word from Colonel Scitovsky.

It was decision time for young Rolf Seiler. In trying to make that decision, he attempted to put himself in the place of the Soviet colonel. Scitovsky's intention had been made crystal clear. He wanted Schellenberg dead.

But how?

Then he remembered Scitovsky's last words to him: "I'm leaving three different weapons, with ample ammunition for all three, in the cellar."

For the first time since Scitovsky had ordered him to maintain a constant surveillance of the apartment across the Rhine, Rolf Seiler abandoned his position in front of the rear attic window. He clambered down the ladder that led to the upstairs corridor of that house and then ran down two sets of stairs to the cellar. The weapons lay neatly arrayed on a table in the middle of the cellar: a pistol, a fully automatic assault rifle, and a carbine.

Rolf Seiler saw two options. He immediately dismissed the one that was implied by the presence of the Sturmgewehr, the standard German assault rifle, and the pistol: a direct raid on the American woman's apartment. That would require an assault team of three men; at the very least, two, if one of them had been Colonel Igor Scitovsky.

The third weapon was the ideal choice for a single assailant: a high-powered, special-issue Mauser Kar 98K rifle with a scope, a weapon with a muzzle velocity that would more than suffice for the purpose he now had in mind. He picked it up off the table to get the feel of it; it was lighter than he had expected. He also picked up six rounds of ammunition and put them in his jacket pocket.

Then suddenly Seiler did not feel at all well. The knot in the pit of his stomach that had been growing over the last hour had brought him to the edge of nausea. Rolf Seiler, barely twenty-two years old, had joined the Rote Kapelle for purely idealistic reasons. The pospect of killing another human being was nothing short of sickening. But then, deliberately, he sought to conjure up images of those atrocities being committed each and every day by the Nazis: the massacre of entire villages in Czechoslovakia and Russia; the increasingly puzzling disappearance of Jews from every single country in Europe occupied by the Germans, and that included most of them. His resolve gradually returned.

Two minutes later he was back in the attic and in front of the open window. Bracing the barrel of the rifle on the sill and adjusting the scope for distance and windage, he began loading his clip. Now it was just a matter of focusing the scope.

The three occupants of the apartment were standing together talking just a few meters beyond the huge window. The problem was that the girl was the closest to him, her back to the window in such a way as to block shots on both Schellenberg and Dulles.

Seiler locked the clip into the carbine's breech.

Then he heard something. In the building. A few seconds later he heard it again, though very faintly. Someone was in the building.

Colonel Scitovsky! He must have returned. But . . . but if it were he, why was it again so quiet? Scitovsky was an impulsive man, a Russian. He would be shouting up to him by now, ready to celebrate.

Seiler continued to hunt for Schellenberg through the scope, but the woman was still standing in front of him. Finally she began moving. Both Schellenberg and Dulles were now exposed. Rolf Seiler chambered a round, took a deep breath, held it.

He fired.

Schellenberg was down immediately. Dulles dived to the floor. Both were still in view.

Seiler was chambering a second round when two things happened: the lights went out in the apartment across the Rhine, and someone burst into his attic through the trapdoor. Seiler turned in the darkness to confront the intruder but was tackled by a huge man whose momentum sent them both flying back. Smashing his head against the windowsill, Seiler slid down the wall unconscious, onto the bare wooden floor.

Seconds later, the man who had felled him was joined by two, then three, then four other members of Basel's political police. Their chief, Dr. Wilhelm Lützelschwab, who, after recovering his balance, had reached to his belt for his flashlight and directed its beam onto the young man lying at his feet bleeding profusely from a scalp wound, was now projecting the beam around the rest of the attic, probing until he was satisfied that he had been dealing with a lone gunman.

But who had been the target?

It took Lützelschwab but a few seconds to come up with an answer. He knew Basel like the back of his hand. Most of the buildings on the opposite bank were institutional—owned by the church, the city, the university—and were occupied only during the day. The exceptions were a half-dozen apartment buildings on the Augustinergasse. The American vice-counsel lived on the top floor of the building directly across the Rhine from the attic window of Rheingasse 37. He had worried about her being a possible target of the Germans, who had already attempted to kill the British ambassador. He had even warned Peter Burckhardt about it after he had seen them together at the Three Kings while that Nazi, Eggen, was watching them. And all the while, it was the Communists he should have been concerned about!

"Somebody turn on the light in here," he said. The light went on immediately. Then, pointing: "You. and you. Take him to the emergency room of the Bürgerspital, get him bandaged, and then lock him up in solitary in the Lohnhof."

Once they were down in the front living room, Lützelschwab ordered one of the policemen to plan on spending the night there. The reason they had come directly to the Rheingasse from Benken was simple standard police follow-up procedure: now that those members of the Basel cell of the Rote Kapelle who had been involved in the attack on the Benkener Schloss were either dead or in custody, it was logical that the base from which they had operated should be occupied—as quickly and as quietly as possible—before the news got out. The objective: entrapment of any remaining cell members who might seek to check in with their now very dead leader in the hours and days that lay ahead.

The last thing he had expected to encounter was a lone assassin at work in the attic . . . although Dr. Lützelschwab would never admit that when this entire operation was inevitably reviewed. Everybody would seek to get into the act—the army, the intelligence service, the federal police—and all with the same thought in mind: covering their backs. All of them had failed where he had succeeded. Single-handedly!

But it had not been a total success. Somebody had been shot just minutes earlier in the center of Basel, i.e., on the territory for which he was primarily responsible. He only hoped to God that if it was the American girl—and who else could it be?—she was not dead.

"Come on," he said to the remaining police sergeant. "We're going across the river to take a look."

# FORTY-TWO

Across the river, after Nancy Reichman had finally drawn the curtains, she again switched on the lights in her living room. Then she knelt beside Allen Dulles, who was at the side of the man who lay shot.

"How bad is it?" she asked in a voice trembling with fright.

The answer came not from Dulles, but from Peter Burckhardt, who was struggling to sit up. "It got me on the right shoulder. Barely."

She could now see the blood dripping onto her carpet from his jacket sleeve.

With the help of both Dulles and Nancy, Burckhardt managed to fully rise to his feet. "We'll get you a new carpet," he said with the trace of a smile.

"Let me . . ." she said, initiating an attempt to remove his jacket to appraise the wound.

"No," Burckhardt said. "We are all getting out of here. Now! You are first driving me to the Bürgerspital. Then, Nancy, you are taking Mr. Dulles back to his hotel, where you will also be spending the night." He added, "If you agree, sir."

Allen Dulles responded immediately. "I agree. Nancy, go down and start your car. We'll follow you."

Peter Burckhardt countermanded that order. "No. Your car's too small. Get the keys to the Mercedes out of my left jacket pocket."

Nancy did as told, and within three minutes, the Swiss Intelligence officer, who looked somewhat like Walter Schellenberg, and the chief of America's espionage operations in Switzerland were in

■

the backseat of Burckhardt's Mercedes as it pulled away into the Augustinergasse. The hospital was less than ten minutes away. Burckhardt insisted that they simply drop him off and proceed immediately to the Schweizerhof Hotel

"To avoid unnecessary complications," he said.

# FORTY-THREE

After both the ringing of her bell and the subsequent pounding on her door had produced no response, Dr. Lützelschwab and his two men broke into Nancy Reichman's apartment and turned on the lights that Allen Dulles had turned off just five minutes before. At first glance, everything appeared normal. On second glance, however, it definitely did not. For what appeared to be a red wine stain in the middle of the living-room carpet turned out to be quite different; thicker, and still warm. Blood. When the curtains were drawn open, they revealed a huge window that again at first look, appeared intact, but under further examination, contained a bullet hole situated almost exactly in its center. Upon measurement, it was a hundred and sixty-five centimeters above the apartment floor.

Shoulder-high. The amount and color of the blood on the rug indicated that the wound had not been serious.

But if it was Nancy Reichman who had been hit, where was she?

"Goddamn it," Lützelschwab swore. "Why would they shoot her?" It didn't make sense.

For the next half hour, the political policemen of Basel went through Nancy Reichman's apartment examining every object in it, looking for an explanation. Needless to say, not one thought was wasted on the propriety of it all. The political police in Switzerland were above laws that might have guarded the privacy of its citizens or residents.[40] In Reichman's case, diplomatic immunity from

---

40. Such acts of Switzerland's political police, it turned out, did not cease when the war ended. Quite the contrary. In 1989, it came to light that they maintained secret card files—"Fichen"—on no less than 900,000 of the nation's residents

■

search or seizure no doubt also applied. On the other hand, she was but a vice-consul. And a woman. Neither gained her much respect in the circles of authority in Switzerland in 1943.

It was well past midnight when Lützelschwab and his men finally gave up and returned to police headquarters. He immediately put out a bulletin to all local police forces to be on the lookout for the missing American woman. Then, just as he was finally preparing to leave for home, the two sergeants whom he had put in charge of the assassin also arrived at headquarters after having delivered their prisoner to the local jail. One of them went directly to Lützelschwab's office.

"Guess who checked into the emergency ward of the Bürgerspital while we were having that young Communist punk bandaged up there. That Burckhardt fellow who is attached to Section Five. He was shot in the shoulder."

Lützelschwab was so excited by this news that bone-tired though he was, he jumped up from the chair behind his desk. "Did you talk to him?"

"Tried to, but the doctor who was treating him interfered."

"Was anybody else being treated?"

"No. Just the Seiler boy and the guy from intelligence."

"Nobody was with him?"

"Nobody."

Lützelschwab looked at his watch. It was almost quarter to one in the morning, but it could not be put off. Vice-consul or not, that young woman was still a full-fledged member of the diplomatic corp, and she was missing. He knew that she and Burckhardt were

---

suspected of being somewhat less than loyal to the Swiss Vaterland. The political police were empowered to spy on their citizens (through wire taps, interception of mail, etc.) by a secret edict of the Federal Council put into effect in 1951 in order to "protect the security of the nation." It remained valid until 1990. This edict further allowed the political police, in times of national crisis (such as an attempted *coup d'etat*, the definition of which remained extremely hazy), to take 'preventative action" in the form of committing Swiss citizens of questionable loyalty to internment camps without any due process of law whatsoever. Denunciations by "loyal" citizens were sufficient cause for the taking of such action, and were, in fact, to be encouraged. Revelation of all this led to the greatest political scandal in Swiss postwar history. Needless to say, no member of the Swiss conservative ruling establishment suffered any serious consequences One of the aftermaths was a proposal in parliament to abolish Switzerland's secret police. The proposal was defeated. See the *Tages Anzeiger* of Zürich for a complete history of this affair.

more than just acquaintances from university days; among other things, hadn't he watched them dancing cheek-to-cheek in the Three Kings Hotel not so long ago?

He pulled the Basel phone directory from a desk drawer, and after finding the number, dialed the Bürgerspital. When he had identified himself and asked about Burckhardt, the switchboard confirmed that the patient was spending the night there. He then had the call transferred to the night resident. He again explained who he was and said that he would be showing up in about ten minutes and expected to see the patient Burckhardt immediately. When the doctor began to protest, Lützelschwab simply hung up the phone. It was too late to put up with any crap from some smartass young doctor.

# FORTY-FOUR

Peter Burckhardt was a bit woozy from the local anesthetic and sedatives that they had given him but still lucid enough to handle the questions that Lützelschwab was firing at him. Yes. it was he who had been hit by that bullet while in Nancy Reichman's apartment. What was he doing there at that hour especially after all that had just transpired in Benken? Meeting with Allen Dulles.

That stopped even Lützelschwab for a few seconds.

"On matters that concern Section Five of the General Staff, and nothing more," Burckhardt added.

"Any ideas about who shot you?" Lützelschwab asked.

"Maybe."

"Well, you don't have to puzzle over it any longer. We not only know who did it, but we've got him in custody."

Lützelschwab then explained. After he was done, he asked a further question: "Now that you know 'who' did it, maybe you can explain 'why'?"

"One explanation more or less leaps out," Burckhardt replied. 'The Rote Kapelle was out to get Schellenberg and was covering all the bases. They knew that he would be meeting with us—with Colonel Masson—in Benken. But they must have also somehow learned about Dulles being in town and concluded that a clandestine Schellenberg-Dulles meeting was also being planned—and what better place to hold such a meeting than in the American vice-consul's apartment? So when I showed up, the shooter assumed, quite logically when you think of it, that I was Schellenberg."

Makes sense, Lützelschwab thought. And we'll find out tomorrow

■

for sure, even if I have to personally beat it out of that young Communist son of a bitch.

Lützelschwab decided to press no further on the matter; Burckhardt appeared totally fatigued. But he had to add a final word. It was now apparent that at least one officer in Section 5 had enough brains to consort with the Americans instead of with criminals like Schellenberg. He was beginning to change his mind about Peter Burckhardt. The young man was no doubt running a great personal risk by meeting with the Americans at the same time as his boss, that fool Colonel Masson, was so focused on cutting a deal with the goddamn Nazis. Well, more power to him.

"We need more of your type, Burckhardt," he said. "And don't worry, I'll leave Dulles out of this."

"I'd appreciate that very much."

"Where's the girl?"

"Staying the night at the Schweizerhof. Dulles is there, too."

"I'll send a man over there right away just in case there is still a loose cannon rolling around. By the way, the driver of the Rote Kapelle van tried to run our roadblock outside of Benken and got shot up pretty badly in the process. So we don't have to worry about him." Then, "Speaking of shots, how's the shoulder?"

"Could be a lot worse. They say I can check out in the morning."

"Take care of yourself, Peter. And thanks again for what you did for us in Benken. I owe you one."

With that, Lützelschwab left. And Peter Burckhardt fell into a deep sleep.

# PART·THREE

# FORTY-FIVE

An incident that was to dramatically affect the final stages of the war occurred in the early hours of March 3, 1945. A man jumped ship—a German ship—up the Rhine from Nancy Reichman's apartment. He swam ashore and was immediately spotted and taken into custody by one of the Swiss border guards. The sergeant of the guard telephoned Lützelschwab's office and explained the situation.

An hour later a black Citroën arrived. In it were two of Dr. Wilhelm Lützelschwab's men. They presented their credentials and waited as various phone calls were made for verification.

After another hour, they pushed the handcuffed man into the backseat and headed back to Basel, to the Speigelhof, where the headquarters of the regional counterintelligence unit was located. There he was put in a holding room.

Dr. Lützelschwab arrived in his office at ten o'clock. The desk sergeant had left a note on his desk to the effect that they were holding a man—a Frenchman, or at least he spoke French—and awaited further instructions as to what to do with him. So far, he had refused to talk to anybody, insisting that he would speak only to someone of high authority.

Normally, Lützelschwab would not have wasted his time on such a petty matter—the arrival of refugees or escapees from both Germany and France was an almost daily event—but following the instinct that had been so important thus far in his career, he decided to take a look at the man.

What he saw when he entered the holding room was a short, thin man in his early thirties, unshaven, haggard, and shivering in mud-stained clothes.

■

"Il paraît que vous voulez parler avec celui qui commande ici," Lützelschwab said.

"Exactement!" the prisoner replied eagerly.

Lützelschwab explained who he was and suggested that if the man had something important to tell him, now was the time to do it. Now or never.

The man said that he was a Frenchman from Strasbourg. He was by profession a sailor and had from his youth worked on the Rhine barges, traveling the river between Rotterdam, the Ruhr, Strasbourg, and Basel literally hundreds of times. In late 1942, he had been pressed into service by the Nazi occupiers of his home town and taken to northern Germany. There he had been given an unusual job, very unusual indeed. Perhaps the Swiss authorities would like to hear more about it.

Aha, Lützelschwab thought, we've already arrived at the quid pro quo stage. And again his instinct led him to show a readiness to cooperate.

"I assume that what you want to tell us must be very important. Otherwise, you would not have gone to so much trouble and taken such a risk to come here, would you? If indeed it turns out to be of value to us, I can assure you, monsieur, that the Swiss government will be most willing to express its gratitude in a concrete fashion. Especially," he added, "where a neighbor from Strasbourg is concerned."

The man seemed to carefully weigh these words before speaking again. Then he made up his mind. "All right," he said. "I will explain. I worked out of two ports immediately adjacent to each other on the Baltic Sea. Their names are Wolgast and Peenemünde. I lived in a barracks on Peenemünde. It's an island."

Lützelschwab had never heard of either port.

"I was assigned to a small coastal steamer. This steamer had only one destination: the port of a small city on the southeast coast of Norway by the name of Skien. It was like a shuttle. Peenemünde and Wolgast to Skien and then straight back. But what was so bizarre was that we always left the German ports completely empty; we carried no cargo whatsoever. And on the way back, we carried just one piece of cargo, a *single* piece."[41]

Now the French sailor had Lützelschwab's full attention. And

41. For the OSS version of this "improbable story," see Richard Dunlap, *Donovan: America's Master Spy* (New York, 1982), pp. 401 ff.

despite himself, he could not help but break in and ask: "Et qu'est ce que c'était?"

"What was it? I tell you what it was. A cask. That's all: a single cask. And you want to know what was in the cask? Eh?"

Lützelschwab waited.

"Water! Can you believe it? One cask of water! One cask per trip!"

Lützelschwab just stared at the man. A crazy. He must be a crazy. Someone knocked on the door.

"Herein!" Lützelschwab bellowed.

The door was opened a crack. 'A Herr Doktor Peter Burckhardt is here to see you, sir," his sergeant said.

Lützelschwab looked at his watch. Of course. They had agreed last night to meet here at ten o'clock. But after what had happened to Burckhardt, he had hardly expected him to show up. At least it meant that he could immediately end any further conversation with this poor demented man.

Without even glancing back at the Frenchman, he left the holding room.

Peter Burckhardt, pale, his right arm in a sling, was waiting for him in his office. When Lützelschwab entered the room, he was still shaking his head.

"What's bothering you?" Burckhardt asked.

Lützelschwab told him. And to his surprise, when he was done, Burckhardt was not laughing. In fact, he had a frown on his face, which prompted Lützelschwab to say, "I thought you got shot in the arm, Burckhardt, not in the head!"

"Hold on," Burckhardt replied. "There's something stuck in the back of my mind. About water. But for the life of me, I can't remember where or when or from whom I heard it, whatever 'it' is. Let me think for a moment."

Burckhardt thought while Lützelschwab stared at him.

Then: "My sister!"

"Your sister?"

"She studies physics at the university."

"What's physics got to do with this, for God's sake?"

Ignoring the question, Burckhardt asked, "May I use your phone?"

"Be my guest."

He caught Felicitas while she was still at home at their parents' place in Riehen before leaving for her lectures at the university. Peter repeated the story he had just heard from Lützelschwab and then asked what the significance, the scientific significance, of it might be. He listened for the next three minutes without saying anything, then thanked her and hung up.

"I think you're on to something," he said to Lützelschwab.

"On to what? What was that call to your sister all about?"

"For the moment, matters that concern only Section Five. But I have to talk to your sailor to be sure."

Lützelschwab led him out of his office and into the holding room down the corridor. When Burckhardt saw the wretched man, he turned to Lützelschwab. "Why don't you get him some clean clothes? And in the meantime, a cup of coffee."

Reluctantly—even resentfully—Lützelschwab left for the coffee and clothes, leaving Burckhardt alone with the prisoner.

"Doktor Lützelschwab told me your story," he began. "Tell me, how in the world did you manage to get all the way here from north Germany without being caught?"

"I got to Rotterdam on another coastal steamer with the help of some of its crew, also Frenchmen. Their ship made regular calls at Peenemünde, which was how I came to know them."

One of Lützelschwab's men arrived with not only coffee, but also two "Weggli," the Basel version of a breakfast roll. Burckhardt watched while the man devoured them. After he had washed them down with the coffee, the Frenchman breathed a deep sigh of relief and continued.

"In the port of Rotterdam, it was easy to find some of my old buddies from the days when I worked the Rhine barges. With their help, I was able to make my way up the Rhine to Basel. Almost got caught once—in Rüdesheim when the crew took me with them to a Weinstube. We were stopped for control by the police on the way back to the barge. Fortunately, nobody had any documents on them and we were so drunk that rather than getting stuck with us for the night, they simply let us go."

"Just a minute," Burckhardt said. "You said that that coastal steamer made regular calls at Peenemünde." Unlike Lützelschwab, Burckhardt knew where the little town was. As a boy, his parents had once taken him to the port of Travamünde, from which they had gone on a Baltic sailing trip and had spent a night anchored off the tiny island of Peenemünde. "What kind of cargo did it carry?"

"Cement."

"And that Norwegian port. What was its name again?"

"Skien."

This time, Burckhardt drew a blank.

"But the origin of the cask of water was another town to the north of Skien by the name of Rjukan.'

"How do you know that?"

"From the guards—heavily armed guards—who always brought the keg to our ship."

A new piece added to the puzzle: heavily armed guards!

"Let's move back to Peenemünde," Burckhard directed. "You said you lived in a barracks?"

"Yes."

"Did a lot of sailors live there, or was it just for foreign sailors who had been forced to come to work in Germany?'

"Yes."

"Yes to which question?"

"The barracks were for foreigners. But not only sailors. There were many barracks. And all kinds of workers from all over Europe, but especially from eastern Europe. Poland."

Another piece had fallen into place.

But now the man Burckhardt was questioning suddenly appeared to be on the point of collapse. The door opened again, and another of Lützelschwab's men appeared, carrying clothes. Lützelschwab walked in behind him.

"How are you doing?" he asked Burckhardt. If he was expecting an explanation of what this was all about, he did not get it.

"We're done. At least for the time being." Burckhardt rose and walked around the table to extend his hand to the French sailor. "Thank you, monsieur. You have told me some very interesting things. I may have to talk to you again."

"That means I can stay in Switzerland?"

Burckhardt glanced over at Lützelschwab, who nodded ever so slightly.

"For the time being, yes." These words brought, for the first time, a smile to the face of the French sailor. He gripped Burckhardt's hand and pumped it repeatedly. "Merci, bien, monsieur. Merci. Merci." Then Lützelschwab's man took charge of him.

Back in Lützelschwab's office, Burckhardt asked, "How do you plan on handling his case?"

The policeman answered, "Normally, we would have no choice but to take him to the frontier this afternoon and hand him back to the German authorities. That's been the official policy under a decree issued by Bern in September of last year. Since then, exceptions can be made only for military deserters, escaped prisoners of war, and for genuine political refugees.[42] The French sailor does not qualify under any of these since there are literally millions of foreign workers just like him who have been forceably brought into Germany since the beginning of the war. And a lot of them tried to escape their fate there by escaping to Switzerland. We could hardly allow that to continue since, as you know full well, Burckhardt, our boat is full. We've already got seventy-three thousand refugees here. So it was stopped. We are now forced by law to send them right back to Germany."

"So they just try again later."

"Not anymore."

"What's that supposed to mean?"

"You don't want to know," was Lützelschwab's first response. Then: "Under a new German law, any foreign worker who remains absent from his place of work for more than forty-eight hours is deemed to be a saboteur. As such, when caught, he automatically receives the death penalty."[43]

"Sorry. I should have known about that new law. I've been busy with other things. And the German courts go along with this?"

"Of course."

"It gets worse and worse over there."

"That's what I keep telling Bern. That's why I am so vehemently opposed to even the thought of consorting with any Nazis for any purpose whatsoever. And I would put Schellenberg right on top of the list of Germans who should be avoided like the plague. Why your boss Masson invited him onto Swiss soil will escape me for as long as I live."

"Sometimes you have to deal with the devil in order to survive.

"You can include me out of such exercises in sophistry, Burckhardt."

"I will try to remember that. But back to the French sailor. We might still need him. And if you need it officially, I am now speaking on behalf of Section Five of the General Staff."

"Then I'll keep him. For a while."

"Thanks." And now Burckhardt prepared to leave.

Lützelschwab decided to get in a last question. "Before you go, allow me to get back to Schellenberg. What happens next, now that we managed to save his life?"

"To use your expression, you don't want to know."

Then he was gone, closing the door behind him.

42. Bonjour, Vol. VI, pp. 25 ff.
43. *Ibid.*, p. 19.

# FORTY-SIX

Burckkhardt knew that just about then a small convoy that included Schellenberg's Mercedes was leaving Benken headed ultimately for a secret rendezvous with Switzerland's general. The Mercedes was now guarded by two Swiss army vehicles manned by heavily armed military personnel that had been brought in hurriedly during the night.

Burckhardt had spoken to Colonel Masson earlier that morning—from the hospital—to tell him that he had had confirmation from two sources that no German attack on Switzerland appeared imminent: first, from the German paratrooper, and then, very briefly, from Allen Dulles. He did not bother to explain why his conversation with Dulles had been so abbreviated, or how it was so abruptly ended. There would be time for that later.

The response of Masson could not have been more cordial. He promised to pass this information on to General Guisan *before* he began his talks with Schellenberg. And then he apologized that he had to hang up. They were scheduled to leave within a few minutes on a trip that would take them first to Bern, where Masson would install the general and his entourage in the Hotel Bellevue, from where, later that afternoon, he would proceed alone with Schellenberg and their army escort to a secret rendezvous with General Guisan.

The meeting of the two generals, one a member of the High Command of the Nazi SS, the other the commander in chief of the Swiss Army, would have been inconceivable to the Swiss citizenry. General Guisan was to them the very antithesis of all that the Nazis stood for, and he had convinced his countrymen that, if necessary, rather than bend to the Nazi will, he would be the first to die for his beloved fatherland.[44]

And now the saviour of their nation was going to have dinner with an SS general on holy Swiss soil!

Knowing the uproar that this would cause were it to leak out and

---

44. The unique status of Guisan can be partially attributed to the fact that Switzerland does not have a general in peacetime. So the very elevation of a military officer to this rank guarantees him a singular place in Swiss history. In Guisan's case, that occurred at 5 P.M. on August 30, 1939.

Guisan subsequently made two moves that established him as the hero of World War II in the minds of all right-thinking Swiss. The first occurred on July 25 of 1940, a month after the surrender of France and thus at a time when it appeared inevitable that the Nazi darkness was destined to descend on all of Europe. The commander in chief, fearing that the Swiss could now well succumb to defeatism, decided to stage what was in essence a theatrical event designed to reestablish the will of both the army and the people to resist the forces of totalitarianism that now totally encircled Switzerland. He organized a "secret" convocation of the 400 most senior officers of the Swiss armed forces and asked that they solemnly renew their oaths of allegiance to their country and the democratic way of life for which it stood. The time: July 25, 1940. The place: the "geheiligte Boden"—the holy ground—of the Rütli meadow in central Switzerland near Lucerne, where, in 1291, the peasant population of the original Swiss cantons—Uri, Schwyz, and Unterwalden—had first declared their independence from foreign tyranny.

Word of the "Rütlirapport" soon spread like wildfire throughout Switzerland, and on August 1st of 1940, General Guisan took to national radio to repeat the message he had given to his officers. The overwhelming favorable response to his appeal allowed him to subsequently usurp the role of national leadership from the seven-man Federal Council that formed the executive branch of the Swiss government, some members of which—especially Foreign Minister M. Marcel Pilet-Golaz—were (correctly) suspected of being not only defeatist, but downright pro-German.

His next move came in the form of his commitment to quickly build, at whatever cost, an Alpine "reduit": a mountain fortress in central Switzerland to which his main military forces would retreat in the event of an attack and from which they would wage relentless and uncompromising guerrilla warfare after having destroyed all north-south transportation and communication links running through their territory.

By spring of 1943, the reduit was already in place. In the mountainous region of central Switzerland, with a sparse population of 300,000 inhabitants, housing facilities for an additional 300,000 soldiers had been erected. Food, clothing, and fuel for 600,000 men had been stored in the fortress, and 40,000 horses stalled there. The supplies and ammunition were deemed sufficient to allow the Swiss Army to withstand a siege of from 6 to 8 months.

For the definitive biography of General Guisan and the role he and the Swiss Army played in World War II, see Willi Gautschi, *General Henri Guisan, Die schweizerische Armeeführung im Zweiten Weltkrieg* (Zürich, 1989).

seeking to avoid giving the meeting any "official" status by holding it at General Guisan's headquarters in Interlaken, it had been decided that the meeting would be held in a small restaurant—the Gasthaus "Bären"—in the village of Biglen in the canton of Bern. The Gasthaus had a reputation for high culinary standards even under wartime conditions, and General Guisan was a regular guest there. Masson had arranged for a small private dining room in the rear of the restaurant to be available at six o'clock on Wednesday, March 3, 1943. The table would be set for eight.

There can be little doubt that the meal was a success. Much of the conversation consisted of light talk about horses, about buying horses, about the cavalry. Although only eight people dined—each general was accompanied by three aides—they downed one bottle of white wine, a 1940 Johannesburg; three bottles of red wine, a 1937 Pommard; and eleven liqueurs. After dinner, they switched to champagne, Moët et Chandon Brut, 1938, and managed to go through another three bottles.

Around ten o'clock that evening, the two generals and their adjutants, Masson and Eggen, withdrew and spent two hours in another private room. At midnight the meeting finally broke up, one hour after the official closing hour known in Switzerland as "Polizeistunde." The Wirt, Herr Berchtold-Schneder, added an additional Fr. 5.50 to the bill for the inconvenience t caused him.[45] Carried away by the occasion, all participants signed the guestbook of the "Gasthaus Bären." Masson, as he paid the bill before leaving, had second thoughts about that and requested that the page be torn out and destroyed. It was torn out, but not destroyed. It and the bill for 259.21 francs were the only paper trail the Nazis left behind.[46]

After midnight, the general's car took him to his headquarters in Interlaken, while Colonel Masson drove Schellenberg back to the Hotel Bellevue in Bern. Early the next day, the two girls from Berlin—who were getting very bored in safe, neutral Switzerland by this time—conspired to convince "Schelli" that they could use a bit of fun before returning to the wartorn German capital. So they sneaked into his bedroom from their adjoining suite and woke the young general with a series of perverse sexual acts that could only

45. *Ibid.*, p. 540.
46. See pages 198 and 200 for copies of that page and of the bill. (Gautschi, pp. 539, 541.)

# Kellereien und Hotel „Bären"
# H. Berchtold-Schneider, Biglen (Bern)

Postcheck-Konto III 1021

Telefon 8 58 64

Spezialität: Feine Waadtländer-, Walliser- und Neuenburgerweine - Franz. Rot- und Weissweine - Fremdweine - ff. Liqueurs

Biglen, den ___ ___ 194___.  **6071** ✱

## Rechnung für _Herrn Direkt. Hauser_

Ihrem freundlichen Auftrage zufolge sende ich Ihnen auf Ihre werte Rechnung und Gefahr per Bahn nachstehend verzeichnete Waren und wünsche guten Empfang.

Bedingungen:

| H. B. | | | | |
|---|---|---|---|---|
| | | Tomate Thomi' 6 Dosen | 12.- | 72.- |
| | 6 | Cyron | -.80 | 4.80 |
| | 1 | fl. Neuenburg 1940 | 8.- | 4.- |
| | 2 | fl. Pommard 1937 | 8.- | 16.- |
| | 8 | Port Koffee ca | .70 | 5.60 |
| | 11 | Liqueurs | .60 | 6.60 |
| | | Cigarren u. Cigaretten 0.15 | | 2.75 |
| | | H. Telefon -.50 | | 2.- |
| | | Tee 4 | 1.00 | 3.- |
| | | fl. Fernuggen 1 | | 7.- |
| | 3 | fl. Mack et Claudon Brut Tag 25.- | 75.- | |
| | | | | 194.55 |
| | 4 | Champagne 1 Dosen | 6.- | 24.- |
| | 1½ | O. Provence, 1 Cyron, 1 Citron | | 7.40 |
| | 3 | Cigarren ½.35, ½.40, ½.25 | | 1.15 |
| | 1 | Kaffee u. Tee | | 0.40 |
| | 4 | Citron | | 0.40 |
| | | 15 % Service | | 352.7 |
| | | | | 353.70 |
| | | | | 6.00 |

Fässer, Kisten u. Korbflaschen bleiben mein Eigentum und sind bei franko Einsendung gut gutzuschreiben. Nach 6 Monaten noch ausstehendes Leergut wird zum Tagespreis fakturiert, diese verrechneten Fässer, Kisten usw. werden dann nicht mehr gutgeschrieben werden.

_Total Fr. 359.70_

have been thought up by two girls who had been born and raised in the world's most decadent city.

Exhausted by fifty-five uninterrupted minutes of depravity, Schellenberg immediately caved into their request to go skiing. Where? Arosa. When? Now. Right away. He crawled out of bed and staggered across the room to his bathroom before they could dream up new ways to express their appreciation.

By four that afternoon, they were back at it in the Hotel Excelsior in Arosa, where upon arrival they had been given the best rooms in the house, thanks to the invisible hand of Swiss Intelligence, which also made sure that they were not bothered by such details as registration or payment. Dinner was served in Schellenberg's suite, and then, having regained their strength from the Wienerschnitzel and Rösti, specialties of the kitchen of the Hotel Excelsior, the general and his companions resumed their activities. As it turned out, Schellenberg stayed in bed for almost all of his stay in Arosa.[47]

At seven o'clock the next morning, Schellenberg was aroused from his sleep by the telephone. It was the front desk. A courier who had asked for him was waiting below. Schellenberg told the clerk to send him up. A few minutes later there was a knock on the door. When he opened it, a man in civilian clothes informed him that he had two messages—one oral, one written—for General Walter Schellenberg. When the German general, clad only in a dressing gown, said that he was Schellenberg, the courier insisted that he produce identification and waited in the corridor until Schellenberg returned with his passport.

After carefully examining it and handing it back, the courier said: "The general has instructed me to tell you that arrangements can be made to transport the cocoa. Colonel Masson will handle the details." The courier then handed him a sealed envelope and left without a further word.

By eight o'clock, Schellenberg and his entourage were already packed and headed for the Swiss-German frontier. Prior arrangements allowed them to roll right through. From there they drove directly back to Berlin, stopping only for a brief overnight layover in Nürnberg.

---

47. To explain his rather odd behavior, Schellenberg told the hotel management that he had an upset stomach and even went so far as to have a local doctor visit him in his room and prescribe "Opiumtröpfe"! (Gautschi, p. 544)

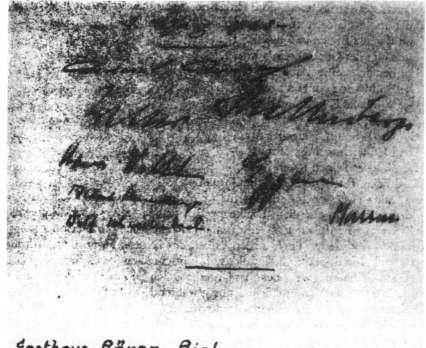

*Gasthaus Bären, Biglen.*

On March 9th, Walter Schellenberg gave his personal report to Hitler. They were later joined by the German foreign minister and the Nazi minister of economic affairs.

General Guisan subsequently acted as if the meeting had been a nonevent.[48] But its main substance was summarized in a secret communiqué sent to the German ambassador to Switzerland, Otto Karl Köcher, by his boss, German Foreign Minister Joachim von Ribbentrop. Ribbentrop quoted from a letter from General Guisan that had been hand-delivered to Schellenberg in Arosa in which Guisan reaffirmed that he, the Swiss Army, and the Swiss populace intended to defend Switzerland's integrity against attack from *any* foreign army at whatever cost necessary, and would take advantage of the unique topography to achieve that end. Guisan had initially

---

48. When, five days after the meeting, Guisan was questioned by Switzerland's civilian minister of defense about rumors of a meeting with a high-ranking German general in Biglen, he said that, indeed, he had met with a German "personality" but that he did not know his name. When then asked if it had been a political, industrial, or military "personality", Guisan replied that he apparently was in the military, in fact, a general, but what kind of a general, he did not know. (Gautschi, p. 548.)

given this same commitment orally to Schellenberg during their talks in Biglen, and when pressed to further define it, he had empowered Schellenberg to "give the Führer his solemn word as an officer that if the Allies attacked Switzerland on its southern flank, the Swiss would defend themselves to the last drop of blood — 'zum letzten Blutstropfen.'"

Schellenberg had quoted Guisan as saying that "since Switzerland wanted to avoid any possibility of Germany mounting a preventative military action against Switzerland, he would seriously entertain the thought of demobilizing a major proportion of the Swiss Army and redeploying the manpower in the civilian sector, allowing Switzerland — under conditions of continuing strict neutrality, of course — to contribute indirectly to the buildup of Germany's war potential."[49]

According to Ribbentrop, it was Walther Funk his minister of economic affairs, who finally convinced Hitler that it would be extremely unwise to attack Switzerland. Switzerland was invaluable to the Third Reich as its international turntable — "Drehscheibe" — in financial matters and as Germany's only major outside supplier of large quantities of industrial and military equipment of the highest quality, with no questions asked as to their ultimate deployment.[50] Funk pointed out that General Guisan's own son was a director of the firm that was supplying wooden barracks with which to house Jews in Polish concentration camps. So from the economic point of view, there could be no doubt that Switzerland was Nazi Germany's most valuable "ally."

Funk concluded that as long as the Swiss continued to cooperate — and, thanks to the Schellenberg mission, General Guisan had given his guarantee that they would, provided the Germans did not initiate a preventative attack against them — it would be folly to change the status quo. Hitler finally agreed. That ended any further consideration of any "Aktion Schweiz."

Funk was a lot closer to the mark than he knew. For the content, much less the meaning, of that cryptic oral message that Schellenberg had received from Guisan in Arosa was never revealed to him or to Ribbentrop. It confirmed a highly secret arrangement wherein

49. For the original text of this communiqué from Ribbentrop to Ambassador Köcher, see the Swiss National Archives, BAr EDI 1005/2. Also, Gautschi, p. 546.

50. See Walter Schellenberg's memoirs, *Aufzeichnungen* (Weisbaden/München, 1979), pp. 313 ff. Also, Gautschi, p. 534.

Switzerland's role as a "turntable" serving the interests of Nazi Germany would reach new heights. It was crucial to convincing Hitler that he should drop any further consideration of waging a preventative war against Switzerland.

It had its origins in an exchange between Schellenberg and Guisan that had taken place at the end of their conversation in the back room of the restaurant in Biglen.

"Herr General," Schellenberg had begun, "as I understand it, you have large trucks that make regular runs between Geneva and Lisbon, thanks, I should add, to our allowing them transit through France."

"We do. Just as you are able to get supplies from Germany to Italy, thanks to our allowing you the use of the Gotthardt tunnel. In our case, our trucks transport principally grain and other foodstuffs that are brought into Lisbon from South America on ships that sail under the Swiss flag. As long as we clear their cargo with the Allies ahead of time, the American and British navies leave our ships unmolested."

"Do your ships ever call at West African ports?"

Guisan referred this question to his adjutant.

"Yes," Masson answered. "As you know, we have a very large chocolate industry in Switzerland, which can keep operating only if it gets regular supplies of cocoa beans from West Africa. As a result, we are able to continue to export large quantities of chocolate to your country. Swiss chocolate often appears in the ration kits of your army."

"We are fully aware of that, and appreciative." Then Schellenberg continued: "We are experiencing great difficulties bringing in any cargo from Africa. In particular, we have one very special type of cargo presently stored in a warehouse in the Belgian Congo. We have found a way to move it to Portuguese Angola. We need help, however, in bringing it back to Europe. It is of vital importance where one of our scientific projects is concerned."

"What is the nature of this cargo?" the Swiss general asked.

"Uranium. It is an exotic ore found in only a few places on earth. This particular ore comes from one of Union Minière's mines in Joachimsthal, the Congo."

"Why can't the Portuguese transport it for you?"

Schellenberg hesitated before answering. "I will be very frank with you, Herr General," he said at last. "It has to do with research into a new area of physics. Theoretically, it could lead to the development of an extremely potent explosive device. It is a project so sensitive that we would want to involve the Portuguese only as an absolute last resort." He then added his clincher. "We know that some of your physicists at the Eidgenössische Technische Hochschule in Zürich are engaged in research in the same field. Particularly, Professor Wolfgang Pauli. He is in regular contact with Professor Werner Heisenberg, who is in charge of our project. They compare notes, so to say. As I understand it, if Pauli is to continue his research, he must have access to those materials essential for his experiments, especially uranium. As I have already mentioned, it is extremely difficult to come by. If we could come to an arrangement, I am sure that our people would be willing to divert some of our uranium to your scientists."

"How much are we talking about?" Guisan asked.

"Herr Eggen," Schellenberg said to his adjutant, "you are more conversant with these details than I."

"Two hundred tons, sir."

"How can it be transported?" Guisan asked.

"In bulk. Or in bags. I would think that the sacks they use to transport cocoa beans would prove quite suitable."

"I understand," Guisan said. "We Swiss are of course very interested in any new weapons research. As we have already discussed at great length, Herr Schellenberg, we intend to defend our country against any intruder with all of the weapons at our disposal. We would naturally be interested in any scientific discoveries that might enable us to further enhance our defensive capabilities." Then he added: "I'll see what I can do."

"How soon can I expect to hear from you or this matter?" Schellenberg asked.

"Within forty-eight hours."

"Excellent. The Führer will be very pleased to hear about this." Then: "I have already indicated that we are dealing with an extremely delicate matter. I would hope that this will not go beyond ourselves and a very limited number of your physicists in Zürich."

"It won't."

On March 25th, after nothing even remotely unusual occurred north of the border, Masson and Guisan declared the "emergency" over and subsequently claimed that it was Schellenberg who had played the key role in "saving" Switzerland.[51]

Peter Burckhardt and his colleagues in Bureau D of Swiss Intelligence, as a result of the information he had received from both the German paratrooper, Major von Göhler, and Allen Dulles, had ultimately become convinced that it had been a false alarm all along and that Schellenberg had duped Masson into believing otherwise. They regarded the entire Guisan-Schellenberg episode as appeasement. It strengthened their resolve to do everything within their power to undermine the Nazi influence upon Switzerland. This resolve was not just a matter of ideology; it grew out of the conviction that Swiss-German cooperation was bound to lead to serious difficulties with the Allied powers.[52]

And it soon did. The root cause was gold. For gold was the key to understanding how the invaluable "Turntable Switzerland" worked, and it represented the reason that the Nazi minister of economic affairs, Walther Funk, had told Hitler that it was essential for Germany's future war efforts that the "Turntable" remain intact and undisturbed.

51. In fact, on the evening of March 22, Rittmeister Eggen met with Masson in Zürich and they stayed up until midnight drinking champagne to celebrate the fact that due to their intervention, the Swiss people had been spared "the bitter cup" of being directly involved in World War II. See Gautschi, p. 556.

52. The ideological split within the Swiss Army's High Command, and especially within Section 5 of the General Staff (intelligence), dated back to an earlier event that occurred on July 21 of 1940, when 37 young officers in the Swiss Army had gotten together to found a secret organization designed to counter the appeasement tendencies that were then becoming rampant in both the High Command of the army and in Switzerland's political leadership. They swore to fight on even if the Swiss government ordered the Swiss Army to surrender to the Nazis. When they were found out, eight of the members of this "Officers' Conspiracy" were given 14 days of "sharp arrest." Max Waibel was among them, since he was among the ringleaders. Subsequently the entire affair was downplayed as a "children's crusade" and Waibel was not only rehabilitated, but was later given a leading position within Swiss Intelligence, directing all of its operations aimed at Nazi Germany. See Gautschi, pp. 235 ff.

# FORTY-SEVEN

The subject of money was unexpectedly raised by Nancy Reichman during a private dinner.

"The amount of money you people take and launder for the Nazis, Peter, is appalling. It goes beyond greed. The sums are astronomical. The Russians swear up and down that after the war, they're going to hang half of you for financial war crimes."

"Our trade agreements with Germany are a matter of public record, Nancy. You know that. Doing business with the Germans is the price of survival."

"I do know that. But there are limits."

"Where else can we sell our products? They have us surrounded."

"I'm not talking products, Peter. I'm talking gold—gold looted from Belgium, Holland, France, Eastern Europe, and Russia. Gold confiscated from the coffers of sovereign countries and ripped out of the mouths and off the bodies of the dead. That's what your people are banking. Not money made from selling the Germans chocolate and electrical power."

"You really think that these Soviets know what they're talking about?"

"According to the Soviets, it comes from 'a very reliable source in Basel.' They will offer no further clarification for fear of 'compromising their account.'"

"Did their 'very reliable source' offer anything concrete? Facts and figures, or just vague allegations?"

Nancy handed him a file folder marked *Eyes Only*. "You'll find facts and figures, names and places, in spades. This stuff is going to mean major trouble for you people. Now and in the future."

■

"Meaning?"

"The war is going to be over someday. When it is, some people are going to want an accounting."

Burckhardt thumbed through the documents, giving a cursory look to the fact and figures. They appeared to be authentic. He let out a low whistle. The source in Basel had undoubtedly communicated via Colonel Igor Scitovsky, he thought silently.

"Why are you showing me this?" he asked.

"Because unless this sort of 'monkey business'—as Mr. Dulles termed it—stops, it could prove to be extremely damaging for Switzerland. It openly invites severe reprisals, he said, and given the magnitude of the gold transfers, there would be very little he could do to ameliorate the consequences."

"I accept that. But I don't know how much I can do about it. We're talking about something *so* delicate that no more than half a dozen people in this country know the details. And all of them are, to use your phrase, in *extremely* high places."

"I understand," Nancy Reichman commented. "The last thing we want—and now I am quoting Mr. Dulles directly—is that you do anything that could put you personally in jeopardy. Because, as he pointed out, the cat is already out of the sack."

"I understand, and I appreciate your concern. But that does not mean that I am going to let the matter rest there. Before I say anything else, Nancy, I will want to look into the matter further. If the situation is as bad as you suggest—both in terms of the facts and the leaking of these facts to the Soviets—you can rest assured that I'll be back to you in very short order. And my reason for doing so is to try to contain the amount of damage done."

All this only confirmed his worst fears and made him increasingly unsure of where he stood. He was Swiss, a member of his nation's banking establishment, a soldier. Switzerland was sworn to neutrality, and he was sworn to defend and support her policies. Yet more and more he found himself questioning his government's policies, and increasingly drawn to the Americans.

After dinner it was a very subdued Peter Burckhardt who drove Nancy Reichman back to her apartment overlooking the Rhine. He even turned down her invitation to stay for coffee.

# FORTY-EIGHT

At seven-thirty the next morning, March 31st, Burckhardt was on the phone to the head of Basel's counterintelligence unit, Dr. Wilhelm Lützelschwab.

"You're calling about that Frenchman we fished out of the Rhine," was the policeman's initial response.

"No, but I assume you've still got him."

"I do. But there are limits to how much longer."

"What I'm calling about is much more serious. I know you briefed us on the Rote Kapelle affair, but I'd like a few more details. How long were you monitoring their transmissions before you closed them down?"

"Not long. Maybe two months."

"I trust you still have the transcripts."

"Of course."

"Did you decipher them?"

"Just those transmissions that took place immediately before the incident in Benken. We've had more pressing matters."

"If I could convince you that there is a strong possibility that some of those transmissions might have contained information that would be extremely compromising to Switzerland, would you put some of your people on it immediately?"

"Maybe. It's a tedious, time-consuming task, and I have a very limited budget. The resources I do have are supposed to be devoted exclusively to our counterespionage in this region. If what you are talking about falls within that category, I might be able to help you."

"What if I tell you that it involves one of the most important

■

single acts of espionage conducted against Switzerland since nineteen thirty-nine? And that it all happened here in Basel."

"I'd say come on over."

"I'll be there in half an hour."

Once behind closed doors in Lützelschwab's office, Burckhardt got right down to business.

"What I am about to tell you is highly secret. I would not even think of discussing it with you were it not necessary to convince you that deciphering every single intercept of the tramnsmissions to Moscow by the local unit of the Rote Kapelle is of the utmost importance. All right?"

"Convince me."

"We're going to be talking mainly about gold. To date, since the outbreak of the war, the Nazis have shipped to us, to Switzerland, over a billion Swiss francs' worth of gold. To put this in perspective, the physical amount of gold involved equals more than a third of the entire world production of gold during this same period. It is gold that has been looted by the Nazis and subsequently sold to our Swiss National Bank or stored in that bank for the account of the German goverment. In accordance with instructions from Berlin, the gold is then transferred to similar gold accounts that other governments maintain with the Swiss National Bank. The recipients are chiefly the central banks of Spain, Portugal, Turkey, Romania, Sweden, and Argentina. These gold disbursements are all directly related to the Nazi war effort. Where the sale of this gold to us is concerned, it is being used to buy weapons—chiefly anti-aircraft guns from Oerlikon, artillery fuses and timing mechanisms for the Wehrmacht from our watch industry—plus machine tools, generators, pharmaceuticals, and aniline dyes from Basel's chemical industry.

"Romania gets Nazi gold, via Switzerland, for oil. Spain and Portugal buy strategic metals from all around the world—manganese, chrome, wolfram—for German accounts, and then reexport them to Germany. According to our information at the BIS, the Nazis get one hundred percent of their mangenese this way, ninety-nine percent of their chrome, and seventy-five percent of their wolfram. Without these exports, and our providing the financing for them, German production of the specialty steels required for such things as shell casings, artillery barrels, and ball bearings would have to be shut down within two months."

Burckhardt paused to see what effect all this was having on Lützelschwab. From the now gray complexion of the man who sat across from him behind his desk, it was apparent that even this tough, cynical policeman, who thought he had seen and heard it all, was shaken.

"Turkey is a special situation," Burckhardt continued. "From what we have been able to ascertain at the Bank for International Settlements, gold held in the 'German account' at the Swiss National Bank is transferred to the Turkish central bank's account there. The Turks then provide the Germans with counterpart funds in Ankara in the form of hard currencies—dollars, Swiss francs, sterling—that are subsequently used to finance the extra-European intelligence efforts of the SS, to pay their agents all around the world via bank transfers from Turkey.

"The proceeds from their gold sales to Argentina—and again, these sales take place here—are used to purchase fuel and supplies for the German submarine fleet in the South Atlantic when it resupplies there. As for Sweden, our fellow neutral," and Burckhardt's sarcasm was heavy, "that country supplies Germany's steel industry with forty percent of the iron ore it requires. The Swedes are also beginning to demand 'Swiss' gold in return, although thus far, the quantities transferred to their account in Bern have been small."

"I think I get the message," Lützelschwab said. "However, before you go on—and excuse my ignorance. since I am but a lowly policeman with a degree in law—would you mind explaining exactly how all these transfers take place? And where is all that gold kept?"

"First of all, the gold never leaves the country. As to where it is kept, the gold that belongs to Switzerland is now dispersed throughout the country. It used to all be kept in Bern, but today most of it is in highly secret vaults in Zürich and Lucerne, as well as in the Alpine reduit. But the gold that the central banks of foreign countries keep here is still stored in a large underground vault beneath the Swiss National Bank's building in Bern. As you must know, the building proper has been totally sealed off since the war began and is guarded by a special, heavily armed unit of our army.

"The vault itself is currently divided into fourteen separate compartments—steel cages. The gold, in the form of twelve-kilo bars, is stacked up inside of these cages. Each gold bar is stamped with the mark of the central bank that had the bars poured, a mark that guarantees its exact weight and purity. On the door leading into each cage there is a listing of the number of bars, and the central bank of origin is given. Once a week, three officials of the National Bank make the rounds to confirm each inventory count."

"Have you been there?"

"Yes. One of those fourteen cages contains gold belonging to the Bank for International Settlements. It is my responsibility to oversee that gold and to give instructions to the National Bank whenever there are to be movements into or out of our depot there."

"How is the gold moved?"

"On a trolley. For instance, say that we at the BIS want to buy fifty million dollars' equivalent in Swedish kroner in exchange for gold. We tell the Swiss National Bank to roll out the trolley. They load up fifty million dollars' worth of gold bars in our cage, wheel it over to the Swedish cage, and stack them up there. Then they adjust the inventory posted outside both cages. Upon confirmation from Bern of the gold transfer, the Swedish central bank credits our account in Stockholm with the kroner. Transaction complete. It's exactly the same setup as they have in the vaults of the Federal Reserve Bank in New York, where there is also a lot of gold being held for the account of other countries. Our country has an immense amount there. When our government buys US government bonds or bills, it pays in gold, and the New York Federal Reserve Bank rolls out the trolley deep under the streets in New York, and gold moves from our vault to that of the US Treasury.

"The one place it can't move, however, is out of the United States. Since June fourteenth of nineteen forty-one, the assets of all continental European nations in the United States, including those of Switzerland, have been blocked, and the reason given was 'to prevent the liquidation in the United States of assets looted by duress and conquest.'[53] In other words, to prevent a recurrence of what has already happened in Europe. If we look at the experience of King Leopold of Belgium, it will give you an idea of the trouble all this can lead to for we Swiss."

"Go ahead."

"All right. On June twenty-sixth, nineteen forty, four weeks after the surrender of the Belgian armed forces, the Belgian king, now a prisoner of the German Wehrmacht, sent a personal message to

---

53. This was done by President Roosevelt under Executive Order 8785. See Paul Erdman, *Swiss American Economic Relations* (Basel, Tübingen, 1959), p. 94.

Hitler. In it he informed Hitler that prior to the outbreak of war, a substantial amount of gold belonging to the Kingdom of Belgium had been shipped to the Banque de France in Paris for safekeeping. That gold was moved to a hiding place in the vicinity of Bordeaux. The amount of Belgian gold that had been sent to France for 'safekeeping' in face of the threat of German invasion amounted to—" Burckhardt stopped talking and removed a folder from his briefcase, opened it, and read "—4,944 cases containing 221,730 kilograms. But in addition, France was also holding fifty-seven thousand kilos of gold belonging to the Polish National Bank, as well as an additional ten thousand kilos belonging to the national banks of Luxembourg, Lithuania, Latvia, Norway, and Czechoslovakia."

Burckhardt closed the folder.

"The problem was that none of that gold remained in France. Four days before France's surrender, all of it—plus all of the gold that France itself owned—was loaded onto two French cruisers in the port of Brest. The gold should have gone out on British warships and been taken to New York. But when the British failed to show up, the plan had to be changed. And so was the ultimate destination. Ten days after the French cruisers had set sail, they entered the port of Dakar, the city from which France governs all of its territories in West Africa.

"After being offloaded in Dakar on June twenty-eighth of nineteen forty, it was put under the guard of the French colonial army. And there it sat for the rest of the year . . . until the Nazis sent an ultimatum to the governor of the Banque de France, Bréart de Boisanger: no more stalling. We conquered Belgium. All rights of the Belgian National Bank are now our rights. Their gold is now our gold. We want it brought back now to a safe place. Berlin.

"The Vichy government ultimately caved in to the German demands. But since the Atlantic was now a full-fledged war zone and British warships essentially controlled the waters off of the west coast of Africa, it was decided to bring the gold by land, through central Africa, and then across the Sahara desert to the Mediterranean port of Algiers . . . from where it could be flown to Marseilles and then on to Berlin. The last ton arrived in Berlin about eight months ago.[54]

---

54. For an exhaustive factual account of the movements of looted gold from Germany into Switzerland during World War II, see Werner Rings, *Raubgold aus*

"Since then, most of it has been transferred to Switzerland, first to the depot of the Reichsbank in the Swiss National Bank. And then it was transferred to the Swiss gold depot in exchange for Swiss francs, which were then used to buy turbines or aluminum from Swiss manufacturers, or to the depot of the central bank of Sweden in exchange for kroner that were used to buy Swedish steel. And so forth. Which takes us full circle. Right?"

"Right."

"Now, so far we have just been talking about the gold the Nazis looted from Belgium. They looted a similar amount from Holland. Most of that gold—in fact, probably all of it—also came to Switzerland in nineteen forty-one and last year. Then there is Czech gold, some of which was brought to the BIS by the Nazis. Schacht himself engineered that one. That is going to prove damn embarrassing for the BIS when it comes out."

"Who knew all this?" Lützelschwab asked.

"The three general directors of the Swiss National Bank, for sure. They engineered it. My guess is that at least two members of the Federal Council must also have been in on it from the very beginning, and one of them is our minister of foreign affairs, Marcel Pilet. You have to also include my boss at the Bank for International Settlements, Per Jacobsson. But there were a few men in not so high places who were fully in the know: me, for reasons that

---

*Deutschland: Die "Goldscheibe" Schweiz im Zweiten Weltkrieg* (Zurich, 1985). This episode was one of the best-kept secrets of World War II, both during and after. The Swiss government had put under seal all references to these matters, and it was only by chance that in the winter of 1978–79, a Swiss student at the University of Bern by the name of Peter Utz stumbled upon a mass of material that documented these events and had somehow by mistake found its way into the Swiss Federal Archives (Schweizerische Bundesarchiv). His findings were subsequently presented before the Historical Seminar at the University of Bern, under the leadership of the Swiss historian, Dr. Walter Hofer.

Much earlier than this, in 1958, I found out how touchy these matters were in the view of the Swiss government. I had chanced upon references to the German-Swiss gold deals during World War II from American sources and included some of that material in my doctoral dissertation at the University of Basel. When the Swiss Federal Council, the collective presidency of Switzerland, found out about this, it tried to block publication of the dissertation. The head of the economics department, Professor Edgar Salin, who was at the time also chancellor of the university, termed this unacceptable interference in the freedom of the university and threatened to go public with the issue. The Swiss government backed down, and the dissertation was published in 1959 in unabridged form.

I've explained to you, and, it seems, a Soviet plant, who also works inside the Bank for International Settlements."

"On what do you base the last part of that statement?"

"At this point, only surmise. But it is not pure conjecture. I think it extremely unlikely that it is somebody in the National Bank since—"

"Hold on. How do you know this information has leaked to the Soviets?"

"Because they passed it on to the Americans."

"How much did the Russians find out?"

"I don't know. That's why I'm here. To discover that, with your help. Assuming, of course, that the information was transmitted to Moscow from that house on the Rhinegasse."

"And how do you know that the Americans knew?"

"I think you ought to be able to figure that out yourself."

"How many Swiss have heard about this leak?"

"Where I'm concerned, only my boss in Section Five, Captain Waibel. I can hardly know if other people in Bern have also been told. Although somehow I doubt it."

Lützelschwab liked that answer. "I'll put young Merian on it right away. And I'll see if I can borrow another cryptologist—Marc Payot—from the police in Geneva. It was these two who cracked their code in the first place. We can only hope that we started our intercepts of their radio traffic with Moscow early enough to have caught this."

"I think the odds are in our favor. I heard about t just last night, and knowing the Russians' attitude toward Switzerland, I doubt that they would have kept this sort of thing to themselves for very long."

# FORTY-NINE

Two weeks later, the deciphering of the Rote Kapelle transcripts confirmed Burckhardt's worst fears. It was all there, and more. The clue to where it originated came from detailed statistics on *direct* gold transactions between Germany and Salazar's Portugal, deals that had been brokered by the Bank for International Settlements, deals in which the Swiss had played no role whatsoever. That information could *only* have come from inside the Bank for International Settlements, a fact that confirmed a Soviet plant there.

Lützelschwab summoned Burckhardt to his office to show him what the team of Merian and Payot had come up with. His own job would now be to find the leak inside the BIS and plug it. Burckhardt's job was either to get to the men who ran the National Bank and convince them of the folly of their ways or to convince the Allies that all gold traffic between Germany and Switzerland had now been halted, permanently.

"Whether it is true or not," the policeman added.

"How do you propose to find the leak?" Burckhardt asked.

"Why not take the obvious course of action?"

"Which is?"

"To ask your boss if we can interrogate those persons who have access to the information that was passed on to Moscow. In fact, that would be the only way, since the Bank for International Settlements enjoys the same status as that of an embassy and is thus otherwise strictly off limits where we are concerned. To get in, we have to be invited in."

"Bad idea," Burckhardt immediately countered. "Even if you found out who it was, what would you be able to do about it?"

■

"Arrest him and charge him with espionage."

"Espionage against whom? All he did was to gain access to some confidential information inside the BIS and make it available to a foreign government. Such action certainly violates the rules of the BIS, but hardly the laws of Switzerland. If you wanted to accuse anybody of espionage, it would be the BIS itself. After all, it was its internal staff that gathered all the information in the first place."

"Is there any way of penetrating the BIS?"

"You've already got somebody inside the bank  Me."

Lützelschwab liked it. "And do you have any suspects in mind?"

"A few, but there is one in particular "

Lützelschwab suddenly slapped his right hand across his forehead. "I almost forgot. We've got that kid!"

"What kid?"

"The one who shot you, Burckhardt "

"So?"

"He was in and out of the house on the Rhinegasse almost every day. If their man inside the BIS delivered documents to Colonel Scitovsky on a recurring basis, it is highly likely that he saw him. Probably even talked to him."

"You're right."

"I assume that the personnel department at the BIS must have photographs on file of all the staff and employees."

"It must. I know that when I was hired, one had to be attached to the forms I filled out as part of the hiring process."

"Who runs the personnel department?"

"A Swiss. He knows the local scene, so he can check out the credentials of new hires. Not that it's such a big job. The bank employs only a hundred and fifteen people."

"How old is he?"

"Around forty, I would guess."

"Healthy?"

"As far as I know."

"Terrific. Then he must be a reservist in the army. Pull rank on him, Burckhardt. Get copies of the photographs of your suspects and I'll run them by that kid. Get their entire personnel files while you're at it."

"And if Seiler refuses to cooperate?"

"He won't."

# FIFTY

It required four hours of interrogation, five broken ribs, and two sessions of "shock therapy" before they got the answer they wanted. The breakthrough came when Dr. Wilhelm Lützelschwab told Seiler about the sixteen men who had already been secretly executed in Switzerland for espionage and that he was going to be Number Seventeen before the sun came up, unless . . .

Rolf Seiler then fingered a Pole by the name of Stanislaus Kryzinski before passing out for the third time that night.

When Lützelschwab telephoned Burckhardt with the news, Burckhardt knew that they had the right man. After the German surrender at Stalingrad, the Pole, in an emotional outburst in his defense of the Soviets and all that they stood for, had quoted a long passage, word for word, *from memory*, from *Das Kapital* to make his final point. From then on, he had become known inside the bank as "Der rote Pole."

So they had him. Dr. Lützelschwab delegated three of his political policemen to break into his apartment. They found a whole stack of documents dealing with international gold movements, the latest dated just two days earlier. All had been stamped "Highly Confidential" and all were on paper that bore the logo of the Bank for International Settlements.

The following morning, Peter Burckhardt was back in Lützelschwab's office. The first thing Lützelschwab did was to hand over samples of the material his men had found in the Pole's apartment and photographed with their Minox cameras. Then he handed him three additional blowup photographs of typescript that summed up

·

the dates and amounts of recent gold transactions involving the German Reichsbank, the BIS, and the Swiss National Bank. They were sizable.

"That comes from a portable Olvetti we also found in his apartment," Lützelschwab explained as Burckhardt read. "Looks like he was getting ready to send off another dispatch to his friends in Moscow."

"Did you find a transmitter there, too?"

"Unfortunately not. If we had, we could have put him behind bars immediately. But I suspect that he will go back to the house on the Rheingasse. This time he will be in for a surprise."

"Don't you think he's heard about what happened there?"

"How? We made sure that nothing was reported in the press about either the shooting in Benken or our raid on their house here in Basel. And everybody connected with the Rote Kapelle in Switzerland, be it here, in Geneva, or Lausanne, is either dead or locked up incommunicado."

"The system works," Burckhardt commented dryly.

"And it is my duty to ensure that it continues to work."

"What does that mean?"

"It means that the Pole now falls under the exclusive control of the political police department of the canton of Baselstadt and that from here on, Peter, matters relating to his person need no longer concern you."

"What about the damage he's already done?"

"*That* falls under *your* jurisdiction."

"I'm not so sure. They might disagree."

"Who are 'they'?"

"The men who run this country, Lützelschwab."

# FIFTY-ONE

At dawn two days later, a body was fished from the Rhine about a half kilometer downstream from the Mittlerebrücke. An autopsy revealed a very high level of alcohol in the deceased and several unusual bruises. The local police made the usual cursory checks of the many bars in that area in the hope that somebody would remember the man and possibly provide information that could lead to his identification. They came up empty-handed.

Then, two days later, they received a report from the personnel department of the Bank for International Settlements that one of their staff was missing. He had not reported for work the entire week, and repeated attempts to contact him at home had proven futile. When the man in charge of personnel went to the morgue later that day, he immediately identified the dead man.

Although going through such an ordeal almost always shook up people, the personnel chief at the BIS seemed unusually nervous. And when the two policemen who had accompanied him suggested that they go back to the bank, where they could take a look through the Pole's file, which they assumed also contained a photograph of the deceased, he became even more agitated. The reason, of course, was that he had given out that file just a week earlier to Lieutenant Peter Burckhardt, under strict orders to tell nobody.

So as a loyal Swiss soldier, the personnel head kept his silence, which gave the police the idea that maybe the dead man had been pushed. Instead of going to the bank, they took him back to the police station and started interrogating him about his relationship with the dead Pole. They finally let him make a phone call to one

■

of the officers at his bank, Dr. Peter Burckhardt, who, he said, could explain everything.

After listening for no more than thirty seconds, Burckhardt asked the man for the number of the phone he was calling from. When he got the answer, he hung up. No more than a minute later, that same phone in the police station rang. It was Dr. Wilhelm Lützelschwab.

The police file on the dead Pole was closed permanently one hour later, with the notation, "Death by accidental drowning. No further action required."

The system worked. The leak had been plugged

# FIFTY-TWO

Getting to Ernst Weber, president of the board of directors of the Swiss National Bank, was not easy. In fact, for a mere lieutenant attached to Section 5 of the General Staff of the Swiss Army, it would have been impossible had it not been for the fact that Peter Burckhardt's father was president of Switzerland's largest commercial bank. Nobody in Switzerland *ever* said no to him. Burckhardt, Sr., made a personal phone call to Weber. An appointment was set for his son for two o'clock the next afternoon.

When Peter Burckhardt entered his office, Ernst Weber did not bother to rise, but simply motioned Burckhardt to a straight-backed chair in front of his desk and uttered the words: "Um was geht es?" Before Burckhardt could even begin to explain what his visit was about, he added: "You have ten minutes." After which, he pointedly looked at his watch.

It took eight of these ten minutes for Burckhardt to describe the bare bones of what was involved. He told of how the Soviets had learned about Nazi gold shipments to Switzerland, described the problems these shipments could create for Switzerland with the Allies, and ended by assuring the central banker that the leak had been plugged.

When Burckhardt fell silent, Weber simply repeated his original question: "Why are you here?"

Burckhardt was so taken aback that for a moment he simply did not know how to respond.

"If you are worried about what the Americans or the Russians think, I am not. *We* run this country, not they. And we run it *our* way," Weber told him.

■

"But, sir, a large part of the gold we have been receiving from Germany was looted."

"Who says that? Wir haben nicht die leiseste Ahnung.[55] We do not have even the slightest idea about who owned or did not own the gold you are referring to. You of all people ought to know, Burckhardt, that it is impossible for us to determine the origin of *any* gold bars that are delivered here from abroad. It is the simplest thing in the world for a foreign government, or a central bank, to falsify the mint-of-origin stamp on the bars, change the numbers stamped there, then provide counterfeit certificates of ownership, or to falsify the dates of changes in ownership on certificates that are not counterfeit. Do you think that we here at the National Bank have either the time or the ability, or, I might add, the inclination, to check out every bar of gold that comes in here? We are not the policemen of the world, Burckhardt. Nor, if you need reminding, are *you*. We Swiss are in a situation that requires—no, Burckhardt, *demands*—solidarity. Solidarity! Understood?"

The president of the Swiss National Bank pushed a button mounted at the edge of his desk, and an usher opened the door of his office. Peter Burckhardt had no choice but to leave. But before he disappeared out the door, Ernst Weber had one last message for him: "E Gruess an Ihre Vater." Greetings to your father.

The audience was over.

This was the signal that the ranks, which obviously also included his father, had just closed. The system worked. Which meant that the case had been closed in *both* Basel and Bern.

But not in Washington, Burckhardt knew. And also not where he personally was concerned. Somehow a way had to be found to undercut the self-righteous hypocrites like Ernst Weber and put to an end, once and for all, their outrageous cooperation with the Nazis.

But in the interim, like it or not, he knew that it was up to him to exercise damage control. To put a lid on this matter for the time being, if nothing more. Not by lying, at least not by lying outright, to the Americans, but by perhaps somehow diverting their attention, even if only temporarily, to something of much more importance to them. But what did he and Section 5 have to offer the Americans?

Burckhardt immediately knew the answer: that French sailor they had fished from the Rhine! Provided they still had him.

55. These are the exact words used by Ernst Weber, president o the Swiss National Bank, in 1943 when confronted with this issue. See *Raubgold aus Deutschland*, p. 48.

# FIFTY-THREE

When Peter Burckhardt called Dr. Wilhelm Lützelschwab the next morning, the policeman confirmed that he still had the French sailor locked up in the Lohnhof, but gently reminded him that he could not keep the man there much longer. This prompted Burckhardt to show up for dinner that evening at his parents' place in suburban Riehen, where he reminded his sister of her promise to follow through on the matter. He did so after dinner, just as they were finishing their coffee.

"What Frenchman are you talking about?" asked Peter's father from his position at the head of the table.

Peter explained briefly about the sailor who had had the peculiar task of repeatedly escorting a single flask of water from Norway to Peenemünde.

"What kind of nonsense is that?"

"Don't ask me," Peter answered. "Ask her. I did a month ago and still haven't had an answer."

"Why in the world would you ask Felicitas?"

That got the girl's dander up. "Because, dear Father," she replied calmly, "we are in the middle of the twentieth century. At least the rest of the world is."

"What's that supposed to mean?"

"That women have brains, too. In fact, in some countries, they are even deemed intelligent enough to vote."[56]

---

56. Twenty years later, the male population of most, but not all, Swiss cantons finally voted to enfranchise Swiss women. The half-canton of Appenzel—Inner Rhoden—held out until 1990 when it was forced to capitulate by court order.

■

"Now, now, Felicitas. *That* is not up for discussion this evening," her mother said.

"All right," Felicitas continued. "Peter asked me because he suspected, recalling what I am currently involved in at the university, that the flask of water had some connection with nuclear physics. the study of the atom." Then, turning to her mother: "As *you* may or may not remember, Mother, that is one of the subjects I am studying."

Her mother's face indicated that she did not appreciate the sarcasm, but she said nothing further.

"About eleven years ago, British scientists found a way to shatter the nucleus of an atom by bombarding it with an atomic particle called the neutron, thus opening up the atom for the first time to closer examination. In our physics laboratory at the Bernoulianum, we have a machine called the cyclotron a rather small one, that does just that—it bombards atoms. But compared to what they are doing in England, Germany, and America. our research in Basel is small potatoes. Even in Zürich at the Federal Institute of Technology, they are way ahead of us. Which is quite natural, since it was there that Einstein got his start."

"What does all this have to do with Peter's story?" her father asked impatiently.

"I can only guess, but it probably relates to the fact that the Germans are working on developing a new weapon. Everybody in the field of physics knows that at least theoretically ways can be found to force the nuclei of atoms to give up some of their enormous energy."[57]

"And?"

"Well, again theoretically, that could result in an enormous explosion. Perhaps even an uncontrollable one."

That silenced the rest of the family

"Explain that," her brother suggested.

"It relates to what they call a chain reaction," Felicitas said. "In chemistry, such a process is self-limiting. But in physics, this is not necessarily true. The bombardment I mentioned could create a chain reaction that could run away in geometric progression—1, 2, 4, 8, 16, 32, 64 . . . 67108868, 134217726, and beyond, indefinitely."[58]

57. See Richard Rhodes, *The Making of the Atomic Bomb* (New York, 1986), p. 23 ff.
58. *Ibid.*, p. 28.

"And the Germans know how to do this?" her mother asked.

"Nobody knows how to do it, Mother. At least not yet," said Peter. "But we believe that the Germans are trying to. That's probably where our Alsatian sailor and his cask of Norwegian water fit in."

"Physicists believe," Felicitas went on, "that the key to making an atomic explosive is uranium . . . that if a neutron hits the nucleus of an uranium atom, something is bound to happen, like the beginnings of a chain reaction. If you use a pound of uranium as the target, you might be able to set off a chain reaction of millions of other atoms and get an extremely large explosion. But "normal" uranium wouldn't work. The chain reaction would fizzle. You need to "enrich" it. And to do that, you need to separate a special type of uranium isotope known as U235 from the much more common U238.[59] One way of doing that is to use a "uranium burner," a separation system that requires the use of a moderator to slow down the movement of the neutrons inside the "burner" to the speed required for achieving that separation. It was first thought that plain water would serve this purpose. But it doesn't. What does work is "heavy water"—a chemically different kind of water, consisting of deuterium, instead of hydrogen, molecules."

"You have totally lost all of us, dear," her mother said.

"It doesn't matter. The point is that 'heavy water' is probably the key to developing the substance that will serve as the material at the core of a device that could set off an atomic explosion. And it was no doubt 'heavy water' that was in those kegs."

"How do you know all this?" her mother asked in absolute awe.

"Wolfgang Pauli comes over from the Federal Institute of Technology twice a month to lecture on nuclear physics. He's Austrian. Before he came to Zürich, he was at the university in Göttingen, where he knew many of the big names in this field: Max Born, Enrico Fermi, Edward Teller, John von Neumann, Walter Elsasser—even an American, Robert Oppenheimer. They all left, because almost all of them are Jews. Pauli and Elsasser came to Switzerland; the rest went to America. One of the giant figures in nuclear physics stayed, however, Walter Heisenberg.[60] And according to Professor Pauli, he is no doubt in charge of the project that is using that heavy water coming from Norway."

59. *Ibid.*, p. 294–297.
60. *Ibid.*, pp. 168–197, where Richard Rhodes tells the story of this "exodus" of nuclear physicists from Germany in the 1930s.

"But why from Norway?" Peter asked.

"You have to distill an immense volume of ordinary H-two-oh to get even very small quantities of heavy water. That takes enormous amounts of energy. Professor Pauli explained that to obtain just one ton of heavy water a year would require an installation that would burn a hundred thousand tons of coal a year. This is impossible in Germany today. So when I told him about your story, Peter, he said that it made complete sense. There was only one source of heavy water in quantity in the whole world before the war broke out. Norway. It was not deliberately being produced there but was simply a chance by-product of a process employing hydrogen electrolysis to produce synthetic ammonia. That was, and no doubt still is, taking place in a huge electrochemical facility known as a high concentration plant, powered by a waterfall at Vemork, a little place near Rjukan, in southern Norway."[61]

"I spoke to that sailor again," Peter said, "after I telephoned you, Felicitas, and what you just told us tallies *completely* with what he told me. They would pick up those casks at a small port in southern Norway by the name of Skien, but when I pressed him further, he told me that the casks were transported there under heavy guard from another town nearby. Rjukan."

"The Norway connection makes obvious sense, Peter," his sister said, "but I should add that Professor Pauli seemed puzzled when I mentioned Peenemünde as the destination."

"Why?"

"Because just last week he had spoken by telephone to the man in charge of Germany's nuclear research, Professor Heisenberg. He and Professor Pauli were colleagues at Göttingen. Anyway, Heisenberg was where he has always been since the war broke out: the Kaiser Wilhelm Institute in Berlin."

Then Peter's father broke in. "That's just a detail Felicitas. Let's

61. The danger inherent in German control of this heavy-water installation had already led to two British attempts to sabotage the installation. The first attempt occurred during the night of November 19, 1942, and involved the landing of two gliders carrying British commandos in the vicinity of the Vemork High Concentration Plant. Both gliders crashed into the side of a mountain, however. The 14 men who survived the crashes were captured by German occupation forces and executed the same day. On February 16, 1943, the RAF tried again, this time parachuting in six Norwegians who were native to the region. They managed to disable the plant, using explosives. However, the plant resumed operations in April, and by the summer of 1943, it was back to full production. See Rhodes, pp. 455–57, 468.

stick to the substance of the matter, one that appears to have extremely serious implications." Then he turned to his son. "What do you intend to do about it, Peter?"

"Talk to my immediate superior in section Five, Captain Waibel. And if he agrees, I will repeat the story to somebody who is in a position to do something about it."

"And who might that be?"

"Allen Dulles."

# FIFTY-FOUR

As usual, the meeting with Allen Dulles was arranged through the American vice-consul in Basel, Nancy Reichman. But this time Dulles was very specific as to the details. He wanted to talk privately to the Alsatian sailor. He knew that German agents were everywhere in Basel, gathering signs and portents, however veiled, meaning that any unusual happening that would provoke their interest—such as a visit to Basel's jail by Allen Dulles—was out. As was a meeting at police headquarters, the American consulate, or Nancy's apartment.

Then Nancy had an idea: how about a chance meeting, followed by a stroll around the zoo in Basel? Dulles liked this solution for its sense of the absurd: it was the sort of rendezvous that seemed to be standard practice in spy fiction.

He arrived in Basel's train station at ten o'clock the next morning. It was a sunny, warm spring day. He spotted Nancy wearing a yellow summer frock for the occasion. To Dulles' delight, the "woman scientist" who accompanied her was an extremely beautiful young woman.

Felicitas Burckhardt was providing the transportation from the train station in her red Alfa-Romeo convertible. Since it had only a front seat, Dulles soon found himself wedged between the two attractive young ladies. He was wearing a dark suit and a hat of the homburg variety. It took them just five minutes to drive to Basel's Zoologischer Garten, where the parking lot was still almost empty, since the zoo had just opened at ten o'clock. One of the few cars there was a black Citröen.

Felicitas Burckhardt paid the entrance fees, insisting that Basel

.

was her home and the Americans therefore her guests. They proceeded down a walk adjacent to a pond half filled with flamingos. Then came the zebras on the right, the giraffes on the left. All of the animals were on display in perfectly natural settings of rocks and ponds and trees. The zoo in Basel, although small by London or Berlin standards, was known throughout Europe as a jewel, an unexpected treat that could be found right in the middle of one of Europe's older urban centers.

The okapis came next, and Felicitas Burckhardt made sure that her American guests learned that Basel was the only place outside of Africa that these rare animals had been bred.

As they passed the okapis, the morning quiet was suddenly broken by a cacophony of loud honks. It was feeding time for the seals and sea lions, and as they approached the railing around the creatures' large pond, they could see one of the keepers standing high on the rocks behind, tossing them fish. Many of the denizens of the sea were clapping their flippers, clamoring for more food. The only other spectators enjoying the fun were three men, also standing behind the rail on the other side of the pond: Peter Burckhardt, Dr. Wilhelm Lützelschwab, and the French sailor.

"There they are," Nancy Reichman said.

Dulles looked in their direction. He was not pleased with what he saw.

"Who is the tall man in the dark suit?" he demanded of Nancy.

"I don't know," she answered, obviously flustered.

"I do," Felicitas Burckhardt interjected. "He is with the Staatsanwaltschaft, I don't know the English for that, but everybody in Basel is afraid of him, since they know that he is head of the political police."

"Then he must be Wilhelm Lützelschwab," Dulles said. He was fully aware of the fact that in wartime Switzerland, the political police were in charge of counterespionage. Was he being set up?

Peter Burckhardt had been carefully watching them since their arrival, and now, sensing that something was wrong, he hurried over. His first words, addressed to Allen Dulles, indicated that he knew what the problem must be. "The third man," Peter explained, "is in charge of the prisoner, and it was only with his cooperation that this meeting could be arranged. He is totally, I stress totally, opposed to the Nazis and completely sympathetic to the cause of the Allies. He has given me his word that as far as he is concerned, this meeting is and will remain strictly off the record."

"He knows who I am?" Dulles asked.

"Of course."

"And he understands what this is all about?"

"I don't think so."

"Will he insist on knowing?"

"Not necessarily. It depends—"

"On me," Dulles interrupted. "His name's Lützelschwab, right?"

"Right. He likes to be called Doktor Lützelschwab."

"Fine with me. Let's go."

They walked over to the two men who had remained at the railing on the other side of the pond. After being introduced, Allen Dulles drew Dr. Lützelschwab aside. He proposed a deal.

"In exchange for your allowing me to talk with this man in private," Dulles said, "I will hand you some extremely damaging evidence on the activities of one of the Nazis' most important agents in Basel—a Swiss lawyer in the service of IG Farben."

"Done," said Lützelschwab.

The two men returned to the group. Dulles suggested that they split up. He would take a stroll with the sailor, while brother and sister Burckhardt served as interpreters. He did not bother to explain that the role of Felicitas Burckhardt was not to interpret language, but to explain the possible scientific import of the matter they were now going to explore.

Lützelschwab invited Nancy Reichman to accompany him to the zoo's restaurant for coffee and patisserie. He suggested to Dulles that he join them when he was done.

It was almost an hour later when the foursome finally appeared at the top of the stairs that led from the zoo to the restaurant's terrace. Lützelschwab, sensing that the less they were all seen together in public, the better, immediately went over to them and offered to once again take charge of the prisoner and return him to the Lohnhof jail. Without any further ado, he put a hand on the sailor's arm and began guiding him back down the stairs. Peter Burckhardt, hurriedly excusing himself, rushed after them.

"Wilhelm," he said when he caught up with the policeman and his charge, "what's going to happen to this man now?"

"I've no choice in the matter. The law dictates that I toss him back over the border within twenty-four hours of his illegal entry into Switzerland, and I've already bent that law rather severely by keeping him here this long. So I'm afraid—"

"I understand. You've got to get rid of him."

"Yes."

"Well, there are ways and there are ways, Wilhelm."

"What the hell is that supposed to mean, Burckhardt?"

"First a question: over which border are you going to toss him?"

"The German one, naturally."

"But he's French. From the Alsace."

"Technically, yes. Although you know perfectly well that the Germans have once again reclaimed Alsace-Lorraine as their territory. But so what?"

"This. As you probably know, our estate out in Benken borders on the Alsace."

"So?"

"Why don't you have him delivered to my custody out there, with the understanding that I will shove him over into France?"

Lützelschwab smiled, then nodded. "As long as you sign on the dotted line when you take custody of him, it's your funeral after that."

"I'll sign whatever you require."

"I'll personally deliver him in Benken at six this evening."

"I'll be there." Then Burckhardt added: "For such a mean bastard, Wilhelm, you sometimes surprise me."

So later that day, Wilhelm Lützelschwab would get rid of a prisoner, while the Burckhardt estate would gain a handyman. But now Peter rushed back up the stairs to rejoin the group on the terrace. It was going on noon, so Dulles suggested that they all stay on for a light lunch and declared—while looking directly at Felicitas Burckhardt, for whom he had obviously developed a liking—that this time, *he* was paying. As soon as they rejoined Nancy Reichman at the table, Dulles called a waitress over and ordered a well-chilled bottle of Fendant.

During the next forty-five minutes, at his request, Felicitas Burckhardt delivered to Dulles the same lecture on nuclear physics, uranium, and heavy water that she had presented at her parents' home in Riehen. While she spoke, Dulles occasionally took notes on the back of a restaurant menu. Lunch came in the form of tiny, open-faced sandwiches—asparagus, smoked salmon, salami, and ham—followed by tarts filled with lemon cream, strawberries, and mocha cream. It was a perfect Swiss lunch, marred only by the coffee: wartime coffee that was mostly chicory.

It was nearing one o'clock when lunch finally broke up. Dulles consulted the abbreviated Swiss train schedule that he always kept in the inside breast pocket of his suit jacket and declared his intention to get the 1:47 train back to Bern.

Peter Burckhardt took him to the station.

# FIFTY-FIVE

After Allen Dulles returned to the embassy early that afternoon, he transmitted a coded message to General William Donovan, head of the OSS in Washington. The message would have far-reaching consequences.

> *From: 110*
> *To: 109*
> *Status: Top secret*
> *Text: Just spoke to a French worker who swam the Rhine from Germany to Switzerland. Told following improbable story. Said he was forced-labor guard for cask of water from Rjukan in Norway to island of Peenemünde in Baltic Sea. End.*[62]

Dulles did not assign the message any special priority. So it sat on Donovan's desk for weeks while Donovan was in North Africa directing the intelligence penetration of Sicily in advance of the planned invasion in July.

It was not until early August that Donovan passed the message along to the man in charge of "research and development" in the OSS, a chemist and investor by the name of Stanley Lovell, known within that organization as "Dr. Moriarty." Matters dealing with science were automatically referred to him.[63]

Stanley Lovell immediately understood the implications. The water was heavy water being used by German physicists in Peene-

62. Richard Dunlop, *Donovan: America's Master Spy*, p. 401.
63. Dunlop, p. 401.

■

münde in an attempt to develop a nuclear bomb. Lovell, under orders from Donovan, flew to London with this information. Two weeks later, on August 17, 1943, the Royal Air Force attacked and devastated Peenemünde.

But the German facilities devoted to developing an atomic bomb escaped totally unscathed . . . due to a fact that would later return to haunt Allen Dulles: there had never been any such facility located on Peenemünde. Neither he nor Peter Burckhardt had listened carefully enough to what the French sailor had repeatedly told them. Although he *lived* on the island of Peenemünde, his ship operated out of *two ports*. Peenemünde and the neighboring port of Wolgast—which nobody had ever heard of. So they all jumped to the wrong conclusion, and with good reason. Constant aerial surveillance had indicated a feverish buildup of mysterious facilities on the island of Peenemünde, activities that logically could only have the purpose of developing and manufacturing the Nazis' "secret weapon," around which so many rumors were constantly circulating.

And the rumors were true: the V-1 and V-2 rockets *were* being developed there.

But not the atomic bomb.

The heavy water was being unloaded at the mainland port of Wolgast, from where it was shipped by rail to Berlin, to the Kaiser Wilhelm Institute, where the German nuclear research was centered all along.[64] Lovell might have caught on to this at the very outset had Dulles relayed to him the apparent skepticism of Professor Pauli that the young Swiss scientist, Felicitas Burckhardt, had detected in her conversations with him and duly passed on to Dulles during lunch at Basel's zoo. But he didn't. And Heisenberg's efforts to make his country the first to develop an atomic bomb continued unabated and unobserved while American Intelligence was being diverted to other matters.[65]

This lack of attention to nuclear matters also explained why no attention was paid to the convoy of fifty Swiss trucks that left Lisbon bound for Geneva on the night of August 24, 1943. The

64. *Ibid.*, p. 402.

65. As Richard Rhodes points out in his definitive history of the development of the atomic bomb: "One of the mysteries of the Second World War was the lack of an early and dedicated American intelligence effort to discover the extent of German progress toward atomic bomb development." *The Making of the Atomic Bomb*, p. 605.

trucks were purportedly loaded with sacks of coffee and cocoa beans. That cargo had arrived at Lisbon two days earlier aboard the *S.S. Schwyz*, one of the eleven oceangoing freighters the Swiss government had bought in 1941 and that had since sailed the Atlantic under the Swiss flag. The coffee beans had been picked up at the Portuguese West African port of Luanda; the cocoa beans at the Gold Coast port of Accra. The ship was allowed to pass through the Allies' naval blockade of continental Europe inasmuch as the Swiss government had issued it a "Certificat de Garantie," attesting to the nature of its cargo and warranting that none of it would be reexported to Germany.

The "Certificat de Garantie" was accurate where the cocoa beans were concerned. But the two thousand sacks that had been loaded onto the freighter in Luanda and then offloaded onto twenty-six Swiss trucks in Lisbon did not contain one pound of coffee beans. Instead, they were filled with two hundred tons of uranium ore.

When the convoy arrived four days later at the French-Swiss frontier, which on the French side was manned by German SS troops, one of the military attachés of the German Embassy in Bern was there to meet it. He was acting under direct orders of SS General Walter Schellenberg, orders sent from Berlin in a coded message. Colonel Masson was waiting on the Swiss side of the frontier. Following his instructions, the trucks carrying the uranium were dispatched to Basel and the cargo unloaded at a warehouse adjacent to the Badische Bahnhof. The warehouse was leased to Extroc S.A. Rittmeister Eggen, one of the managing directors, personally signed the documents acknowledging receipt of the cargo.

The next day, most of the sacks were loaded onto German railroad cars. The rest stayed in Basel. In the months that followed, in a facility especially designed for the purpose by a consortium of Swiss chemical companies, all of them headquartered in Basel, the ore the remaining sacks contained was refined into pure uranium oxide. It was then transported in drums to Zürich . . . to the laboratory of the physics department of the Swiss Federal Institute of Technology.

# PART·FOUR

# FIFTY-SIX

In the period that followed, Nancy Reichman devoted many of her days and nights to evaluating German train traffic. It did not take her long to confirm Allen Dulles' worst suspicions: the Swiss were playing both sides to their own advantage. It was not for nothing that Switzerland had remained an untouched island in the middle of a Europe totally dominated by the Nazis.

The sheer volume of freight passing through Basel on its way south had swollen to immense proportions. From an observation point she had established in the outskirts of Basel alongside the main railroad line that led from the Swiss-German frontier through Basel to the Gotthardt tunnel and then to the Italian frontier, she saw train after train moving south, often only minutes apart. All of the railroad cars, many of them tankers, were either German or Italian. All were sealed. All were under heavy guard. They were at the core of the "understanding" between the Nazis and the Swiss, an understanding that had been struck at the very outset of the war and that was the real reason for the abandonment of Hitler's plans to incorporate Switzerland into his Thousand Year Reich.

Those trains, Nancy Reichman knew, were absolutely essential to the German Army, which was now going it alone against the Allied forces north of Rome and engaging them in some of the most bitter fighting of the war. The trains were loaded predominantly with fuel, which was now in extremely short supply in Italy. In return for providing the Nazis with transit through neutral (and thus safe) Switzerland, the Swiss were able to buy from Germany, on a ton-for-ton basis, coal and oil for their own use

Equally important, the Swiss were allowed to freely transport

·

foodstuffs—especially grain bought in North and South America and brought by ships sailing the Atlantic under the Swiss flag—into neutral Portugal and Spain, and from there through Nazi-controlled territory to Geneva. Transit for transit.

Her report was duly noted in the Swiss section of the State Department back in Washington and added to a growing body of evidence that Switzerland stubbornly remained Nazi Germany's last important economic ally.

Nancy Reichman also tried to pursue the matter of what the Nazis were getting in return for the immense amount of gold they were selling Switzerland. She spliced together a newspaper item here, a dinner conversation there, with information deliberately provided to her by Swiss who were in violent disagreement with their government's policy of providing Germany with everything from precision machine tools to turbines to ball bearings to anti-aircraft guns to artillery shells. It gradually became clear that Swiss industry continued to provide key support to the German war effort in late 1944, at a time when it should have become increasingly clear to any sensible Swiss that they were supporting a losing effort and running the risk of serious retaliation if such practices continued unchecked.

Her conclusions—again duly noted and filed in Washington—were that forty per cent of all Swiss exports were still going to Germany and that half of them could be classified as "war materials." Furthermore, although this volume of "war materials" represented no more that one per cent of the output of Germany's defense industry, they were often high-precision products that, due to their unique state-of-the-art quality, had become essential and irreplaceable components in German tanks, aircraft, and U-Boats.

In the tense fall of 1944, the Swiss sourcing of such high-tech military hardware became increasingly important—in fact, critical—as the Allied bombings of Germany gradually destroyed the ball-bearing factories in Schweinfurt, the Krupp weapons-producing facilities in the Ruhr, and the Siemens electrical equipment plants in Berlin. The production gaps were often now filled by imports from such companies as Georg Fischer in Schaffhausen, which supplied diesel engines for U-Boats; Brown-Boveri in Baden, where heavy electrical equipment such as generators and turbines were being manufactured to German specifications; or the Bührle concern outside of Zürich, one of the principal suppliers of anti-aircraft weapons to the Nazis, as well as cannons for the Wehrmacht's Panzer units. They could all be relied on to meet their delivery deadlines, since their factories were, of course, immune from Allied bombardment.

One day there came a request from Washington that Nancy look into a holding company registered in Basel under the name Societé International pour Participations Industrielles et Commercials S.A., popularly known as Interhandel. A background memorandum explained that Interhandel's holdings were mainly in the chemical industry. Its principal asset was a huge chemical concern in the United States, General Aniline and Film — Kodak's chief competitor in the film industry in the nation. Ironically, GAF also supplied the khaki and blue dyes for the American Army, Air Force and Navy uniforms.

In 1942, the United States government had seized GAF under the Trading with the Enemy Act, claiming that despite the purported Swiss character of this holding company, it was in fact merely a front for the notorious German chemical cartel, IG Farben. The Swiss had vehemently protested this action, the memorandum went on to say, and would undoubtedly try to reclaim the property. As the United States government's only official representative in Basel, Vice-Consul Nancy Reichman was to collect such information and documentation as possible to back up the American seizure and block a potential Swiss counteraction.[66]

Where to turn? A phone call to Professor Salin produced a suggestion: a lawyer whom Nancy had met at one of Salin's dinners in late 1943. His name was Karl Meyer. Meyer had many corporate clients in Germany. He was also a major in the Swiss Army.

Nancy met Dr. Meyer in his offices on the Freie Strasse. At the outset, Meyer responded to her questions with curt, precise answers. Who owned Interhandel? The Sturzenegger Bank of Basel, a bank whose ownership was one hundred per cent Swiss. Its board of directors was also one hundred per cent Swiss, composed

66. For a full history of this episode, see Chapter 11. "The Strange Case of General Aniline and Film" of Joseph Borkin's *The Crime and Punishment of I. G. Farben: The Startling Account of the Unholy Alliance of Adolph Hitler and Germany's Great Chemical Combine* (New York 1978), pp 200–222. Also, Chapter 8, "The Film Conspiracy," of Charles Higham's *Trading With The Enemy: An Exposé of The Nazi-American Money Plot 1933–1949* (New York, 1983), pp. 130–153. Also, Erdman, *Swiss-American Economic Relations: Their Evolution in an Era of Crises*, pp. 158–166.

chiefly of partners of Basel's leading law firms. That alone guaranteed that Interhandel was above reproach.

Then he began to bridle. "Why are you here, Miss Reichman? It is one thing to use Basel as a place from which to spy on Germany, but it is quite another thing to misuse our city's hospitality to spy on Switzerland."

Meyer picked up a book, a thin one bound in red, and offered it to her. *Handkommentar zum Schweizerischen Strafgesetzbuch.*

"What you have is the short commentary to the Swiss criminal code. Some of the laws it describes are peculiar to Switzerland, and perhaps even offensive to Anglo-Saxons, but that in no way affects the will of Swiss courts to impose penalties on anyone who violates them. I suggest that you turn to page one hundred sixty-three of the commentary."

She did so.

"You see Article two hundred seventy-three of the Swiss Criminal Code there. Why don't you read it—out loud."

In spite of herself—her inner voice screamed that she should just throw the little red book at him and leave—she began to read. "*Wer ein Fabrikations—oder Geschäftsgeheimnis auskundschaftet, um es einer fremden amtlichen Stelle zugänglich zu machen.*" It went on and on, ending with the words, "*wird mit Gefängnis, in schweren Fällen Zuchthaus bestraft.*"[67]

"Good. For an American, you read German very well. But just to make absolutely sure that you understand what is at stake here—for *you*, Fräulein—let me bluntly summarize in English what Article two hundred seventy-three says in no uncertain terms. Anyone who tries to spy on a Swiss business—any business—in order to make its confidential affairs available to foreign governments is subject to the penalty of prison and, in severe cases, to a minimum of five years at hard labor. All that is required to set in motion a criminal investigation is a complaint by a Swiss citizen like myself."

He paused for a moment to let this sink in.

"From the smirk on your face, Fräulein, I cannot help but conclude that you think I am bluffing."

She finally spoke up. "I don't think. I know." What she knew for sure was that her diplomatic immunity protected her from any criminal investigation. What she did not know, however, was

67. Oscar Härdt, *Handkommentar sum Schweizerischen Strafgesetzbuch* (3 Auflage, Bern, 1943).

whether a complaint by Herr Doktor Meyer might not lead to the withdrawal of her credentials by the Swiss Foreign Office, and ultimately to her expulsion from Switzerland. But she was too mad to give a damn about that possibility. The way the war was going, even the Swiss would have to think twice before deliberately antagonizing the United States.

So Nancy Reichman rose from her chair and slapped the little red book down on the Swiss lawyer's desk.

"I don't know if you are aware of it or not, Herr Doktor. but we are putting together a blacklist of individuals and companies in this country who have been trading and consorting with the enemy. They will be barred from conducting any commerce with the United States and its allies after this war is concluded. I am going to make the recommendation that this list be extended to certain law firms. Needless to say, a complaint by any member of the American Foreign Service should suffice to add someone to the list."

The Swiss lawyer sprang to his feet. For a moment. Nancy Reichman thought he would hit her.

"Raus!" he shrieked at her.

So she left.

# FIFTY-SEVEN

The next day Nancy Reichman received a call from Peter Burck-hardt at the consulate.

"I hear you had a run-in yesterday with one of the pillars of our local legal establishment."

"How did you hear so soon?" Nancy asked. "Don't tell me he's some big friend of yours." Before waiting for an answer, she went on. "That pompous ass not only threatened me, but I swear, Peter, if he had been able to get at me, he would have slugged me."

"My father told me about it."

"Figures."

"Now take it easy, Nancy. You've kicked up a hornet's nest. Every bank in this little city has a big financial interest in Interhandel."

"But it's controlled by IG Farben."

"No. It's owned by the Sturzenegger Bank."

"Come on, Peter. That little bank! It probably doesn't even have twenty employees. All it does is act as a front for the true beneficial owner, which I know, you know, your father knows, and certainly the Sturzenegger Bank knows, is IG Farben. It's that simple."

"Maybe. But you'll never be able to prove it. Not one document pointing in that direction will ever be allowed to leave this country. Every document is protected under both the bank secrecy laws and those designed to prevent economic espionage."

"I know about those laws from your pal, Herr Doktor Meyer."

"He's not a pal, Nancy. He is, in fact, an arrogant, pompous ass. But then, most lawyers in this city are. On top of that, they can be bought. And in the case of Interhandel, they have been totally and irrevocably bought. As are the banks. We're talking hundreds of millions of dollars here."

■

"So what do you advise me to do?"

"Lay off. Otherwise you will find yourself totall*y* ostracized in this community, discredited, eventually expelled. Tha , in my judgment, would be much too high a price to pay for continuing the pursuit of Interhandel, especially since such a pursuit will fail in the end."

For a few seconds, Nancy Reichman said nothing. "I'll think it over," she finally told him.

"Would you like to go to the opera tomorrow night? The Fledermaus—"

"No, thank you. I'm not in the mood."

Later that afternoon she telephoned Allen Dulles and asked if she could come over to Bern the next morning and talk to him very briefly. He immediately agreed. She slept badly that night and was up before dawn to make sure to catch the first train to Bern.

After listening to her story. Dulles had but one comment: "Peter Burckhardt is right. Lay off. There are more important issues at stake—life and death issues, not just money. Save yourself for them."

When she got back, although it was already late in the afternoon, she telephoned Peter Burckhardt at his bank.

"It's me," she began. "Is that offer for the opera still on?"

"Of course."

"Will you pick me up at seven?"

"With pleasure."

"By the way, I'm forgetting about Interhandel. So you won't have to be ashamed to be seen with me in public."[6-]

68. The advice of Allen Dulles proved absolutely right. The Swiss bankers and lawyers fought to reverse the seizure of General Aniline and Film for the next 20 years in the American courts. During this period, the Union Bank of Switzerland managed to acquire control of the Swiss holding company, Interhandel, by paying an unknown amount of money to the Sturzenegger Bank and the German interests behind the facade of that bank. In 1959. the Chairman of UBS, Dr. Alfred Schaefer, got himself appointed general manager and vice-chairman of Interhandel and single-handedly took up the crusade. Well, not quite single-handedly: in August of 1961. he recruited the help of a certain Prince Radziwill, the brother-in-law of President Kennedy. Radziwill. as a member of the Kennedy clan, of course had direct access to the President's brother, Robert Keneddy who, by chance, was the attorney general of the United States. In October of 1961, Robert Kennedy met with Alfred Schaefer. A deal was worked out tha eventually led to the United States government selling the (seized) stock of GAF in the largest competitive auction in Wall Street history. The sale netted $341 million. Interhandel got $124 million of this. A few years later, Dr. Alfred Schaefer was elected to the board of BASF, the giant German chemical company that was one of the postwar successors of—guess who?—I. G. Farben. See Borkin, pp. 210 ff.

# FIFTY-EIGHT

During the intermission between the second and third acts of the opera, Peter Burckhardt was ordering two glasses of champagne when he was encountered by a man who had obviously just come into the theater, for he was still wearing his topcoat. Peter excused himself and left Nancy Reichman standing in front of the bar while he retreated into a corner with the man and entered into an intense, whispered conversation.

He returned a few minutes later alone. "Something urgent. I have to leave. Do you want to stay, or should I—"

"I'll stay, and don't worry. I can walk home from here. You'd better get going. It sounds important."

Peter Burckhardt drove to the headquarters of Section D of Swiss Intelligence, located on the Petersplatz, across the wooded park from the university. Upon entering the building, he was approached by the sergeant who had the night shift in the communications center located there.

"Here," the sergeant said, handing Burckhardt a slip of paper.

It was an urgent request that Lieutenant Peter Burckhardt arrange a meeting with Rittmeister Eggen; it included various telephone numbers in Berlin where Eggen could be contacted, day and night.

Burckhardt reached Eggen on the first try. The Rittmeister was still in the offices of SS headquarters, situated in Berlin not far from the burned out Reichstag building.

"It is so extremely kind of you to call at this very late hour, Herr Doktor," Eggen said.

■

"Bitte," Burckhardt responded. He did not like this man.

"It is imperative that we meet as soon as possible," Eggen said. "A prototype of an advanced version of one of our fighter aircraft, A Messerschmidt 100 Cg + EN, which had been engaged in an air battle over southern Germany, landed by mistake at the Dübendorf airport outside of Zürich two hours ago. It is powered by radically new engines and is equipped with highly secret and extremely advanced instrumentation that gives the plane a unique capability where night operations are concerned. The pilot tried to take off again when he realized where he was, but was prevented from doing so. We must have that plane back, Herr Lieutenant.

"To that end, one channel has been established between General Schellenberg and your Colonel Masson in Lucerne. I have been instructed to establish a second line of communications between the two of us. We are to work out the details."

"I have similar instructions," Burckhardt responded.

"I feel obliged to inform you that General Schellenberg and I are acting under direct orders of the Führer. He has told us that he expects us to resolve this matter within forty-eight hours.[69] In keeping with that, I plan to leave Berlin for Basel first thing tomorrow morning, which should mean that I will arrive in your Badische Bahnhof in the late evening. You might want to make your plans accordingly."

"I shall certainly take that into account, and I shall consult with my superiors and get back to you within the hour," Burckhardt said.

As soon as Eggen hung up, Burckhardt rang Section 5 headquarters in Lucerne. He was immediately connected with Colonel Masson. After he had repeated his conversation with Eggen, Masson's response was curt and explicit. "Tell Eggen that you will meet him when he arrives. General Guisan and I are going to fly over to Dübendorf at dawn tomorrow in his Fieseler Storch to take a look at the machine and will then return to Bern to consult with

---

69. What the Führer had told Schellenberg and Eggen was that if a deal for the return of the ME 110 could not be worked out within 48 hours, SS Intelligence should immediately determine the exact location of the aircraft. Then it was to be destroyed either by a bombing attack on the Dübendorf airport by the German Luftwaffe, or by the dropping of a unit of German paratroopers that would include a demolition squad. This information was revealed in a secret deposition given by Eggen in Switzerland on August 10, 1945. See the Swiss Federal Archives, *BAr 2809/1.4.*

the Federal Council as to how to handle this matter. By late afternoon—well before Eggen gets here—we will get back to you with further instructions."[70]

The German with many titles—Rittmeister, Sturmbannführer, Major—arrived at the Badische Bahnhof at 21:07 that evening and was met by Lieutenant Peter Burckhardt as soon as he had cleared Swiss customs. Burckhardt came equipped with the outline of a deal that had been relayed to him by telex just one hour earlier. The telex had also contained orders, issued by no less than the commander in chief of the Swiss Army, General Guisan himself, authorizing him to negotiate the details of the deal for the Messerschmidt 110 with Eggen on his behalf. But Burckhardt should proceed only if Eggen came equipped with a similar authorization, in writing, signed by someone in an obvious position of authority in the upper hierarchy of the Nazi regime.

Eggen had booked a room at the Three Kings Hotel, overlooking the Rhine in the center of Basel. Burckhardt, who had driven him there in his Mercedes, insisted that rather than join him in his room, as Eggen had suggested, the German take his time to unpack and get refreshed. He would wait for him in the bar . . . the same bar, of course, where he had first seen the man prior to the Schellenberg meeting at the Benkener Schloss.

The bar had not changed, but the bartender had; the one who had been there before had gone down in a hail of bullets a year earlier when he had tried to evade a police roadblock on the outskirts of Benken. Something else was different. This time, the head of Basel's political police, Dr. Wilhelm Lützelschwab, was nowhere to be seen. Which was just as well. Lützelschwab tended to get upset when he saw SS on his turf.

Burckhardt sat alone at a corner table for ten minutes. Then the German reappeared, carrying his briefcase. He sat down and

---

70. For a complete history of this incident, see Gautschi, *General Henri Guisan*, pp. 563–567. Here Gautschi gives the complete text of the message that Schellenberg sent to General Guisan. In it, Schellenberg indicated that he wanted to personally come to Switzerland and meet with Guisan in order to work out the details of the return of the Messerschmidt 110. Guisan knew that the political fallout of his meeting yet again with the SS general would be devastating should it become known to the Swiss public. So this suggestion was immediately rejected, leaving Schellenberg no choice but to put the entire matter into the hands of his deputy, Sturmbannführer Eggen.

handed Burckhardt a sheet of paper. It contained the authorization that Burckhardt required and carried two signatures: that of Marshal Hermann Göring, the head of the German Luftwaffe, whose prize plane had gone astray, and that of General Walter Schellenberg, the head of SS Intelligence and the man whom Hitler had charged with retrieving the plane. Burckhardt read the authorization and then withdrew from the breast pocket of his jacket that portion of the telex he had received earlier that evening containing General Guisan's orders. Eggen read it and nodded.

"It looks like it will be the two of us, doesn't it?"

"At least for the moment," Burckhardt replied.

"Then why not get right to it? The issue is very simple. We want that plane back. You will want something in return. What is it?" All of his cloying charm had disappeared.

"The plane will not be returned. That decision has already been taken by the general and the Federal Council, and it is irrevocable," was Burckhardt's response, and from the expression it evoked on the face of the SS major, it was totally unexpected.

"Are you Swiss crazy?" he hissed at Burckhardt. "Don't you realize that it is Hitler you are dealing with?"

"We are not dealing with Hitler. We are dealing with you, Herr Eggen."

"But you just said that there can be no deal. That—"

Burckhardt interrupted. "I said no such thing. I just said that we will not be returning the Messerschmidt. Doing so would be incompatible with the recognized rules governing the conduct of neutral nations during times of armed conflict."

"I can tell you right now, Herr Lieutenant, that this will be totally unacceptable to the Führer. He will not tolerate a situation in which there would be even the slightest chance that the British or the Americans might gain access to this plane."

"That will not happen."

Eggen looked puzzled. "But how in the world could you guarantee that?"

"By destroying the plane. In the presence of whomever you choose to witness its destruction."

Now the suave Rittmeister Eggen resurfaced. "How ingenious, Herr Doktor! And how very typical of you Swiss. You always find a way. If need be, I am sure that you would even find a way to square the circle. When will this demolition occur?"

"As soon as the quid pro quo is worked out."

"What does that involve?"

"In exchange for the desctruction of the Me 110, we want twelve of your standard fighter aircraft, Me 109 Gs, for our air force. We would expect them to be delivered within two days of the demolition of your prototype night fighter, and flown into the same airport where the Me 110 landed: Dübendorf."

"I assume the 110 is still there?"

"I doubt it," Burckhardt replied, although he didn't have the slightest idea of whether it was still there or not.

"There is one more detail," Burckhardt added. "We are fully prepared to pay for these Me 109s. Full price. Cash. In Swiss francs. On delivery."

"Aha. This is becoming very interesting," the German said, and Burckhardt could almost hear the wheels spinning in his head. "What price did you have in mind?"

"A half million francs per plane."

"Five hundred thousand francs each," Eggen repeated, savoring the words. "And cash, you said."

"Cash."

"I think, Herr Doktor Burckhardt, that we already have the essential elements of a deal, at least as far as I am concerned. I am sure that Herr General Schellenberg will second me in this. The problem will be Marshall Hermann Göring. To convince him that his Luftwaffe must give up twelve fighter planes under the current circumstances will not be easy." Then he hastened to add, "But do not misunderstand me. Difficult it will be. But not impossible."

Then: "Might *I* now make a suggestion, Herr Burckhardt?"

The Swiss braced himself. "Certainly."

"That we drink a nicely chilled bottle of Dom Pérignon. Agreed?"

Once the champagne had arrived and been poured, Eggen lifted his glass. "To your twelve Me 109s, Herr Lieutenant, and our six million Swiss francs."

The man is utterly shameless, Burckhardt thought as he also raised his glass. And as if to second his thoughts, Eggen's next question was: "Now when you said cash, did you mean bank notes, or a cash balance in a Swiss bank account?"

"Either. That depends on you."

Eggen mulled that one over. "Bank notes might tend to draw a lot of attention, wouldn't you say? I mean, it would require a steamer trunk!"

"Not a trunk, but maybe two large suitcases. We could pay you in thousand franc notes."

"Still." Then: "The more I think about it, the more I tend toward using a bank. But not just any bank. Where such a large sum is concerned, we would want you to make the funds available at a very large bank, ideally the largest. If your father still—"

Burckhardt interrupted him. "Yes. He is still chairman of our largest bank, the Swiss Bank Corporation."

"Well, that would make it all the easier, wouldn t it? I mean, you could, so to say, keep all this in the family."

Peter Burckhardt remembered that the last time Eggen had tried to get his foot inside the door of the Swiss Bank Corporation on behalf of his "clients" back in Berlin, his father had adamantly refused to have anything to do with him. Instead Eggen had been referred to the bank across the street in downtown Basel, one that specialized in German financing. But this time, Burckhardt knew, if Eggen insisted, his father would have no choice but to cooperate.

As if reading his mind, Eggen continued to pursue the matter. "Which reminds me of a related subject. You were kind enough to facilitate my establishing certain financial arrangements at the Basler Handelsbank after our conversation in your study at the Schloss a year or so ago."

"I assume they are taking good care of you. And your clients."

"Yes. And no, frankly," the German said.

"I'm surprised to hear that."

"Don't misunderstand me, Herr Doktor. They are always most courteous and professional at the Handelsbank. But what has begun to worry a few of my clients who have accounts there is the fact that the bank's loan portfolio is very heavily concentrated in one country."

Yours, Burckhardt was about to say, but kept his silence.

"They feel that given the uncertainties of the future, they might be better advised to keep their money in a bank that is more diversified geographically."

So that their Swiss bank does not go down with the sinking German ship, leaving you and your "clients" without a financial nest egg abroad, Burckhardt thought, a nest egg that will allow you to fight again on another day. And to think that he and his father had no choice but to deal with this scum!

His words were quite different from these thoughts, however.

"I'm sure that something can be worked out, Herr Eggen. Provided there are no new complications in the basic deal we have just been discussing."

"That is now up to me."

# FIFTY-NINE

It took longer than either the Germans or the Swiss had anticipated, but on November 18, 1944, the Me 110 Cg + EN was blown to smithereens on the tarmac of the Dübendorf airport outside of Zürich (using German explosives that had been brought in by Eggen), and just to make sure, gasoline was poured over the fragments and set ablaze. There were six official witnesses: from the German side, SS Major Eggen and Captain Brandt of the German Luftwaffe (the personal delegate of Marshal Herman Göring, who, upon direct orders from Hitler, had signed off on this deal); from the Swiss side, two brigadiers from the Swiss High Command, Rihner and Wattenwyl, as well as Colonel Masson and Lieutenant Burckhardt of Section 5 of the General Staff of the Swiss High Command.[71]

Exactly two days later, on November 20th, twelve German Me 109s were flown into Dübendorf and turned over to the Swiss Air Force.

That evening, the son of General Guisan, Colonel Henry "Gigi" Guisan, put on a banquet to honor Rittmeiser Eggen for his role in bringing this incident to such a successful conclusion, and in his toast offered the opinion that Eggen "a rendu d'immenses service à notre pays."[72]

71. Gautschi, pp. 563–567.
72. Ibid., p. 565.

■

251

# SIXTY

Early the next morning, Peter Burckhardt showed up unannounced at his father's office at the Swiss Bank Corporation.

"Sorry to bust in this way," he began, "but it is urgent official business."

"Please pull up a chair, Peter," his father said. Peter sensed from the tone of voice that his explanation had better be good.

The young Burckhardt spent the next ten minutes describing the Messerschmidt incident, concluding with a listing of the terms he had agreed to with Eggen.

"You realize that you people are presenting me with a fait accompli," his father said when he had concluded his narrative. "Despite the fact that you, Peter, know full well my attitude about doing business with the Nazis."

"I'm sorry. If you prefer, I will go down the street and talk to the Union Bank of Switzerland."

That was unexpected.

"Don't come in here and address me that way, young man," his father said. "We are talking principles. Not how I might or might not fit into the tactics of your Colonel Masson. His dealings with Schellenberg seem to never end."

Peter Burckhardt got up from his chair. "Maybe it's best we stop right here."

"No. You'll sit right down again while I think this through."

Now it was the banker who got up, and during the next three minutes paced the floor of his office while Peter watched him in silence from his chair.

"All right," he finally said. "We'll do it."

■

# SIXTY-ONE

On November 22, 1944, at precisely eleven o'clock, SS Major Eggen entered the headquarters of the Swiss Bank Corporation in Basel. Alone and carrying a briefcase, he was escorted to the office of that bank's chairman, Dr. Maximiliar Burckharct-Von der Mühl. The banker did not offer his hand, but indicated that the German should sit in the chair in front of his desk.

"I would suggest that we get right to the business at hand, Herr Eggen," he said while pressing a buzzer next to his telephone.

The door to his office was opened almost immediately, and a man in a dark suit entered carrying a dossier. He looked at Dr. Maximilian Burckhardt, who responded with the sightest of nods, whereupon the bank executive opened the dossier and handed it over to Eggen. It contained two pieces of paper.

"You have there, Herr Eggen," Burckhardt saic, "our notification that six million Swiss francs are available for payment in full for the twelve Me 109 aircraft that were delivered yesterday to the Swiss military authorities in Dübendorf. The second document, which requires your signature, confirms that you have the authority to accept these six million francs as payment in full for the twelve aircraft, that you also have the authority to dispose of these funds as you see fit, and that you release the Swiss government and this bank from any further claims in this matter. Our only other requirement before we release these funds to you is that you produce documentation from your government authorizing you to act in this manner on its behalf. I assume you have brought that."

Rittmeister Eggen, visibly nervous, reached into his briefcase and extracted a document bearing the seal of the German Reich and

■

the signatures of Marshal Hermann Göring and General Walter Schellenberg. Again the bank executive, standing at Eggen's side, looked to his chairman for instructions, and after receiving a second nod, took the German document in hand. So far, Dr. Maximilian Burckhardt-Von der Mühl had not touched a single piece of paper related to this transaction, nor would he. He merely watched as his man stood and read what Eggen had handed to him.

"In Ordnung?" Burckhardt asked impatiently.

"In Ordnung, Herr Doktor," came the reply.

Burckhardt turned his attention back to Eggen. "Then all we need are your instructions in regard to the disposal of these funds, Herr Eggen."

"I want to keep the funds here at the Swiss Bank Corporation," was Eggen's reply.

"I see. I assume that they will then be used at a later date for settlements within the framework of our two countries' bilateral trade-compensation agreement," the banker said.

"Not exactly. I would like to open three new accounts—numbered accounts—at your bank and have the six million francs disbursed equally among them."

The eyebrows of Dr. Maximilian Burckhardt rose ever so slightly. "And these three new accounts, are they—"

Before he could finish his question, Eggen interrupted. "They are to be personal accounts. One for Marshal Göring, the second for General Schellenberg, and the third for myself."

Burckhardt again turned to his executive. "Any problem with that?"

Without even reexamining the document describing Eggen's authority in this matter, the man immediately said, "No, sir. Herr Eggen has clearly been granted a full power of attorney by the German authorities."

Left unsaid was that the same authorities who had given Eggen these powers—Göring and Schellenberg—were now also to be beneficiaries of that grant of authority. They were in essence stealing from themselves. Since in the Third Reich, "they" and the state were synonymous from the viewpoint of an outside institution that was merely facilitating the movement of funds from a client's right hand to his left, there was no problem.

So on behalf of the Swiss Bank Corporation, Dr. Maximilian Burckhardt said just that. "Then there is no problem. You understand that the proper signature cards must be filled out and that we will also require mailing instructions. You can either have us notify you at your addresses in Berlin as to the status of your accounts, or if you prefer, we will hold back all such correspondence here at the bank, where it will, of course, be available for your review when you are again back on these premises.' Not that there was any question in the banker's mind as to which option these three new clients would go for! Again he turned to his assistant "Get three sets of account-opening documents."

As the man hurried out of the office, Burckhardt continued. "You can execute these documents for your personal account immediately. As to the other accounts, as an exception, we will also open them up right away on an interim basis since, in this instance, we already have valid samples of the signatures of the two beneficiaries of these accounts, don't we?"

"Vielen Dank, Herr Doktor," Eggen said. Then: "There is one other matter, Herr Doktor."

"Yes. Those accounts at the bank across the street."

Burckhardt's assistant returned at this juncture with the three sets of account papers, and Burckhardt addressed his next words to him: "That can be taken care of in your office. And I have already spoken to you about some accounts that are to be transferred from the Basler Handelsbank to ourselves. You will go over there with Herr Eggen as soon as you are done here and arrange it."

Dr. Maximilian Burckhardt then stood up, leaving Rittmeister Eggen no choice but to do the same. Again the Swiss banker did not offer his hand, but merely said, "I think that does it. I wish you a good day, Herr Eggen, and a pleasant trip back to Berlin."[73]

The German had no sooner left the room than Dr. Burckhardt picked up the phone and asked his secretary to connect him with Ernst Weber, head of the Swiss National Bank the country's central bank and thus the one that set and enforced the rules governing commercial banks such as the Swiss Bank Corporation.

"Ernst," he began, "this is Maximilian Burckhardt."

"Salü, Max. Is this business or private?"

---

73. This was a classic example of how intelligence service personnel use Swiss banks for their own enrichment. The East German Stasi followed the same practices during the Cold war. And, of course, it was at the Geneva branch of the Credit Suisse where the principals involved in the Iran-Contra affair kept their accounts, not necessarily for their own enrichment, but to further their own causes, which were hardly synonymous with those of the United States government.

"It is business, and very private."

"Then hold on for a minute."

When Weber came back on the line, he explained, "There was someone in my office. Now, how can I help you?"

"I'll be blunt. It concerns some very sizable deposits that we have accepted from some of the leading persons running Germany these days."

"How leading?"

"Right at the top."

"I thought that your policy was—"

Burckhardt interrupted him. "It was. It changed yesterday."

"Why?"

"It was in the national interest. It involves Section Five of the General Staff."

"Your son works there, doesn't he?"

"Yes."

"As you must recall, you set up an appointment for him with me. At that time, we discussed a matter that is not dissimilar. He was worried about our gold transactions with the Germans. Apparently the Russians and the Americans have gotten hold of some vague information about them, and your son was worried about the consequences. I'm afraid I was a little rough on him. In essence, I told him it was none of his or their business."

"And what was his response?"

"I had the impression that he thought we were consorting with the enemy here at the National Bank. It seems rather odd that now his Section Five has just induced you to do the same."

"I'm doing it for good reasons," Burckhardt replied, "reasons that I am not at liberty to disclose."

"Fair enough. Maybe now you—and your son—might suspect that appearances are not necessarily reality where *our* dealings with the Nazis are concerned either."

"What's that supposed to mean, Ernst?"

"I'll tell you. But to use the words you began this conversation with, it is business and private. And were you not running the largest bank in this country and now finding yourself in the same quandary that we have been in for years, I would not pursue this conversation further."

"I understand."

"All right. We in essence act as the clearing bank for all of Germany's international gold and currency transactions. This is hardly news to you. Right now we are holding just over two billion Swiss-franc equivalent of their gold and are expecting what will probably be their last shipment to us in just a few days, which should add another half billion to their stockpile here."

"What's going to happen to it?"

"It's going to stay right here."

"What do you mean?"

"We're going to freeze it . . . for the duration of the war, which can hardly be much longer, the way things look now."

"Then what?"

"We are going to keep it."

"On what grounds?"

"We don't need any grounds. The gold's here."

"And what if the Allies lay claim to it?"

"They are already starting to put the pressure on us, as you surely know. But we'll work that out. They can hardly come and get it, can they, Max? Now back to your problem . . . those deposits."

"I think our minds work very much alike, Ernst. What I am proposing is that we do exactly the same thing. Freeze them. Indefinitely."

"On what grounds?"

"The same grounds you are using in regard to the gold."

"What will you tell them if they want to make some transfer to, say, Argentina?"

"Stall. As you already said, the war is almost over. And once it ends . . ."

"As you know, Max, our banking law requires a ten-year waiting period before unclaimed deposits officially revert to the bank."

"I was thinking that perhaps that period could be appreciably shortened, or even waived—on a one-time basis only—provided, say that twenty per cent went to the Red Cross."

"And what if the Allies go after these funds?"

"As you so elegantly put it, Ernst, we'll work that out. Provided you back us up."

"You can count on it, Max. As I pointed out to your son, in difficult times like these, we Swiss must stick together. Solidarity is the watchword."

"Thanks, Ernst."

# SIXTY-TWO

That solidarity was soon to be put to the test. For as Ernst Weber had pointed out, the pressure on Switzerland was mounting.

It had begun in earnest on July 7, 1944, when the Swiss government received a "strong telegram"[74] from the American secretary of state, Cordell Hull, warning them against entering into any new trade or financial deals with the Nazis, deals that the Americans said would only help to extend the war. During that same month of July, 1944, a conference designed to establish the postwar international financial framework was taking place at Bretton Woods, a New Hampshire resort, and one of the main items on the agenda was the fate of the Swiss-based Bank for International Settlements. Thanks to the activities of the Basel cell of the Soviet Rote Kapelle, the whole financial world now knew of the games that the BIS had been playing in cahoots with the Reichsbank and the Swiss National.

On July 10th, a resolution was introduced by a Norwegian economist, Wilhelm Heilhau, calling for the dissolution of the Bank for International Settlements "at the earliest possible moment." He was fully backed by Henry Morganthau, the American secretary of the treasury.[75] However, after initial support, one of the key figures at this conference, and the preeminent economist of the century, John Maynard Keynes, now Lord Keynes, backed away from this

---

74. For the complete text, see Bonjour, Vol. V, p. 350.

75. Morganthau, for whom the BIS had become a bête noir, felt the bank "should be disbanded because to disband it would be good propaganda for the United States." See Higham, *Trading With the Enemy*, p. 13.

■

proposal and called for a postponement of any action, suggesting that the BIS be kept going until a new world bank and international monetary fund was set up; once this was done, the BIS could be closed down. Dean Acheson, representing the American State Department, sided with Keynes, and a resolution to this effect was passed at the close of the conference on July 20, 1944. There could now be no doubt but that the continuing existence of the BIS was hanging from a very thin thread.

Then there was a dramatic hardening of the British stance vis-à-vis Switzerland. On July 27th Anthony Eden, the British foreign secretary, warned the Swiss ambassador in London that unless Switzerland stopped exporting war materials to the Nazis, the Allies would cut that country off from any further supplies of raw materials and, yes, even of foodstuffs.[76]

As Peter Burckhardt soon learned, this was not an empty threat. On August 29th of that year, the Allies landed in the south of France—three months after their invasion of Normandy. Within fourteen days, they had captured not only the entire Mediterranean coast from Marseilles to Nice, but had spearheaded all the way north to Grenoble, just a hundred kilometers south of Geneva. This meant that the Americans had now cut off all communication and transportation routes between the German troops in France and those German divisions still fighting the Americans in northern Italy. It also meant that maintaining a direct line of supply between Germany proper and Italy—through Basel and the Gotthardt tunnel under the Swiss Alps—had become absolutely imperative for the Nazis if the war in Italy were to be continued. Yet the Swiss government insisted that the supply line remain open, invoking an international treaty signed by both the Germans and the Swiss in 1907, which, the Swiss said, precluded its closing.[77]

Peter believed the move to be imprudent—in fact, counterproductive—and within a month, his opinion was confirmed. With the capture of Bordeaux by the Americans in September, 1944, all rail and road routes between Switzerland and the Iberian peninsula were in Allied hands. This cut to the quick where the Swiss were concerned, for the Allies now made it clear: unless the Swiss

76. Reported in a cable sent by the Swiss ambassador in London, Ruegger, to the Swiss foreign minister, Pilet, on June 29, 1944. Bonjour, Vol. V, p. 351.

77. The treaty, the Haager Landkriegsordnung, excluded all war materials, however. *Ibid.*, p. 351.

stopped helping Hitler, the Allies were going to starve them to death.

To Peter's dismay, the Swiss continued to stonewall.

Still worse was then threatened. In the late evening of October 16, 1944, the political department of the Swiss government received a most urgent and highly secret message from the Swiss ambassador in London, which it immediately passed along to Swiss Intelligence. It dealt with a conversation that had taken place in Yalta between Winston Churchill, Franklin Delano Roosevelt, and Josef Stalin. Stalin had brought up the subject of Switzerland, and later that evening, Churchill, in briefing the Foreign Office personnel, had said, "I was astonished at Uncle Joe's savageness against Switzerland. He called them 'swine,' and he does not use that sort of language without meaning it."[78]

Then Stalin had made an astonishing proposal to Roosevelt and Churchill, one that he insisted would greatly shorten the war and save innumerable Russian lives, one that was, however, potentially lethal where Switzerland was concerned. His logic was impeccable. Stalin pointed out that after the Allied landing in Normandy in early June and the subsequent capture of Paris, the progress of the Allies in their eastward march on Germany had slowed to a stop. Ahead of them still lay the "Siegfried Line," the "impenetrable last line of defense," according to Hitler, which would stop them short of German territory. What Stalin proposed in the face of this was simple: to outflank the Siegfried Line to the south by invading Switzerland from France and then sweeping through into south Germany—into Baden and Württemberg—across the Swiss border. Stalin was further quoted as saying that "the Swiss had played a false role in the war and should be made to cooperate."[79]

All of this naturally put a strain on American diplomatic personnel in Switzerland, especially on Nancy Reichman. For while she was in complete agreement with the harsh measures now being imposed on her host country by the Allies, she, better than most Americans, knew that the majority of the Swiss people were violently anti-German. They were, very simply, at the mercy of a Swiss govern-

78. Winston S. Churchill, *The Second World War*, Vol. VI (London, 1954), p. 616.
79. This was first revealed on March 16, 1954, with the publication by the U.S. State Department of the secret Yalta Conference documents. See Bonjour, Vol. V, p. 408.

ment that was stubbornly clinging to policies that had been totally overtaken by events.

The citizenry saw their allotment of gas for heating and cooking cut to one-quarter of normal peacetime usage. They watched meat and sugar vanish from the shelves. They even saw their daily ration of bread cut from 250 grams to 225 grams, and now that all food and grain imports had been sealed off by the Allies, their bread contained as much "potato additive" as it did flour.

And all the while, Nazi gold piled higher and higher in Swiss vaults.

All of this increased Nancy Reichman's sense of isolation. She could hardly wait for this dreary war to end. About the only thing that kept her going was the steady relationship with Peter Burck-hardt. But even there, the spark was in danger of going out, suffocated by her growing frustration in a Switzerland cut off from the world and where, as the old year ended and the new began, the lights were growing dimmer, the food scarcer, and the future so very uncertain.

# SIXTY-THREE

On January 9, 1945, Allen Dulles phoned Nancy Reichman.

"I have to leave for a quick trip to Paris within the hour," Dulles said, "and must be brief. You can expect a call from Peter Burckhardt. He will alert you as to the time he expects his boss at the Bank for International Settlements, Per Jacobsson, to arrive at the Badische train station. He's returning from a trip to Berlin."

"Yes, sir."

"Jacobsson's trip to Berlin was my idea. We have reason to believe that the Germans are ready to manufacture an atomic bomb. For a while, we mistakenly believed that this was taking place at Peenemünde, which we subsequently bombed off the map. Then we found out that their nuclear research and development has always been going on exclusively at the Kaiser Wilhelm Institute in Berlin. Professor Werner Heisenberg runs a research team there, made up of some of the world's leading atomic scientists, including Otto Hahn, Carl von Weizsäcker, and Max von Laue. A week ago we learned that they have all disappeared. So I asked Jacobsson to go to Berlin and make inquiries. I told him that we urgently needed answers to two questions. How close are they to production? And where have they gone?"

"I understand."

"I will be back in Switzerland late tonight. If Jacobsson turns up, I will expect to hear from you first thing tomorrow."

One hour later, another call came in for Nancy, this time on the regular consulate line. It was Peter Burckhardt, and he was all business.

■

"I talked to a mutual friend early this morning who told me that he has had a change in plans. I expect that you have also heard from him."

"I have."

"Regarding that other party, here at the BIS we just received a telex from the Reichsbank in Berlin informing us that we can expect his arrival back in Basel at nine fifty-five this evening. I was told that you will want to meet him there."

"Yes."

"Then I will pick you up at your apartment at nine-thirty."

"I'll be waiting downstairs."

She hung up, and so did the man who monitored her phone calls at his post in the headquarters of Basel's political police. He duly reported what he had heard to his boss, Dr. Wilhelm Lützelschwab.

# SIXTY-FOUR

At shortly after ten that evening, Per Jacobsson walked out of the Badische Bahnhof. Spotting Peter Burckhardt and Nancy Reichman in front of the restaurant "Kleinbasler Weinstube," he hurried across the street to join them.

Once inside, they sat down at a table and ordered a carafe of Dole. "Mr. Dulles," Nancy explained, "was unable to come over from Bern this evening, so he asked me to come instead."

The Swede nodded. He knew that the American woman worked with Dulles. In fact, the three of them had even dined together in Basel on one occasion.

"Were you able to find out where Heisenberg is?"

"No," answered the Swede. "Mr. Dulles' information was correct. Heisenberg, Hahn, von Weizsäcker. They have all disappeared from Berlin. And all of the equipment they were using at the Kaiser Wilhelm Institute has likewise disappeared."

"Did you get any indication of how close to their goal they were before they disappeared?"

"Very close. I don't quite understand exactly what it means, but I was told that for a while there was a lack of heavy water,[80] and

---

80. The problem with heavy water stemmed from the effects of British commando raids and bombing attacks on the Norsk-Hydro facility in Norway, Germany's principal source of heavy water. However, none of these raids were totally successful, and all they did was to periodically diminish the output to about 50% of what it would have been otherwise. See the chapter titled "The German Atom Bomb" in William Casey, *The Secret War Against Hitler* (Washington, DC), 1988, pp. 48 ff.

.

also a minor design problem. They now have an adequate supply of heavy water, and the design problem will be corrected shortly."

"Mr. Dulles will want to hear about this immediately."

Peter Burckhardt dropped Nancy off back at her apartment before taking Jacobsson to the Three Kings Hotel, where he now lived. At eight the next morning, she telephored Dulles on the "safe" line from the consulate. He told her to make no plans for the next few days that could not be easily canceled. He might have to call upon her for help in this matter "one last time."

After he hung up, he wished that he had not used that phrase.

# SIXTY-FIVE

Dulles immediately put all of his intelligence resources inside Germany to work on the search for the missing nuclear scientists. In addition, he personally met with the head of the D section of Swiss Intelligence, Captain Hans Waibel, Lieutenant Peter Burck-hardt's immediate superior, to enlist his help in the search.[81]

Waibel did two things. First, he activated the "Viking Line," Switzerland's highly secret intelligence link, which led to a man in the innermost circle around Hitler. But he could hardly forget that the same source had been dead wrong about German plans to invade Switzerland in March of 1943. So, on a hunch, he put out the word to the Swiss community that lived in southern Germany, and despite the risk, acted as informants for Swiss Intelligence throughout the war. He asked them to report on any strange construction projects or any strange influx of scientists. Within forty-eight hours, Waibel had the answer. It came from a Baumeis-ter, an architect/builder, who lived in the Black Forest. In the fall of last year, this man had been involved in a very unusual project: the construction of a concrete pit, the specifications of which required wall thicknesses of a magnitude he had never encountered, or even heard of before. Not only that, the pit was built in a cave

81. Dulles had developed a close working relationship with Waibel, one that bore enormous fruit. For it was Waibel who later set up the negotiations in Switzerland (in Zürich, Lucerne, and Ascona) in March and April of 1945 between Allen Dulles and SS General Wolff that led to the surrender of the German Army in Italy on May 2, 1945. This was done without the knowledge of either the Swiss government or General Guisan. See Gautschi, pp. 645 ff., especially Dulles, *The Secret Surrender*.

■

in the side of a cliff! Moreover, the missing scientists had now resurfaced. A dozen of them at least. And this in a sleepy little town in the Black Forest.

The name of the town was Haigerloch. It was situated exactly a hundred and twenty kilometers northeast of Basel: just seventy-five miles.

Waibel immediately reported these facts to Dulles. The next day, Sunday, January 14, 1945, Dulles began the implementation of a plan that he hoped would ascertain how far the scientists had progressed in their work, and then, if it was determined that they had made a breakthrough (which the Americans still had not), to convince them to come out of Germany into Switzerland before it was too late, thereby allowing them a last-ditch opportunity to build a new life and to continue their scientific research almost without interruption.[82]

These men must surely realize that the Russian army was rapidly approaching from the east and that if the Russians got to Haigerloch first, the consequences for them personally, and for *both* Germany and the West, would be unthinkable. One would have to appeal to their sense of solidarity with their former colleagues at Göttingen in the twenties and thirties, almost all of whom were now in the West—in Britain, in the United States, in Switzerland. Not one had headed east.

The first step, however, was to get them into Switzerland, which would require that they be officially offered asylum there and that this offer be given on the spot . . . by a Swiss. It would also require that they be convinced that the United States would not seek retribution, but would be willing to help them out in any way they requested, including financial support as well as travel documents that would allow them to settle permanently in the United States. They would have to be convinced of this again on the spot . . . by an American carrying the proper credentials. But a prerequisite to all of this was determining how close they were to developing an atomic bomb . . . which would require the judgment of a Western scientist, a settlement that could be rendered only on the basis of an on-the-spot inspection.

All of these considerations flatly ruled out the commando raid advocated by General Leslie Grove and his right-hand man, Boris

82. For the complete history of the "resettlement" of German scientists in the United States, see Tom Bower, *The Paperclip Conspiracy* (New York, 1987).

Pash, who were officially in charge of intelligence and countermeasures aimed at German nuclear projects. They were the reason that Dulles had gone to Paris: to meet with them and specifically discuss this matter.

A year ago, Dulles had been warned off from any interference in their area, but now they wanted him back. After having been stunned by the first attack on London by V-2 rockets on September 8, 1944, and then the appearance over the skies of Germany of the Messerchmidt 262—the world's first jet fighter that could fly at a speed of 540 miles per hour, as compared to the top speed of 358 mph of the American B29 bomber, and the 302 mph of the Flying Fortress (B17G)—they were increasingly concerned that German science was about to spring another surprise on them.

When the German Army mounted its fierce counterattack in the Ardenne Forest before Christmas of 1944, their concern turned into acute worry that this might be a coldly calculated attempt to buy enough time for the final manufacture and deployment of a German atomic bomb. Grove and Pash became even more nervous when they received word that the German nuclear scientists had disappeared from Berlin. That was when they had appealed to Dulles for help, and when Dulles had recruited the aid of Per Jacobsson. In return for his renewed cooperation, Dulles had asked that he be granted a free hand for a few weeks before they came down on the problem with a sledgehammer.

General Grove had reluctantly agreed.

# SIXTY-SIX

For Dulles' plan to work, he needed the unqualified support of the D section of Swiss Intelligence. However, its head, Captain Hans Waibel, was skeptical of the operation.

Yes, Waibel explained, Switzerland did have a network of friendly Swiss nationals already on the ground in the Black Forest. And, yes, they might be of assistance in infiltrating the nuclear site at Haigerloch.

"These 'friendly Swiss nationals,' however, are not paid agents," Waibel said to Dulles in the offices of the Base consulate. "You can't simply order them around. They have to *want* to help, and quite frankly, most of them are in this to help their own people. They won't want to go out on a limb for a bunch of Allied agents."

"Which is why I would recommend sending people they can trust, people they will want to work with." Left unsaid was the fact that these people were known within the OSS as Dulles' "Swiss Account."

"Like who?"

"There are two people we can get in with no problem—Peter and Felicitas Burckhardt. They have relatives there who will help, and Felicitas can reconnoiter the reactor. She's studied under Pauli, and Pauli and Heisenberg have always been close. They'll trust her."

"In other words," Waibel said, "you recommend that we send in *my* people."

"Plus an American who can pass for Swiss. This is an American mission. It is the American government that is prepared to make an offer to Heisenberg in return for his cooperation—should it get that far. That offer, if it is to be credible, can be made only by a representative of the American government, with bona fide credentials."

Waibel smiled at the idea. "You mean the Reichman woman? She's perfect for it . . . though I can't imagine why she would want to do it."

"She'll do it."

"Allen, this job is as dangerous as hell. She could end up dead, or in the camps. This could be a terrible mistake."

"No problem."

"Are you sure?"

"You don't know her. She'll want to do it."

# SIXTY-SEVEN

At eight o'clock on the night of January 17 1945, the Swiss "Schubboot" *Corviglia* left the Rhine harbor in Basel. It was pushing three barges containing six thousand bags of Swiss cement bound for the Ruhr. It was also taking along three passengers: two Swiss and one American. During the cursory search of the vessels by the German authorities, which had taken place in the harbor, they had hidden in a "cache" which the crew that loaded the barges had rigged under the cement bags on one of the vessels.

An hour and a half later, when they were ten kilometers downstream and approaching the village of Weil-am-Rhein, the tugboat and the barges drifted toward the right bank and slowed almost to a halt. The three passengers boarded a small dinghy and were quickly rowed to shore—barely fifty meters away—by two deckhands from the tug. The banks of the Rhine were not guarded, for at this point the river ran through territory that was under German control on each side.

The three passengers wore heavy boots and overcoats, all of them well-worn. In fact, the overcoats bordered on shabby. They also bore small backpacks containing provisions for what was designed to be a forty-eight hour trip. After they had scrambled ashore, they walked through a pasture, lightly dusted with snow, to the main road, which ran through the tiny German village. In the middle of that village was a small inn, and in front of it stood a man in peasant clothing. As they approached him, he turned without saying a word and disappeared into the darkness behind the inn. They followed him. There, leaning against the building, were three bicycles, two of which were designed for women. Again without anyone saying a word, the three wheeled the bicycles onto the road, mounted them, and then rode off in the darkness.

Staying to deserted rural roads, they pedaled east. Shortly before eleven, they approached the village of Fahrnau. After they had passed through it, Peter Burckhardt, who had the lead, looked back at the two young women who were trailing him and signaled that they were approaching their destination: a Bauernhaus on the northern outskirts of town.

Burckhardt suddenly veered off the road into a narrow lane leading to a barnyard behind the house. Motioning to the two women to stay behind, he went to the back door and knocked.

The door was opened, and a big man in his mid-sixties peered out at him. "Peter," he roared. "Gott sei Dank du bisch heil ako."

He stepped outside and embraced him. The Swiss "network" had gotten word to him to expect his nephew.

Then he spotted Burckhardt's sister. "Felicitas! Du bish au do!" He bounded down the steps and gave her a bearhug.

"Uncle Ernst," Peter Burckhardt warned, "I think it best we go inside."

# SIXTY-EIGHT

The four, Nancy Reichman trailing, entered the kitchen of the Bauernhaus, which dated back to the fifteenth century. There the scene outside was repeated by Tante Emily, who embraced her nephew and niece; the difference was that now a few tears were shed, for it was the first time that the young Burckhardts from Basel had seen the sister of their mother since the summer of 1939. To be sure, Fahrnau was no more than fifteen kilometers from Basel, but after the war began and the border was sealed, it could just as well have been light-years away.

Then, all of a sudden, everybody seemed to take notice of the outsider in their midst. It was Felicitas Burckhardt who stepped in to bridge the awkward moment.

"Onkel Ernst and Tante Emily," she said, "this is a very good friends of ours—of both Peter and myself—and her name is Nancy Reichman. She's an American."

"En Amerikanere!" Tante Emily repeated. "Do in Fahrnau!" She took the hand of this exotic visitor from another world, vigorously shook it, and said, "Willkommen in unserem Heim, Fräulein Reichman." Her husband, looking equally astounded, then did the same.

Tante Emily now insisted that the visitors take off their backpacks, overcoats, and boots and come into the living room. So they might warm up, she guided them to the bench that circled the "Kachelofen." Then she brought a tray with three steaming bowls of hot soup—potato-and-leek soup—from the kitchen. It was, of course, first offered to Nancy Reichman. As soon as the soup had disappeared, which was almost immediately, Tante Emily went

■

back into the kitchen and reappeared this time with two huge pies, apple and cherry. She insisted that everybody try both. Then came the coffee, and with the coffee, the Kirschwasser that Onkel Ernst had personally distilled from their own cherries.

The conversation turned serious. What was going to happen to Germany, Onkel Ernst wanted to know from his nephew, when this war was finally over? He added that everyone knew it was only a matter of months before Germany would have to surrender. Everyone, that is, but the madman Hitler.

Peter Burckhardt replied that this was still very unclear. There were some, like the American secretary of the treasury, Henry Morganthau, who wanted to reduce Germany to an agrarian state. He doubted that a reasonable man like President Roosevelt would go along with this. The Russians, no doubt, wanted to convert the country to a socialist state. But he was sure that the British, especially Churchill, would not stand for that. There could be no doubt, however, that Germany would never be allowed to threaten the world again.

Onkel Ernst nodded silently until Peter Burckhardt had finished expressing his views. Then he gave his. "It all started to go bad in Germany when Hindenburg forced the Kaiser into exile. That was the mistake that led to everything that followed. First, the Treaty of Versailles and the reparations we could never afford to pay. Then, the disastrous inflation. And finally, the equally disastrous unemployment. These were all things we Germans had never experienced before. Then there was the so-called democracy of the Weimar Republic. We Germans neither understood nor wanted it, so it was bound to fail. All this made a Hitler inevitable sooner or later. Ach, Peter, if only they had let our Kaiser be. Then this calamity would never have happened."

Tante Emily, who had no doubt heard this a thousand times, broke in and wanted to know all about her relatives in Basel, how they had spent the war and what they planned on doing when it was finally over. It was Felicitas Burckhardt who responded, and soon the mood shifted back to one of joyful anticipation of the time not far off when they could all once again plan Sunday trips across the border to visit with each other.

At midnight, Peter Burckhardt brought the evening to a close. They had to get going early the next morning, he explained. As he understood it, he said to Uncle Ernst, the Postbus, which followed the northeasterly route through the Black Forest left Lörrach every morning at seven and came through Fahrnau a half hour later. Was it still running on that schedule?

It was. But it did not stop in Fahrnau. One had to wave it down. Where? Anywhere. On the road right in front of the house would be as good a place as any. If fact, it would be a better place than farther back in the center of the village. The Gestapo informant, who owned the butcher shop there, watched everything. In fact, everybody now watched everybody else. It would be best if the three of them stayed in the house until he himself had flagged down the bus. Then they should board quickly. Uncle Ernst did not ask where they were going, or why. His nephew was obviously operating under higher Swiss authority, and as a good German who yearned for the return of legitimate authority in his own country, he was not about to question that.

Onkel Ernst escorted his nephew to one of the two spare bedrooms on the second floor of the ancient Bauernhaus, while Tante Emily took the two "girls" to the other one farther down the hall. Stopping at a huge wooden cabinet, she extracted heavy woolen nightgowns that looked to be almost as ancient as the Bauernhaus. Then she bade them good night, kissing and hugging each of them. It was ice-cold in the bedroom, so Felicitas and Nancy took but seconds to don their nightgowns, turn out the lights, and dive under the huge Federbett.

At first neither said a word, but then Felicitas broke the silence. "Do Jewish people say a prayer before they go to sleep?"

"Yes. We call it 'Shmah.'"

"Do you pray?"

"Sometimes."

"Same here. Are you afraid?"

"I was until I got here. Now I feel safe. It must be the nightgown."

This produced a laugh from both of them.

"How would you like Peter to see you in *that* outfit?"

"Onkel Ernst probably has him in one, too."

Another giggle.

"Are you serious about Peter?"

"Sometimes. But lately I'm not too sure about him."

"He likes you an awful lot, Nancy," his sister said. "He doesn't have any other girlfriends, you know."

"Still." Then: "Don't tell him now, Felicitas, but I'm planning on going back home. I've already talked it over with Mr. Dulles, and he said that he can arrange it with the State Department when this is over."

"You mean when the war's over?"

"No. When this trip is over."

"Well, I hope you change your mind. In fact, I'm going to include that in my prayer."

"You're awfully nice."

"I do wish you'd stay."

# SIXTY-NINE

At six-thirty the next morning, Tante Emily knocked on their door. She brought a tray with two steaming cups of coffee. Bauernbrot, butter, and cherry jam. She insisted on serving them in bed, chattering away the whole time. She disappeared, then returned fifteen minutes later with two bowls, a huge pitcher of hot water, and towels. By seven, the girls were dressed and fed.

When they came down the stairs, the two men were waiting. Their faces were serious and the atmosphere tense. The radio was tuned to Beromünster, Switzerland's German-language national transmitter.[83] The seven o'clock news was just coming on, and the lead story dealt with the most recent events on the Eastern front. The Red Army offensive in Poland that had begun just five days earlier seemed about to produce its first huge success: the surrender of Warsaw.

"They're coming much faster than any of us thought," Onkel Ernst said.

Then events on the Western front were summarized. The Americans had begun to reverse the tide in the Battle of the Bulge and had just captured Houfallize, in the heart of Belgium.

"Let's hope they get here first," Peter Burkhardt commented. By "here" he did not mean just this village of Fahrnau on the edge of the Black Forest, but also that other village sixty kilometers farther into the forest, Haigerloch.

---

83. The French-language transmitter is located at Sottens; the Italian-language transmitter is atop Monte Ceneri.

■

At the end of the news broadcast, as always, came the weather forecast:

*"Kalt, mit zunehmender Bewölkung. Heute Nacht und Morgen Schneefall, teils schwer, bis in die Niederungen."*

*"Cold, with increasing cloudiness. Tonight and tomorrow snow, at times heavy, even at lower elevations."*

"Not good," Onkel Ernst said. Peter Burckhardt said nothing. But the two girls could not help but exchange glances.

Five minutes later, Onkel Ernst put on his overcoat and left the house through the front door. Peter Burckhardt likewise put on his coat, but instead of leaving the house, he stood at the living-room window next to the front door, facing the road. After another five minutes, he looked at his watch and suggested that the two young women put on their boots and coats.

Tante Emily's chatter had ceased. She just sat there in front of the Kacheloffen, trying to look brave and unconcerned, but not succeeding.

Then it happened very fast. Peter Burckhardt saw his uncle wave, and seconds later, the bus—yellow, with the insignia of the postal service, the "Posthorn," on its side, came to a halt in front of the house. Peter signaled to the women. Opening the front door, he led them to the gate. They waved back to Tante Emily, who stood silently at the front door, and then boarded the bus. Peter Burckhardt, after shaking hands with his uncle, did the same.

"Hechingen, dreimal, retour," he said to the bus driver, adapting as best he could his Basel patois to the local "Badische." Hechingen was the jumping-off point for Haigerloch.

"Acht Mark, fünf und siebzig Pfennig," the bus driver told him after consulting his fare book.

Burckhardt fished the exact amount from his wallet (one of Waibel's men in Section 5 had told him what it would be) and then motioned to the two women to proceed toward the back of the bus, where most of the seats were empty. They stopped at the row second to the last, took the two seats on the left and stuffed their backpacks below their seats. Peter, keeping his backpack at his side, took the window seat across the aisle, and as the bus began to move, once again waved farewell to his uncle and aunt, who were now both standing in the doorway of their Bauernhaus, waving back. It was a typical scene in the Black Forest as relatives from different villages took leave from each other after a short family visit.

The bus, a diesel Mercedes, belched smoke as t gradually picked up speed, and within minutes it was up to a respectable forty-five kilometers an hour. This soon proved to be its top speed, since the road became increasingly narrow, winding, and steep the farther into the Schwarzwald they went. Furthermore, although there was no snow on the road, there were frequent patches of ice, forcing the driver to become extremely cautious lest his bus skid into the snowbanks that now lined the road on both sides.

The first stop after ten kilometers was the small town of Schönau. Two people got out, one in. Then came a brief stop at Tocnau, and after laboriously climbing another fifteen kilometers, they reached their first major destination, Feldberg. The bus stopped for fifteen minutes. This wait was apparently part of the normal schedule and intended to give passengers enough time to load and unload their skiing equipment, since Feldberg was the center for that sport in this region of southwest Germany. However, in January of 1945, there were no skiers to be seen. The young German men who would normally have been there, either alone or with their girl-friends and wives, were dying in such diverse places as Belgium, Poland, Italy, and Yugoslavia. The average age of the bus passengers, apart from Peter's group, must have been seventy.

They left Feldberg at nine o'clock, and soon they were alongside the Titisee, an Alpine-like lake. Here most of the passengers debarked, carrying their pathetic-looking suitcases. A like number of elderly Germans climbed into the bus. Titisee offered the facilities and therapy of a centuries-old spa, famed for its curative powers, especially where rheumatism was concerned. It was there that the three young passengers in the rear of the bus saw their first German policeman. He seemed totally uninterested in the bus. But suddenly realizing that such an heretofore overlooked factor as his age could raise suspicion, Peter Burckhardt hunched down in his seat so as to become as inconspicuous as possible.

# SEVENTY

The bus arrived at Hechingen at precisely eleven-thirty. Peter Burckhardt, his sister Felicitas, and Nancy Reichman were the only passengers who got out there. The bus stop was in the middle of the small town, right in front of the post office.

Peter Burckhardt spotted what he was looking for almost immediately. Parked directly across the street from the post office was a van, and on its door the sign: HÄBERLEIN TIEFBAU DONAUSTRASSE 11 HAIGERLOCH.

There was a man in his mid-fifties sitting behind the steering wheel of the van. As soon as he noticed Burckhardt staring in his direction, he put his left arm out the van window and waved. This surprised Burckhardt, but then he realized that the safest way to establish contact in this country full of suspicion was to be natural and relaxed. So he waved back. Taking each woman by the arm, he headed across the street to the truck. The man sprang out, and as Peter Burckhardt approached him, moved forward to grasp his outstretched hand and shake it vigorously. Next, he embraced Peter's sister, and then Nancy Reichman. Although there were a lot of people in the street, many of them on their way to and from the post office, no one paid the slightest attention to them.

Nor did anyone find it strange to see four people climb into the small van, since transportation in Germany in January of 1945 was reduced to the barest minimum. Peter took the seat next to the driver, while the two young women made themselves comfortable on the van floor behind. It was only after the truck had pulled away from the curb that the driver spoke. He used the Basel dialect.

"Es freut mi dass Sie do sin, Herr Doktor. You are right on time.

■

I was starting to get worried. The radio this morning said that the weather is going to be changing."

"No problem," Burckhardt replied. "The sun was even shining on Feldberg. How far is it to Haigerloch?"

"Eighteen kilometers. In fact, we turn off the main road right here." He proceeded to make the turn onto a much narrower road in bad repair.

"Are there any control points?" Burckhardt asked.

"No. Nobody around here has the slightest idea that anything unusual is going on in Haigerloch. The authorities don't want to set up unusual security arrangements that might draw attention to the village. But still, one never knows. What is your story if we are stopped?"

"I'm with the Grenzwache, the border guard, stationed in Lörrach. I'm on a forty-eight-hour compassionate leave to attend my grandmother's funeral in Trilltingen, which is a tiny farming village just outside of Haigerloch. My two sisters are with me. We are staying with you since you are a friend of the family, and have room and transportation for us."

"And your documents are in what name?"

"Sempach. Peter, Felicitas, and Ursula Sempach."

"Good. In fact, very good."

"Our people in both Basel and Lucerne greatly appreciate what you are doing, Herr Häberlein, and have asked me to tell you that. We know the risk you are running."

"When I grew up in Basel, our family lived right next door to the Waibels on the Gempenstrasse in the Gundeldingerquartier. You must know where that is."

"Of course."

"Although Hans is much younger than I, somehow we've stayed in contact over the years, even after I moved here. I was going to come home when the war started, but you know how difficult it is to just leave everything behind that you have built up over the years. But I still try to do my bit." He swerved abruptly to avoid a pothole, and immediately turned to the women in back to apologize.

"Sorry about that. But if you just hold on, we should be there in about twenty minutes." Then he again addressed Peter Burckhardt. "What is your plan once we get there?"

"One of us is going to try to contact Professor Heisenberg right away. Your friend, Captain Waibel, told me that you know him."

"Yes. As you must know, my little company did the basic

underground construction for the project he is working on. When it requires minor repairs or modifications, they call on me. So I see Professor Heisenberg regularly."

"At work."

"Yes. But just last week I also went over some plans for a major new project with him at the house he lives in. It is just down the street from our home in Haigerloch."

"He lives alone?"

"His wife and children stayed in Berlin, as I understand it. But he has a full-time housekeeper here."

"Does she know you?"

"Yes. She is a local woman, and Haigerloch is a small town. We go to the same church."

"Does Heisenberg come home for lunch?"

"Normally, yes. The place where they work is very uncomfortable. We almost always see his car—one of the few now operating—in front of the house between noon and two o'clock."

"Herr Häberlein, I think you missed your calling. Your friend Captain Waibel could have used you in Section Five."

Burckhardt could see that the expatriate Swiss was pleased to receive the compliment.

Five minutes before twelve, the van crossed a bridge over the Eyach River. Arriving at a fork, Häberlein bore right, taking what he explained was the "low" road. He followed the river's course to the small Black Forest town of Haigerloch.

"I see where it got its name," Burckhardt said. "Loch" in German means "hole," "gap," or "opening," and it was into just such an opening between cliffs on both sides that they had entered.

Herr Häberlein slowed the van almost to a halt and pointed the finger to his right hand up to the left. "See the church on top of the cliff?"

Burckhardt had to crane his neck to see it. "Yes."

"That's where it is. In a cave, under the church."

"Amazing!"

"Ingenious, actually. There is no way that you can spot anything from the air, and even if you could, the cave is absolutely bomb-proof."

"How big is it?"

"The main chamber is thirty meters long, fifteen wide, and twelve high."

"How do you get to it?"

"Through a concrete tunnel that we built. The entrance to the tunnel is just behind the church."

Häberlein turned the van into a side street and stopped in front of a large stucco house. As soon as the van stopped, the door to the house opened. The woman who emerged was obviously Frau Häberlein. She did not appear pleased. The four hurried from the van into the house, and her husband introduced the new arrivals to her one by one. She acknowledged them with only a few curt words—in high German, not in the Swiss dialect. Herr Häberlein also switched over to Hochdeutsch.

"Maria stammt aus Mannheim," he said, explaining that she was originally a native of that German city. "We met while I was studying engineering there. After we were married, we lived in Basel for a while. Then I got a big job here in the early thirties—as a member of the construction team building a dam on the Eyach River about five kilometers upstream. We liked it so much here that we decided to settle in Haigerloch, and eventually I started my own firm."

To some extent, this sounded more like an apology than an explanation to his listeners from Basel, and this was confirmed by Herr Häberlein's next words, which were addressed to his wife: "But when this is all over, we will probably return to Switzerland, won't we, Maria?"

"We shall see."

An uncomfortable Herr Häberlein then suggested that she prepare some coffee while he showed the visitors their rooms. As soon as she disappeared, Peter Burckhardt said, "The rooms can wait. I sense the concern of your wife, and it is fully understandable. We also want to get this over with as quickly as possible. You said that Professor Heisenberg usually comes home for lunch."

"Yes," Häberlein replied.

"Would you mind taking one of us over to his house? My sister has a letter of introduction to Heisenberg from one of his colleagues who now teaches at the Federal Institute of Technology in Zürich, Professor Wolfgang Pauli."

The Swiss engineer nodded his head, indicating that of course he knew the name.

"You mean right now?" he asked.

"Right now," Burckhardt replied.

This appeared to come as a shock to Häberlein, but he immediately agreed. "Fine, Herr Burckhardt. If you're ready—"

"My sister will be going alone, at least on this initial visit. We have very carefully thought this over. A young woman will attract the least attention. Especially if she is in the company of a local man who is well known in this town. That you are personally acquainted with the professor's housekeeper makes it all the better. We must depend on you, Herr Häberlein, to get my sister past the front door without creating any suspicion in that woman's mind that might prompt her to do something foolish."

Like alarming the local police was the thought Burckhardt left unspoken. If Häberlein's wife acted the way she did, who could know how Heisenberg's housekeeper might react to the sudden appearance of a stranger at her front door?

"I will do my best, Herr Burckhardt," Häberlein answered, but one could now detect a tightness in his voice.

Peter Burckhardt reached into his backpack and lifted out a leather pouch that had been given to him by one of Dulles' men. A red string protruded from it. One firm tug on the string would set off a chemical reaction, resulting in the immediate incineration of the contents of the pouch, which included the American diplomatic passport of Nancy Reichman as well as his own papers identifying him as an officer attached to Section 5 of the General Staff of the High Command of the Swiss Army. Peter Burckhardt now withdrew a third document from the pouch, an envelope bearing the insignia of the Eidgenössische Technische Hochschule in Zürich.

"Here, Felicitas," he said as he handed it to his sister. Then he gave her a hug and a quick kiss on the cheek. Nancy Reichman stepped forward, and without saying anything, did the same.

"Let's get it over with," Häberlein said to Felicitas. Then to her brother, "We'll be going out the back door, as we always do. The front door is for visitors. I'll tell my wife that the two of you will be staying here in the living room. I'm sure she will have your coffee ready in a few minutes."

# SEVENTY-ONE

As Häberlein had mentioned in the van, Professor Heisenberg's house was just down the Donaustrausse from his own home. Felicitas Burckhardt, walking at his side, could not help but think that this was probably *the* street in Haigerloch where the rich folk lived. It ran between the main road and the bank of the Eyach River. They stopped at the last house on the street. A large BMW was parked there.

"He's home," Häberlein said.

He took a deep breath, proceeding to the front door with Felicitas Burckhardt, and pressed the buzzer.

A woman in her fifties, dressed in black, opened the door almost immediately. She smiled when she saw who was there.

"Ach, Herr Häberlein, what an unexpected pleasure! Is the Herr Professor expecting you?"

"Not really, Fräulein Schmidt. And I do hope that we are not intruding. But my niece here," and he nodded in the direction of Felicitas Burckhardt, "is visiting us just for the day. She studies physics at the university, and when I told her that the famous Professor Heisenberg lived just down the street from us, she asked if she might meet him." In these parts, when one talked about "the university," it was naturally assumed that one was referring to the ancient university in Tübingen, located just twenty kilometers to the northeast of Haigerloch.

These words of Häberlein produced, if anything, an even broader smile on the face of Fräulein Schmidt. "Oh, I'm *sure* that the Herr Professor will have time to see her. You know, he really misses his students. I hear him say that all the time. Because as you and I

■

know, Herr Häberlein, as much as we love our Haigerloch, it is hardly Berlin, is it? So both of you come in. The Herr Professor is eating his lunch, and of course we cannot disturb him until he is done."

Once they were inside, she said, "Now let me take your coats, and you can both make yourselves at home in the living room. I'll bring you some coffee. It's awful stuff these days, but its very cold out there today, so you need something to keep you warm. Especially you, young lady," she added after Felicitas had taken off her coat. "My, how slender you are! What is your name, dear?"

"Felicitas Burckhardt." Häberlein was surprised that she gave her real name, but the housekeeper was so busy chattering away that she noticed nothing.

Ten minutes later, Herr Professor Werner Heisenberg entered the living room. The two visitors immediately rose. Felicitas Burckhardt was surprised by his appearance. He was much younger than she had anticipated—barely into his forties. And he was quite the opposite of the ascetic she had expected to meet. Heisenberg more resembled an athlete than a professor. And as he moved forward to greet Herr Häberlein, he moved with energy and grace. The fact that he had red hair added to his aura.

"Herr Häberlein," he said, "I'm glad you're here. I was going to telephone you this afternoon in any case to suggest that we get together once more to finalize the plans for the new construction. Now that won't be necessary. If you have the time, we can go directly from here to the site. The blueprints are there, and anyway, I think it would be a good idea to examine them on the spot, just to make absolutely sure that it will fit. I still have the feeling that it will be a very tight squeeze."

Then he turned to Felicitas Burckhardt, and he was obviously pleased by what he saw. As he greeted her, he kept her hand in his just that slight bit longer than was necessary.

"Fräulein Schmidt tells me that you are studying physics, young lady," he said.

"Yes. And my Doktor Vater is an old colleague of yours from Göttingen."

"Really! Who?"

"Professor Wolfgang Pauli."

She could see his eyes flicker as the import of this sank in, but he said nothing. Then she reached into the pocket of her jacket and withdrew the envelope.

"Professor Pauli asked me to give this to you."

Still not responding, Heisenberg opened the envelope and read the two-page letter that was inside. Folding the letter, he tucked it back into the envelope and put the missive into the breast pocket of his jacket.

"Our last problem seems to be solved," he said to Häberlein. "It will be shipped to us from Switzerland next week. That makes it all the more urgent that you begin your construction immediately."

Turning again to Felicitas Burckhardt, he said, "Next time you see Wolfgang, would you please tell him that his invitation is appreciated but that it is simply not practical. And tell him not to worry about me. I'll manage. By the way, he speaks highly of you. Which should please you, because Wolfgang has always had very high standards." Then: "Burckhardt. You are not by any chance related to the historian Jacob Burckhardt?"

"Yes. He was my great-uncle."

"How interesting. This began as a very uninteresting day, and your visit has suddenly changed that. You said that Wolfgang is your Doktor Vater. What is the subject of your dissertation?"

"The measurement of the critical mass of uranium."

Again she saw that speculative flicker in his eyes.

"Rudolph Peierls' specialty. I knew him well, before he left Berlin for Cambridge. I assume that one of your starting points must be that paper he published in nineteen thirty-nine in the *Proceedings* of the Cambridge Philosophical Society."

"Yes, sir."

"Did Wolfgang suggest this thesis?"

"Yes, sir."

"I assume that he has you concentrating on the difference, the potentially radical difference, between U238 and U235 where critical mass is concerned."

"Yes, sir. Tons versus pounds."

The tons and pounds Felicitas referred to were the amounts of fissionable material necessary for the manufacture of an atomic bomb. That answer seemed to have satisfied whatever lingering doubts Heisenberg might have been harboring as a result of this very strange encounter in his living room.

"Would you like to see my little factory—for making U235?"

"I'd love to, Herr Professor!" She smiled warmly.

"Good. Then, Herr Häberlein, we'll take her with us. She can look around while we go over those blueprints one more time."

in the middle of the graveyard. It was apparently a storage place for the caretaker's gardening equipment. The door over it, however, was made of heavy steel. The padlock on it hung loose. Heisenberg swung open the door, and gallantly bowing to his comely visitor from Switzerland, said: "Welcome to my humble workplace."

They found themselves at the top of a concrete stairwell, wide and well-lit. Heisenberg leading the way, they descended for about twenty meters. At the bottom of the stairwell there was another steel door. Beside it was a buzzer, which Heisenberg pressed. The door was opened by a man in uniform bearing the insignia of the Waffen SS. A submachine gun was slung carelessly over his right shoulder. Upon seeing Heisenberg, he drew to attention.

Heisenberg addressed him immediately. "Hans, you know Herr Häberlein, of course. And this young lady is one of my students who is going to be visiting us for an hour or so."

He took the arm of Felicitas and stepped into the huge cavern that for centuries had served as a wine cellar for priests from the castle church. Situated in the middle of it was a concrete pit about ten feet in diameter. Within the pit hung a heavy metal shield covering the top of a thick metal cylinder. The latter contained a pot-shaped vessel, also of heavy metal, about four feet below floor level. Atop the vessel was a metal frame.[84]

"Here it is," Heisenberg said to Felicitas as they stood beside it. "My uranium machine."

This was the phrase that German scientists used at that time to describe an atomic pile. Heisenberg went on to explain at length the details of his "machine," pointing out the key components of it as he went along.

"The liquid in the vessel is, of course, the moderator, heavy water. One and a half tons of it. The fuel consists of six hundred sixty-four cubes of metallic uranium. They are attached to seventy-eight chains suspended from the metal shield that you see there on

---

84. This description is identical with that found in Boris T. Pash, *The Alsos Mission* (New York, 1969), pp. 206 ff. Pash was the man whom General Grove, the ranking military officer in charge of the Manhattan Project (the code name of the American project aimed a developing an atomic bomb), had put in charge of intelligence in that area. Pash and his men discovered the Haigherloch cave containing the German reactor on April 23, 1945. See also Rhodes, *The Making of the Atomic Bomb*, pp. 609–610: Malcolm C. MacPherson, *Time Bomb: Fermi, Heisenberg, and the Race for the Atomic Bomb* (New York, 1986), pp. 275–276.

top of the pile, and they hang down into the water. Simple, yet elegant, wouldn't you agree, Fräulein Burckhardt?"

The young Swiss scientist stood mesmerized by what she saw in front of her. "Oh, yes, Herr Professor." Then she asked the question: "What level of neutron multiplication does it achieve?"

Heisenberg hesitated. But finally he answered: "Just sevenfold, I am afraid."

"What level is necessary to produce a sustained chain reaction?"

Here Felicitas was referring to the process she had described a year earlier over dinner at her parents' place: the bombardment of a uranium atom by neutrons could release energy in a geometric progression — 1, 2, 4, 8, 16, 32, 64 . . . 67108868, 134217736, and so forth, in the form of an atomic "explosion."

Heisenberg hesitated again before answering, but again he did respond. "One that is substantially higher. But we now know that we can achieve that by simply increasing the size of the reactor by fifty percent. As you can see over there, we already have a new cylinder and a new vessel that meet these specifications. The only missing component is the metal lid. It must be made from a special steel, "maraging" steel, which is no longer available in Germany. But we have even solved that problem, and all we need now is a much larger concrete pit, in which to house the new reactor. That is why we are here today, to go over the blueprints for its construction. In fact, Herr Häberlein and I must get to work and I must get to work. While we do, perhaps you might like to go to my little office in the back and read an article I just wrote on fission cross-sections for fast neutrons. It's not published yet, and the way things now look, it probably won't be for a while. But it might give you some ideas for your dissertation.'

The audience was over.

For the next hour, Felicitas Burckhardt sat in Professor Heisenberg's office while he and Herr Häberlein, now joined by two technicians in white coats, huddled over blueprints that they laid out on a long wooden table beside the reactor. The typescript of Heisenberg's article lay in her lap. But it lay there unread. For Felicitas Burckhardt sat there totally stunned by the import of what she had just seen and heard.

The Germans were a lot closer to developing an atomic bomb than anyone had thought.

She would, of course, ask Herr Häberlein how long he estimated it would take to construct that new reactor. It had to be fifty percent larger than the existing one, but even so, she knew that it could be built within weeks.

And most important of all was Heisenberg's own statement. After reading the letter from Pauli, he had announced that his "last problem" had been solved. He was clearly referring to a missing component for the larger reactor: the reactor shield. The Swiss would ship it to him next week. Unless it could be intercepted.

Now all she had to do was to get back to Peter with this information. After that, they had to return home. Quickly. Before their luck ran out.

At three o'clock Professor Heisenberg returned to his office to fetch her. She was shivering from a combination of excitement, mounting apprehension, and the penetrating cold of the cavern. Heisenberg noticed this.

"Girl," he said, "we must get you home. You're freezing."

When they emerged from the cavern into the graveyard of the Schlosskirche, the weather that greeted them added to her growing discomfort. For now it was snowing, and snowing heavily. Ten minutes later, Werner Heisenberg pulled his BMW to a stop in front of the Häberleins' house on the Donaustrasse.

"Give my very best to Wolfgang Pauli, Fräulein Burckhardt. Tell him that I look forward to seeing him soon, and under happier circumstances. Perhaps back where we nuclear physicists all got our start. Here in Germany. In Göttingen."

The proud German professor got back into his BMW and drove off. Felicitas Burckhardt and Herr Häberlein hurried through the falling snow to the front door of his house. His wife was waiting just inside.

"Walter," she said, "come with me. I must talk to you."

As they disappeared down the hall and into the kitchen, Peter Burckhardt came out from the adjacent living room. He saw that his sister was pale and shivering, and was immediately alarmed.

"What happened, Felicitas? Is something wrong?"

"No, no. It's just . . ." She could not continue.

"You look frozen. Come into the living room. I'll get you something hot to drink and then you can tell us what happened. Are you sure everything's all right?"

"I'm sure. It was just all of a sudden too much. And now that I think of it, Peter, I haven't had anything to eat since last night in Fahrnau."

"I'll fix that."

Her brother headed for the kitchen, and Felicitas went into the living room to join Nancy Reichman, who was anxiously waiting for her. Minutes later, the three of them sat close together on the sofa in the living room while Felicitas Burckhardt described what had happened.

"We've got to get back immediately!" she finally said.

"But how?" Nancy asked. "Did you see what is happening to the weather? We could be stuck here for days."

Just then Herr Häberlein reappeared in the living room, went straight to Peter Burckhardt, and drew him aside. "My wife has asked me to talk to you, Herr Doktor. She is very upset. She says that because of you, we are all going to end up in either a concentration camp or before a firing squad. She wants you out of here."

"How? There's no bus back until tomorrow morning."

"That's one of the problems. Forget about the bus. We know the Schwarzwald. With snow like this, there is no way that the bus will run tomorrow. By dawn, there will be a meter of snow on the road up by the Feldberg. It will take them days before they can remove it. I'm not sure there are enough men and machines available now to even manage that. You must realize that this country is on the edge of chaos."

"So what are we supposed to do?"

"There is a train that still runs once a day between Stuttgart and Freiburg-im-Breisgau, where it connects with the main line between Frankfurt and the Badische Bahnhof in Basel. It stops at Horb, which is exactly sixteen kilometers north of here. It leaves at seventen in the morning. I will take you there in the van in time to make tomorrow's train."

"What about the snow?"

"I've got chains. And the problem is not the snow *here*. We'll get enough, but nothing like they will get in the high country to the south. Don't worry. I'll get you to Horb. And then you are on your own, Herr Doktor. There are limits to what any of us can do. And I tell you, no, I warn you: my wife has reached her limit. In fact, she just told me that she does not want to have anything more to do with you. You told us your sister needs food, so I will be bringing you supper here in the living room as soon as I can. It will be just soup and bread. You can stay down here as long as you want, but I suggest you go to bed early. I will show you where your rooms are now. I want you all ready to leave by six tomorrow morning."

He took Peter upstairs, showed him the two spare bedrooms, brought him back to the living room, and then disappeared into the kitchen. As Peter explained the new situation to his sister and Nancy Reichman, they could periodically hear the voice of Häberlein's wife—loud, shrill, hysterical—as she continued to work on her husband back in the kitchen.

Once Peter had finished speaking his sister asked, "You don't really think that we can simply go to Freiburg and take the train to Basel, do you?"

"Of course not."

"Then what *do* you think?"

"We will get off at the last stop on the German side before Basel, in Lörrach."

"And then what?"

"Don't worry. The original plan is out. But other arrangements have been made."

That original plan had called for them to follow the same route out of Germany that they had taken in, getting off the bus in Fahrnau, where they could wait in his uncle's house until darkness fell, after which all four of them would have cycled to Rhine to meet up with a Swiss barge headed upstream toward safe haven in the port of Basel at the preappointed hour of ten o'clock. The fourth cyclist would have been Heisenberg and his bicycle, one borrowed from Onkel Ernst. Now all of this had been turned topsyturvy: no Heisenberg, no bus to Fahrnau, and even if there had been a bus, there was no way that they could have cycled to Weil-am-Rheir through this amount of snow, either tomorrow or even most probably for the rest of the week. Which would probably be too late for them to stop the shipment of the reactor shield.

But Peter Burckhardt had arranged for a backup plan. His people would be there ready to help. The time and the signal that would set the plan in motion had been agreed upon. Provided they could get there in time.

The soup and bread arrived a half hour later, and even though it was getting dark outside and in, Herr Häberlein insisted that there be no lights on in the living room lest they attract attention. In Haigerloch, the use of living rooms was usually reserved for entertaining guests, now a very unusual event, and thus one that could arouse the curiosity of neighbors. So they ate in the dark. Häberlein did turn on the radio, however, and tuned in the German national sender, which at least provided classical music for the next two hours. Then it started to get very cold in the living room, which was obviously not heated except for special occasions. At seven o'clock, Peter Burckhardt suggested that they go to bed, no matter what the hour, simply to keep warm. And the sooner they got some sleep, the better. Tomorrow would start very early, and might end very late.

At six the next morning, the unwelcome visitors sat in the Häberlein kitchen sipping the coffee that Herr Häberlein had prepared. His wife was nowhere to be seen or heard. Shortly after six, they emerged from the house. It was barely dawn. In the early light, they could see that there was at least half a meter of new snow on the ground, and more was coming down. The engine in Häberlein's van was already running. He let out the clutch a split second after Peter Burckhardt closed the door on his side of the van, and after sliding around a U turn, headed out to the main road, where he turned right, driving slowly through the lower town of Haigerloch. It was still completely deserted. On the northern outskirts of town, the road rose sharply as they emerged from the valley floor. Twice the wheels of the van began to spin out of control, but then the chains caught and they were off again, soon on level terrain, a condition that Herr Häberlein assured them would continue all the way into Horb. Six kilometers later they went through the village of Weildorf, and five kilometers after that, Emfinger.

"How much farther?" Peter Burckhardt asked. It was six twenty-five.

"Another five kilometers. We should reach the train station in twenty minutes. Unless we get stuck."

They were back in the country, proceeding at a careful thirty kilometers an hour. There were no tire tracks up ahead, meaning that theirs was the first vehicle through the snow, which was growing deeper by the minute. Häberlein kept the van in the middle of the road as best he could, which was not easy; it was becoming increasingly difficult to see out, since the wipers could no longer clear the snow from the windshield.

"Do you see that little bridge up ahead? It must take us over a stream. Would you mind stopping on it for just a moment?" Peter Burckhardt asked.

"That would not be a good idea," Häberlein replied. "In snow like this, the idea is to keep the vehicle moving. Once you stop, you might not be able to get going again. Especially on an icy bridge."

"Nevertheless, it is very important that you stop, Herr Häberlein."

As the van slowed, Peter Burckhardt opened his backpack and withdrew the leather pouch from it. The moment the vehicle stopped, he jumped out and moved to the side of the bridge. Holding the pouch on the railing with one hand, he yanked the red string that protruded from it with the other hand. There was a hiss, and then the pouch burst into flame. Peter Burckhardt involuntarily flinched backward.

It was all over within seconds. He then took one of his leather gloves and flicked at the charred remnants of the pouch until they had all fallen from the railing into the partially frozen stream below. All that remained was a black scar on the bridge railing. When he got back into the van, nobody said a word. They all knew that what they had just witnessed was a signal that they were getting near the danger zone of the German railroad system, where suspicious eyes at checkpoint were ever-present, on the lookout for deserters, or for potential saboteurs in the employ of the approaching Allied armies.

At six-fifty they pulled up in front of the train station in the center of the town of Horb. The two Burckhards and Nancy Reichman scrambled out of the van, while Häberlein remained behind the wheel with the motor running. There were no hand-shakes this time. Once they were out, Häberlein just waved good-bye, once, and pulled away.

Inside the small station, Peter Burckhardt approached the ticket window. He had decided to purchase tickets just to Freiburg. That was no doubt the destination of most of the passengers along this feeder line, and thus one that would not arouse any particular attention. The train arrived twenty minutes late, the delay obviously due to the snow. No one paid any attention to them. They found a second-class compartment occupied by two older women, both dressed in black, sisters as their conversation soon revealed.

After greeting them with the usual "Guete Tag," Nancy and the two Burckhardts kept their silence. They occasionally glanced at the Stuttgart morning newspaper that Peter had bought at the kiosk in the station, but for the most part during the hours that followed, they just stared out the window.

The train pulled into the Bahnhof in Freiburg at twelve-twenty. Upon leaving their compartment. they hurried down the Bahnsteig to the main hall of the station. The huge "Zeittafel" that hung there indicated that the next train south, coming from Frankfurt am Main and bound for Lörrach, left in twenty minutes and that it was on time. The one after that left five hours later.

There was a line in front of the ticket counter, and it was twelve twenty-seven before Peter Burckhardt reached the front of it.

"Dreimal Lörrach, Zweite Klasse einfach," he said and pushed a fifty-mark note under the window.

"Bahnsteig seven. And you'd better hurry," the woman behind the glass advised as she pushed three tickets and his change back to him.

They ran toward platform seven, and as they approached it, they could see why they had been advised to hurry. A long line of people were queued up at the gate, waiting while their documents were checked by the military police.

The train from Frankfurt was pulling in just as Peter Burckhardt reached the head of the line.

He handed the guard on the right his military papers that identified him as a sergeant in the border guard stationed in Lörrach. He also gave him his travel papers, indicating that he was on a forty-eight-hour compassionate leave to attend a relative's funeral in Trilltingen and was allowed to travel in civilian clothes. And handed over the three tickets he had just bought.

"Where's Trilltingen. Sergeant?"

"Just outside of Haigerloch."

The guard then looked at the tickets.

"Who are the other two?"

Burckhardt pointed to the two women standing behind him. "My sisters." They stepped forward and handed him their ID cards.

"I don't understand something," the guard said. "Why are these tickets issued here, and why are they one-way?"

"Because we came up to Haigerloch from Lörrach by bus yesterday, through Titisee and Feldberg, and had planned to take it back today. But—"

The guard interrupted him. "The snowstorm." Then: "In Ordnung." He handed them back their papers and turned his attention to the next person in line, saying, "Ausweis, bitte."

The train was packed; there was standing room only. In contrast to the bus they had taken into the Black Forest, the majority of the passengers were not old and they were not civilians. Most of them were men in uniform, and they were either very young—some looked to be barely sixteen—or very old for soldiers, men with gray hair and stooped shoulders. Germany was scraping the bottom of the barrel.

The trip to Lörrach was mercifully short: fifty-nine minutes. This train did not go on to the Badische Bahnhof in Basel, so when it stopped at Lörrach-Stetten, it was the end of the line, and everybody got off. There was just one platform, and it was outside. What greeted them there was nothing short of a howling winter blizzard. It had brought everything to a halt; there was no traffic whatsoever on the streets.

The two Burckhardts and their American companion, like most of the passengers who had disembarked, began to trudge through the snow toward the center of town. Nancy Reichman waited until she was sure they were finally by themselves before asking: "How are we going to get home, Peter?"

"We can't get back by water. Getting from here to the Weil-am-Rhein by foot today is out. Even if we could get to Fahrnau somehow and go into hiding there until the storm clears and a new rendezvous could be arranged, I wouldn't do it. We've already exposed Onkel Ernst and Tante Emily to enough potential risk. So we are going to go back into Switzerland by land."

"Where?" his sister asked. "That border is sealed by barbed wire and land mines. Everybody knows that, Peter."

"One place isn't. I'll show you."

He led them to the Basler Strasse, the main street of the frontier town of Lörrach. Streetcar tracks ran down the middle. Until the end of August, 1939, the tram that ran down these tracks, the No. 6, had been part of the city of Basel's transport system, and it took passengers from Lörrach to the center of Basel. One had barely noticed that one was going from one country into another except for a cursory border check. You got off the tram, showed your ID, and then got right back on the same tram a few minutes later. It then continued down the middle of the same street, except that the street was now called the Aussere Baselstrasse, and it was on Swiss territory. That border-crossing was the only one in the region that had remained open during the entire war.

Now, however, the tram had stopped running. Barriers like those at railroad crossings had been erected on both sides of the line that marked the border, with a narrow no-man's-land of about twenty meters in between. And there were guardhouses beside these barriers, but no barbed wire and no land mines. This was, of course, the same border-crossing that General Walter Schellenberg had used two years earlier.

At Basler Strasse 90, about a hundred meters from that border-crossing, there was a cafe and restaurant, "Zum Kranz." It was two forty-five when the three of them entered it. They ordered not only coffee, but Wurst and bread as well. Peter Burckhardt also ordered a beer. They wanted to see his ration coupons before taking the order. Fortunately, Section 5 had thought of that and had provided him with a supply.

At exactly two fifty-five, Peter Burckhardt excused himself, telling his companions not to worry, that he would be back almost immediately. At precisely three o'clock, he walked across the Basler Strasse, and upon reaching the other side, turned and walked straight back. Standing once again in front of the restaurant, he looked intently down the street. It was still snowing, although it seemed to be letting up. Even so, at precisely five minutes past three, again on the second, he saw the light blink three times. It came from a window on the third floor of the first building on the left on the other side of the Swiss border, an apartment building. Upon seeing it, Burckhardt immediately went back into the restaurant, where he ordered another beer, and a half carafe of the local Badische white wine for his sister and his American friend. He also paid the bill.

Then it happened very quickly.

At two minutes to four, he told the two young women that they were going to leave immediately. They were to leave behind both their backpacks and their overcoats, which they had hung on the rack just inside the door.

"When we got onto the street, I want you both at my side. All right?"

They nodded.

"We're going to walk briskly toward the border. You're going to hear an explosion. It will be on the left side, behind the German guardhouse. There is a parking lot there where the border guards inspect the trucks coming into Germany from Switzerland. The explosion will go off when we are about twenty meters this side of the crossing. When you hear it, run straight ahead keeping to this side of the street, duck under the barrier, and then keep running until you are on the Swiss side. That barrier will be open."

When they stepped out of the restaurant onto the street, dusk was falling, and with the snow still coming down, visibility was becoming increasingly limited. Yet it was too early for the lights that illuminated the border-crossing at night to come on. The moment had been carefully chosen, though nobody had even thought of factoring in the possibility of snow.

There were only two German guards standing outside the guardhouse in the falling snow. When the explosion went off, it sounded like mortar fire. They turned in the direction of the blast and went into a crouch, their submachine guns at the ready. In that second, Peter Burckhardt grasped the arms of his companions.

"Go!"

Their walk broke into a run. They had almost reached the barrier on the German side when the second explosion went off. Like the first one, it was a Swiss-army mortar shell that had been set off just meters inside Swiss territory by Peter Burckhardt's accomplices. Now the border guards dived forward for better cover in front of the gray cinder-block guardhouse. That's when the three ducked under the first barrier. The third blast came while they were sprinting across the no-man's-land in front of the second barrier, which now opened.

A man stood there waiting on the other side. It was Wilhelm Lützelschwab.

"Down!" he shouted. "Down!"

As they dropped to the snow-covered street, so did he. He later told them that he expected they might be the target of machine-gun fire from the other side of the border. But it never came. Confused shouts were heard, but no gunfire. Soon they were surrounded by a half-dozen uniformed Swiss soldiers, plus four of Lützelschwab's men in plainclothes, and in the middle of that massive protection, the four of them walked to a black Citroën that was waiting a hundred meters farther down the Aussere Baselstrasse. Captain Max Waibel of Section 5 of the General Staff of the Swiss High Command emerged to greet them.

"Congratulations, Peter," he said. "Your backup plan worked perfectly."

There were handshakes, pats on the back, and kisses exchanged.

"Where's Heisenberg?" Waibel asked.

"He decided not to come," Peter Burckhardt answered. "But

that's the least of our problems. My sister will explain why. Then we will have to talk to Allen Dulles."

"That will be easy. He's been in constant touch with us during the past three days. He called this morning to say that he was on his way to Basel."

# SEVENTY-THREE

Earlier that day, Dulles had received a phone call from Basel.

"This is Maximilian Burckhardt," the caller began. "We've never met, but I am informed that you know my son, Peter."

"I know exactly who you are, Dr. Burckhardt."

"Good. Well, something came up this morning in the bank that prompted this call. Normally I would have relayed what I am about to tell you through Peter, but he is incommunicado for the moment, as I understand it."

"He is."

"I'll come right to the point. The adjutant to General Walter Schellenberg, Rittmeister Hans Wilhelm Eggen, was in my office this morning. He wants to defect. He specifically wants to talk to you, Mr. Dulles."

"Where is he now?"

"He left the bank no more than a quarter of an hour ago. He's staying at the Three Kings Hotel."

"I will call him there. Thank you, Dr. Burckhardt."

"My pleasure."

Dulles got hold of Eggen ten minutes later and arranged to meet him in his hotel room at three o'clock that afternoon.

When the Nazi opened the door leading into his suite on the fourth floor of the Three Kings, Dulles did not shake hands with him. He just nodded his head when Eggen introduced himself and then proceeded into the living room.

"I am extremely grateful that you have come, Mr. Dulles," Eggen began.

■

Again, Dulles just nodded as he shed his overcoat.

"I would like to propose what you Americans call a deal. I shall fully brief you on the current German situation as I know it from my position inside SS Intelligence in return for your arranging transit to Chile, where I have relatives."

"We shall see. First, a few preliminary questions. Are you acting solely on your own, or as an agent for General Schellenberg?"

"Solely on my own. Schellenberg knows that I am in Switzerland, but he has no idea that I intended to contact you."

"What is the official purpose of your visit to Switzerland?"

"To visit my bank. And to review the current status of a trading company I am associated with here in Basel."

"You are referring to the Swiss Bank Corporation and Extroc S.A.?"

Eggen could not mask his surprise at hearing the second name. "You are well informed."

"That is my business," Dulles responded "Let's start with the military situation on the Eastern front. What is the current SS intelligence estimate?"

"That Warsaw will fall to the Russians within hours. And that the Red Army will be on German territory a week later."

"Is that the reason you are here?"

"One of them," Eggen replied.

"Has Hitler been given this same intelligence estimate?"

"Yes. Two days ago. By General Schellenberg."

The grilling continued relentlessly for the next two hours. At just before five, Dulles asked to be excused for a short period. He took the lift down to the lobby and used the public phone there to check in with his aide back in Bern.

"I'm glad you called, sir. It's imperative that you get hold of Peter Burckhardt."

"Has something happened?" Dulles responded with alarm.

"No, no. They are all safely back. But they want to talk to you immediately." He gave Dulles the number that Burckhardt had left with him.

Peter answered the phone on the first ring. "I think it best if we get together as soon as possible, sir," he said.

"All right. How about in one hour? At Nancy Reichman's apartment," Dulles said.

"Perfect."

"I'm tied up at the moment Would you mind calling Nancy and arranging it?"

"I will. My sister will also be there."

"Then I'll see the three of you shortly after six."

Dulles returned to the fourth-floor suite of Rittmeister Eggen and told the German that something urgent had come up that would demand his presence during the next four hours. He would be back at nine o'clock.

"Will you then be prepared to discuss my request for safe passage?" Eggen asked.

"We shall see," Dulles responded.

# SEVENTY-FOUR

When Dulles arrived at Nancy Reichman's apartment an hour later, the three young people were still dressed in the same clothes they had worn for the past three days. They were a haggard, tired lot. But they did not waste any time before getting down to business. Peter Burckhardt, who was trained in the process of debriefing, took Dulles through their trip, step by step, to the point where Felicitas went to the home of Heisenberg in the company of the Swiss engineer.

"Now, Felicitas," Peter said, "I want you to tell exactly what happened next. And in the process, I want you to repeat verbatim, if you can, your conversations with Heisenberg, both in his home and subsequently at the site of the nuclear reactor."

Felicitas told of how she had visited Heisenberg in his home, and even repeated his exact words after he had read the letter from Wolfgang Pauli, words that had been addressed to the Swiss engineer: "Our last problem seems to be solved. It will be shipped to us from Switzerland next week. This makes it all the more urgent that you begin your construction immediately."

Felicitas then related how Heisenberg had taken them to the church overlooking the town of Haigerloch, and then down to the cave that housed his experimental nuclear reactor. She carefully described the reactor, and told of the admission by Heisenberg that it had proven too small to go "critical." That the problem was size, a problem that would be solved when a reactor of the same design, but fifty percent larger, was built. Every component of that larger reactor was present, except for the shield.

"And that is when he said, and I quote exactly, 'It must be made

■

from a special steel, "maraging" steel, which is no longer available in Germany.'" Felicitas paused. "Then Heisenberg repeated the same words he had spoken to the Swiss engineer at his house: 'But we have even solved that problem.'"

"Hold on for a minute, Felicitas," Dulles said. "If the larger reactor is now built and goes 'critical,' what will that mean?"

"That within weeks, it will produce enough weapons-grade uranium to make a bomb."

Dulles' next question: "What is 'maraging' steel?"

Nobody knew.

He turned to Felicitas. "Why would the reactor shield have to be made from a special steel?"

"Because of the enormous stress it is subjected to. Seventy-eight chains are suspended from it. Attached to the end of the chains are six hundred sixty-four cubes of dense metallic uranium oxide submersed in heavy water."

"Who makes speciality steel in Switzerland?" Dulles asked.

"Just one company. Von Roll," Peter Burckhardt replied.

"Where is it?"

"Schaffhausen."

"We bombed Schaffhausen once before," Dulles said. "By mistake."[85]

That produced silence, which was finally broken by Peter Burckhardt. "There must be another way."

"But is there?" Dulles responded. "Do you *really* think it possible that Pauli, the Federal Institute of Technology, and now Von Roll have all been cooperating with the Naxis on nuclear matters without somebody at the highest level of government here approving of it? And do you think for one moment that if I confronted them with your story, they would admit it? They'd probably arrest you, make Pauli disappear, and try to kick me out of the country. Come on, Peter."

"What do you think?" Peter asked.

"Somebody must have approached Von Roll on behalf of the

---

85. On April 1, 1944, twenty-four American bombers attacked Schaffhausen with fire bombs, killing forty civilians, injuring hundreds of others, and destroying 66 buildings, principally factories, this city being the base of one of Nazi Germany's other suppliers of war materials, the firm of Georg Fischer. For a definitive history of the American air attacks on Switzerland during World War II, see Chapter 5 "Neutralitätsverletzungen durch angelsächsische Flugzeuge," in Bonjour, Vol V, pp. 106–135.

Germans," Dulles said. "There must be contracts. Arrangements for payment. This is, after all, Switzerland." He rose to his feet. "I think I know how to find all that out. And right now. From an old acquaintance of yours, Peter. Rittmeister Hans Wilhelm Eggen. The Nazi wheeler-dealer. He's back in town. And he wants to defect to us. He's over at the Three Kings Hotel. Your father put me onto it. Look, I know what you've all been through, but can I ask you one last favor? Stay here for another hour."

Then Dulles left.

# SEVENTY-FIVE

A very nervous Rittmeister Eggen opened the door to Allen Dulles for the third time that day. Dulles started talking before he had even taken off his coat.

"I'll arrange transit for you to Chile with one proviso: you provide me with specific information, right now, on a very specific matter."

Relief mixed with continuing worry could be seen on the Nazi's face. "And if I don't have it?"

"Then you'll go back to Germany and get it."

"Agreed."

"Has your firm, Extroc, had any dealings with a Swiss speciality steel company by the name of Von Roll?"

Now the relief on Eggen's face was overwhelming. "That's it?"

"That and a lot more."

"Of course. That metallic shield for Heisenberg's operation. The contract is with us."

"Do you know what's involved?"

"Of course. Our nuclear research."

"But how did the Swiss get involved?"

"It all started with the uranium shipments from the Belgian Congo back in the spring of nineteen forty-three."

The entire story began to tumble out. The meeting between Guisan and Schellenberg in Biglen. The deal in the back room of the restaurant there. The use of a Swiss ship to and Swiss trucks from Lisbon. Extroc handling the transshipment of the uranium into Germany, as well as the diversion of some of the uranium ore to a Swiss refinery in Basel. Heisenberg and Pauli in constant

■

contact with each other, apparently proceeding on parallel tracks in developing an atomic reactor. Heinsenberg turning to Pauli's supplier of reactor components, Von Roll, after his German supplier had been bombed out of existence.

"And when will that shield that you contracted for with Von Roll be shipped?"

"I don't remember exactly. But I think next week."

"I want copies of your contract with Von Roll. As well as the documentation related to your firm's handling of that uranium shipment."

"No problem. It must all be on file at the office here."

"Get it. Now."

"What do you mean?"

"You must have keys to Extroc's offices. Go get what I need. Right now."

"But—"

"No buts, Eggen. General Guisan's son is affiliated with Extroc, is he not?"

"Yes."

"I don't want him to know about this. Or anybody else in that company."

"There's really only a bookkeeper and a secretary."

By this time, Allen Dulles was putting his overcoat back on.

"I'm staying at the Euler Hotel. I'll be expecting you."

Dulles did not go directly to the Euler, but instead took a taxi to Nancy Reichman's apartment, where he told of what had just transpired.

"I think we can spare Schaffhausen," Dulles said to Peter Burckhardt, "provided I get to see General Guisan right away. Can you and Captain Waibel help me there? If there is any question as to why, you might merely tell the general that Rittmeister Eggen is defecting to the Americans and has told them some very unpleasnt details about what transpired in Biglen. Some of these details involve his son."

# SEVENTY-SIX

The Guisan-Dulles meeting began two days later, at ten A.M. on Sunday, January 21, in a room in the Schweizerhof Hotel in Bern. It took place under four eyes and lasted less than one hour. Like the Guisan-Schellenberg meeting in Biglen almost two years earlier, no protocol was ever made of the contents of this meeting.

The next morning shortly after daybreak, at the Von Roll plant complex on the outskirts of Schaffhausen, a huge metal shield was transferred by crane from the foundry to a waiting rail flatcar. It took another hour for the component to be secured and a tarpaulin placed over it. The operation was witnessed by four people: Rudi Schneider, the plant manager; Rittmeister Hans Wilhelm Eggen of Extroc S.A.; General Henri Guisan; and Allen Dulles.

When the loading process had been completed, the two Swiss climbed into a waiting Swiss army staff car; the American and the German into a car provided by the American Embassy. The flatcar was then attached to a locomotive of the Swiss National Railroad. As it pulled out of the rail siding onto the main line, the two cars followed it on the highway that paralleled the rail line. Three kilometers north, they approached two parallel bridges—one for rail, one for vehicular traffic—that crossed the Rhine into Germany.

The cars stopped at the barriers on the Swiss side, manned by Swiss army personnel. All four men got out. The locomotive and the single flatcar it was pulling was waved through and proceeded slowly to the middle of the railroad bridge, where it stopped. The locomotive engineer—a Swiss army sergeant—got out and jogged back onto Swiss territory.

General Guisan stepped briskly forward to a point on the bank

.

of the Rhine overlooking the full sweep of the river. The bridge had been mined by the Swiss on the day that World War II broke out, and apparently the demolition crew knew what they were doing. When Guisan raised his hand, the explosion blew the central span of the railroad bridge sky high. Then the entire bridge collapsed into the swift-flowing river below, carrying with it the locomotive, the single car behind it, and the Nazis' last hope to win the war.

# SEVENTY-SEVEN

That evening all of the principals whose wartime espionage activities had been assigned the code name "Swiss Account" by OSS headquarters in Washington gathered for dinner in Basel in the Schützenhaus restaurant: Allen Dulles and Captain Waibel; Per Jacobsson and Peter Burckhardt; Felicitas Burckhardt and Nancy Reichman. The final toast of the evening was given at eleven o'clock by the master spy, Allen Dulles.

"To the Swiss Account, and to your remarkable achievement of developing, at enormous personal risk, what is undoubtedly the most significant single piece of intelligence of the war. My country extends to you all its eternal gratitude."

Peter Burckhardt drove Allen Dulles back to his hotel and then took Nancy Reichman home to her apartment on the Augustinergasse. When they arrived, Nancy turned to kiss him good night.

He stopped her, took her hand, and said, "Would you mind if I came up for just a few minutes? I know you are exhausted, Nancy, but—"

"Of course, Peter."

Once they were inside and had taken off their coats, Peter Burckhardt again took her hand and said, "Felicitas told me that you are going home."

"Yes."

"Please don't."

She said nothing.

"I want you to stay, Nancy, because I want to marry you. Will you?"

■

"But, Peter, you know I'm Jewish," she said, "What would your family think?"

"You know what Felicitas thinks. And where my parents are concerned, I have fully discussed this matter with them. Their position is very simple. They will welcome you with open arms. They would be proud if you would now also bear the Burckhardt name."

They were married one month later in the small chapel on the grounds of the Benkener Schloss.

# EPILOGUE

The activities of all those personae associated with the Swiss Account of course continued until the end of the war, and during this period, two episodes in particular stand out.

The first involved Allen Dulles and Captain Max Waibel. Through the intermediary of the Swiss intelligence officer, Dulles established contact with the commander of the German armed forces fighting the Allies in Italy, Field Marshal Albert Kesselring, as well as with the chief of the SS units there, General Karl Wolff. The operation was given the code name "Sunrise." Meetings arranged by Waibel at various places in Switzerland culminated in the German surrender of all their forces in Italy, one million men, on May 2, 1945.

Of Waibel's role in this, Dulles later wrote: "As we proceeded to develop our secret and precarious relations with the German generals early in 1945, we would have been thwarted at every step if we had not had the help of Waibel in facilitating contacts and communications and in arranging the delicate frontier crossings which had to be carried out under conditions of complete secrecy. In all his actions Waibel was serving the interest of peace."[86]

After the war ended, Waibel remained in the Swiss Army, serving for a while as a military attaché at the Swiss Legation in Washington, and eventually becoming chief of infantry. He retired with the highest military rank available in Switzerland in peacetime, that of *Oberstdivisionär*. But then his luck ran out. Jozef Garlinski, an expert on the subject of espionage in Europe during World War II, describes Waibel's latter days as follows:

---

86. Allen Dulles, *The Secret Surrender*, p. 27.

■

"After leaving the service, he gave himself over to his beloved horse riding, organizing and running clubs for children. He also went on the board of directors of a private bank unaware that this bank was engaged in illegal and dishonest transactions. When this became common knowledge, Max Waibel, after trying to repay the shareholders, took his own life on 21 January, 1971."[87]

In fact, this decent and brave soldier was hounded to death by the local press and the ungrateful citizenry of Lucerne.

The second episode also involved Allen Dulles, and was also related to the desire of one of the warring parties to negotiate a surrender in the spring of 1945. But this time, it was the Japanese who sought negotiations with Washington through Dulles. And in this instance, the intermediary was not Waibel, but the Swedish economist and banker attached to the Bank for International Settlements in Basel, Per Jacobsson. Describing the origins of this incident, Jacobsson's biographer (his daughter) writes:

"Per Jacobsson was approached by two Japanese bankers, Kojiro Kitamura, a board member of the BIS, and Kan Yoshimura, head of the Exchange Section of the BIS. Would PJ be prepared, as a neutral with good connections, to try to arrange peace for Japan? They were talking on behalf of Lieutenant-General Seigo Okamoto, military attaché in Bern, who (through an intermediary) could go directly to Emperor Hirohito. PJ suggested that the right person to approach was Allen Dulles, then head of the European branch of the American OSS, and a close personal friend."[88]

Dulles picks up the story from there: "In April, 1945, while the Battle of Okinawa was at its peak. [I was] approached in Switzerland by Japanese army and navy spokesmen there and also by some Japanese officials at the Bank for International Settlements in Basel. They wished to determine whether they could not also take advantage of the secret channels to Washington established for 'Sunrise' to secure peace for Japan. Per Jacobsson. the able Swedish economic advisor at the Basel bank, was brought into these talks, and there was an active exchange of communications between Washington and Bern.

"On July 20, 1945, under instruction from Washington, I went to the Potsdam Conference and reported there to Secretary Stimson

87. Jozef Garlinski, *The Swiss Corridor* (London, 1981), pp. 193–194.
88. Jacobsson, Erin E., *A Life for Sound Money, Per Jacobsson, His Biography*, p. 170.

on what I had learned from Tokyo—they desired to surrender if they could retain the Emperor and the constitution. By this time the news of the Italian surrender and the story of how it had been brought about had been widely publicized in the press: its effect was contagious. Unfortunately, in the case of Japan, time ran out on us."[89]

Time ran out, of course, when the US dropped atomic bombs on Hiroshima and Nagasaki, leaving the Japanese no choice but to immediately surrender unconditionally.

Against that historical background, another chronicler of this episode concluded his account of these Swiss negotiations as follows: "When the fateful day of capitulation came at last, Commander Yoshiro Fujimura recalled with chagrin the blindness which had contributed toward his government's failure to follow to good advantage the Swiss path of negotiation; and in Zürich, Lieutenant-General Seigo Okamoto indelibly inscribed his name upon the sacred registers of the samurai by taking his life with his own hand. Both of these men had been involved in the Swiss talks. If there had been a little more time to develop this channel of negotiation, the story of the Japanese surrender might have had a different ending."[90]

After the war, Allen Dulles returned to the United States and remained in private life until 1950, when he once again took up his career as a spy with the newly created Central Intelligence Agency. He became its head in 1953 and remained in that post until 1961. Per Jacobsson remained with the BIS in Basel until 1956, when he was made managing director of the International Monetary Fund, the world's most prestigious financial post, which he held for the next six years. He wanted to return to Basel upon retirement, but died in 1963 before this final dream could become reality.

One more note on Jacobsson: although he traveled extensively in Germany during the war and had contacts in Berlin at the highest level until the very end of the conflict, my description of his final trip there in January of 1945 is fictitious. Also: although he undoubtedly was fully aware of the dubious role that the BIS was playing during World War II, he never became personally involved in such matters as the secret transfer of looted gold from Germany to Switzerland.

89. Dulles, *The Secret Surrender*, pp. 255–256.
90. Robert J. C. Butow, *Japan's Decision to Surrender* (Stanford, 1954), p. 111.

Where that gold was concerned, even before the war ended, the Allies threatened to maintain an economic boycott on Switzerland unless it was turned over to them. The Swiss government agreed, and also promised to relinquish all other German assets in Switzerland, such as bank accounts, once it was determined how much was involved.

So no embargo was imposed. This promise was subsequently reaffirmed in a formal agreement signed in Washington, after which the Swiss simply stonewalled. There was no proof, they claimed, that they had received any looted gold from Germany. And as to the Nazi bank deposits, there was no way under Swiss law that private property could be seized. They insisted that the entire matter be turned over to an international court of arbitration . . . which would have taken years.

In the end, the Allies caved in. On August 28, 1952, in return for a lump sum settlement of ninety million dollars, the Allies consented to declare all of their claims against Switzerland arising out of World War II as satisfied. That amount represented no more than five cents on the dollar. The rest was simply kept by the Swiss, although a small amount was eventually given to the Red Cross.[91]

The two generals in this novel, General Henri Guisan and General Walter Schellenberg, could hardly have been cut from more different cloth, so logically they spent their postwar years quite differently. Guisan, upon retirement as commander in chief of the Swiss armed forces on August 20, 1945, became a national monument who remained by far and away the most admired man in Switzerland until the day of his death in 1960 at the age of 86. His biographer, in the last sentence of his exhaustive study of this man and his career, summed up why he received such adoration: "The General's ultimate contribution to his nation was that under his command, the army played a decisive role in maintaining the political and cultural independence of Switzerland."[92]

By contrast, SS General Walter Schellenberg remained the slippery, elusive character until the end. He managed to travel to Stockholm, purportedly on a peace mission, just forty-eight hours before the German unconditional surrender in early May, 1945. He subsequently asked for asylum in Sweden and was given it, thanks to the intervention of Count Bernadotte, whom he had helped to

91. Erdman, *Swiss-American Economic Relations,* pp. 147–158.
92. Gautschi, *General Henri Guisan* p. 765.

get a certain number of Scandinavian political prisoners out of German hands. His stay in Sweden was short, since the Allies demanded his extradition, so in June, 1945, he found himself back in Germany. In January of 1948, he came up before an American military tribunal and was sentenced to six years' imprisonment, including his confinement since June, 1945. It was one of the lightest sentences given to a leading figure in the Third Reich. By this time, Schellenberg was a sick man and was released from prison in June of 1951 by an act of grace.

Jozef Garlinski picks up from there: "He then got in contact with his wartime associate, Roger Masson, and appealed to his generosity. Masson . . . facilitated a secret entry into Switzerland and introduced him to a friend, Dr. Lang, who hid him not far from Romont. However, the Swiss police very soon found him and ordered him to leave the country, so he crossed the Italian frontier and settled in the small town of Pallanza, on Lake Maggiore. There, with the help of a German journalist, he began to write his memoirs, but the work was constantly interrupted by a liver complaint, from which he had suffered since childhood. He died in Turin on 31 March 1952, aged barely forty-one."[93]

Schellenberg's SS associate, Rittmeister Hans Wilhelm Eggen, stayed in Switzerland until October 1, 1945. On that day, according to the Swiss authorities, he crossed the border into Italy. Then he simply disappeared.[94]

Roger Masson, head of Swiss Intelligence in World War II, who fondly referred to Schellenberg as "Schelli," paid dearly for that friendship. In September of 1945, he gave an unauthorized interview to a reporter from the *Chicago Daily News* and told him about his meetings with the SS general. Thanks to this, what had been heretofore a top secret, known only to the highest-ranking political and military authorities in Switzerland, was no longer such. Two members of the Swiss parliament now attacked Masson, demanding an inquiry. The investigation was carried out by Judge Couchepin, who rendered his opinion in January of 1946, completely clearing Roger Masson of all suspicions and wrongful acts. Nevertheless, Masson was now a marked man, and as in the later case of his former associate, Max Waibel, he was now subject to constant harassment from the Swiss press and citizenry. He could not defend

93. Garlinski, *The Swiss Corridor*, p. 196.
94. Braunschweig, *Geheimer Draht nach Berlin*, p. 322.

himself, for he was bound by the secrecy of his service even after he left the army and went into retirement. He died in 1967 an embittered man.[95]

Wilhelm Lützelschwab was a real-life person, although I must confess that I took some liberties with him. There is no evidence that he ever reverted to beating confessions out of prisoners or did a few other things that Swiss policeman aren't supposed to do. The real-life Lützelschwab actually left his post as head of Basel's political police in 1943 and was promoted to the position of Erster Staatsanwalt, or chief prosecuting attorney, for the half canton of Baselstadt, although he did not give up his counterespionage activities and was often called in to help in special cases. In 1945, at the age of forty, he resigned from government service, deciding that it was time to have a go at the private sector. He joined the management of a Swiss life insurance firm, Pax. Predictably, he ended up as head of the company He died a very successful and respected man in May, 1981.[96]

Heisenberg was captured by the Americans at a lake cottage in Bavaria, to which he had fled shortly before the advance team of American army specialists reached Haigerloch on April 23, 1945.[97] There they found the now-abandoned atomic pile in the cave in the cliff behind the church; construction on the larger pile had never been started. After being transported to England, where he was held for a brief time, Heisenberg was allowed to return to his old university, where he resumed his nuclear research under British supervision. In February of 1947, he was interviewed in Göttingen by a reporter from the *Washington Post*, where it was reported that he had received an "offer" from the Russians. According to Tom Bower, in his book *The Paperclip Conspiracy: The Hunt for the Nazi Scientists*, upon hearing this, "the Pentagon now feared that he and eleven other German nuclear scientists, including Otto Hahn, would be recruited by Moscow. To protect American security, the Joint Intelligence Committee (of the Joint Chiefs of Staff) recommended that the nuclear scientists be brought to America, but not employed. The British, annoyed that [President] Truman

95. Garlinski, *The Swiss Corridor*, p. 192.
96. Braunschweig, *Geheimer Draht nach Berlin*, p. 36.
97. See Rhodes, *The Making of the Atomic Bomb*, pp. 609–610; General Leslie M. Groves, *Now It Can Be Told: The Story of the Manhattan Project* (New York, 1962), pp. 240–244; MacPherson, *Time Bomb: Fermi, Heisenberg, and the Race for the Atomic Bomb*, pp. 275–290.

would not share America's atomic secrets, rejected the proposal."
So Heisenberg was allowed to remain at Göttingen, where he
stayed until his death. For his version of some of the events
described in this novel, see his article in the June, 1968, *Bulletin of
Atomic Scientists*, "The Third Reich and the Atomic Bomb."

Which bring us finally to the fictional characters in this story.
There were really only three major ones: Peter Burckhardt, Felicitas Burckhardt, and Nancy Reichman. Felicitas Burckhardt, the
lovely and refreshing Felicitas, never married. She stayed with her
academic career and ended up as the most ravishing professor to
ever grace the halls of the over five hundred-year-old University of
Basel.

A year after the war ended, Peter Burckhardt resigned from the
Bank for International Settlements and accepted an offer by his
father (also a fictional character) to join the management of the
New York branch of the Swiss Bank Corporation. He eventually
became head of that operation (showing once again that nepotism
is not all bad). He retired in 1980 and moved to California with his
dear wife, Nancy, where they bought a vineyard in the Dry Creek
Valley of Sonoma County. They produce both an excellent Caber-
net Sauvignon and a Chardonnay (very similar to those of the
Jordan winery) and bottle it under the label "Domaine Burckhardt"—a label that, if examined carefully, reveals both the Swiss
and American flags in the upper left-hand corner.